LORD

IN TWO WORLDS

JOHN E. WEBB JR.

ACW PRESS
Phoenix, Arizona 85013

Cover design by WalljasperDesign
Interior design by Pine Hill Graphics

Packaged by ACW Press
5501 N. 7th Ave., #502
Phoenix, Arizona 85013
www.acwpress.com
The views expressed or implied in this work do not necessarily reflect those of ACW
Press. Ultimate design, content, and editorial accuracy of this work is the responsibility of the author(s).

Printed in the United States of America by Bethany Press International,
Bloomington, Minnesota 55438.

ISBN 1-892525-27-5

This book is dedicated to my beautiful daughter Brhiannon (my little Sharineas). Who, by the very act of being born into this world, has taught me to love in a greater capacity than I ever thought possible. And has also given me a little better understanding of how much God loves His children.

Chapter

1

Matthew Adams, Jr. sat on the window seat in his bedroom gazing out at a somber sky, which, at the moment, was sending down a fine drizzle. It was evening now, that time between day and night when everything loses its distinction. The only way he could tell that it was still drizzling was by looking at the street light across the road. Matthew had just gotten out of the shower, his hair was still damp and he now sat with only a towel wrapped around him.

His twenty-first birthday had finally arrived, and his two best friends insisted on taking him out. Pete and David were great, but their taking him "out on the town" to celebrate his coming of age was not really setting well with Matthew tonight. It was not really anything new; the three of them had been getting into bars and drinking since they were seventeen. Matthew had spent most of the day looking back at his life, which made him as somber as the sky outside and not really ready for a night of bar hopping. Still, they had been friends through-out high school and were still together three years after graduation. *I suppose I had better humor them,* he thought, with a roguish smile on his face. *They only want to show me a good time and make this a night to remember in our race for manhood.*

No matter what his friends did it would be more meaningful than anything Matthew's mother had done for his last three birthdays. Amanda Adams had pretty much forgotten about both of her children. Though Matthew still lived with his mother, it seemed he was more of a house-sitter than a son. Of course, it had not always been that way. At one time they had been the ideal family, but that was when his father had still been alive.

Six years had gone by now since his father was murdered. Matthew felt guilty because with each passing year it was getting harder to remember him. Sometimes at night he would awake from a bad dream and realize he could not remember what his father's face looked like. Frantically, with tears in his eyes, he would jump out of bed and turn on the light, only to stare at the picture of his father on the dresser. With every ounce of strength Matthew would try to hang on to the memories and the image of his father that he could feel slipping away.

Matthew Adams, Sr. was the main thing Matthew Jr. had been reflecting on all day—as well as his own life up to this point and the current condition of the world. He could still remember what it was like having family meals with his father, mother, and older sister Sarah. Matthew Sr. had loved God with his whole heart and if there were such a place as heaven, Matthew was sure he was there. His father had always insisted that they pray together as a family before every meal and usually had either Sarah or Matthew say grace over the food. It was a warm memory and Matthew wished he could hold on to it forever. Matthew believed that if there had ever been a Christian who was one-hundred percent sincere, it was his father. He had been a kind and gentle man, six feet four inches tall and very muscular, although Matthew never saw him take advantage of his great stature. On the contrary, he put everyone before himself and always stood up for those who could not defend themselves.

Matthew had many heroes he looked up to, but his father was at the top of that list because he was the most real. One instance Matthew remembered was when he had been ten years old. He and his father had been doing some evening Christmas shopping downtown. As they were walking past an alleyway they heard a short cry, barely audible, but it was enough to make them both look down the alley. What happened next was a blur of motion. Matthew could barely make out a man with a gun in his hand. He had it pointed at a woman's head and was grabbing her purse. Having seen the same thing, his father never hesitated. He shoved Matthew, bags and all, away from the mouth of the alley and ran toward the struggle. Matthew decided later that it must have been the thick blanket of snow on the ground that kept the mugger from hearing his father coming until it was too late. Just as the man started to turn, his father ran into him full-force sending them both to the ground. The gun went off as it flew from the man's hand. The bullet hit the wall at the mouth of the alley near where Matthew had crawled back to watch and now sat in stunned amazement. He watched as his father struck the woman's assailant in the face with a blow so hard Matthew could hear the sound of it from where he sat. The man collapsed under the force of the crushing blow. Matthew saw his father raise his fist to strike a second time—yet he hesitated and did not let his fist fall again when he realized the unconscious man was no longer a threat. Instead, he went over to the woman who lay on the ground curled up in fright, to see if she was all right.

It turned out that she was not hurt, just shaken and scared. The woman was so grateful that she offered Matthew's father a reward. He declined, saying that it was a blessing just to be able to help. The police arrived and hauled the gunman away in handcuffs, which had all been very exciting for Matthew. They took statements from the woman, his father, and even from himself. Later, on the way home, he asked his father if he had been afraid. "Son," he answered, "at first all I felt was anger when I saw that man victimizing that lady. I didn't think, just reacted. But I have to admit, just before I reached him that anger turned to fear. Not so much fear for myself, but a fear of what might happen to my family if I were to get hurt or killed. I just thank God that His Spirit was with me and His angels were there to keep us safe."

Yeah! Matthew thought, *God was with him that night, but he must have been busy somewhere else the night Dad really needed Him.* It had been five years after the incident in the alley and Matthew slept right through it. His father had awakened in the middle of the night because of a noise he heard downstairs. Matthew's mother did not want her husband to go check on the sound, but he did anyway. Later, the police told the family that his father must have surprised a burglar. They had found the lock on the kitchen door broken from the outside. All Matthew remembered was waking to the sound of a gunshot. Afraid and confused, he threw on his robe and headed for the stairs that his mother and sister were already descending. His mother turned on the lights and screamed, then yelled for him and Sarah to get back up stairs. Of course it was too late. He and his sister were already there and could see their father lying in a puddle of blood, a sight Matthew would never forget. He could never understand why his father had to die such a senseless and meaningless death. Matthew Adams, Sr. had gone to check on a noise in his own home and paid for it with his life.

For a while, Matthew had been angry at his father for leaving them alone. Eventually though, he came to grips with what had happened, even admiring his father for always thinking of his family before himself. It was God he really blamed, or more to the point, Jesus. God was a far away being, aloof and unreachable in Matthew's mind. He did not believe God had all that much to do with people's lives. Jesus though, He was supposed to be God's Son—and supposedly had come to earth to live as a man and represent God. Since he was small Matthew had been taught that Jesus had been tortured and crucified, paying for sins He never committed to make the way open for everyone who believed to enter heaven. His father had continually talked about Jesus, sang about His rising from the dead, and praised Him for saving his soul. He always told Matthew that it was Jesus who had forgiven him, set him free, and changed his whole way of thinking. The way Matthew saw it, Jesus was the one responsible for his father's welfare and He blew it, big time.

After his father's death everything changed. At first he and his mother and sister had been drawn closer together out of the need for comfort. His father though, had been the strong one in the family, and it was he who had held them together. Matthew Sr. had faithfully taken his family to church every Sunday, and Matthew had to admit to himself that he felt love and security whenever they had been there. Soon after his father's death, Matthew, along with his mother and sister, quit attending church or even seeing any of the friends they knew from there. Matthew missed many of the people at church but more than anyone else, he missed Rick.

Rick was several years older than Matthew and had always tried to help him along spiritually. The last he heard about Rick was that he graduated from some university with a big degree in physics and was back here in Indiana working at a giant research center. Those days, and the people that went with them, were now all a part of his past. His family had drifted their separate ways, trying to fulfill their lives. What his father feared most that night in the alley with the gunman had finally come true.

Matthew's mother started dating again. She was still quite attractive, and there seemed to be no lack of men in her new life. He was never sure from one week to the next just whom she was seeing, and by the time Matthew was nineteen his mother was rarely home. When she was home she was always polite, like one would be to a paper boy or sales clerk. A very large gulf had formed between them.

His sister had married and moved to Chicago. She and her husband started a photography studio and spent most of their time chasing after the good things in life. The only thing that Matthew thought had any real meaning in his sister's life were her two adorable daughters. He truly loved them and regretted not seeing them more. Sarah was always so busy running here and there that Matthew did not know where she found the time to be a mother to her girls. *But*, he thought, *it's her life and I'm only the little brother. What do I know?*

When his family had gone down the tubes, Matthew's morals had gone with it. He and his friends spent a lot of time experimenting with drugs, though none of them had really given their lives over to it. They drank just about every weekend and spent the remaining time looking for women.

With a sigh he drew his gaze away from the window and looked at, but did not really see, the electric guitar in the corner. It was just one example of the many things he had started but never finished. Matthew started to play when he was sixteen and like almost everything else, picked it up quickly. Once he had mastered playing bar chords and learned a few songs, he lost interest. It seemed to be the same with everything he tried. Sports, music, writing, working on cars;

he would pick it up quickly, but always lost interest before he ever got good at anything.

Matthew was six feet tall, muscular, and looking more and more like the man in the picture on his dresser every day. No matter how many drugs, how much alcohol, music, sports, or women he had, none of it made him feel as if he had any purpose in his life. Deep down inside what he really wanted was to be a man like his father had been. A good man ready to lay his life on the line for what he believed. The problem was that Matthew did not know what he believed in. He had some physical strength, but neither the inner strength nor courage he saw in his father, and he had no idea where to find it.

The one thing in his life that did seem to give him some purpose was Angela. She was the only girl Matthew had ever gone out with for more than a couple of weeks in a row. They had been dating now for six months and his feelings for her were getting stronger every day. He felt that he had finally met someone he could trust, someone who would not let him down. Once in a while, lately, ideas of marriage had even been floating through his head. That was the reason he had been looking for a real full-time job, something with benefits and a good salary. Unfortunately, jobs like that were just about non-existent these days, and so far nothing had come his way.

This night was supposed to end up at the 747 Club where all of his friends gathered on the weekends. He was looking forward to that; Angela said she would be there waiting for him. Matthew was hoping they would get to spend some time alone tonight.

Thinking of seeing Angela again was the best medicine to alleviate his melancholy mood. As if suddenly coming out of a trance, Matthew realized that he had spent way too much time thinking and daydreaming again; the guys would be here soon. He still needed to get ready, so he quickly went into the bathroom to run a comb through his medium-length brown hair, and get dressed. He wore his favorite black jeans and the new shirt Angela had given him for his birthday. He headed out of his room, flipped off the light, and took about three steps before the phone rang.

"Well that must be Sarah, right on time," Matthew said out loud, although no one was listening. His sister, Sarah, called twice a year without fail. She always called on Christmas and on Matthew's birthday. They were not the closest of siblings, but at least they kept in touch, even if it was only a couple of times a year. He walked back into his room, turned the lights back on, and picked up the phone. "Hello, if you've got the dime, I've got the time."

"Matt, are you still using that tired out old line to answer the phone?" Matthew cringed. Sarah always insisted on calling him Matt, and he hated it. It always made him feel as if he should be lying in front of a door with "WELCOME" written across his chest.

"Only on you, sis. How are you doing?"

"I'm fine, Matt. Mark and the girls are doing real good too. I just thought I'd call and wish you a happy birthday."

"Well thanks, sis, it sure is good to hear your voice again." There was a hesitation on Sarah's end of the line.

"Have you...seen Mom lately? I haven't heard from her since Donna's birthday five months ago." Their mother was a touchy subject between them. Sarah never wanted to face the reality of the way their mother was acting and the kind of person she had become.

"She was home for two days last month, but I'm not sure where she is now."

"You mean she hasn't even called you for your birthday?!" Sarah was incredulous.

"No, but you know, I'll probably get a card or a call in the next week or so."

"Yeah, I guess. Well you're twenty-one today, a full grown man. It doesn't seem like the time should be going so fast. Just be careful tonight, and I hope you're not too sick in the morning," she said with a laugh. "The girls have an open house at school tonight so I really have to be going, but it was good talking to you again."

"No problem, sis, I've got to be going too. Say hello to Mark, and give Diane and Donna a big hug and kiss for me."

"I will. You have a good time tonight and be careful. Matt...I love you."

"Uh, I love you too, Sarah; thanks for calling. I'll give you a call next month."

"Okay, Matt. Bye, and have a happy birthday."

"Bye sis." Matthew held the receiver a little away from his ear, listening to the sound of the dial tone. *Well, she was a little more sentimental than usual, but still on the go. Sometimes I wish we could have gotten to know each other a little better.* Just then he heard two short, then one long blast on a car horn coming from the street out front. That was Pete's traditional signal that he had arrived. Matthew quickly replaced the receiver and raced downstairs. *It's time to forget about life and have a good time,* Matthew thought, as he closed the front door behind him.

At the same time Matthew was walking out his front door, a meeting was taking place not far from his home, just outside Gary, Indiana. It was not far in miles, but it was separated by a virtually impenetrable dimensional barrier. In the council chambers of Peridon Japax Silvanthia, High King of all the Elven people, a private council of two had been called. The King was meeting with his top counselor and expert in the Elven law, Alexthna Chenorea. King Peridon was stating his position; "Alexthna, I am going to have to make an attempt to reconvene the war council of the combined three races. I do not know if the old alliances will hold today. It has been over fifty sun-cycles since we have needed to band together. I know it's a desperate action, one that you do not see the need of, but something must be done."

"My King, I do not believe it will be necessary because of the rate at which all of the major prophecies are being fulfilled. They all point to the Time of Calburnathis being at hand."

"Ha! That is what the priests and experts in the law said fifty sun-cycles ago, when that mad Traul, Chetick, turned the entire Traul race against our people. He slaughtered thousands of Elves and almost took over the valley. Although, with the help of the Humans and Dwarie, we were not only able to stop his insanity, but regained our portion of the valley that we had been denied for so long. It was our might that won that war, not the prophecy of a sword that is still where it has always been. And it will be our might that wins the war that's brewing right now."

"But, my King, must I remind you that the prophecies of Ishmanah, given over three thousand sun-cycles ago, have up to this point *all* come true. This cycle's Festival of the First Season is tomorrow, the day foretold that Calburnathis would be drawn forth."

"Yes, yes, I have been hearing very little else from you of late." The King went on, "You experts in the law, prophets, and priests have never been able to agree on anything. From the time the prophecy was given until sixteen hundred cycles ago, the sword of King Dragrasia was safely locked away in the temple vault. Your kind argued about the meaning of the prophecy for hundreds of sun-cycles, until the High Counselor and the Keeper of the Amulet of Truth stole the sword and disappeared with it. They never returned, but the sword reappeared one day imbedded in the Great Tree with the Amulet of Truth draped around its hilt.

I have always been curious as to what happened with the sword during the thirty or forty cycles that it had disappeared, but that did not seem to be a concern at the time. You experts in the law and priests went at it again, completely disregarding your earlier interpretations. You began to argue over the new meaning of the prophecy, and when the sword would be drawn from the tree. I do agree, the prophecy will someday be fulfilled, but we cannot be sure that time is now. We also cannot afford to take the chance.

This mysterious Enlightened One, as he calls himself, is stirring up trouble in the north again. From all the reports that have come in, he is preparing for war with us. From what we know, he has convinced the entire Traul and Nomie races that we are evil; there are even many Humans in his camp. They believe that it is our worship of the Creator that is causing all of the famine, ground shakes, and other disasters we have been experiencing in the land. It sounds much as it did fifty sun-cycles ago. I believe it is time for us to unite with the other races of the valley to protect ourselves from certain hostility."

"What makes my King believe that the other races will believe there is a threat and join us after so long a time of peace?"

"The Dwarie are honorable and have always stood by us before. As far as the Humans go, you know the majority of them in the valley are followers of the Path. As much as I hate that religion, they do believe that we Elves are the Creator's chosen, and will come to our aid. Besides, this Enlightened One supposedly hates the Path followers even more than he hates the Elven people."

"Bah! Why are we always being associated with those fools?" Alexthna said, through clenched teeth. "They were the ones responsible for attacking and killing our people only a few hundred cycles after Calburnathis reappeared. At that time they said we were hated by the

Creator, now they say we are His chosen. I do not think any of them know what they believe."

"I cannot abide their blasphemies either, but if we do not fight this Traul evil together—we may all be destroyed. The only ones I will not work with are those Elves that have converted to that religion. Those heretics are banished from this kingdom, no longer considered alive, and will not be allowed back in." Alexthna bowed his head.

"I know it still pains you that your father's brother rejected the traditions of our fathers, that he gave up his position and his family to convert to that blasphemous religion. I too grieve over that decision. He was my mentor, and taught me almost everything that I know about magic and the Creator's law for our people."

"Yes, I am still pained, also angered at what he did. That is why I wish never to hear his name spoken again. I once loved him as a father, but now he is exiled from this kingdom for the rest of his days. I wish to speak no more of this! Is it agreed then? I will send word to the leaders of the other races to reconvene the war council. Together we will march to the north and put a stop to the evil there."

"I will agree, my King, but I beg you to wait until after tomorrow's celebration, just in case the Creator has different ideas."

"So be it," the King said. "I will wait, but only until after tomorrow. After so many years stuck in that tree, I don't really believe the sword will be pulled out tomorrow. Even if Calburnathis is drawn, we will still need a combined races' defense army, which I will propose to the Human and Dwarie leaders. I do not see how one Elf with a sword, even Calburnathis, can defeat an entire army by himself. I have also gotten reports that say the Enlightened One has great control of magic, greater than anyone has ever seen before. My scouts have told me that the force he is gathering may be the largest in history, bigger than it was in the last war. I will not be caught unprepared."

"As you say, my King," Alexthna said bowing from the waist. "So shall it be done." At that moment, one of the huge doors at the far end of the council chamber flew open, and a young Elven female walked into the room.

"Father, here you are! I've been looking all over for you."

"Sharineas!" The King said as sternly as he was able. "You know you are not to come into the council chamber when council is in session." Sharineas answered with mock scorn in her voice.

"It's only you and Alexthna, and you've been in here far too long as it is. Father, you know how much has to be done before the celebration tomorrow. Why don't you come out now before your brain is filled with cobwebs from being in here so long?" She then beamed her most disarming smile at them. Both were under her spell and could not help smiling back.

Sharineas was the Princess of the realm, court favorite, and only child of the Elven High King and his Queen, and meant the world to them. Peridon and his wife, Jasmantha, had only one child left. They had a son, eight cycles older than Sharineas, but he had been killed thirteen sun-cycles ago in a hunting accident. Now Sharineas was the light and joy of the King's heart. He was understandably over-protective of the only child left to him. Peridon would give up his kingdom, even his life, to keep her from harm. *She is so excited about tomorrow,* the King thought, *that she is oblivious to the world around her. If I have anything to say about it, she will stay in that place of innocence.*

Every fifty sun-cycles a new Keeper of the Amulet of Truth was chosen. Unlike the days of old, the title was mostly ceremonial now. Two days before, all of the Elven maidens that were of age presented themselves to the current Keeper of the Amulet. One by one they walked before her and touched the amulet. When Sharineas had touched the amulet, it began to glow, signifying that she was to be the new Keeper.

High King Peridon did not know whether he should feel pride or fear over his daughter's new title. The days were so uncertain with war brewing in the land once again. They were all going to be called on to make grave sacrifices. He did not want one of those sacrifices to be his daughter, but for now he would celebrate her good fortune with her. Tomorrow was the Festival of the First Season, when Sharineas would go through the ceremony that would make her the new Keeper of the Amulet.

"My beautiful daughter, how could I ever deny you anything? Alexthna and I were just finishing anyway. Let us go finish the preparations for your big day tomorrow."

"It's not just a big day for me, father. It's going to be a big day for everyone."

"Who knows?" Alexthna said, catching the King's eye, "It might be an even bigger day than we think."

An old Elf sat on the side of a mountain by himself. Near where he sat was a pieced together cottage that looked as if it was as old as the mountain itself. Stretched out below him at the foot of the mountain was a giant valley that was surrounded on every side by mountains; a magnificent thing to look upon. A full moon illuminated the entire side of the mountain; and with the acute eyesight of his people, the old Elf could see the area surrounding him almost as if it were day. At the moment however, he was not looking at the view. He sat on the ground with his knees drawn up to his chin; face tilted toward the sky; eyes closed.

If anyone had been there to observe him they would have thought he was asleep except for the near imperceptible movement of his lips. After a long time in that position a slight smile formed on his lips and he then spoke as if talking to the sky. "Yes, my King, as you say, so shall it be done." Immediately he stood up, went into the old cottage, and began putting select items in a traveling sack. When he had finished gathering his things, the old Elf began to descend the mountain— toward the Valley of the Gold.

Chapter

2

Matthew ran the length of his front porch and jumped over the three steps to land on the sidewalk below. He then came to a dead stop. Sitting on the street in front of his house was a brand new silver-blue Pontiac Grand Prix. *I wonder where Pete is*, Matthew thought. *That's not his car.* As he finished that thought, two short blasts and then a long one sounded from the Grand Prix, and Pete jumped out smiling. Pete was a little shorter than Matthew with red hair and a few freckles across his face. Matthew, Pete, and David jokingly referred to themselves as the three musketeers and did everything together. Out of the three, Pete was the least sure of himself and, therefore, least lucky with the women. Like Sarah, Pete thought the meaning of life was in how much you could accumulate. He worked full-time during the week, and part-time at another job on the weekends. Pete was always buying the best of everything, even if he could not afford it.

"Well, what do you think of my new car?" Pete asked. "I just got back from picking it up."

"It's great!" Matthew exclaimed. "But why didn't you tell us? And how in the world can you afford it?"

"I just thought I'd surprise you guys with it. My dad co-signed for me. I had to go in hock for five years, but I think it's worth it." Matthew was taken back.

"You mean you're going to be paying on this thing for the next five years?"

"Well yeah," Pete answered, "that's how everyone does it. Besides, women really go for a nice car, and just between you and me, I need all the help I can get."

"Well if you think it was worth it, I think it was worth it," Matthew said with a chuckle. Inwardly he could not help wondering where Pete was going to get the time to pick up women in his new car. He would have to be spending all of his time working to pay for the car. Of course, everything was bought on credit these days.

The world had gone to a one-world money system not long ago. When America saw how well it helped stabilize the other countries' precarious economies, her people wanted in as well; so the United States had changed with the times. The majority of people had so overextended themselves financially that the country was on the verge of collapse. The government took complete control of the money system, doing away with cash, and issuing everyone a money card. Now everyone's paychecks were deposited straight into an account, and they had a personal credit card to use instead of cash. Most people loved the new system. It not only made transactions easier, but gave everyone a stronger credit base. So now, even more than before, people could go out and buy whatever they wanted, whenever they wanted. However most people were farther in debt than they had ever been in the past. The average work week for men and women in America was now up to fifty-two hours. The only problem with the universal credit card was the old story of theft and forgery. The person behind the start of the whole system had assured the public that the problem was well in hand and that a system for making it impossible to tamper with each person's identification number was almost ready.

The one-world money system was the brain child of, and implemented by, the newly elected president of the United Nations,

Carmine Ishmali. It was through the United Nations that the new money system worked. It had stabilized the world economy, eased manyof the strained diplomatic relations and had succeeded in giving the U.N. considerably more power than it already had. The U.N. was also now the recognized police force of the world and boasted the largest single military force ever assembled. The U.N. "Peace Keeping Force," as it was called, had members from almost every country in the world; the most notable exception to this being Israel.

All of this was headed up by the charismatic and very intelligent Carmine Ishmali. Part European and part Arabian, he held to no certain religion yet believed in a supreme being and that all human beings should live in harmony with one another. The pro-life activists were against him because he did not stand with them on that issue. The fundamentalist Christians were calling him the Anti-Christ. Those two groups, however, were only an ever-shrinking minority who did not have much voice any more. Everyone else was calling him the savior of the world. World conflict had diminished, while international goodwill was continually on the rise. Not many seemed to notice that disease, famine, and natural disasters were out of control. Moral decline, drug abuse, as well as violent and sexual crimes were also on the increase. "So, what do you think of the car?" Pete broke into Matthew's thoughts.

"I think she's a real beauty. Do I get to ride in it or do I have to run along side wherever we go?"

"Of course you get to ride in it, as long as you don't have any mud on your feet," Pete answered half jokingly. "Let's go get David."

"All right, let's ride," Matthew said as he jumped in the passenger side door.

They drove the six blocks to David's apartment. He was waiting for them out front, as always, wearing his stylish black-leather jacket and smoking a cigarette. David was the best looking of the three musketeers and had always been the lady killer. He was a little taller than Matthew and had black wavy hair. It was always David who caught the attention of the best looking females wherever they went, making Pete and Matthew feel like leftovers. Actually, Matthew had quit looking for the one night stands even before he had met Angela. He had simply lost interest in going out with women just to use them. Not David though.

He was worse than ever and would probably never change. Even with the number of people dying from the AIDS virus rising at such an alarming rate, David was not frightened; he thought he was indestructible. When Pete gave his trademark honks as he and Matthew pulled up, David flicked his cigarette butt and walked toward them. "Whoa, where did you guys steal this thing?"

"Pete just bought it," Matthew yelled from the open window. "He's really moving up in the world, isn't he?"

"Hey buddy," David said through the open window, "you're really leaving us in the dust. Pretty soon we won't even be allowed to talk to you."

"Come on you guys, you know it's not like that, I just like having nice things."

"Well," David said as he got in the back seat, "I don't care one way or another as long as you still haul us low-life types around. Let's go, the night's growing old and we've got a birthday to celebrate." All three began to hoot and laugh as Pete pulled the car away from the curb.

They decided to start the night by heading down to the Drag. The Drag was the name the area young people had given to the street where all the main activity took place. Clothing stores, shoe stores, restaurants, bakeries, and a bar on every block. It was a big deal even at their age to ride up and down the street to see who was out running around. Since tonight was Matthew's birthday, they had plans to hit every bar on the Drag. After a couple of hours the boys had hit quite a few of the drinking establishments and were feeling pretty good. The next stop was Brett's Bar and Grill which was down the block, just past the antique shop. Being so close they decided to walk, even though all three were beginning to weave a little. Before they could make it to Brett's, Matthew stopped and was looking at something in the antique shop window. It was a full suit of medieval armor that the shop had just purchased. "Boy, wouldn't that be cool to have?" Matthew asked his ghost-like reflection in the glass.

"What? That piece-of-junk tin suit?" David asked.

"Yeah, you know, to have on display in your entryway, or something like that."

"It's a good thing you don't have a lot of money," Pete offered his opinion. "You would probably have a whole house full of weird, useless stuff."

Ever since he was young, Matthew had read about the knights in shining armor and wished he could have lived back then. Every male friend that Matthew knew had some kind of hero they wished they could be like. Pete had told him once that he always dreamed of being a fighter pilot back in World War II. David had always seen himself as a gunfighter back in the old west, although Matthew did not know on which side of the law David wanted to be. Matthew had loved to read ever since he could remember. Comic books, auto-biographies, history; he loved it all—his favorite reading though, was science and fantasy fiction. In Matthew's mind, out of all the reading he had ever done, nothing could surpass J.R.R. Tolkien's *Hobbit* and *Lord of the Rings*. As much as he loved that story though, his favorite had its roots in reality.

The story of King Arthur and his Knights of the Round Table had always awed and inspired him. The chivalry of the knights, the purity of their motives, and the quest for the Holy Grail were just part of it. These things, along with the great love and loyalty that Arthur inspired, were things that did not seem to exist in today's world. All of these things touched the part of Matthew that wished he could be more like his father. He felt that living such a life would have brought him fulfillment, although Matthew knew that like everything else man had put his hand to, the concept of knighthood had degenerated. It had not been long after its conception that the knights were feared by the very people they had once sworn to protect. The knights had turned to pillaging towns, raping, and even killing innocent people who could not protect themselves. Still, the early days of the knighthood had been glorious, and Matthew would have loved to live back then. The suit of armor had brought back all of these childhood dreams and shed an uncomplimentary light on his present life. "Come on," David said. "We have things to be, places to see, people to do, and a birthday to celebrate."

"All right, all right." With one more backward glance at the suit of armor, Matthew followed his friends into Brett's.

The antique shop had brought Matthew's sullen mood back, causing him to think about his life and what he wished it could be. He did not have much to drink at the rest of the bars they went to, even though many of the people he knew offered to buy him birthday drinks. At Matthew's insistence they skipped the last bar and headed for the nightclub. He was hoping the different atmosphere and seeing Angela would help to get him back in the party mood. They finally reached the 747 Club at about ten o'clock, the magic hour when everyone began to crawl out of the woodwork.

The club had gotten its name five years before, when a Bowing 747 crashed right there outside Gary, Indiana. Forty-seven people in the plane had been killed, as well as nine on the ground. The plane landed in a field, but part of the tail section had come off and landed on the restaurant killing nine people, including the owner. The owner's son used the insurance money to rebuild what had been destroyed, and turned the place into a nightclub. Not having much discretion or taste, the son named his club after the plane that had crashed into his father's restaurant. The building even had a mock tail piece of a Bowing 747 coming out of the roof, making it look as if a plane had just crashed. The tacky idea worked. The 747 Club was now the most popular night-club in the area. The fact that they were very lax in checking I.D.'s, had live bands, and always had plenty of drug dealers floating around, helped their business immensely. The most popular features of the club were the backrooms; just a long hall with a series of small rooms on each side. These rooms were available to regular, well-known cus-tomers, who were willing to pay for their use. Once behind the doors, customers could use the rooms for whatever he or she wanted; whether legal or illegal.

The band was already playing music so loud a person could barely think, with lights flashing in time to a pulsating beat. There was already a thick haze of cigarette smoke hanging over the table area, and beginning to infiltrate the dance floor. Even though Matthew drank less at the last couple of bars, he was still lightheaded, which only added to the air of confusion that always permeated this kind of place. They heard a female voice shout over the din: "Hey, over here, you guys." All three turned as one to see a very pretty blonde who obviously commanded attention wherever she was without having to say a word.

"Angela," David yelled, "save us some seats, we're on our way over." When they finally made it over to the table, Angela put her arms around Matthew and gave him a long kiss, wishing him a happy birth-day as she pulled away. Matthew blushed at the laughter of Pete, David, and Angela's two best friends, Jennifer and Melissa.

"You sure look good in that new shirt," Jennifer said to Matthew.

"Well the person who picked it out for me has good taste," Matthew responded. After the preliminaries were over they all hit the dance floor. Matthew was doing his best to rid himself of the mood he was in, but it seemed as if these thoughts that kept running through his mind were out of control. He was tired of faking it and said he was going to sit out a couple of dances. Angela did not want to sit, so she danced to one song with Pete and a couple with David. When the band went on break they all came back to the table where Matthew was, laughing and out of breath.

"Hey Matthew," David said. "Steve just told us that Phil has got some really good toot for sale in his usual room. Why don't we go partake of a little refreshment?" Everyone else, including Angela, was enthusiastic, and Matthew did not want to ruin their night.

"You guys go ahead, I can't really afford that right now."

"Come on," Pete said. "We'll all pitch in and buy you a quarter for your birthday."

"That's okay, you all go ahead, I'll stay here and keep our table for us."

"Okay, suit yourself," David said. "Come on you guys, my nose is getting itchy." Angela put her arm around Matthew.

"You sure are being a bummer tonight, what's wrong?"

"I'm just feeling kind of sick tonight," Matthew lied. "You go ahead with everyone else and have some fun, I'll be waiting for you right here."

"All right, but I won't be long so don't go anywhere."

"I won't." As Angela started to turn away Matthew added in a stammering voice: "Hey Angela…uh…I love you." Angela smiled and hesitated.

"Luv you, too…see you later," Matthew wanted to kick himself. He had been wanting to tell her how he felt for a while now, but was waiting for the right moment. Now he had gone and blurted it out at definitely the wrong time.

As the blush that was caused by his foolish blunder disappeared, Matthew started to become more aware of his surroundings. The whole scene was alien to him tonight. For some reason he seemed to be seeing things for what they really were. The too-loud laughter, tight-fitting, revealing clothes, the alcohol, drugs, and haze of cigarette smoke—it was all just a cover up for people who were just as frustrated and disillusioned with life as he was. He looked down at a bottle of spilled beer on the floor and recoiled at the sight of roaches crawling in the liquid. If there was one thing he hated and almost feared, it was cockroaches. He raised his foot and grimaced at the crunch he could feel through his shoe as he stepped on the two bugs who were lapping up beer.

The band began to play again, so Matthew watched and listened for a while. The flashing lights and rhythmic beat were almost hypnotizing, and he felt himself getting very sleepy despite the loud music. He lay his head in his arms and tried to pull his disjointed thoughts together. The same question kept coming back to him. *What is my purpose in life? I just don't see it.*

In the last couple of years he had tried different religions. Eastern mysticism, the New Age philosophies, he even thought once about Satanism, but discarded that idea. None of these religions or schools of thought had answered his questions, or brought him fulfillment; they had only succeeded in making him more confused. Matthew thought at times he had felt something real when attending church with his father, but could never seem to grasp what Matthew Sr. had.

Matthew's thoughts wandered to his Aunt Nancy, whom he had not thought of in a long time. He thought the world of his father's sister, who was also a strong Christian. The year before his father died; Nancy's husband had left her for another woman—leaving her to raise three children alone. It was very traumatic for her and the children, but they eventually adjusted. Nancy was almost back to acting like her old self again when her brother was murdered. Since both parents were dead, Matthew Sr. and his sister had been very close. So when he was killed it affected Nancy tremendously; many people thought she would not make it. But make it she did, staying strong for her children, and not giving up on life. She always claimed it was the Lord who helped her through it, and continued to give God and His Son the glory for everything. No matter what she said, though, Matthew could see that painful expression come over her face every once in a while. She was making it, Matthew admitted to himself, but just barely.

Matthew's thoughts melted into the haziness of a dream, then the music suddenly stopped. He sat upright rubbing his eyes. *The band can't be stopping already; they just started.* The band was, indeed, on break, and Matthew realized he must have fallen asleep for a while. *Where is Angela? She said she would be right back.* Unable to figure out why his friends had not come back for him, Matthew went to look for them. He saw Pete at the edge of the dance floor talking to Melissa and made his way over to them. "Hey Pete, why didn't you guys come back to the table?" Pete was grinning from ear to ear.

"Oh, hey man, I'm sorry. We must have all forgot. You know what it's like when you're buzzed, it doesn't even seem like we've been gone long."

"Yeah, I guess," Matthew mumbled. "Do either of you know where Angela is?"

"Gee, we haven't seen David or Angela since we were all with Phil. Maybe they went back for seconds," Melissa said with a giggle.

"Thanks guys, I guess I'll look for her there," Matthew said as he headed for the back rooms. He reached the long, dimly lit hallway with doors up and down it on either side, and knocked on the one he knew Phil always used for dealing drugs. Two short raps, then two with pauses in between, that was the knock regulars knew would get them entry. Matthew heard the lock click, the door opened a crack, and an eye looked out at him. When he saw who it was, the person behind the door let him in the room. Matthew began to check out everyone in the too-small room. It was very crowded and filled with cigarette smoke, but there was no sign of either David or Angela. Phil was sitting on the single bed that every room had, with a card table in front of him and a smile on his face.

"Hey Matthew, I'm glad to see you changed your mind, what'll ya have?"

"No thanks man, not tonight," Matthew answered. "I was just wondering if you knew where David or Angela were?"

"Afraid not, I haven't seen them since they were in here about a half hour ago, sorry. Are you sure you don't want any? It's real good stuff."

"No, I'm not feeling too well tonight, maybe tomorrow night, though. I'm going to keep looking for Angela, thanks."

"See ya!" Phil and everyone else in the room said as he left. *If I know David, he's already found some babe and has her back in his favorite* room. Matthew started down the hallway, past doors with either laughter, moaning, or both, coming from behind them. He had spent plenty of nights in these rooms looking for comfort and forgetfulness. Tonight though, he felt uneasy being here, and the thought of all that was going on behind these doors sickened him. He finally made it to the last door on the right and heard David's voice along with a female giggle in response. *I hope he doesn't get too mad at me for interrupting, but he's the only one left who might know where Angela is. At least they're not in the middle of anything serious at the moment,* Matthew thought, as he knocked on the door.

"This room's occupied," came David's voice.

"David it's me, Matthew. Look, I'm sorry to bother you, I was just wondering if you knew where Angela went after you guys left Phil?" The door opened a little and a head with black, wavy, messed-up hair popped out of the crack.

"You've got real bad timing, man."

"Do you know where Angela is?" Matthew asked again, with just an edge of irritation in his voice this time.

"No I don't, what am I, a babysitter? We did a couple of lines with Pete, Jennifer, and Melissa, then she split. How am I supposed to know where she went? Now do you mind, I'm kinda busy."

"All right, I'm sorry I bothered you. Carry on." Just before David closed the door, Matthew got a whiff of a very familiar perfume. He got a tight feeling in his stomach, and a wave of anger hit him. Normally he would have taken his friend's word for it, but between the drink and the frustrations building inside him all day, Matthew became reckless. He shoved the door open, knocking David back onto the bed. The light from the hallway illuminated two figures. David sprawled out in his underwear and a pretty blonde covering herself with a sheet. Matthew stood there in shock and disbelief. "Angela, what are you doing?" Was all he could manage.

"I…" she stammered, looking for words.

"Hey buddy, you know, all's fair in love and war and all that stuff," David cut in. "Don't take it personally."

Matthew was so hurt and angry that his first reaction was to kill them both. He had never been a violent person, nor irrational, but it took every ounce of strength he had to turn and run instead. He bolted past the dance floor into the table area, pushing the tables and people out of his way as he went. He was hoping someone, anyone, would start something; giving him an excuse to fight and release his anger. Everyone who saw his flushed angry face though, had sense enough to back off and let him go. Matthew made his way outside. It was cooler and quieter out here, with a heavy mist in the air. Once outside, the tears began to escape. He ran through the parking lot into the field behind the nightclub so no one coming in late would see. He ran a little erratically due to the alcohol and the tears that were blurring his vision.

After all of the losses in his life, this was the final cut. Matthew felt he could take no more and needed to lash out at someone. The bitterness and frustration poured from his soul just as freely as the tears flowed from his eyes. In the middle of the field he stopped and raged at the sky.

"All right God, I've had enough of this life, I'm ready to quit now! ...Can't You hear me? Are You there? Why don't You strike me with lightning or something? ...I don't even know why people believe You exist. If You were really up there You would care about us! Where were You when my uncle ran out on my aunt? She believed in You, but You didn't stop her from being hurt. You weren't there when my father was murdered either, he trusted in You and Jesus, and You just stood by and watched."

Matthew began to run again toward a stand of trees, but slipped in the wet grass and fell before he made it to them. Between the light rain that was now falling and lying in the wet grass, his clothing was soaked. Matthew neither cared nor noticed the discomfort of his clothes as he spoke to the ground through clenched teeth. "The Bible says You made this world. Well, mister high and mighty Jesus. I'm willing to give You the credit and the blame for this mess if You would just show Yourself. If You really existed you wouldn't have let things get so screwed up down here." Matthew's anger was almost spent. He slowly got to his feet again and made his way to the trees. The cool, light rain that fell, plus the adrenaline of his anger, had burned off some of the alcoholic haze in his brain. He leaned against a large tree and half clung to it. With his face against the cool wet bark, Matthew did the only thing he had strength left to do. He wept.

The area surrounded entirely by a mountain range called the Dragon's Jaw, was vast. The Valley of the Gold, the name was as old as history itself. This area was named after a certain tree that grew in the huge forest covering three quarters of the valley. The biggest and oldest of these trees was located in a very large clearing, between the Elven kingdom and the main Human villages. If anyone would have been in the clearing this night, he would have seen a multicolored glow come from near the huge tree. If anyone had been there he would have noticed the unnatural silence of the forest creatures, and small flashes of blue lightning in the center of the clearing. If anyone had been there this night, the hair on the back of his neck would have risen on end. He would have felt the crackle of power in the air all around him. However, no one was near this night.

Matthew leaned against the tree, oblivious to time. The rain was running down his face, mixing with his tears. Suddenly he saw a flash of light out of the corner of his eye. He jerked in surprise, turned toward the light and tried to wipe the rain and tears out of his eyes. It seemed as if he had used up all of his tears. *Now if my nose would just quit running,* Matthew thought as he walked toward the small circle of light. The circle was only a few feet in front of him and growing. Swirling and dancing in the circle of light was every color he could ever have imagined.

The circle's size seemed to be holding now at about five feet in diameter. The colors grew brighter and swirled more quickly the closer Matthew got. He reached over and picked up a stick, noticing in a detached sort of way that the rain had almost stopped and a fog was beginning to rise. He threw the stick into the swirling colors to see what would happen.

Nothing…

The stick just disappeared into the circle of light.

Matthew walked around the back side of the light. It looked the same from this side; a round, flat, sphere of swirling colored lights. He could not find the stick anywhere, and it had been big enough to spot easily. Matthew walked back around to the other side. *Well, what have I got to lose?* He thought to himself. *No real family, no real friends—if this thing kills me it won't be any great loss.*

He cautiously reached out his hand and touched the moving, colored lights; nothing happened, just a warm sensation on his finger tips. He reached farther in with his hand, then all the way to his forearm. A warm, good feeling flooded through him. He pulled his arm out and looked at it. *No dire consequences yet*, he thought, *what the heck.* Balancing on his left foot, Matthew proceeded to put his right leg into the circle of light. He felt around with his foot, but could find nothing solid in the circle. That same warm, secure feeling came over the part of his body touching the light. Losing any feeling of fear that he previously felt, Matthew leaned the front part of his body farther into the swirling colors.

He opened his eyes and saw nothing but swirling colors. Matthew did not want to lose the feeling he got from the light, but still could not find anything solid on which to bring his foot to rest. *Maybe if I try just a little farther.* He stretched his foot a little moor; still nothing.

Not wanting to take any more chances, he began to pull himself out of the strange circle. Just as he did, his left foot slipped in the wet grass. Matthew tumbled forward into the light, regretting his foolish curiosity.

Chapter

3

Matthew did not fall very long. He felt foolish over the scream that escaped his lips, after falling only two feet before hitting the ground. When his body hit the ground he immediately began to roll. Wherever he was, the ground was steep and Matthew could not stop himself. All he got for his efforts were skinned hands, elbows, knees, and a couple of good bumps on the head. When Matthew finally came to a stop, the ground had leveled off and he saw huge stones all around him. That was all he could tell about his surroundings because he was too bruised, battered, and weak to even sit up.

Matthew could taste blood, and his left arm was throbbing with pain. The mixture of alcohol and tumbling down a hill, had his head spinning like a top; he could feel himself losing consciousness. He fought to keep his eyes open, trying to stay awake. He concentrated on the stars and full moon above, trying to figure out where the hill came from and where the rain, fog, and wet grass had gone. Just as Matthew's eyes were closing, and his mind was slipping into a state of unconsciousness, he saw a face looking down at him. *My eyes must be playing tricks with me,* Matthew thought, as he slipped off into sleep. *That face looked like something out of my Elfquest comic books.*

As consciousness returned, Matthew's first thought was that the sun must already be up, because he could feel warmth on his face. He tried to open his eyes. One of them opened all the way; the other only a crack. He lifted a hand to the left side of his face where his eye would not open all the way. He could feel the swelling there, and it was very tender to the touch. Gingerly, he propped himself up on his right arm and moved his legs a little. They were sore and stiff, but not broken. He was not so sure about his left arm though. It did not seem broken, but it hurt so badly he could hardly move it. There was a rip in the sleeve and somehow a rag with a little blood stain had been wrapped around his arm. *The blood is probably from hitting one of those rocks on the way down, but where in the world did that bandage come from?* Matthew was able to see his arm so clearly for the same reason he thought the sun had already risen. About five feet away someone had built a small fire. Matthew looked around the area as best as he could from his propped up position, but could see no one.

The sun was indeed starting to come up though. Everything around him was becoming more distinct and he could even see a little way beyond the fire. Matthew turned as much as he could and saw sunlight just starting to peek over the mountain he had just rolled down. Then it hit him. *Mountain I rolled down! There aren't any mountains in Indiana.* He turned himself back around; it was getting light enough now that he could just start to make out the valley below. Totally mystified was an understatement of how he felt at that moment. He scooted himself over to a small boulder near the fire and looked down at the beautiful valley that was becoming even more clear as the sun rose higher. *Someone had to build this fire and bandage my arm. I guess I'll just sit here and hope they're coming back. I don't know where I think I'd go even if I could walk. I can barely sit as it is, and I have no idea where I am.*

Matthew sat for a while longer looking out over the valley, but soon began to doze off again. Before actually falling asleep he was aroused by a faint noise off to his right. He tried to stand up in case he had to defend himself, but was still a little too dizzy. Matthew finally settled for looking as fierce as he could while sitting on top of the stone he had been sitting against. There were several huge boulders off to his right, so he was not able to see very far in that direction. Soon he heard the sound again, only louder this time. Something was definitely coming his way and Matthew was desperately wishing he had some way to defend himself.

From around a boulder about twenty yards away came an old man with white hair and a long beard, softly humming to himself. He was carrying a sack over one shoulder with some kind of water skin over the other. He also had many pouches hanging from his belt. "Hello! I see that you have finally awakened, my young friend," the old man said, looking right at Matthew. "When I found you I feared that you were at death's door. I am truly glad to see that you are not." Matthew sat there dumbfounded; somehow he knew the old man was not speaking English, yet he could understand every word that was said. *This must have been the face I saw over me last night.* "You poor lad, can you not talk? Did some foul person cut out your tongue, or were you born this way? Do you know any sign language?"

Matthew could tell by the twinkle in his eye and the smirk on his face, that the old man was playing with him and knew perfectly well that he could speak. Matthew grinned in spite of himself and was just about to speak, but when his mouth opened nothing came forth. Not because of any problem with his vocal cords, but because of his shock. The old man had come close enough for Matthew to see him clearly, and he did, indeed, look like an Elf. He was about six inches shorter than Matthew—thin faced, with big almond shaped eyes, and pointed ears sticking out of his head through the long, white hair. *This just can't be happening.* "My young friend," the old Elf said with a slight smile. "It is becoming quite clear that your brains were damaged in your fall down the mountain, but it is still not polite to sit there with your mouth hanging open like that. Not to mention that you are bound to have some kind of insect fly in." Matthew immediately closed his mouth and tried to clear his thoughts. Finally he was able to talk.

"Please, could you tell me where I am and who you are?"

"Praise the Creator, the boy does speak! For a moment there I was beginning to think maybe you really could not, in which case I would have felt bad about having teased you."

"Yes, but can you tell me where I am?" Matthew asked again.

"Well look around you my boy, you're on the side of a mountain, Mount Easil to be exact, the highest mountain in the Dragon's Jaw. That is the name of this mountain range encircling the valley you see below. As for who I am, well…I have had many names, but my friends these days call me Deeli; just an old hermit living up here in the mountains. Now, my slow-witted young friend, can you tell me who you are?"

"I'm not really slow-witted, I was just shocked by your features. My name is Matthew Adams and I think I'm going crazy because you look like an Elf."

"Of course I look like an Elf, probably due to the fact that I am an Elf. Why does that surprise you?"

"Because where I'm from Elves don't really exist. Hey! You can understand me when I'm speaking English."

"I do not have the slightest clue as to what English is, but I have been wondering about how we are communicating," Deeli replied. "That is why I have been speaking to you in several different languages, and you have answered me in the same language with which I spoke to you. That in itself is remarkable, but I also spoke in the ancient speech of the Elves and you answered me in it. There are only a handful of Elves alive that can speak that language, and they are all priests."

"Everything I'm saying is coming out to my ears as my own language," Matthew said earnestly. "Believe me, I don't know any of your languages, or even how I got here."

"Where are you from that Elves do not exist?" Deeli asked.

"I'm from Gary, Indiana, if that helps any. I'm afraid only Humans exist there."

"Is that what you are? You look half Elf, half Human, and I have never heard of Indiana. I am afraid I cannot tell you how to get back there. Maybe you are not supposed to." Deeli made this last statement with an air of mystery. "I do not know what world you are from, but I am not convinced that you are not a powerful sorcerer. Being able to understand the ancient Elven speech, and the way you entered our world are two of the most remarkable things I have ever seen."

"You saw the way I got here?" Matthew asked eagerly. "Please tell me about it, I'm not really sure how it happened."

"I guess I can tell you what I know. I was hiking down this mountain last night to the valley below, when I saw a light in the corner of my eye."

"You were hiking down a mountain at night?" Matthew asked, finding this almost as strange as talking to an Elf.

"I see that it is not impolite to interrupt someone where you come from. But to answer your question, yes, Elves have much better eyesight than Humans, and there was a full moon out last night. Besides, I was on an errand for someone that could not wait."

"Then why have you stopped to help me?"

"The one I am running the errand for would have it no other way. Besides, I do not know that you are not part of that errand. May I finish my story now?" Deeli asked with eyebrows arched.

"Oh, I'm sorry," Matthew apologized. "It's just that I have so many questions. Please, go on."

"Now, where was I? Oh yes. The light caught my eye, so I walked toward it. I got up close and could see that it was a large circle of colored lights, kind of like a bowl of soup turned up on its edge, but not spilling out. Anyway, I was standing in front of this thing contemplating the strange phenomenon, when out flew a big stick and hit me square in the chest." Matthew had to hold his hand over his mouth so as not to laugh. Normally it would not have been that funny, but the animated way Deeli was telling the story—and the thought of him standing there getting a stick thrown at him from out of a circle of light—was too much.

"At the time," Deeli continued, "I had no idea it was a stick, you understand. I only knew that something had flown out and hit me. Well, I found the stick and picked it up; then I decided to move out of the way in case any more sticks were going to follow. No more sticks came through, but before I knew it a hand popped out. Well, I tell you; this really got my curiosity going. So I decided to stay around long enough to see what else would happen. I did not have to wait long. After the hand came a little farther through, it disappeared back into the light. Then a foot came through with a leg behind it. The foot looked as if it was searching for something to set down upon. But the circle of light being a little off the ground, combined with the mountain sloping away from the circle, made it impossible for the foot to come to rest. You can imagine my disappointment when the leg started to retreat back into the light. But just as it started to, out you popped, rolling down the mountain as if you were having the time of your life. I watched for a bit to see where you came to rest, then looked back at the light. It grew smaller and then disappeared. That is when I rushed down here to see if you were still alive. Thank the Creator you are, and that you have finally arrived."

"The fall down the hill was not exactly the time of my life," Matthew stated. "What do you mean I've finally arrived?"

"I just mean that I have been expecting something out of the ordinary to happen and I believe that you might be it." Matthew was more than a little perplexed. He still had no real answers as to how he got here. Now here was this old Elf suggesting that his appearance might not be accidental. The only thing Matthew knew for sure was that he had a headache and his mouth felt as if it was full of cotton. These things only brought back memories of the night before, which already seemed like a lifetime ago. *That's all right with me. I would rather forget about last night anyway*, he thought. "I was on my way to a village at the foot of this mountain," Deeli broke into Matthew's thoughts. "I am meeting a Human friend of mine there; would you like to come along?" With the circle of light gone, Matthew knew he would not be going back soon; and was not so sure he really wanted to.

"Well, I need to find out what I'm doing here and why. It doesn't look like I'll find the answers here, so I might as well tag along with you."

"Splendid!" Deeli cried. "I think if you stay awhile you may just find those answers." Matthew tried to get up from his sitting position on the large rock, but his head pounded worse and his stomach threatened to leave him. He quickly sat back down.

"I don't think I can make it to the fire, let alone down the mountain," Matthew said, holding his right hand to a throbbing head and cradling an aching left arm in his lap.

"I can see the arm still pains you from your roll down the hill," Deeli said looking at Matthew closely. "But your other ailments, combined with your coloring, remind me of someone who has had a little too much fruit of the vine." Matthew had to smile at the old and very astute Elf.

"I guess you could say I had been trying to escape my world through those means."

"It seems to me that you escaped a little farther than you had planned," Deeli said smiling. "But you are here now and lucky for you I came along. I have some things with me that should get you feeling better in no time." Deeli proceeded to minister to Matthew. He unwrapped, then cleaned the hastily bandaged arm and re-bandaged it, putting some herbs from one of his pouches on the cut. The pain seemed to fade almost instantly. Deeli then set a tin cup full of water on a rock just inside the fire, pouring herbs from another pouch into it. When the concoction was warm he made Matthew drink it. Deeli then pulled some bread and dried beef from his sack and they both ate. Miraculously, the food stayed down. By the time they were done eating, Matthew felt much better and was able to get up and walk around.

"Thank you Deeli. Boy, my head and stomach feel a lot better; that stuff you made me drink worked like magic."

"No, I have sworn an oath not to use my magic anymore. That drink was made from crushed flowers and bark from one of the trees you see in the valley below."

"I didn't really mean magic.... Wait a minute, are you telling me that you can do real magic?" Matthew asked in disbelief.

"Why yes, can no one in your world work magic?"

"There is no such thing as magic in my world."

"Most of the beings in this world have the potential for magic," Deeli explained. "The only ones who really stay adept in it these days are the Elven priests and some of the Traul race. I have sworn to my Dearest Friend that I would not use it anymore." A sad look came over Deeli's face. "Of course I have not always been successful at keeping that promise. But that is nothing for you to concern yourself with," Deeli added, brightening. "I think it is time we were on our way; I am going to be quite late meeting my friend as it is." Deeli grabbed up his water skin and sack. He then slung them over his shoulder and extended his hand to Matthew. They started down the mountain at an angle so it would not be so hard on their knees. Matthew had to put his arm around Deeli's shoulder, leaning slightly on the tough old hermit.

"I bet we look like quite a pair," Deeli said. "A tired old Elf, creaking his way down the mountain, helping a small Human who looks like he got in a fight with an ill-tempered Traul." Matthew had no idea what a Traul was, but the statement still struck him funny and they both began to laugh. *I think I'm going to like this guy*, Matthew thought as he headed down the mountain into the unknown.

Good, the sun is finally coming up, thought Chamiel, the High King's chief steward. *It's hard enough to get the entire royal household ready for a day like today, but when it has to be done by oil lamp it's nearly impossible.* The royal house had been busy for two hours already, making preparations for the Festival of the First Season. This was the biggest event of the sun-cycle and needed much attention. This festival was also the most difficult to prepare for. All other Elven holidays and festivals were held right here on the castle grounds and in the city. This festival though, was held in the clearing of the Great Tree; almost half a day's ride. The chief steward had been hustling about all morning giving orders this way and that. He stopped at a window and looked out into the courtyard for the fourth time in fifteen minutes.

"The trip to the clearing takes four hours on a good day, and Lord Gamilon has not yet arrived," Chamiel said aloud to no one visible. "The King gives me nothing to work with but boys; none of which have a brain in his head. You there in the green tunic, finish loading that food quickly and then help the others get those carriages in line." As much as Chamiel complained, he was good at his job and the royal entourage was ready to leave by the eighth hour. The King and his family had been told that all was ready and were on their way down to the courtyard. Before they got there, Lord Gamilon and six of his men came riding swiftly into the courtyard. They spooked the horses that were in the processional line and sent many a stable hand running to restore order.

Lord Gamilon, son of one of the highest nobles in the land and engaged to the High King's daughter, Sharineas Leasha Silvanthia; was on his way to becoming the next High King. He was considered handsome by most, a little arrogant by all, but an Elf of the most noble character. Gamilon had long black hair that he let flow down to his shoulders most of the time, and a short well-kept beard. He was a very serious person and knew the Elven law almost as well as the experts and priests. Being the eldest son of a noble he had the finest education and was also a trained warrior. Today he was dressed in his finest riding clothes, deep forest green and black, trimmed in gold. He also had on a deep green riding cloak and looked every inch the royalty that he was.

"You there," he yelled at one of the stable hands. "Take charge of my horse while I go to meet the royal family." Gamilon met the King and Queen as they were entering the courtyard. "My Lord King," he said with a bow. "And Lady Queen, such a beautiful day for a celebration."

"Yes it is, Lord Gamilon, and we are very pleased that you will be riding in our carriage with us," said the Queen. Gamilon looked behind the pair with a quizzical look on his face.

"Is Sharineas not coming to the festival on her big day?" Just as he said this, Sharineas bounded up behind her parents; cheeks flushed with excitement. Gamilon and Sharineas had known each other since childhood and had been matched for marriage by their parents since before they could walk. To Sharineas, Gamilon was her best friend, and marriage some distant event that she could not comprehend. Gamilon's feelings however went much deeper. He was twenty-six cycles and she twenty-five, more than old enough to be wed in his mind.

"Gamilon! Where have you been? I thought you'd never get here," Sharineas said excitedly. "We've been waiting for you forever."

"I do not think we have been waiting quite forever, my dear," King Peridon said with a wink toward Gamilon.

"I truly am sorry, Sharineas. My father was supposed to have come with us, but he has fallen ill and I had to stay long enough to make sure it was not anything serious. At his advanced age one can never be sure."

"Oh, I'm sorry to hear that," Sharineas said. "Will he be all right?"

"Yes, I'm sure he will be. He just was not up to traveling today. He felt bad; this will be the first festival he has ever missed since we were able to begin celebrating them again."

"It grieves me to hear this of your father," said the King. "He is one of the last Elven officers left alive who served in the war that returned to us our land. Truly a great figure in our history, you should be proud of him, my son."

"Oh I am sir, I love my father and wish to make him proud of me. If the rumors that I have been hearing are true, maybe I will get the chance to prove myself to him."

"Those kinds of rumors will always be around when people are bored with life," the King said looking at Gamilon and giving him a slight shake of his head. "Pay no attention to such talk, you are young, concentrate on living your life in peace." With that the King and Queen made their way over to the royal carriage. Gamilon and Sharineas followed a few paces behind.

"I'm sorry I was late, Sharineas, I hope you can forgive me."

"Of course I can, Gamilon, you could not help the circumstances with your father. I was just worried about being late for the ceremonies; they start right after the midday meal."

"Yes, I know you must be there on time, and you will be." Gamilon could see in Sharineas' eyes the excitement of her newfound appointment as Keeper of the Amulet. He could not help feeling that these newfound responsibilities would only prove ill for their relationship. "This is a bigger day for you than for anyone else and I hope it will be the second happiest day of your life, next to our wedding day, of course. By the way, have you thought anymore about setting a date for our wedding?" Sharineas did not answer right away, but cleared her throat and looked straight ahead. After a moment she answered without looking at her betrothed:

"Gamilon, I must ask you to please wait a while longer. I just do not feel that I am ready yet." At that moment they reached the carriage, thus ending their private conversation. Gamilon was grateful for this because he knew it would not be wisdom on his part to speak the reply that had been about to come out of his mouth.

They stepped up behind the King and Queen into the first carriage of the line. It was drawn by six horses and decorated in royal splendor. An entire legion of the royal mounted guard led the procession. The royal family was next with their servants behind them. After that came the carriages of relatives of the royal family, other various nobles, and their servants. Fourteen carriages and wagons in all, a very impressive sight for the common Elves. With the royal family arriving, the procession was finally able to get under way. The lead soldiers began moving from the courtyard out into the street. The street was already full of

Elves heading for the festival, but all stopped to make room for the royal procession.

The screaming of children, the noise of animals, talking, shouting, and laughter, all combined to make up the atmosphere for traveling to the biggest celebration of the cycle. This was the one time of year when all of the races that inhabited the valley came together. It was not only a religious holiday for the Elves and Path followers, but a celebration of the dead seasons' end, and entrance into the season of life.

Sharineas sat in the carriage, quietly looking out the window. She had always been excited about going to the festival, but this was a special one for her. Finally she would have responsibilities and a position that she was not born to; something that she was supernaturally called to by the Creator, something the Princess had been waiting for all of her life. Sharineas enjoyed being Princess and heir to the Elven throne and never took advantage of the position. Somehow though, she did not feel that this was her call in life. She looked ahead on the road, wondering why the people were not moving faster. Her eyes full of anticipation, her mind on only one thing. *Yes,* she thought to herself. *This is the most important day of my life.* Gamilon watched her face out of the corner of his eye. He said nothing; his countenance dark, his thoughts kept to himself.

Matthew and Deeli had made their way to the foot of the mountain and stopped at the edge of a huge forest. Matthew could not believe the variety of colors in the forest. There were trees that looked like pines, but were baby blue. It was springtime here as well as at home, and the leaves were still small on the trees. Matthew could see red, yellow, and even purple in them. It was an amazing, beautiful sight. He was awed.

On their way down the mountain the two had done a lot of talking, and both agreed that Matthew must have stumbled through some kind of dimensional gateway. Deeli told him that he had many books and scrolls at his home and remembered reading something about this same kind of thing before. He promised Matthew that tomorrow he would take him to his home and maybe they could find some answers there. Matthew was still not convinced that he was not laying on a hospital bed somewhere in a coma and all of this was an illusion in his mind.

At Deeli's insistence, Matthew quit gawking at the forest and they started walking north along the tree line. They walked for about an hour before seeing the first Human dwellings through the trees. "The village is right through these trees," Deeli said. "When we get there, you can take that soggy shoe off and let it dry a little. I warned you when we were crossing that stream that the rock you were about to step on was slippery. But did you listen? No, of course not. At least I know the youth are the same in your world as in mine."

"I've always been the kind who wants to find things out for myself; that way I never have to wonder about it later," Matthew said, as he grimaced at the cold water squishing between his toes in the soaked shoe.

"Well, now you will not ever have to wonder if that rock is slippery, and you have the wet shoe to prove it," Deeli retorted, causing them both to chuckle. They broke through the trees and Matthew got his first clear look of the Human village. The houses were not shacks, but neither were they like anything Matthew was used to. The whole village looked like something out of the late middle ages, complete with little patches of grass between the huts and dirt roads winding throughout. *It's also like something out of the twilight zone*, Matthew thought, *the place seems deserted.* "This is just what I was afraid of," said Deeli. "The whole village has already left for the festival and we have missed them. Haub has probably gone as well. I am much later than I said I would be."

"What festival? And who is Haub?"

"Oh, did I not tell you about the festival? It is to celebrate the first season after the snows are gone. It is also a religious holiday for the Elves and the followers of the Path. That is where we are going, and it is several hours' walk from here. Most in the village do not own horses, so they have already left. Haub is the friend I told you I was meeting, the most kind and gentle Human you could ever know. Unless, of course, you tried to hurt a friend, or his family. Wait, there is Haub's dog, Brut. Haub would not have left without him; maybe he is still here."

"That's the biggest dog I've ever seen," Matthew said. Lying in the shade of one of the buildings, was a huge animal that looked like a cross between a Saint Bernard and a Doberman Pincher. The dog raised its head, saw that it was just Deeli, and promptly put its head back down.

"I will go and check his home to see if he is there. You go and check in that long building over there. That is the village hall where all the people have their meetings. Haub is one of the town elders, so he might be in there."

"All right," Matthew said as he started off toward the long structure. The village gave him an eerie feeling, empty of all its inhabitants. *It's as if the plague came through, or a mass murderer who hid all the bodies of his victims. I think I've been watching too much T.V. What could happen in a peaceful world like this?* It was so quiet that all Matthew could hear was the sound of his own breathing and his still-wet shoe slapping the dirt as he walked. Then he heard a noise in the building he was headed for. Thinking it was probably Deeli's friend Haub, Matthew yelled out his name as he continued toward the building.

He walked up to an unusually high, large door and reached out his hand to open it, intending to introduce himself to Haub. Just as he reached out his hand, the door flew open hitting Matthew squarely in the face and knocking him to the ground. He lay there stunned, pain shooting through his nose and behind his eyes. He could hear through the ringing in his ears that someone had walked up to him and was just standing there.

Matthew had been holding his hand over his eyes and nose to help stop the pain. He now took away the hand and forced his eyes open. Matthew's heart leapt into his throat and his mouth hung open in a silent scream. Standing not two feet away was a giant wearing an animal skin vest. He had to be at least nine feet tall, with a protruding forehead and big bushy eyebrows, although it was the huge, short-handled axe the giant held that Matthew could not take his eyes away from. He did not need to be any closer to see that on the blade of the axe was fresh blood.

Chapter

4

Even though the pain was great, his fear of the giant wielding a bloody axe was greater. *What kind of world is this?* Matthew thought as he crept backwards on his hands and feet. When he had gotten a few yards away and the giant still had advanced no farther, Matthew decided to make a break for it. He jumped up and turned in the same motion, running at full speed from the very start. He ran all of three feet before colliding with something else. All that he could think on his way to the ground was, *my God! No wonder he didn't come for me, there was another one behind me. I must be surrounded.*

"Deeli, help!" Matthew cried loudly as he scrambled back to his feet, ready to run again. But when he looked at his new assailant, there was the old Elf himself sprawled out on the ground. Deeli was trying to sit up and working on getting his breath back.

"What is all the blessed yelling about, and why did you knock me down?" Matthew grabbed his hand trying to get him to his feet.

"There's a murdering giant after me, come on!" As he did this, Matthew looked back at the giant and dropped Deeli's hand. The old Elf was laughing; the giant was sitting on a bench alongside the building from which he had emerged. He was watching Matthew and Deeli with his head cocked and a questioning look on his face.

"You mean the Human sitting on that bench over there?" Deeli asked through his laughter.

"Human, how can that be a Human, he's gigantic!"

"My dear Matthew, I said earlier that you looked part Elven because you were too small to be all Human. That is my friend, Haub." Deeli motioned for Haub to join them, and the giant man got up with his axe in hand and walked over to them. "I can see that the two of you have already met, but I do not believe you have been properly introduced. Haub, this is my new friend Matthew. Matthew, my *Human* friend, Haub." Matthew gave Haub a weak, nervous smile.

"I'm sorry I was afraid of you, it's going to take me awhile to get used to things around here."

"Well met, Matthew," Haub said. "Deeli my friend, may His peace rest upon your shoulders."

"I had no idea that the Humans of this world would be so big," Matthew said looking at Haub.

"They are all very big," Deeli said from his position still on the ground, "although Haub is one of the biggest I have ever seen. Now will you please help me up?" Matthew leaned over to help Deeli up and whispered in his ear.

"Why does he have blood on his axe?" Deeli gave Matthew a frightened look.

"I do not know, maybe he has murdered the inhabitants of this village." Matthew's eyes bulged in fright, but Deeli gave him a smile and a wink to let him know he was just kidding. "Friend Haub, how is it that you have come to have blood on your weapon?" Haub was not quite in the mood for talking yet—instead, he bent over and gave Deeli a hug.

"I am glad you are all right, I was getting worried about you being so late; especially after what just happened in the meeting building."

"What did happen?" Deeli asked with much concern in his voice. "I hope none of that blood on you is yours."

46

"No, none of the blood on my clothing is mine. I only received a few bruises and a little cut on my neck, but I don't think you will like what I have to tell you."

"Let us go sit down and you can start from the beginning," Deeli said. All three went over to the bench Haub had been sitting on and he began his story.

"The other villagers left for the festival, but you had not yet arrived, so I decided to stay behind and wait for you. I was doing a little cleaning up outside this building when I heard a noise from within. In the back of this building are rooms where we keep our extra food supplies, medicines, and village records. Once inside the building I could tell the noises were coming from there. The noise grew louder as I got closer to the rooms, they must have believed every one had gone."

"It sure did seem that way to me," Matthew interjected.

"Continue on Haub," Deeli said giving Matthew a wink. "Where he comes from it is not impolite to interrupt someone while they are talking." Matthew blushed under the joking rebuke.

"The little monsters were making enough noise that they didn't hear me coming. I caught two Nomies, one in the records' room and another came in from the food stores. The first one I killed right away, but while I was getting my axe out of his skull, the other one came at me from behind. It hooked one of its claws in the back of my neck. When I was finally able to reach around and pull it off, I threw it against the wall and it crumpled to the floor. I gave the thing a good crack on the head to make sure it was dead. I was trying to figure out what they would want with our records when I heard my name being called. That's when I came out and knocked you down Matthew."

"Oh don't worry about that, I'm feeling better. It was more the shock than anything. Then seeing you with that bloody axe; it scared the pants off me." Haub gave a smile in return which helped Matthew to relax some, but now Deeli was in a more serious mood.

"You said that it put a claw in you, but Nomies do not have claws."

"That's the part I knew you wouldn't like to hear. They were the mutated, winged Nomies." Deeli's face changed to an even more serious expression. Matthew was dying to find out what all of this meant, but was afraid to interrupt again. Deeli could see this written all over his face so he explained a little.

"The Nomie and Traul races have always worked on the side of evil. One of their number has risen up as of late and organized them into an army. I am afraid he intends to use this army to take over our valley and destroy its inhabitants. He is very powerful in magic and rumor has it, totally ruthless. There have been not only rumors, but also sightings of Trauls and Nomies that he has mutated through his magic. The mutated Nomies have claws, fangs, and black leathery wings that enable them to fly. The evil being, who calls himself the Enlightened One, uses these flying Nomies mainly as spies. And now they are this far south into the valley." Talking now more to himself than to Matthew, Deeli asked. "I wonder what he is up to?"

"I don't know," Haub replied. "The only thing I know is they were either pretty hungry, or for some reason very sure of themselves, to take a chance on being discovered like that."

"How do you know so much about what he is up to?" Matthew asked Deeli.

"I am not without my sources. But I really do not know enough about him, no one but his minions have ever even seen this Dark Lord. We do not even know for sure what race he belongs to. Now Haub, let me have a look at the cut in the back of your neck." Matthew just about fainted when he saw the long bloody gash.

"It's just a scratch," Haub insisted.

"I agree," said Deeli, "that it looks worse than it is, but it is definitely more than just a scratch. Haub, where would we be able to get some clean strips of cloth?"

"There are some in the back room where the medicines are kept. I will go get some."

"No, you stay right here. Matthew will you please go look for the cloth? I will go to the well and get some water for cleaning this up and mixing some more of my special tea."

"Sure, no problem." Matthew got up and headed for the door that Haub had used to exit the building. The room he walked into was long and narrow, with many long tables in it. He made his way to the back of the room and went through the door. Matthew gagged on bile and nearly regurgitated. The room was a mess from the fighting and in the middle of the floor lay a hideous looking creature with wings. Its head was split open, blood and brains oozing out onto the floor.

There was also a lot of blood on one of the walls, but Matthew saw no second creature. There was, however, a trail of blood that led into the next room, so Matthew cautiously followed it. The trail led to an open window with blood on the sill; no winged creature in sight. *The other Nomie must not have been dead. I better get back and tell Deeli.* In his excitement Matthew ran back into the other room almost forgetting the cloth strips. Running back he found them in a drawer and headed back out to the others. Deeli had already gotten the water and had his hands on Haub's head, obviously praying for him. Deeli heard Matthew come out and opened his eyes. "What took you so long?" He asked.

"I'm sorry, but the Nomie that Haub threw up against the wall must not have been dead," Matthew answered as he handed Deeli the cloth strips. "It's gone and there's a trail of blood leading to an open widow." Deeli looked up from tending to Haub's neck, an alarmed expression on his face.

"That is bad news indeed, they are nasty little creatures. We had best keep a sharp eye out for it."

"It has probably crawled off to die somewhere," Haub said. "I did hit it pretty hard." Deeli did not look convinced. When he had finished cleaning the wound, the elderly Elf packed it with some of his herbs and bound it. Haub had already drank the same concoction that Matthew had, so his pain was much less.

"If you do not mind, Matthew, I would like to say a prayer for Haub's healing."

"Sure go ahead, whatever you think will help." While Deeli was praying, Matthew's thoughts were wandering. *It seems as if I'm doomed to spend the rest of my life running into religious people. He really does seem sincere, like dad. Maybe his God is the real thing.* In just a short time Deeli was done praying.

"Haub, I am not sure you should be trying to walk all that distance to the festival"

"Well I'm not staying behind, my wife and children are waiting there for me. Marth would be very worried if she thought I was too ill to come."

"You are right," Deeli submitted, holding his hands out in front of him, "you are much too big for me to argue with. But Haub, please, no bravery. If you need to rest along the way tell us and we will stop."

Haub rested while Matthew and Deeli cleaned up the back room as best they could and burned the winged Nomie's body outside the village. When they were finished, all three started out through the woods, taking food from the village stores with them. They traveled for a while before coming to a well-traveled dirt road that Deeli said would take them to the festival. Once on the road the three companions began talking. Deeli related how Matthew came into their world from his own. When Deeli was through, Matthew thought he would try asking some questions.

"Deeli, you said that this power was rising in the north, and that no one has ever seen this person. Have your people done anything to stop him?"

"I am afraid that most people are not too alarmed about the threat. The prophecies have foretold a being like this arising at the end of time, but the same kind of thing happened about fifty sun-cycles ago. At that time many priests and experts in the law were saying that the end of the world had come, that the end time prophecies were about to come true, but they did not. So the people now are taking no notice of the signs. Much of it is my fault. I was the loudest voice back then telling people it was the end. Of course I was a very different person back then. Now I continue my warnings, but I let the Creator do things in His own time."

"Boy! This is a lot for me to take in all at once. It's going to take me awhile to get used to all this stuff. By the way, what's a sun-cycle?"

"It is the time it takes our world to revolve around the sun," Deeli answered. "The time it takes to go through all four seasons."

"Oh, in our world we refer to that as a year. It seems like a lot of things in our worlds are the same and yet so many things are different."

"It is as if the Creator had so many ideas left after finishing with one world that He had to make another one. That way his creativity would not go to waste," Deeli said, hoping to get a response out of Matthew. Matthew did not know what to say, so he just shrugged his shoulders and remained silent. They walked that way for some time; Matthew contemplating his situation and wondering about these two people with whom he was traveling.

"Deeli, on our way here you told me that the Elven kingdom and the Human villages were separated by a huge forest. You also said that the races did not mix very much, only on special occasions like this one. How did you two get to be such good friends?"

"What has really brought us together as friends is our common belief in the same God. But I think I will let Haub tell you how we met." Haub looked a little taken back and hesitated for a moment. Matthew could tell he was not the kind to tell stories and it seemed he did not talk much unless he was spoken to first. *The strong silent type*, Matthew thought. After a long pause, Haub began.

"It is true that we believe in the same God, but I did not come to know Him until I met Deeli. He found me one day about five cycles ago. I was hunting up in the mountains above us when I came upon three Trauls. To this day I don't know what they were doing there, unless it had something to do with what is going on now. The three attacked me. It was a long battle, but I managed to win and kill all three. I was hurt badly and could not walk. I thought for sure that I had won, only to lie there among the rocks and die. Deeli insists that it was at the summons of the Creator that he came. He was hiking in the area and heard the noises of battle. He got there after the fighting was over, but stayed and tended to me for three days and nights. Praying over me, washing my wounds, and feeding me. When I was able to walk, he led me to his house, which was closer than my village. I spent several more days there recuperating and listening to stories about the Elven God, called the Creator. He also told me about the way of the Path—a way to which my soul responded wholeheartedly. He told me all his God had done to wash away the evil from us so that we could be with Him after we die. I truly felt His presence then and became a follower of the Path. When I was finally well enough to make it down the mountain, we came back to my village where all the people thought I had died. Deeli was deemed a hero. After they heard about all that had happened to me, most of the village came to believe, including my family." Haub talked of his family with such emotion that Matthew could tell he loved them very much. In a way, it made him a little jealous.

"Since then we have been like brothers," Deeli added.

"It is so refreshing to minister to Human believers. When they convert it is not halfway like most of the Elves, but it becomes a whole-hearted way of life."

"Matthew," Haub said hesitantly, "does your world believe in gods, or a single God, or none at all?"

"The people of my world believe in many gods," Matthew answered, trying to find the right words, "including a supreme God who created the world. But there are so many variations that I think people are more confused than anything. So the majority of the people worship themselves as gods and spend their lives looking out for their own interests."

"What about you?" Deeli asked.

"I'm really not sure what I believe. At one time I thought I was sure, but that's long past. Actually I am half hoping I can find the answer to that question here. But please, don't try to force me to believe what you believe, I've had enough of that in my life. Like I told you before Deeli, I'm the kind that likes to find things out for myself."

"In this case there is no other way my young friend," Deeli said with a smile. "At one time I would have tried to coerce you into believing as I do, but my Lord has shown me the error of that way. Haub and I will respect your wishes and beliefs. And no matter what, we will continue to unconditionally love you and be here for you. We may not necessarily think your beliefs are right, but no one can force another to change his heart. Only the Spirit of the Creator can do that." Matthew could not help himself from loving these two back. Their very attitude toward him and respect for what he believed made him more interested in finding out about this "Path" that they followed.

Matthew's thoughts could go no further. The sound of flapping wings suddenly filled the air and Matthew was knocked to the ground. He tried to push the creature off, but it already had a strong hold on him. The monster had a claw in Matthew's left shoulder and its jaws going for his throat. In the next moment the winged Nomie was ripped off him. Haub had grabbed the thing by its neck and threw it to the ground away from Matthew. Haub swung his axe at the creature missing anything vital, but cutting off one of its legs. As he was going for a second swing, another of the Nomies landed on his back catching him right on his wound. Haub grunted in pain, his eyes rolling back in his head as he fell to his knees. With his free hand he tried to reach up and pull the creature off his back.

Matthew got up to go help Haub, but Deeli was ahead of him. He had rushed up and pulled the Nomie off Haub's back. Haub turned around, weak as he was, to fight this second attacker. The first, almost forgotten, Nomie threw himself at Deeli, knocking the Elf up against a tree and leaving him unconscious. The first creature would have killed the elderly Elf, but Haub had taken care of the other one and came to Deeli's rescue. Just as the thing was about to rip Deeli open with its claws, Haub came up from behind and put his axe between the winged Nomie's shoulder blades. Everything happened so fast that Matthew did not know what to do; he was simply not used to this kind of thing. As Haub was taking care of Deeli's would-be killer, yet another of the winged Nomies dropped out of the tree onto Matthew. Haub turned and recognized the wounded Nomie he had fought back at the village. It had landed on Matthew so hard that he was almost unconscious.

The creature wanted to kill Matthew desperately, but when it saw Haub coming it flew up and circled above them. Matthew saw Haub standing over him, shaking his huge axe at the mutated Nomie. Finally Matthew heard a screech and the sound of leathery wings flapping away into the distance. When the sound was completely gone, he saw Haub collapse beside him. *He must have been keeping himself going by sheer willpower; just to protect me,* Matthew thought, as his mind slipped into silence.

Chapter

5

W hat's the hold-up this time?" Sharineas yelled out the window of the royal carriage to a mounted soldier. The soldier could hear the irritation in her voice and thought again before giving her a glib answer.

"I beg your pardon, Princess, but it's the priests again. They will only go so far without stopping to offer sacrifices to the Creator."

"Well that doesn't have to stop the rest of us from going on ahead. Tell whoever is in the lead to go around them." The soldier looked as though he would rather be anywhere else but here dealing with impatient royalty, but stood his ground.

"The problem, your Highness, is that they are very specific in the number of steps taken before stopping to offer up their sacrifice. At this time they are in the center of a very narrow stretch of road and no one can get around."

"Oh, those priests," Sharineas said infuriated. "You may go now." The soldier gratefully trotted his horse farther down the road. "We should have left before the priests," Sharineas continued her tirade. "It seems that all of Elven life is centered around the priests and their law."

"Now dear," the Queen said trying to soothe her daughter. "The ceremony cannot start without your father being there, so don't worry about being late." Gamilon, very quiet the entire trip thus far, spoke up in defense of the priesthood.

"Sharineas! I am surprised at you. The Elven race finally has an established kingdom back after all these generations. We finally have our temple, sacrifices, and priesthood back after being denied them so long, and you would wish it all done away with? We must show our thankfulness to the Creator. It was your grandfather who was the first King of the newly established Elven kingdom. It was he who made provisions for the sacrifices to begin again."

"I know, I know," Sharineas said accepting the rebuke. "It just seems that sometimes the priests have more power than the King."

"You know we must follow the law to the letter; it is what sets us apart from the other races. We are the Creator's chosen people and must never forget it."

"Yes," the King added, "Gamilon is right, we must please our God so that He will be with us in the times ahead."

"What do you mean, father? Our land finally has peace, we rule ourselves again, and there are more of our race coming back to live in the valley all the time." *She is so young and naive*, the King prayed. *Oh God of heaven, please spare my daughter and her offspring the horrors of war.*

"I only mean, Sharineas, that if any of the other races did rise up against us again we would need the Creator's blessing to be on us, and for Him to intervene on our behalf." Gamilon, back to his usually quiet self, was watching Peridon's expressions and thinking: *Ah, My King. Once your daughter wears the amulet you will not be able to hide the truth from her for very long.*

"No one had better attack the Elven people again," Sharineas said hotly. "We are stronger than ever and would not stand for it."

"No one will come against us," her mother interjected. "Besides, I'm sure our old alliances with the Humans and Dwaries in the valley would still hold true. I think it is only a matter of time before peace come to the people outside the valley. Oh look, the line is movii again, the sacrifices must be finished."

"Praise the Creator!" Sharineas said. "Maybe now we can get there on time."

Mother and daughter spent the rest of the journey talking together. They talked of the festival and especially about the ceremony that would bestow upon Sharineas the Amulet of Truth. They were so excited about the upcoming events that neither noticed the silence of the other two occupants, or the frowns they wore.

Matthew awoke feeling wet slime on his face, and a burning pain in his left shoulder. He was still trying to decide whether or not he should attempt to open his eyes, when he felt something rub against his face and leave more wet slime. In a panic he opened his eyes to find a monster with huge fangs and very bad breath hovering over him, its mouth wide open. Matthew froze in fear. *This is it. I've lived through everything else just to be eaten by this monster. I wish I hadn't woke up. This would have been a lot easier to take if I were asleep.* Suddenly an enormous tongue came out of the monster's mouth and licked Matthew's face. "Yuuck!" Matthew yelled. "What the heck is going on here?" The monster, surprised by Matthew's outburst, jumped back.

"I'm sorry, Matthew," Haub said with a little laugh in his voice. The big Human was sitting up against a tree and looking very pale. "He sometimes gets a little zealous when I ask him to do something. I would like to introduce you to my friend, Brut."

"Yes, I recognize him now. I saw him back at the village. Where did he come from?"

"He is usually not too far away from where I am, but he does prefer to be by himself most of the time. He is not my pet and I do not own him. That is the kind of relationship we have, although I think he will stick a little closer from now on. Brut was here standing guard over us while we were out, but I think he feels bad about not being here for the fight."

"Well, thank you for watching over us, Brut. And thank you, Haub, for saving my life, twice. How are you feeling?"

...must admit, but I think Deeli will be able to help
...nd." Haub sent Brut over to awaken Deeli, which
...do in the same fashion he woke Matthew. The two of
...y crawled over to where the dog and Elf were. Deeli was
...around by the time they reached him, pushing Brut away and
...plaining about his breath. Deeli was able to get up, but was feeling
very weak. Matthew looked and could see a large lump and some blood
on the back of Deeli's head where he had been slammed up against the
tree. Matthew cleaned Deeli's wound with water and strips of cloth
from the village. Deeli gave them all a piece of tree bark to chew on to
help the pain.

"I usually like to brew these in a tea, but under the circumstances
I think this will have to do." Once Deeli was tended to and the dizziness had gotten better, he ministered to Matthew and Haub; redressing
Haub's shoulder and bandaging Matthew's claw wound, packing them
both with his medicinal herbs. When he was done, all three sat down
to try to regain some of their strength.

"I'm sorry," Haub said. "I recognized the last one that attacked
Matthew as the one I fought back at the village. It is my fault it got
away and brought the others."

"It's not your fault Haub, you thought it was dead. Deeli and I don't
blame you."

"Of course not," Deeli added reassuringly. "You cannot blame yourself for the attack. If we were to blame anyone it would be Matthew."

"How could it be my fault!? I just got here, remember. I've never
even seen one of these things before today."

"Now I am not really blaming you, so calm down. I am just trying
to point out that the creatures seemed to be after you specifically. You
were between Haub and myself as we walked. Yet when they attacked,
the creatures went for you first."

"But why would they want to kill me?" Matthew asked horrified.
"I've never done anything to them."

"I do not know," Deeli answered honestly. "Maybe it is only my
imagination. I have been worried ever since I found out the Dark One's
spies were this far into the valley. We can only hope that their appearance on the day of the festival is a coincidence." At that statement
Haub's eyes grew wide with alarm.

"We must leave for the clearing at once. If the evil from the north should try anything…"

"Do not be worried for your family, dear Haub," Deeli said. "Could he bring his whole army through the valley without anyone noticing? I do not think so, but I do agree that we should be leaving. Matthew, do you feel up to it?"

"I'll sure do my best," Matthew answered with as much enthusiasm as he could. All the talk of evil armies, being attack by winged Nomies, and the fact that they might be hunting him for some reason, was giving Matthew second thoughts.

The three started out again, more slowly this time because of their wounds. Soon, the beauty of the forest made their fight with the winged Nomies seem farther away and talk turned to lighter things. "Between our stiff walk and bandaged wounds, we look like something out of an American Revolution or Civil War movie," Matthew said with a laugh. Both Deeli and Haub looked at him with blank expressions on their faces.

"What is a movie?" Haub finally asked.

"Never mind, it would be too hard to explain. I guess you had to be there," Matthew said still grinning as they walked on toward the clearing.

Sharineas was fighting a losing battle to keep herself calm. They had finally arrived at the clearing, the carriages were being unpacked, and it all seemed to be proceeding at a snail's pace to Sharineas. "Mother, father, may I please go ahead and see to the preparations for the ceremony? Everyone's probably been wondering if we were even going to show up."

"Sharineas," said the Queen with a patient smile, "the amulet ceremony is the last thing on today's agenda. There are many more events before that, you need not be in a hurry." Sharineas was adamant and persistent in her asking. Finally her father gave his permission.

"Very well, you may go. But the feast will be starting soon and you are to sit with us at the head table."

"I'll be there. Thank you, father." With that, she ran off toward the Great Tree where the ceremony would take place. Gamilon took his gaze from her retreating form and looked at the King.

"She is as giddy as a school maid today."

"This is her big day," the King replied. "I guess we just have to make allowances for any odd behavior. It is a very great honor she is receiving today, and maybe it will be good for her in the long run."

"What do you mean, sire?"

"Well, I have always been afraid that because of her hard-headed ways and lack of things to do as the Princess of the realm...well...that they would cause her to leave home some day; to seek adventure and a place of her own. But now, with this new found responsibility, she will have to stay within the Elven kingdom. Besides, the prime duty of the Keeper of the Amulet is to stay with Calburnathis. As long as it still resides in the Great Tree, she cannot go anywhere."

"That is true," Gamilon agreed. "That part of the prophecy concerning Calburnathis is just as hard to understand as the drawing forth part. I mean the only time in history when the Keeper ever really had anything to do with the sword, was the time when she stole it and disappeared."

"Yes, the sword reappeared, but the Keeper and High Counselor did not. I do not claim to know why the Keeper must stay with the sword, but as long as it keeps my daughter safe within the kingdom, I'll not argue."

Meanwhile, Sharineas had found the present Keeper of the Amulet. Lieanea was telling Sharineas what she needed to know for the ceremony. "The transference of the amulet will take place on that platform they are raising over near the Great Tree, so that Calburnathis can easily be seen. After everything else is through, I will make a short speech and then introduce you. I will then place the amulet around your neck and you will say a few words of acceptance. That is all there is to it. Of course, for the next few moon phases I will be tutoring you on the powers of the amulet and how to use them."

"Have you had many occasions to use the powers?"

"I've used its minor properties some, and other powers have been triggered by accident at times. We only regained the amulet fifty cycles ago, after the war. Many of the things we knew about the amulet's powers were lost over the long period our people did not have possession of it. It took quite some time for me to learn about it on my own, and there are many things I'm sure I still don't know. But as long as our people are at peace, you should have plenty of leisure time to experiment. The only major service I've done for the kingdom has been recently."

"What was it?" Sharineas asked, eyes round with excitement.

"That is too much to go into at the moment, there will be plenty of time for questions later. As you know, our part of today's events happen only every fifty cycles, so we are last on the agenda. You have plenty of time before you must be dressed and ready."

"I wish we didn't have to wait for the test of the sword. It always takes so long, and Calburnathis is never withdrawn from the tree."

"Yes I know, but you must have faith in the Creator. When we need it the most, the sword will be drawn. Unfortunately for you, this is the biggest turn-out I've ever seen for the festival in all of my seventy-seven cycles. Which means the line will probably be longer than ever." Sharineas just gave a low groan and rolled her eyes in mock despair. Lieanea smiled and put her arm around the young Elf maiden. "There must be other things you can spend the time doing. Go enjoy yourself; this is a time of celebration remember?" They turned toward the long tables set up for the Elven royalty. The trumpets were blowing to let the people know that prayers were about to begin.

"Oh no, I'm supposed to be at the head table right now, I better hurry. Thank you, Lady Lieanea, I'll see you later."

"Yes, you best hurry, child. I have to as well. I'm supposed to be with the priests right now." Both laughed as they hurried to attend to their responsibilities. Sharineas was moving so fast she almost ran into Chamiel.

"Your mother and father are over there," he said pointing to where Sharineas should be. "They were looking for you earlier, so I would think you should be quick about it."

"Thank you, Chamiel," the Princess said, as she ran to the banquet area. *That's Chamiel, always knows where everyone is, or rather should be, every minute of the day.* When Sharineas got to her parents' side they were already kneeling in the direction of the temple, as were the priests. "I am sorry, father, I misjudged the time a little."

"I hope your new office as Keeper makes allowances for such tardiness and irresponsibility," the King replied with a stern expression. Sharineas felt the reproof and dropped her chin to her chest. *I seem to be getting in trouble a lot today,* she thought to herself. The Princess looked up once again at her father, whose expression had softened. He leaned over and kissed her cheek. "You will do well. I know your heart is in the right place."

The priests began their prayers, thanking the Creator for His blessings and that the Elven people were His chosen. To the discomfort of most, the priests continued to thank Him for everything else they could possibly think of. The prayers were very lengthy and most people were squirming by the time they were done. Once the ritual prayers were over, the feasting could begin. There was so much food and drink flowing that no one went hungry. It was the Elven custom for everyone to bring what food they could, and the King's household provided what anyone was lacking. Sharineas was so excited about the upcoming ceremony that she hardly touched her food. She spent most of the feasting time sitting next to her father, observing what was going on around her.

It seemed to her that every Elf in the valley was there. That was impossible, of course; they would not all fit—although many were there, including some of the forest Elves. Hydrian, their King, was sitting at the head of another table. When the population of Elves kept growing and the kingdom became crowded, many Elves wished to live closer to the land. These Elves left the city and retreated into the forest. They were allowed to have their own King, but were still subject to the High King, and paid taxes to him.

There were also more Humans than she had ever seen before in one place. Sharineas had heard rumors that more and more of the Humans were converting over to being followers of the Path every day. It would seem that those rumors were true. This festival also marked their biggest holy day of the sun-cycle. The Path religion had held the Great Tree and this clearing as sacred even before Calburnathis appeared here.

On the other side of the clearing, almost out of sight even for her Elven eyes, were the Dwaries. There were never very many Dwaries at the festival. Being the least religious race that dwelled in the valley, they did not have a lot of use for this celebration—but the Dwarie King always made an appearance with a sizable party. Sharineas looked intently in that direction to see if she could pick out the Dwarie King. He never distinguished himself from his subjects. The King looked like any other Dwarie, except Sharineas knew him to be very old. As she was looking, Sharineas caught sight of an old Elf at the Dwarie table. He seemed to be looking at her, but then turned his head away. The strange part was that the face had seemed familiar, but try as she might, she could not remember why.

"Sharineas, can you not hear me?"

"I'm sorry Gamilon, my mind was elsewhere I'm afraid. What did you say?"

"I said that I wish there were a way to keep the other races, and religions, from attending this festival. It is supposed to be a very sacred time for our people, and we have to share it with anyone who shows up, including followers of the Path."

"You know this land is outside the Elven borders, we have no right to keep anyone away. We should count it a blessing that the clearing is neutral ground, or it might be the Elves that were not allowed to be here."

"I cannot for the life of me figure out why the sword appeared here of all places," Gamilon said more to himself than Sharineas. "At one time this ground was the most accursed spot known to our race. Now we must hold our most sacred feast here, with followers of the Path, no less."

"You know this ground has been considered sacred to the Path followers for many, many generations. They were meeting here even before the sword appeared in the tree. Gamilon, you must learn to be more tolerant of people that are different than you."

"I don't mind the Dwaries and their God of the mountain, nor the many gods of the Humans—although I know they are false, but the Path religion takes our God and religion—then perverts it. That is what I cannot tolerate."

"Well there is only one way the Elven people can have this celebration to themselves. That would be to go to war with the other races and take the land as our own." Gamilon wanted to say that maybe they should do that very thing, but thought better of it and instead changed the subject.

"Look, the Test of the Sword is about to begin." Alexthna, High Counselor to King Peridon, advanced to the small stage that had been erected near the Great Tree. Trumpets sounded again, announcing the beginning of the event. Alexthna read the prophecy of Calburnathis, which was the custom once every cycle on this day.

All of the Elven males had lined up to try their luck. In turn, each walked up to the sword embedded in the tree, gripped the hilt, and pulled for all they were worth. Two hours had gone by and no one had been able to draw the sword. Most went away in good humor, the sword had been in the tree for almost sixteen-hundred sun-cycles, and very few really expected it to come out now. Finally the last in line tried and like those before him, failed. High King Peridon watched the face of his counselor drop. *Alexthna truly believed the sword would be drawn today. I feel sorry for him, but now maybe he'll be more willing to listen to the voice of reason.*

Gamilon was once again sitting next to Sharineas; his brows furrowed, and a look of disgust on his face. He had secretly believed that this was the year he would pull Calburnathis from the tree. *I will be King when I marry Sharineas,* Gamilon thought. *I hoped I would pull the sword free before then. With the sword and the kingship I will be able to establish the natural order of things, the way the Creator intended it to be.* Then Sharineas broke into his thoughts.

"This is it, Gamilon, the Ceremony of the Amulet is next," Sharineas said with barely controlled excitement. "I must get dressed." The Princess sat fidgeting through the entire Test of the Sword. She now hurried off without a backward glance at Gamilon. Sharineas practically ran to the portable dressing booth that Chamiel had made sure to bring. Gamilon watched her go with frustration. The young noble had always gotten whatever he wanted. So far the sword and Sharineas were the only things that had been able to elude him.

Sharineas made her way to the stage in a long flowing white dress, which was the traditional garb for this ceremony. The stage was about five feet high and somewhat shaky, as it had just been constructed this morning and was only a temporary platform. Nonetheless, it was strong enough to hold everyone necessary for the ceremony. Alexthna, King Peridon, the High Priest, and present Keeper of the Amulet Lieanea, were already on the stage when Sharineas got there.

After ascending the stairs, Sharineas paused behind a curtain that would keep her out of sight for a good part of the ceremony. Alexthna signaled when he saw that she was ready, and the trumpets began to sound the beginning of this very special occasion. The High Counselor, still with disappointment evident on his face, stood and began the proceedings.

"People of all races," he shouted so that the whole gathering could hear. "You are about to witness an event that has been handed down through the generations to the Elven people, and happens only once every fifty sun-cycles. Today the Keeper of the Amulet of Truth will transfer that office and the amulet to her successor. Three days ago the amulet itself chose the new Keeper. I now present to you the High King of all the Elven people, Peridon Japax Silvanthia." The crowd had quieted during Alexthna's speech, but when the King was introduced they applauded loudly.

"It is my pleasure as your King to watch over these proceedings this day, especially considering who they are for." The majority of the crowd, knowing it was for his daughter, laughed. "I would love to be the one to introduce her to you, but that privilege goes to Keeper Lieanea. So, I now present to you our High Priest, Raneish."

There was a spattering of applause as the High Priest took center stage and went into his speech and then a very lengthy prayer. By this time some of the glory of the moment had been lost to Sharineas. She was tired of standing in one spot and was busy shaking her feet trying to get the blood circulating again. *This is taking so long*, she thought. *And this priest prays forever. He always prays the same things over and over using different words. I wish I could get this tingling in my leg to stop. Oh good, he's finally done.* The applause for Lieanea when she was introduced was much louder than it had been for Raneish.

"I will not speak long, for the amulet has revealed to me that many of you are about to fall asleep," she began with a large grin. All of the people, including Sharineas and her father, laughed. Lieanea had always been able to make the people feel comfortable. "I only wish to say that it has been a great honor to serve my people in this way. It is also a great honor for me to introduce my successor, heir to the Elven throne, Princess Sharineas Leasha Silvanthia."

The crowd clapped and stood to their feet as Sharineas appeared from behind the curtain. Her cheeks were on fire, she was used to being in front of people, but this was somehow different. This was her day and nothing could ruin it. Lieanea and Sharineas faced each other and

Lieanea began to speak. "Sharineas, Princess of the Elven people, do you accept this office and the Amulet of Truth?"

"I do."

"And do you promise to use the powers now given you to protect the people of your race and of this valley?"

"I do."

"Then as Keeper of the Amulet of Truth, I now pass this talisman of our people to you." Lieanea then placed the amulet around Sharineas' neck and it began to glow. The crowd applauded and cheered for her. The new Keeper faced them, trembling a little and waiting for quiet so that she could speak. Sharineas had closed her eyes while she waited, but now opened them wondering why the people had not yet settled down. She realized that the crowd had stopped clapping and were now looking around with puzzled expressions on their faces. They were silent, but the noise was still there and growing louder.

The ground was beginning to shake and fear worked its way into the whole assembly. The sound was coming from the forest. Just as that realization struck Sharineas, she had a glimpse of what was causing the ground to tremble. *But how can I know that? Of course, the amulet has let me know.* But the vision of what she had seen was too horrible to contemplate. The people were scattering in fear and the temporary stage under her feet was beginning to shake apart. *I have to get off this thing and get to safety,* Sharineas thought as she turned to see which way she should go. Suddenly the vision from the amulet flashed through her mind again and froze her in place. At that moment part of the stage collapsed and Sharineas found herself falling through the air toward the ground below.

She had time to do nothing but scream before two arms reached out and caught her. She did not know who her rescuer was, only that he was carrying her to the Great Tree, to try to find cover. *It doesn't matter anyway,* she thought, *we're all about to die. No one could have been prepared for this.* The ground was shaking wildly now and the sound was like continuous thunder. Sharineas' rescuer held her in such an awkward position that her face was toward the forest. As she watched, leaves began to fall and branches to shake. It looked to Sharineas as though the trees were coming alive. Then, with a sudden burst, hundreds of black shapes emerged from the forest and entered the clearing.

Chapter

6

Haub, Deeli, and Matthew saw no more of the winged Nomies, but were still determined to be on better guard this time. They had not been making good time because of their injuries; it was almost midday and they were still not at the clearing. Inwardly, Deeli was concerned about the Enlightened One's spies being in the valley at this time. Outwardly, he was trying hard not to show it for the sake of Matthew and Haub.

Matthew's memory of the attack was already on the back burner of his mind. The enchantment of the strange forest with sunshine streaming through the branches gave him an almost euphoric feeling, and his wound was beginning to feel numb due to Deeli's herbs. Being raised in the suburbs of Gary, Matthew had never seen much of the country; except on family vacations when he was young. He had never been to the mountains, and certainly had not seen a forest like this one with its strange colored trees. Matthew was intently studying the forest when Deeli made an announcement from up ahead of him. "We are very nearly there."

"Where is it?" Matthew asked scanning the trees ahead.

"Oh, we are not close enough to see it from here, but if you look off to your right you will see the first sign that we are approaching the clearing." Matthew looked to where Deeli was pointing and saw something shining through the trees.

"What is it?"

"It," answered Deeli, "is what this valley is named after. It is one of the huge gold trees that populate this part of the forest. This is the only place in our world where they grow." By this time they were closer to the tree, and what Matthew saw made him catch his breath. Before him stood the biggest tree he had ever seen.

It was at least as big as the giant redwoods in California that he had seen pictures of, but the bark of this one looked like pure gold. He went up to the tree and touched the smooth bark; now that he was up close Matthew could see that the leaves were a lime green color. They had veins of gold running throughout that caused them to sparkle when the sun hit.

"This is wonderful," Matthew said in a hushed voice. "I've never seen such a beautiful tree."

"You don't have any like this in your world?"

"No, Haub, we don't. We have some as big, but they are reddish and not as pretty."

"This is just one of the small ones," Deeli said with pride. "Wait until we get closer to the clearing if you want to see some big ones. We really should not take anymore time here. Besides, I am hungry, and if we do not hurry we will miss the feast." Haub voiced his agreement and the three started off again. Matthew was awed by the gigantic gold trees. The farther they walked, the bigger and denser the trees became. Soon they could hear the sound of many voices, and knew the clearing was just ahead. The trees began to thin out again, and all three could see people up ahead laughing and having a good time.

"Praise be to the Creator and Shesea," Haub said with relief. "Everything seems to be all right." They reached the clearing and started to wind their way through the crowd of people. Matthew could scarcely soak it in. The Humans he saw were all huge; the shortest females were taller than he was. They walked by fires with meat roasting on spits; the rising smoke made the air hazy in areas, and the delicious aromas made Matthew's mouth water and stomach growl. There were bright colors and laughter on every side as they made their way through the crowds. They had entered on the east side of the clearing, but Matthew's attention was now on the north side; gathered there were hundreds of Elves.

I can hardly believe this; Deeli isn't some freak of nature. Elves really do exist in this world. Then Matthew stopped walking and stared ahead of him. Deeli had not been exaggerating when he had told him about the tree in the clearing. This tree was so big around you could have built a highway through it and the tree would not have even noticed. It was a good sixty feet before the branches even started. Matthew could not tell how high the tree went after that because he could not get far enough away to see the top.

"I can see that you have met the Great Tree," Deeli said, startling Matthew. "Haub and I were halfway across the clearing before we realized you were not with us and turned back. Quite remarkable, is it not?"

"It's breathtaking," Matthew agreed. "I'm sorry that I didn't keep up with you—this is all so new. But please don't lose me, I wouldn't have the slightest idea where to go."

"Come along then, we are going over to Haub's family, and then I want you to meet another friend of mine." Matthew followed behind the two. As they drew close to the giant tree, both Deeli and Haub knelt down in reverence to it. Matthew was confused. *Could this be the God they worship? What have I gotten myself into?* Both stood back up and noticed Matthew looking at them.

"Is this tree the God you guys have been talking about all this time? I mean it's okay and everything," Matthew rushed on, not wanting to offend his new friends. "There are people where I come from that worship trees and all kinds of stuff."

"No, my friend," Deeli answered. "This is a very holy place to us, but just a place none the less. Our God created the trees and everything in this world. It would be silly to worship the creation instead of the Creator. Hopefully we will have time today to tell you why this is such holy ground. Now, however, we must find Haub's wife before she dies from worry over why we are so late."

"I told them to be looking for us by the Great Tree, so they should be close," Haub said scanning the area from his great height. While the other two were looking, Matthew's curiosity got the better of him again. He began to walk around the tree scanning the area around him. He was so intent on watching the people, that he walked into something hard and fell back in surprise.

There, quivering slightly, was a sword buried in the tree almost to its hilt. The hilt seemed to be made of gold, with black stones embedded in the handle. The hand guards swirled up to make two elaborate dragons with bright red gem-stones for eyes. At the end of the handle was a three pronged claw that held what looked like a huge diamond. Matthew could see every color of the rainbow in that clear, flawless stone.

"Pretty sword, is it not?"

"Deeli! You scared me to death."

"I would not have been able to sneak up on you if you had not been so absorbed. Or if you had been where you were supposed to be."

"I know, I'm sorry I wandered off again," Matthew said, apologetically. Deeli thought Matthew's apology came a little too quickly to be convincing. "Why is the sword stuck in the tree? Why hasn't anyone gotten it out?"

"Slow down my boy, you are going to give yourself gray hair. The young, they are always so impetuous," Deeli said looking at the sky and shrugging his shoulders. "To tell you the truth, only two people have ever known the whole story behind that, and they have been dead for over fifteen centuries. I can tell you that the sword's name is Calburnathis. It is an ancient talisman of the Elven people that belonged to one of our earliest kings, and was said to have been given to him by the Creator Himself. About sixteen hundred sun-cycles ago the sword was stolen from its place of safety in the temple. It was not seen again for over thirty cycles, until it reappeared stuck in the tree. No one has ever been able to pull it out yet, but I believe that day is coming soon. You are very fortunate; the sword is tied very closely to another talisman of my people. It is a crystal amulet, the ceremony to transfer ownership happens only once in every fifty cycles, and today is that day."

"Will we be able to see the ceremony?" Matthew asked.

"I do not see why not. Unless of course we never get to eat because of your fooling around," Deeli scolded with a smile. "I think it is time

you got up off the ground Haub has certainly found his family by now."
Matthew gave one last longing glance at the sword. He could not help
thinking of how it would look with the suit of armor he had seen in the
antique shop.

They walked back to the other side of the tree and saw Haub waving at them from some distance away. They made their way over to him
and his family. Haub, beaming with pride, began to introduce them to
Matthew. "This is my wife Marth. My son Wil, who will be thirteen
sun-cycles soon. And this beautiful little girl is my daughter, Cas."

"I am very pleased to meet you," Matthew said to each of them.
The only one that was shorter than himself was the young daughter.
Seeing this kind, selfless man with his family caused Matthew to think
of his father and the family he had been denied. He could feel a lump
rising in his throat, so he tried to get his mind on other things. He
noticed that all the Humans had the same coarse hair and bushy eyebrows. *Man! I feel like a midget among all these Humans. Even a twelve-
year-old kid is taller than me.*

Suddenly, a very large commotion began on the other side of the
clearing where the Elves were gathered. A large troop of Elves dressed
as soldiers and riding what kind of looked like a small horse, came into
the clearing; followed by a very fancy carriage. Matthew started to walk
off in that direction to get a better view; Deeli caught him by his good
shoulder. "The High King of the Elves has arrived, I think it would be
best if I introduced you to my other friend right now."

"But you're going the wrong way," Matthew protested. "All the
excitement is over there."

"And that is precisely where you do not want to be. Now come
along." Matthew reluctantly followed Deeli to the opposite side of the
clearing. He noticed as they walked that the Humans were generally
not as well dressed as the Elves that he had seen and asked Deeli about
it. "The Elves have a king, an organized government, and an organized
religion. Through history they have been the chosen of the Creator.
And so they have been the recipients of His blessings, as well as His
correction. The Humans lead a much simpler existence, living in many
small villages like the one you saw. Each village is autonomous and has
its own leader and council of elders to help him. Haub is the youngest
elder of his village. The Dwaries also have a king, but are governed in

a much more relaxed way than the Elves. Their king does not put himself above his people. He is also their battle chief and leads them in time of war."

"Where do the Dwaries live?"

"They dwell in the mountains you see all around this valley. Most of them are gathered in the northwest part of the mountain range, that is where their king rules from."

"Am I ever going to get to meet a Dwarie?"

"You are going to meet one right now. Matthew, I would like you to meet King Moark Natund of the Dwaries." Matthew, intent on the conversation, had not even noticed that they were near a table. Sitting before him at the head of the table was a very short, very stocky old man. He had a long white beard attached to a wide face and very rough features. The King looked like what a person would expect a Dwarf to look like. Then it struck Matthew: *Dwarf could have come from the word Dwarie. Dwarves and Elves, could the legends of my world have somehow come from knowledge of this one?*

"What's the matter boy, are you slow-witted or something?" The King of the Dwaries broke into Matthew's thoughts.

"That was the first impression he gave me as well Moark, but he really is a little brighter than it would seem."

"No, sir," Matthew came to his own defense. "I'm just having a hard time adjusting to some things. I'm very pleased to meet you; my name is Matthew."

"That's better, now why don't you have a seat?" the King said gruffly. Before they could sit down however, trumpets began to sound.

"What is that," Matthew asked in alarm, "some kind of warning?"

"No, boy," Moark said. "The Elves are being called to prayer. Deeli, for those who are of your religion around this table, would you lead in worship and say the blessing?"

"It would be an honor, King Moark." All stood; some bowed their heads, while others lifted their hands and faces to the sky. Deeli began with a prayer of thanksgiving that blended into a kind of worship service. Matthew was a little uncomfortable. He looked toward the King and saw that he had his head respectfully bowed, but not actively joining in.

Almost everyone at the table was a Dwarie—their average height being about four and a half feet tall; each with the same rough features as their King. All of them had their heads bowed except a few. These few had their hands raised in worship—as did Deeli and most of the Humans.

They were singing, and most had tears on their cheeks, including Deeli. All of this reminded Matthew of going to church with his father when he was younger. He felt the same tingling sensation he had felt back then. Also the same warm feeling he had when touching the circle of light that brought him to this world. Matthew did not understand it, but let the feeling wash over him. *The God in my world doesn't seem to exist anymore, but maybe there's a God here I can believe in like my father did.* When it was finished, Matthew found himself wiping tears from his own eyes and Deeli looking at him with a smile. "I would like to find out more about your God, Deeli."

"Knowledge will come in the Creator's own time, my friend, but I think you were just introduced to Him. Right now it is time to eat, I know that I am starved." Matthew looked around and saw that everyone was digging in, and for the first time noticed all the food on the table. The sight of it made his stomach growl once again; letting him know it wanted to be fed. He and Deeli sat down and began to eat. There were all kinds of meats, vegetables, cheeses, bread and fruit. Some of the foods Matthew thought he recognized as the same as in his world and others he could not, but it all tasted good to him.

When Matthew felt too stuffed to continue, he leaned back on the low Dwarie bench that he was sitting on and listened to the King telling stories. "Yes, I can remember when I was just a lad, my father telling me stories about Deeli here. One time…" The King was cut short by Matthew's outburst:

"You mean that you are younger than Deeli!" All the eyes at the table turned to Matthew and looked at him in silence.

"Matthew," Deeli whispered, "it is one thing to interrupt me in the middle of a sentence, but quite another to interrupt a king. I am sorry, King Moark, I have gathered that it is not impolite to interrupt when someone else is talking where Matthew comes from."

"Ha! I like that, boy," Moark barked. "Mind you don't do it too often. I like someone who doesn't treat me like some fragile thing up on a pedestal. And yes, I'm a lot younger than Deeli. I just don't look it because Elves live so much longer than the rest of us. I've seen one hundred and one first seasons."

"A hundred and one," Matthew said astonished. "Well then, how old are you Deeli?"

"I am one-hundred and fifty-eight sun-cycles; that is getting up there even for an Elf. From the look on your face, I would guess that the people of your world do not grow that old."

"Heck no, we're considered very lucky to live as long as King Moark."

"How old are you Matthew?" King Moark asked. Matthew felt like an infant next to these two.

"I am twenty-one years, I mean sun-cycles old."

"Why you are barely untied from your mother's apron straps," the King said slapping the table. "You are only a cycle younger than my youngest. Telick," the King said to his eldest son sitting next to him, "go bring Pheltic here so we can introduce him to Matthew." Telick went over to another table and brought back a young version of the King with a short, scraggly, reddish beard and introduced the two young people. Pheltic had a war hammer strapped to his side and a huge grin on his face. He was continuously trying to prove to everyone that he could be a warrior, but was too lovable and naive to convince anyone. Pheltic made himself at home sitting next to Matthew, and the two began to talk.

Pheltic told Matthew about the Dwarie way of life and his home in the mountains. He talked about how his older brother, Telick, had taken over his father's duty as battle chief; and he being the youngest, was always being over-looked. In turn, Matthew told him about how he came to be in this world and a little about his own. It soon seemed as if they had known each other for a long time, and Matthew was grateful to have found a friend his own age. The sound of trumpets coming from the other side of the clearing made them break off their conversation. "What's happening now?" Matthew asked.

"That means it is time for the Test of the Sword," Pheltic replied.

"Deeli, could we go see what's happening over there?"

"I suppose so," Deeli said with a sigh. "Just stay out of trouble and do not get too near what is going on. There are some Elves who would not be as understanding of your differences as I am." Matthew was not sure what he meant by that, but still wanted to go. He had not noticed that Haub and his son had joined them at the table until the big Human invited them to go watch the next event with them.

"That would be great, Haub, thanks. Are you going, Deeli?"

"I do not think that would be wise, besides I have seen this event many times in the past. You young people go and have a good time," Deeli said shooing them away. The four of them walked to the other side of the Great Tree and got as close to it as they could. An Elf in long white robes was on a small stage getting ready to read something.

"This is where all the Elven males try to pull the sword from the tree," Pheltic told Matthew. "It's fun to watch at first, but usually gets pretty boring because no one ever succeeds."

"What is this thing he's about to read?" Matthew asked.

"He is the High Counselor to the Elven High King," Haub told him. "He is about to read the prophecy concerning the sword Calburnathis, written down in the Elven Holy Words thirty-five hundred sun-cycles ago." This made Matthew very interested and he listened to the Elf closely.

"Hear now the word of our Creator!

'So saith the Lord your Creator, in the last days, after their exile, I will draw the chosen of My heart back to the holy land. Many will come against her and she will be under much persecution. Fear not, My child, for I the Lord will be with you and the Sword of Kings will be drawn forth from its imprisonment to do battle for you on the first day of the First Season. If he who wields the sword overcomes, then the people who are called by My name will see a new day and turn their hearts unto Me like no other time seen before. The light of Truth shall follow the Sword Bearer as his eyes and ears. Let those who have ears to listen not grow faint of heart in the time of trial. So saith the Lord your Creator.'

It is now time for the Test of the Sword. May the Creator choose his worthy champion this day."

Matthew did not understand what it all meant, but thought it sounded very dramatic. Most of the people around him did not seem too interested, as if they had heard it a hundred times before. Matthew watched as one by one each male Elf from the long line tried to pull the sword from the tree. He was certain that someone would be able to do it, but after a while with no successes he and the others began to talk.

Haub and Pheltic told Matthew all they knew about the background of the sword, most of which Deeli had already told him. Matthew told them the story of King Arthur and his knights of the round table. All three were amazed at the part about Arthur drawing the sword from the stone. "He had to do this to prove he was the rightful heir to the throne," Matthew explained.

"It seems so similar to this situation," Pheltic said with wonder, "except this sword has been stuck for sixteen centuries and in a tree instead of a stone."

"Another difference is that this sword is fact and the one in my world is just legend. There is nothing magical in my world. One thing I've been wondering about this sword though, is who put it in the tree, and why?"

"That is a question that no one, even Deeli, can answer," replied Haub. Pheltic quickly offered his view:

"Maybe it's to humble those haughty Elves, they think they're so much better than the other races."

"They are the chosen of the Creator," Haub came to the Elves' defense.

"That's what your religions say, but we Dwaries don't buy it. We don't believe they are better than anyone else. I don't mean to say they're bad, just stuck on themselves." Haub just smiled to himself and let the discussion drop. Matthew used the following silence to interject another question.

"Why would the sword being stuck in this tree, in this clearing, humble them?"

"Well," Haub started thoughtfully. "The sword is a matter of great pride to the Elven people. It was given to one of their first kings by the Creator God, almost thirty-five centuries ago. It has much power and is very much a part of their history. Over two-thousand sun-cycles ago my race allied themselves with the evil Traul race and built an empire. They ruled the entire world, and this valley was the most beautiful part of that empire. They persecuted the Elven people, torturing and killing many of them. That is also when the Path religion began, hated by the empire as well as the Elves. They, along with the Elves, were forced to stay in the valley and work for the empire. This very clearing was used as an arena where followers of the Path, and the Elves were torturously killed for punishment and sport. They were made to fight each other to the death. Those found guilty of crimes against the empire were hung from the branches of this tree. The worst criminals were nailed with spikes into the trunk and left hanging there to die. Our history says that sometimes there were so many being executed that you could not see the gold bark because of all the blood."

"Your history sounds as violent and bloody as mine. I can see why the Elves would be touchy about their heritage being stuck in a place like this." With having so much to talk about, the time had gone quickly for all of them. Soon they were watching the last Elf in line grunting and straining, trying to pull the sword loose, but to no avail. All four were disappointed that the sword had not been drawn, especially Matthew. They arose and stretched their legs, then began walking back to the Dwarie tables. Before they had gotten far they heard the Elf who read the prophecy talking in a loud voice. Matthew and Pheltic wanted to find out what was happening now.

"Come on, let's go back," Pheltic said to Matthew.

"I need to go back and let Deeli know the sword has once again not been drawn, and that the Ceremony of the Amulet is about to begin," Haub said.

"Why don't you go get Deeli, and we'll stay here, near the spot where we watched the sword ceremony?" Matthew offered. Haub agreed after telling them to stay out of trouble. He headed back, leaving his son Wil with Matthew and Pheltic. They stood for a while listening to speeches and getting very bored. Wil was getting very restless and asked if he could go back to where his family was eating.

"I guess it's okay," Matthew said, not knowing what he should do. After the boy left, Matthew got an idea. "Pheltic, why don't we try to inch our way up a little closer, so we can see better."

"Sure, this is something I've never seen before." They slowly made their way through the crowd until they were positioned almost in front of the stage. Neither of them encountered much resistance because everyone's heads were bowed and a priest on the platform was saying prayers. Next, an older Elven female stood up and began to speak to the crowd. She was very funny and did not speak long. Everyone, including Matthew and Pheltic, appreciated that.

At the end of her talk she introduced the Elven Princess. A young female Elf came out from behind a curtain; she had long dark hair and seemed a little too thin to look healthy in Matthew's mind. *She also looks way too young to hold an important government office like this.* The older female Elf took an amulet from around her own neck and placed it around the Princess' neck. The amulet began to glow and the crowd applauded wildly, so Matthew and Pheltic naturally did likewise.

The young Elven girl was standing at the front of the stage with her head lowered and her eyes closed, obviously waiting to speak. Matthew thought he could hear a rumbling besides that made by the audience. He looked around as the crowd stopped clapping. Instead of the clearing becoming more quiet, it was getting louder. He could feel the ground begin to shake, and thought immediately that it must be an earthquake.

Matthew looked toward the stage and saw that the Elven girl was just opening her eyes in confusion. The crowd was running around in a panic and Pheltic was tugging on Matthew's arm and motioning to follow him.

"All right, lead the way, I'm right behind you." Pheltic took off toward where his father would be, thinking his new friend was with him. Matthew though, had looked back and saw that the girl was still standing at the front edge of the stage. He also saw that it was falling apart. She was losing her balance and no one else seemed to notice. Matthew ran in the direction of the stage as fast as he could. Sliding on his knees he caught the girl just before she hit the ground.

He did not know what to do, so he held her tight and headed for the shelter of the huge tree. The Elven girl stiffened in his arms, telling him something was wrong. He turned to see black shapes emerging from the forest and realized this was not an earthquake. He set the girl down next to the tree and turned back, freezing in horror. The clearing was filling up with monsters. Some were huge and wearing black armor. Others were smaller; all were mounted on some kind of black steed. He also saw some of the winged creatures they had fought in the forest. It was as if some terrible nightmare had come true.

These must be the Trauls and Nomies, Matthew thought. *But how? They don't live in the valley, how did they get here?* The creatures were armed with swords, axes, and spears, wading through the people and killing them without mercy. It all happened so fast; the clearing was now full of these things killing Elves, Humans, and Dwaries alike. Matthew felt sickened at the sight, and he thought for sure he was going to throw-up. He turned his head gagging and then saw it. The biggest creature he had seen yet, sitting on top of a huge black steed, a black helmet on his head with horns sticking out the sides, staring right at Matthew.

The Traul pointed at Matthew, or the girl still at his feet, he was not sure which. Suddenly, several of the black clad warriors began to advance on them. Matthew grabbed the girl's hand, pulling her up and with him, trying to edge their way around the tree. He wanted to get to the other side and make a break for it. Finally they stopped. Matthew could see that no matter where they went the creatures were already there, bloody weapons raised. They were so close now that he could hear them breathing and see murder in their red eyes. Eyes that were looking straight at him.

Chapter

7

A moment ago we were on our way to see a ceremony, Haub thought, *now we are fighting for our lives.* Haub was fortunate he had kept his axe strapped to his side; many of those in attendance did not even think of bringing their weapons to a religious festival. *This is going to be a slaughter!* Already the grass around him was slick with blood, almost entirely Traul and Nomie. As he looked farther out though, Haub could see that most of the bodies on the ground were Human, Dwarie, and Elven. *God of heaven*, he prayed, *please protect my family for me. You know that I am not able.* With blood in his eyes, blurred vision, and feet slipping in the wet grass, Haub fought on, trying to reach his family.

When the attack started, it came from the north and east sides of the clearing. It came so fast, and without warning, that most people were caught right where they were. When Haub headed back to find his wife and daughter, he had been separated from Deeli and the

Dwarie King. King Moark's bodyguard had immediately made a ring around himself and Deeli. They now fought bravely against Traul and Nomie warriors, but the odds were not with them.

A huge Traul finally broke through and came up quickly behind King Moark. Deeli saw him coming and instinctively raised his hand. A burst of crackling energy shot from his fingertips, and the Traul was reduced to nothing but ash falling to the ground. Deeli's guilt threatened to wash over him; once again he had used the magic that he had sworn to his God he would never use. *There is no time now to dwell on yet another failure—they could wipe out half the inhabitants of the valley. I must find a way to stop it.* From his position with the Dwarie King, Deeli could see that the Elven soldiers were fighting hard, but swiftly losing ground. He could see the signs of magical resistance from where the priests were, but even that would not be enough. He saw the Traul war leader with his black helmet that signified his rank. The leader of this invasion was pointing at the Great Tree, but from where he was Deeli could not see why.

"Of course!" Deeli exclaimed. "They have come to try to remove the sword. My Lord, no! With Calburnathis the Dark One would be able to conquer all." The Spirit of the Creator had led him to believe that something momentous would happen concerning the sword today. He had been very disappointed when Haub came back with word that no one had drawn it from the tree. *I could never have imagined that the Dark One would be he who fulfilled the prophecy. If he gains the sword, there will be no one to stand against him. But how will he get it out of the tree? Could his magic possibly be that strong?*

Then Deeli saw it. From the other side of the tree came flashes of colored light and blue lightning. There was a cracking noise louder than any thunder he had ever heard. "My God," he prayed aloud. "They do have strong enough magic. Is all lost? Is this how it is to end?"

A loud cracking noise brought Pheltic around. He had been laying on the ground, knocked out from a smack on his head by the flat of a Traul blade. Pheltic looked at the tree and shook his head, trying to clear his eyes. What he was seeing could not be happening.

Haub heard the loud noise and saw the flashing lights, as did those whom he was fighting. The distraction was all it took for Haub to gain the upper hand. He lay the last few to waste; still not being able to see his wife and daughter anywhere, he took off at a dead run for the Great Tree.

Sharineas was in a low crouch, her back and the palms of her hands were pressed as close to the tree as she could get them. She looked in every direction, but there was no where to run. The amulet had let her sense the evil that was approaching, but not how to do anything about it. She had thought this was going to be the biggest day of her life, but instead it would be her last. Her thoughts were interrupted by an ear splitting crack and the tree vibrating violently against her. For a while, all she could see were colored lights and blue lightning. The cracking sound was so loud that it caused a ringing in her ears, blocking out all other sound.

Matthew was on his feet and backed up against the tree. He was cold with fear, and could feel the sweat running down his back and sides. His sense of survival was kicking into high gear, but he and the girl had nowhere to go—no way to fight back. He moved a little more to the right and his shoulder bumped into something. Matthew had not realized that he and the girl had made their way this far around the tree. There, in the corner of his eye, was the sword hilt.

He forgot the fact that no one had been able to get the sword free; nor did he think about the implications of what he was about to try. Only that he and the girl were about to be cut to pieces, their blood mingling with the blood of long dead martyrs. Matthew reached up with his right hand, hoping beyond hope that his fear-enhanced adrenaline would give him enough strength to wrench the blade free. As his hand gripped the hilt, a warm familiar tingle went through Matthew. With almost no effort at all, the sword slid out like the tree was made of butter.

Everything seemed to stand still in time for just a moment. It was a silence like he had never experienced before. Matthew seemed to be the only one who could move. A Traul stood over him frozen in time, his blade halfway through an arc that would have split Matthew's head open. Matthew stepped aside, and suddenly a deafening, ripping sound hit his ears. A shudder came from the tree, so huge that Matthew almost lost his balance. The Traul sword came whistling down, missing Matthew and embedding itself in the tree. Blue lightning ran the length of the sword he held in his hand, and colored lights danced all around him.

The first Traul backed off quickly, not being able to get his blade free. But other Trauls and Nomies, shock on their faces, kept coming. Matthew had no choice but to try to defend himself and the girl. The sword seemed to leap up of its own accord, slicing off the head of a Nomie. Another Nomie had gone for the girl. Her amulet was glowing madly, but she was too frightened and wild-eyed to notice. Matthew stepped in front of her and raised his sword, which seemed as light as a feather. The Nomie raised his blade to parry Matthew's, but when Calburnathis came down it cut right through the Nomie blade and then the warrior himself, without any hesitation.

Matthew felt his stomach turn over. He had never hurt anything in his life; let alone killed. He did not want to kill or be killed; just run away from all of this. Then he heard the thing with the black helmet yelling in a very loud and gruff voice.

"Kill him! Gain the sword for the master and a special place in glory will be yours." The warriors had been confused with the drawing of the sword. But now, with that command, their leader had brought them back to the task at hand. It seemed as though every black shape in the clearing was now headed for Matthew.

The blue lightning running along the blade intensified. Matthew could feel the power surging through him now, as if the sword were hungry to stop this injustice. He stepped away from the tree and met his attackers, the sword rising and falling with perfect rhythm. The dark troops continued to advance on Matthew and the girl, yet were slain just as quickly as they came. Many of the warriors were now falling back in fear and confusion. This small Human with the sword was more than they had bargained for.

Matthew became braver and went on the offensive. The power of the sword caused the very air to crackle about him. This rallied the Elven soldiers, as well as the Humans and Dwaries that were still alive. They began to fight back with even more ferocity than before. The Traul and Nomie warriors began to fall over themselves trying to get away from the terrible sword. Many of them were in a head-long flight to the forest. The commander, seeing they had been routed, had the retreat sounded.

Matthew gave chase for a few yards, but suddenly felt very weak and began to stumble. Before he fell however, he was caught and held up by his stocky friend, Pheltic. Matthew stood with his friend's help; sword held limply in his hand. Deeli and King Moark had made their way over to his side with Haub coming up just behind them. They all stood there watching the retreating form of the commander wearing the black helmet. Suddenly, at the edge of the forest, he turned. He looked back at Matthew and bellowed in a barely controlled rage:

"Our races are now at war! We will obliterate you from this land, and the valley will be ours again. You may possess the sword, but my master's power is still greater. If you dare to face him, he will crush you like the bugs that you are!" This last statement was said like a challenge, and with so much hate, that Matthew shrank back from it. The Traul then turned his steed and fled into the forest.

"Thank God you are all okay," Matthew said. "How is the girl?" They all turned their heads to look. The Elven girl seemed unharmed, but she could not hold their attention. Deeli and Haub both fell to their knees crying out in anguish. The rest of them gasped in amazement. From the place in the tree where Matthew had pulled Calburnathis, a huge split ran upward to the top. The crack was even now making more cracking and popping noises as it grew longer. Sharineas screamed and ran toward the group clustered around Matthew. Deeli yelled for those still alive to get out of the path of the two halves. As they watched, the split in the tree ran its course. The tree made unbearable groaning sounds as the two halves fell away from one another. They fell whistling through the air, crashing down into the forest on either side of the clearing. The two halves landed with such force that everyone still standing was thrown off their feet. It took a few moments for people to come out of their shock and begin to pick themselves up off the ground.

Deeli, Matthew, and the rest looked around at the horrible carnage. There were dead bodies of every race lying throughout the clearing. People were finally starting to move again. Moans and cries could be heard from all over the clearing; those still whole began tending to the injured. Everyone moved as if they were in a dream, shock apparent on every face. Haub expressed gratitude that his friends were all right, and went off to look for his family.

"You drew the sword from the tree," Sharineas stated, looking accusingly at Matthew. "That cannot be, you are not Elven. All of these people dead, how can this be?" Sharineas was nearing hysterics by now. "Where are my mother and father!?" Before Deeli could make any reply, a loud voice came from behind them.

"Napdeeliate!" The word was spat out as though it were some foul thing. "I should have known you would have something to do with this," the High King of the Elves said furiously. King Peridon was limping and had a cut on his arm that was oozing blood.

"Ah, nephew," Deeli said. "I have had nothing to do with any of this, I am only here for the celebration—a festival that is being held outside the Elven kingdom that you exiled me from."

"Exiled!" Sharineas exclaimed. "Father, you told me that uncle Napdeeliate left us on his own, saying that he would never return. Are you really my great uncle? You do seem familiar."

"Not now Sharineas; we will discuss this later," the King replied, with a look that ended any more questions. "Now tell me, Napdeeliate, how did you get the sword out of the tree?"

"I told you, I had nothing to do with it. The prophecy has been fulfilled, and Matthew here is rightful heir to the sword Calburnathis."

"He's only a half-breed and has no right to the property of the Elven people!" Alexthna raged as he walked up behind them. "He is not fully Elven, therefore must turn the sword over to us." Alexthna reached out to snatch the sword. Matthew, not sure what he should do, let him take it. As soon as Alexthna took the sword, it fell to the ground taking him with it. The High Counselor rose to his feet red-faced. "What kind of magic have you put on the sword, Napdeeliate? It is too heavy for me to hold, or even pick it up!"

"Move aside, I will pick it up and claim it once again for the glory of the Creator and His people."

"I see that you are even more arrogant now than when you were a lad, Gamilon," Deeli said to the young Elf, as Gamilon reached over to retrieve the sword.

"Quiet, old one. You have betrayed your forefathers and your people, we do not recognize you anymore." Gamilon struggled with the sword, but he too failed to lift it off the ground. He stood, red-faced and glaring at Deeli.

"So the proud shall always be humbled," Deeli said looking Gamilon straight in the eye. "Do you all so quickly forget the legends?

No one but the Creator's chosen vessel may lift the sword when it is out of its scabbard. The young boy's name is Matthew, and he is not a half-breed. He is from another world where only Humans dwell, and all are small as he is. I believe the Creator has been preparing Matthew, and brought him to our world for just such a time as this." Matthew looked at Deeli with a startled expression, but said nothing.

"We do not believe anything you would tell us, Path follower!" King Peridon spat out as he also tried and failed to pick up the sword.

"Well I believe it," Pheltic quipped. "What's wrong with Matthew having the sword anyway?"

"Quiet, Dwarie," Gamilon said fiercely. "This is none of your concern." King Moark took a step toward Gamilon, a low growl in his throat; no more comments were forthcoming from the brash young Elf.

"We just want you to undo the magic you have worked on the blade, so that it can be claimed by the Elven people once again," Alexthna said to Deeli.

"I have used no magic in the last fifteen sun-cycles, except for self-defense." Deeli was getting very agitated by this point and could not hold back. "Look around you, blind fools! People from every race are dead or dying, you should be glad the sword was used in your defense this day. If the Creator had not used Matthew we would not be here right now, certainly not Sharineas." King Peridon looked at his daughter and his face softened.

"Young man, we are grateful for what you have done this day. But you must understand, this sword has belonged to the Elven people since the dawn of history."

"And you cannot expect us to believe you're from another world," Gamilon added.

"I think it could be possible," Sharineas spoke quietly. "I don't know how to use the powers of the amulet yet, but I can sense they are telling us the truth, or at least what they believe to be the truth. I also feel that it is the power of the sword that brought him here, and enables him to understand us." Matthew and Deeli looked at each other in surprise.

"Thank you my dear," Deeli said. "That is a question we could not answer before, but you have shed some light on it for us."

"Sharineas, how can you side with them?" Alexthna asked. "This could be construed as treason."

"No, Alexthna, this is not treason. All three of you, as well as the other council members and priests, are going to have to accept that this boy is our Creator's choice to be the Sword Bearer. I have no idea why, but I can feel that this is true." Matthew was a little taken back by the Princess calling him a boy. Alexthna spat on the ground and stalked off without another word, Gamilon right behind him. Pheltic, who had been trying his hand at picking up the sword, fell backward to the ground seat first.

"Oops, guess my hands slipped off." Matthew could not help but grin at his friend.

"I don't think it belongs to the Dwaries anyway," King Moark said with a grunt. Matthew bent over and picked up the sword as if it weighed nothing.

"I don't know who it should belong to, but at the moment it seems that I am the only one who can lift it. Unless you want to leave the sword in this field for the rest of time, I am going to have to carry it; which would be a lot easier if I had a scabbard."

"I do not understand it," King Peridon said rubbing his beard. "I also cannot deny that you are the only one who has control over Calburnathis. There is a scabbard for the blade at the temple. If you are truly the one, then you will be given the scabbard. For now though, we must tend to the dead. This clearing will be a proper place to bury them after so many of our people have died here. King Moark, I am calling together once again the war council of the races, will the Dwaries be allied with us again?"

"We've all been attacked by this foul thing from the north. You better believe the Dwarie will be a part of this fight, with a vengeance!"

"Good! I am sure the Humans will want to be a part also. I will ask them to send their representatives to the meeting. We can set the meeting for evening at my castle, three days hence, if that will give you enough time."

"I'll be there in time, as long as the boy will."

"I guess we will need you there," Peridon said looking at Matthew. "Will you be able to attend the council, ah…I'm afraid I have forgotten your name."

"My name is Matthew, and I guess I can. As long as you will start using my name, and of course Deeli is with me."

"What!?" Peridon said immediately flushing with anger. "He is not even allowed in the Elven kingdom, let alone the castle or my council chambers."

"If Matthew and your precious sword aren't there, then there's no need for me either," the Dwarie King spoke up.

"Please father, with all that has happened you must make allowances." Sharineas boldly looked her father in the eye. *She already looks and acts older*, the Elven King thought to himself.

"Very well, I rescind your exile Napdeeliate, only until this is over. Do not forget!" With that, King Peridon turned and headed for the collapsed stage where a commotion had begun among the priests. The group followed to see what was going on, Alexthna and Gamilon were already almost there.

"This is indeed a dark day for the Elven kingdom," Alexthna said to the King as he walked up to the scene. There, near the platform, was the body of the dead High Priest. A few yards away lay the body of Lieanea, who had up until today been the Keeper of the Amulet; a short Nomie spear still protruding from her body.

"Lieanea, no!" Deeli ran over to the body weeping, pulled the spear out, and held her head in his arms. No one said a word, finally the sobs stopped and Deeli stood. "I am sorry, Lieanea," he said in a quiet voice. "I know you had many plans for after your term as the Keeper, but you have accomplished what the Creator wanted you to do. Rest in the peace of His arms, dear child."

"How could you have known what her plans were?" Alexthna asked, steel in his voice. "Have you been in the kingdom to see her?"

"There are many things you do not know," Deeli spoke without anger. "The two of us have worked very closely in the past, many secrets were entrusted to us when I was still the King's counselor. Lieanea came to visit me as often as she was able, and kept me informed of what was going on."

"Treason!" Alexthna barked.

"Will you quit seeing treason behind every bush?" Sharineas said in an annoyed voice; tears over the kind Lieanea's death trickled down her face.

"It was not treason," Deeli said. "I was the High Counselor appointed by God; you were given the title by man after my exile."

King Peridon was about to rebuke Deeli until he saw the look on his daughter's face. He had told his daughter things about her great uncle that were not true, and would now have enough explaining to do without making it worse with a rash statement. Alexthna was so infuriated that he could not even speak. Sharineas was full of guilt.

"Lieanea could have saved herself with the power of the amulet if she hadn't already given it to me. What did I do? I hid behind someone else in fright. Her death is my fault, I am not worthy to wear the amulet."

"You do not know that," Deeli said soothingly. "The amulet is not much as a weapon, mainly a revelator of truth. Unfortunately most of the secrets of its power have died with Lieanea. You, my dear Sharineas, are going to have to discover those secrets for yourself as she did. The Spirit of the Creator will guide you, if you let Him. I can also help. Lieanea has shared a few of the secrets with me."

"You!" King Peridon shouted. "You can be present at the war council, but you will stay away from my daughter."

"We will see, my King," Deeli said looking thoughtfully at Sharineas. "We will see what the Creator's will is on that subject." Deeli turned and walked over to where Elven soldiers were digging a line of special graves. There would only be a few hours of daylight left, so the usually lengthy ceremony for the dead could not be held. Instead, they would hold one short service for all the dead, and then go back and mourn for the customary three days, although on this occasion it was likely to be much longer. After the service, Deeli knelt beside Lieanea's grave and made a mark in the dirt.

"Do not put that mark on the grave of an Elf," Alexthna said menacingly.

"She was a follower of the Path," Deeli answered quietly.

"She was not!" King Peridon exploded. "And you will not profane her name in that way again."

"She could not wear the amulet for long and deny that I spoke the truth," Deeli said. "When she converted, Lieanea wanted to give up the amulet and come with me into exile. I told her she would best serve our Lord by staying in the kingdom and giving you godly counsel, my King. She submitted herself to my authority, and has served you and the Creator well over the cycles. Could you not see the look of peace on her face as compared to those priests that died?" Deeli's question met only silence. "Until the council meeting, my King," Deeli looked into King Peridon's eyes for a moment longer, then left for the other side of the clearing with Matthew following behind him.

King Moark and Pheltic had already headed back to check on the number of their dead. Not many of the Dwaries had been killed. They were not only smaller targets, but their lives on and under the mountains had made them tough. Most of those present had been male, and a male Dwarie always carries his weapon.

The biggest loss had been to the Humans. There were more of them at the gathering, the majority women and children. Some of the men had brought their weapons, giving them something to fight with and to protect their families. Though like Haub, many of the men had been gathered in groups, talking and laughing as at any other social gathering, and were not with their families when the attack came. All together, sixty percent of all the women and children had been slain.

Deeli and Matthew finally found Haub at the south side of the clearing. He and two other Humans were digging shallow graves with their weapons. "Haub?" Deeli asked quietly. Haub just looked up, his face red from crying. With sorrow in his eyes he nodded to a spot about fifteen yards away. There lay the bodies of his wife, daughter, and Brut. Brut was very mangled, and it was obvious he had fought savagely to protect Marth and Cas.

"I'm so sorry, Haub," was all Matthew could think to say. Just then another Human walked up carrying the body of a young boy.

"Nooo!" A screamed ripped from Haub's throat. The man lay Wil at Haub's feet and backed away. Haub was bent over the boy crying for a long while, when he raised his head his eyes had changed. They were no longer full of sorrow, or even hatred. They were the eyes of a dead man who had lost all hope and meaning in life. Matthew turned to Deeli, his eyes full of hurt and disappointment.

"I see that the God of your world doesn't protect His children any better than the God of my world." Then he turned, and with tears streaming down his cheeks, Matthew walked into the forest to be alone.

Chapter

8

By the time Matthew emerged once again from the forest, Haub's family had been buried and prayers were being said over them. He could hear Deeli praying: "Mighty Creator, we commend these, Your children, to You and their eternal rest. We thank You, Shesea, for making it possible that we might all be reunited again on the last day. We thank You, oh God, that even through our loss there is victory, and that the time of Calburnathis has finally come."

The simple faith of this kindly Elf, helping him find good even in bad, made Matthew feel small. *Maybe I shouldn't be so quick to write off the possibility of a supreme power after all,* Matthew thought to himself. After the little service Matthew walked up to Deeli.

"I'm sorry I talked to you that way and wasn't here to help. When it comes to understanding about a god and his ways, I get very confused."

"My son, you were forgiven the moment it happened and we will speak no more of it. As for not understanding our Creator, all I can say is 'join the rest of us.' I have tried to serve the Creator all my life and have come into a real relationship with Him only these past fifteen sun-cycles. The thing I am most sure about is that most of what makes up my God is still a mystery to me. As a matter of fact, the longer I walk with Him the more I realize how little I truly know."

"Thank you, Deeli. Hearing that from you makes me feel a lot better. If there really is a god up there, I do want to know more about Him."

"Matthew, my young friend, He has had His eye on you for a long time. He has brought you to this world for a very special purpose."

"Me?" Matthew asked in bewilderment.

"Yes, He has brought you here to draw the sword from the tree and use it to save our world."

"Wait a minute. I know I pulled it out of the tree, but that doesn't mean I'm the one who's going to save your world. What could I do?"

"Only the one whom God has ordained can bear the sword and you are he. You are the fulfillment of the last major prophecy about the end of our world, and who knows, maybe yours as well." Deeli's last statement made Matthew shiver.

"I don't know about what happens in this world affecting mine, but I do think you're putting more importance on me than you should."

"Well, in time I am sure we will learn the answers to our questions. Maybe that is what life is all about," Deeli said smiling, "asking, seeking, and finding answers." Meanwhile King Moark, Telick, and Pheltic had come over to give their condolences to Haub, whom they knew through Deeli's friendship. "Matthew and I are going back to my cottage to rest before starting out for the war council," Deeli announced.

"I will go talk to Roak, the head of my village," Haub spoke slowly and determinedly. "He will gather those needed at the war council. I am not going back to the village. Deeli, I will go with you."

"Certainly, my friend," Deeli said gently. "You go talk to Roak while we gather up some food for the journey." As Haub started away, Deeli yelled after him. "We will need to leave soon, I think the farther away we are by dark the better."

"Can Pheltic go with us, Deeli?" Matthew asked. "It would be great to have him along."

"I'm afraid I have to go back with my father and brother," Pheltic answered for Deeli with a dejected look toward his father. King Moark made a frumping noise that made his long beard shake.

"Yes, he does have to go back with me now, but you will see my son at the war council, young man." Matthew and Pheltic smiled at each other and thanked King Moark. "You have earned the right this day, son. You have been in your first battle...and survived." Pheltic, ever seeking to make his father proud, was pleased at these unexpected words.

They all gathered provisions for the journey from what remained and then said good-bye. Then Deeli, Haub, and Matthew headed back through the forest toward mount Easil and the little cottage. The group did not make it far before it began to grow dark. When it had become so dark they could not see anymore; Deeli called a halt.

"If I had known we would be sleeping in the woods tonight we could have brought bedrolls with us from the village this morning," Haub said in a voice that sounded miles away.

"There was no way any of us could have known this was going to happen," Deeli said in a comforting tone; concern for Haub etched in his face.

"Wow! Was it really only last night when I came through the gateway?" Matthew asked rhetorically. "So much has happened it seems like a long time ago."

It was still what Matthew would call springtime and with the dark came very chilly air. He lay on the hard ground with a tree root for a pillow and his arms wrapped tightly about him for warmth. *Every muscle in my body aches*, he thought. *The ground is hard and I'm freezing. I'll probably never get to sleep tonight.* In the end though, exhaustion won out; and not long after that thought, Matthew fell asleep.

Morning came with sunlight peeking over the mountains and filtering through the lime green leaves of a giant gold. Matthew cracked open his eyelids, and quickly shut them again. *How can it be morning already?* "I know that you are awake, young man," came Deeli's voice. "It is time to get up and come over here by the fire." Matthew reluctantly opened his eyes and propped himself up on one elbow. Deeli and Haub sat next to a small fire they had started near the path. Haub sat there with many bandaged wounds and a faraway look in his eyes. "I only let you sleep so late because I know you were exhausted from all you had been through," Deeli said as Matthew made his way over to the fire. *How true that is,* Matthew thought. Every muscle in his body was screaming in protest. He had always kept his body in good physical shape, but it had never been through anything like the last two days.

"It seems like a lifetime ago that I was running through the rain behind the 747 Club."

"The day I met you seems to me a lifetime ago as well," Haub said.

"I'm very sorry about what happened to your family," Matthew returned. "Is there anything we can do for you?"

"Thank you for your sympathy, but no. I have nothing left in this world but my desire for revenge against the Dark One and his followers."

"Haub!" Deeli said in shock. "I know you grieve, but vengeance belongs to our God. You must rid your soul of this foul emotion. We will put an end to his evil, but it must not be out of revenge."

"I will not forget the sight of my loved ones being laid in the ground, nor will I forgive the one who put them there. I must do what I must do."

"My friend Haub, I will stay by you no matter what. But I will also be praying that the Spirit of the Creator will enable you to forgive, so that you might have peace in your soul once again." When no more words came from either Deeli or Haub, Matthew cleared his throat and spoke.

"Deeli, I have many questions about what happened yesterday, about the sword."

"And I hope to answer as many as I can, but let us eat something now and then we will set off for my cottage. We can talk along the way, although, I think that if there are any answers they are in my books and scrolls back home."

They ate some food and then made sure the fire was out before starting off toward the eastern mountains. The trip through the forest was in silence, each keeping his own thoughts. As they came out of the forest Matthew was once again taken with the majestic mountains before them. That, and the full sunlight on their faces, did much to lighten Matthew and Deeli's spirits. Haub seemed unchanged though, remaining quiet as the other two talked.

"Deeli, why were you exiled from your home, and what was that name they called you?"

"The name they called me was Napdeeliate, it was the name given me at birth. I am actually High King Peridon's uncle, his father's brother. His father was King before him and I was his High Counselor. Fifty sun-cycles ago the Traul race, who controlled the valley at the time, decided that all Elves should be obliterated and started a huge war. My brother and I led our people. Together with the Humans and Dwaries we beat the Trauls, sending them back north to their own land. That freed up the valley again, and so the Elven kingdom was reborn as foretold in prophecy long ago. The reason I was exiled is a painful one to me, but I will tell you what I can. When my brother died, his son Peridon inherited the throne. I had been tutor to both him and his present counselor, Alexthna."

"He was the one who seemed to hate me the most," Matthew stated.

"Yes, he is the one. I loved them like sons, and they felt the same about me. I had been bringing Alexthna up as my successor, but was not given time to teach him even half of what he needed to know. I was an expert in the Elven law and very powerful in magic."

"Do the Elven people really have magic powers?" Matthew asked. "I mean besides what I saw the sword do."

"Yes, all Elves, and some of the Traul, have the ability to do magic, but for most it is a lost art. Only the priesthood continues to practice it these days. When we finally gained access to the temple, we discovered many old books and scrolls that were thought to be lost. I spent many sun-cycles studying them. Peridon had been on the throne only two cycles when I discovered the writings of what was thought to be a heretical sect of our own religion. A religion that had been started by Elves, but now belongs for the most part to the Humans. After careful study of these writings and our own Elven Holy Words, I was convinced that the Elves had missed what the Creator had wanted for them. That is when I rededicated my life to my God as a follower of the Path. He has become more real to me every day since then. That is also when I swore to the Creator that I would not use my magic again. I came to believe that using it was not trusting in Him. I am thankful that He is merciful. There have been many times, including yesterday, that I have failed Him in this.

That is also when I was sent into exile. My people have such a hatred for the Path follower religion, that any Elf who converts is shunned and expelled from the kingdom. In my case—being so closely related to the royal family and holding such a high office—my conversion and exile were very messy indeed. The King gave me a chance to renounce my new found faith and remain, but I would not—nor would I if I had it to do all over again. You do not have any magic at all in your world?"

"No. We have very advanced science, which would seem like magic to you, but it's not. We also have people who claim to have magic abilities, but they never have any proof. We do have stories about magic, Elves, Dwarves, Trolls, and Gnomes which seem to have come straight from this world."

"Really," Deeli said thoughtfully. "Maybe our worlds have touched at other times, and your stories did originate from here. I believe there may be the possibility that the God of your world and mine are one and the same."

"I don't know, some things are similar, but a lot of things are different. I know in my world He forbids even dabbling in magic. I don't think God would do that in one world and make it such a prevalent thing in another."

"Maybe there are different tests for different worlds. As I told you, I do not believe we are supposed to be using magic if we believe on Him. It sounds as though He might have just been too creative to be satisfied with only one world."

"Do you really believe our worlds have made contact before?" Matthew asked, trying to figure out this Creator God.

"From what you have told me about your stories, it seems to me that maybe they did meet sometime before recorded history. I strongly believe that they touched about sixteen-hundred sun-cycles ago, when the sword you are carrying disappeared from the temple." When Deeli did not continue, Matthew became agitated.

"Well don't stop now, tell me what you know."

"We will have to wait until we are back at my home, where I can look up some things in my books. When I was sent into exile I brought all of those old writings with me, including some that were handed down to the Keeper of the Amulet. Throughout history those writings have been known only to the Keeper, until Lieanea showed them to me. They tell a lot of what happened at that time, but have been kept secret because of what they reveal. Also because they say much that cannot be understood. If what I believe is true, you might be able to shed some light on the more confusing parts."

By this time the steep incline had both Deeli and Matthew breathing hard, so they stopped for a lunch break. All three sat on large flat rocks, eating the food they had brought. Deeli tried to engage Haub in conversation, but the big man was still stony and quiet. After lunch they started out again. The sword was not getting any heavier, but Matthew still found himself having to stop quite regularly to rest. "I can't understand why I'm so tired," Matthew said apologetically.

"Are there no mountains in your world?" Deeli asked.

"Oh yeah, we have mountains, but I've never climbed anything bigger than a large hill."

"That is why it is affecting you so much. You are at a very high altitude here and the air is thinner. You would get used to it, given time. For now though, we will simply have to stop and rest or you will get sick; fortunately my cottage is not much farther."

Deeli was right; they continued on and soon the ground leveled off and the cottage came into view. It was a long stone structure built better than the Human dwellings, but looked as if it had been there since the beginning of time. "It's not much," Deeli said, "but I call it home."

"I know you were exiled, but why do you live here, so far from everyone?" Matthew questioned Deeli.

"Actually, I did not mind my exile all that much. Being someone important still meant a lot to me at the time so it hurt my pride very much. But it gave me a chance to be alone and study the Holy Words in a whole new way. So my new brethren told me of this abandoned cottage and helped me fix it into a habitable dwelling place. I have lived here for the last fifteen sun-cycles, studying, praying, and exploring the surrounding mountains. I had expected to spend the rest of my days here."

"Don't you expect that anymore?" Matthew asked with a confused look.

"Well," Deeli hesitated, searching for words, "now that the sword has been drawn from the tree.... Let us just say that I do not believe any of our lives will ever be the same again."

Haub took off for a cluster of bluish pine trees saying that he would find some firewood for the evening meal. Deeli was growing more worried about him, but said nothing out loud knowing that only Haub and his Creator could resolve this problem. He was aware that his friend wanted to be alone because Haub knew very well that there was always plenty of firewood stacked against the cottage.

Deeli led Matthew inside. As Matthew's eyes adjusted to the dimness, he saw that the walls were lined with shelves full of paper scrolls and leatherbound books. Without even asking, Matthew collapsed on a bed. The bed was on the floor and made of pine needles with an animal skin thrown over them. The cottage was a fairly big, one room stone house, with a very large stone fireplace. He could see Deeli in the gloom, gathering up some food for the evening meal and then going to his precious books. Matthew was too tired to help and soon fell into a blessedly dreamless sleep.

Matthew awoke to Deeli's shaking. Looking out the western window he saw the sun hanging just above the distant mountain peaks. "I'm sorry, I didn't mean to fall asleep. Do you need any help?"

"No, no, I thought it best to let you sleep while I prepared dinner. It is nearly ready, so you had better get yourself out of bed. Haub was a long time in coming back; I was about to go look for him just as he returned. It turns out that he had sharpened a long branch and speared a couple of fish for us. There is a lake on the other side of the pines which he loves to go to."

"That sounds good to me." Matthew could now smell the fish sizzling over the fire outside; his stomach responded with a loud growl. All three sat around the fire, eating the fish and some dried vegetables that Deeli had in his cottage. They ate a quiet meal, each reflecting on his own thoughts. By the time they were finished it was almost dark.

When they entered the cottage Deeli lit two oil lamps and set them on a wooden table. On the table lay an open book and several yellowed scrolls. The scrolls appeared to be very old and had been wrapped in oiled leather. Deeli carefully picked up one of the scrolls. "This scroll had been sealed for over fifteen-hundred cycles with a very strong magic. It took me a long time to open once I had it in my possession. It has been handed down to each Keeper of the Amulet ever since Calburnathis appeared in the Great Tree. This scroll was actually written by the High Counselor who disappeared with the Keeper and Calburnathis."

"How can that be?" Haub asked. "I thought they never returned when the sword did."

"So everyone believes, but they did return and lived the rest of their lives on this mountain in secret. They had married while they were away and built this very cottage upon their return." Matthew and Haub looked around, disbelief in their eyes that the cottage could be that old. "Of course it has fallen apart and been rebuilt many times since then, but this is the site upon which they originally lived. His name was Melthanis and hers was Jaspinea; they were both followers of the Path."

"What!" Haub exclaimed in disbelief. "Are you sure?"

"Yes, it is revealed in the scroll very clearly." Deeli went on with his narrative. "Jaspinea gave the scroll to her replacement in secret. She made the new Keeper swear a binding oath to pass it on and never try to open it. Jaspinea said that someday in the distant future the scroll was to be given to the High Counselor. She also said that the amulet would reveal when. And so it was until Lieanea, God bless that brave lady, gave it to me. I opened it and studied the contents. I found it all very interesting and kept it a secret, not knowing what to do with the knowledge until now."

"You said there might be something in there about our worlds having touched before," Matthew said excitedly. "What does it say?"

"I do not know if it is your world that the scroll talks about. But I hope in light of the sword being drawn and your being here, we can determine that. Mind you, it does not say a lot, and not in much detail. Now, if you will allow me to read these passages to you…"

"Yes, of course read them," Matthew said, both he and Haub on the edge of their seats. Deeli was enjoying his role as storyteller and was dragging things out just to watch Matthew squirm.

"Ah youth," Deeli said as he began to read.

'The Creator called to me, Melthanis, in a vision. I saw Shesea and fell to my knees. He bade me gather up and take the Keeper of Truth along with the sword Calburnathis, to the Clearing of Death. So I obeyed, being secretly a follower of the

Path, I could do no less. Jaspinea removed Calburnathis from the temple and we made our way to the clearing. We came upon the Great Tree and began praying on our knees. No instruction came, but a circle of light appeared before us. We stepped through and found on the other side another world, not unlike our own. Yet it was a world of only small Humans. No Elves, Dwaries, Trauls, or Nomies dwelled there. And there was no magic. In our world no one but the Creator's anointed can lift the sword apart from its scabbard. In this world though, the power of the sword was greatly diminished and anyone could lift it; though only two could use it. Jaspinea's and my magic was greatly reduced as well, though the people of that world still thought of us as powerful, magical beings. Once in that world our Lord appeared to us again, saying that the sword was needed by these people as a unifying symbol. Even though we wore our hair to cover our ears, the people were still in awe and even frightened by us. I dwelled with the Humans and did what my God directed me to do with the sword. I also helped the people of that world in other ways. But now, thirty-seven cycles later, we have returned with the help of a young man from that world. He, along with Calburnathis, has brought us back home. The sword is now in the Great Tree, for how long only the Creator knows. I Melthanis, write these words that they might help him whom the Creator calls to be the next Guardian of the Sword Bearer.'

And that is where it ends," Deeli finished.

"That's all?" Matthew asked. "Doesn't it say anything about what actually happened with the sword? It sounds like it could be my world, but there's no way to say for sure."

"Well I did have to skip over a part that is not legible enough to read." Deeli answered him. "Let me see if I can make out any of the words. Here is a part, 'in this world…called…Calburnis.' Does that tell you anything?" Deeli looked up into Matthew's blank expression. "I take it that the name means nothing to you?"

"No, I'm afraid not. It does sound a little familiar, but that's probably because that name is so similar to what the sword is called in this world."

"There are only a few more words that I can make out. 'Also called...' that is all I can read."

"Can I see it?" Matthew asked. Deeli handed him the parchment. Try as he might; Matthew could not make out the word either. For some reason—he knew not why—Matthew walked over to the bed where he had left the sword and picked it up. He brought it back to the oil lamp and began studying the paper again. This time the words seemed darker and brighter. The word he had been trying so hard to see came blazing to life. The excitement and flood of emotion that flowed through him made Matthew drop the paper and almost the sword. He leaned back in the chair with an awestruck look on his face. Matthew could only whisper in a rough voice the name of the sword that he had seen on the parchment.... "Excalibur!"

Chapter

9

Matthew's mouth hung slack and his eye's bulged; appearing to his companions to be in a trance. *How can this be? Was the legend of King Arthur really true? Could this be the same Excalibur?!* Somewhere there was a small portion of Matthew's brain that could hear Deeli talking to Haub. "I think something must have rung a bell, the boy has that same dumbfounded look he had when I first met him."

"You don't understand," Matthew said shaking his head, trying to get over his shock. "If what this says is true, then this sword is famous in my world. It is the sword from the story I told you at the festival, Haub. It was carried by a legendary King and used to unite the Celtic tribes into a country known since that time as Great Britain. My world considers the story to be a myth, but the time that it was supposed to have happened lines up with the disappearance of this sword. It just seems so unbelievable."

Matthew went into greater detail of the King Arthur story and Deeli found it profoundly interesting, especially the fact that Matthew told the story with such passion. Deeli realized that this legend of Matthew's people was something that struck a deep cord in the young man. It also gave the Elf a little better understanding of why the Creator had chosen this Matthew. The three of them stayed up late discussing the significance of the discovery and what it would now mean to Matthew, as well as this world. Deeli went into greater detail of the self-proclaimed Enlightened One, and all that he represented.

"He has swayed the Trauls, Nomies, and many Humans by saying he has been sent by the Creator. He says that his main goal is to unite the races under one rule, thereby bringing peace and prosperity. But he is telling them that we Elves and the Path followers have a distorted concept of God and that the Creator is angered at all the races because of it. His doctrine says that we must all be exterminated—including the Dwaries if they have allied themselves with us—or world peace can never be accomplished. Our Holy Words told us this day would come. Many have tried to make it come about in the past, but have always failed; though none have shown the power that this one has. The drawing forth of Calburnathis is fulfillment of a major prophecy, and tells us that this might just be the final battle."

"What do you mean, final battle?" Matthew asked.

"All I can tell you for sure is that the Lord God has chosen you to carry the sword into the world once again; and that you must use it to face this evil which would destroy us. If not, then this may be the end of time."

"But how can I represent God in this; I'm not even sure yet whether I believe He exists."

"His Spirit will lead you," Deeli said confidently, "just open yourself up to Him."

"But I have heard so many in my world say that they know the true voice of God, and yet do totally opposite things. How will I know what to do and who to listen to?"

"Do not fret, my young friend, He is faithful and will lead you Himself down the true path. I do not know if you trust us yet, but Haub and I will be here to help."

"I do trust you both and thank you for all you've done," Matthew said, his panic starting to subside.

"You do realize, Matthew, that you hold the most powerful weapon our world has ever seen," Deeli said quietly. "You might even be able to use it to go home." Matthew sat there thinking for a long while, his life's story running through his head. Deeli was even beginning to wonder if he had heard him.

"Actually, I don't know how to use the sword's power, so far it's kind of been using me. It brought me to this world, allowed me to understand the languages, and then came to my aid in the clearing when I was about to be killed. It seems to me that I might have a purpose in this world, and that's a lot more than I felt in my own. I think there might be even bigger mysteries to solve than the sword. ...I plan to see them through 'til the end. I don't think...I don't think I would use the sword to go home right now even if I knew how." Matthew paused again; his mind wanting to explore all of the possibilities this new turn in life had to offer. "Do you mind if I go to bed now?"

"By all means, use my bed tonight. Tomorrow will be here very soon," Deeli answered with a knowing smile. Matthew did not even argue about Deeli giving up his bed, just went over and lay down as if no one else was in the room. Closing his eyes, he began examining his life. Haub lay down on the floor using his vest for a pillow, his thoughts on his family. Deeli blew out the oil lamp and went outside to pray; there would not be much sleep for any of them tonight.

Fall asleep they did. It was almost mid-morning when they finally awoke. Deeli, who was used to rising early, could not believe he had slept so late. The plan had been to be leaving by now, so he quickly woke the other two. They walked to the lake near the cottage to clean up, but the water was so cold that no one stayed in long. After getting back to the cottage they ate a quick meal and packed what would be needed for the trip.

Matthew spent some of the time examining the sword. It was gleaming brightly, and looked brand new instead of thousands of years old. Deeli had told him the sword was said to have been made by the hand of God Himself. "God," Matthew began praying under his breath, "if You're really there, if You're the God who created my world too, I just want to apologize for yelling at You the other night. You know, by the nightclub. And for challenging You. I was kind of drunk and didn't really mean all those things I said. If You are there I sure would like to know for sure…the way my dad did. Could You be the same one? And what about this Jesus that my dad believed in, where does He fit in to all of this?" Matthew waited, but nothing happened. *Well, I don't know if He heard me, but if He is real I sure hope God's not the kind to hold a grudge for long.*

Deeli was calling his name from inside the cottage, so Matthew got off his knees and headed out of the pines where he had gone for privacy. Deeli had rags to wrap around the sword so no one would get hurt on the journey. He tied twine around the sword to hold the rags on and make a more convenient way for Matthew to carry it. They shouldered their packs, rolled blankets for sleeping on, grabbed water skins and headed out the door. "We will not be able to poke along on this trip if we want to make it to the war council on time," Deeli said, looking sternly at Matthew as they started down the mountain. Matthew was admiring the beauty of the view before him when Deeli stopped and turned around.

"What's wrong?" Matthew asked him.

"I just wanted to take a look at my home once again, in case I do not make it back." Deeli then turned and started to make his way back down the mountain.

"Why wouldn't you make it back?"

"The three of us will be walking a dangerous path in the days to come. You do remember the flying Nomies, you saw how savage the Trauls can be. And at the end of this road you must meet the Dark One himself, not a small adversary."

"But I have Excalibur now," Matthew said with confidence. "You saw what it did in the clearing."

"The prophecy says that you will meet the evil and *if* you overcome, our world and my people will be given another chance. Confidence and trust in God are necessary for what you are going to be undertaking, but being too cocky might get you into trouble. The prophecy does not say that you will overcome."

"But I'm the one who must face him, how will that put you in danger?"

"If you remember what we read last night, Melthanis did not use the sword in your world. Nevertheless, he was considered the Guardian of the Sword Bearer. That duty has now been passed on to me. So wherever you go, I go; that includes going into danger. Make no mistake Matthew, even if you choose not to go to him, the Emissary of the Evil One will come for you. He wants that sword and your destruction."

Matthew spent the next few hours contemplating Deeli's words in silence. Since Haub was still not talking much, the hike down the mountain was a very quiet one. When they got to the base of the mountain the three struck south for a short distance until they came upon a dirt path. The path led them west and finally ended up connecting to what Deeli called a road, which just looked like a wider dirt path to Matthew. Except for a short break for food, the trio walked until almost dark. By this time they were amongst the giant gold trees and made their camp in the midst of them. Matthew was thankful that this time they had blankets with which to cover themselves and lay upon. Still, the reality of sleeping outside on the hard ground was wearing off some of the novelty he had found in this world.

They awoke the next morning a little stiff. The sun was still hidden by the eastern mountain peaks, but according to Deeli it was light enough for them to get started. Tendrils of mist snaked along the ground, their life not yet burned away by the rising sun. Matthew, teeth chattering, took note for the first time that considering his age, Deeli did not seem affected by his sleeping arrangements. They made a small fire and Deeli brewed some of his tea. The food they ate cold from their packs, in a hurry to begin the day's journey. They made very few stops to rest along the way, but it still took them most of the day to reach the castle on foot. All three had been keeping their eyes peeled for signs of attack, especially from the sky, but none ever came.

As they drew closer to the castle, more and more Elven dwellings were coming into view. The road was in much better shape here, and the people they passed were watching them closely. Rumors had already spread about the return of Napdeeliate, the half-breed who withdrew Calburnathis, and their huge Human friend. Some of the Elves they passed seemed to hold them in awe; others acted outraged by their presence.

Matthew was too enthralled by all that he saw to let the reaction of the Elves bother him. It seemed as if he was living in a fairy tale, walking through a medieval-looking town full of Elves with a huge castle just ahead. Matthew had never seen a castle before, except in pictures. This one had mountains rising in the background and a high stone wall surrounding it.

"Matthew, you have that slack-jawed look again," Deeli said from in front of him. "May we continue on now?" Matthew had stopped before the gates without realizing it and was staring up at the castle. When he heard Deeli's voice, it brought him back from his daydreaming and made him realize he was not moving anymore. He hurried after the other two as they began to enter the front gate.

The soldiers were stiff and formal with them, knowing who they were and that the King was not happy about having them here. As the trio walked through the gate, they realized how many sentries were on top of the wall. They also saw many Elves polishing armor and weapons, but the majority were in the courtyard practicing battle maneuvers. There was a lot of hostility in the air and the message was apparent—it was time for war. "It would seem," Deeli started, "that the King has already made up his mind."

"Well, having a Human boy walking around with their sacred Elven sword is not what they had expected. I can understand why they wouldn't want to just rely on me."

"Words of wisdom, young Matthew," Deeli said. "In my zeal to see the Creator move through the sword and prophecy, I forget to look at the situation through other people's eyes." They had walked through the courtyard unattended, but as the three neared the main entrance two soldiers came up alongside them.

"We have been ordered to take you to your rooms," one of them said. "You are the last to arrive, the council will be starting soon."

"It looks as though we made it in time," Deeli said as they followed the soldiers, "which is good because I do not think they would have held things up for us."

"The way everyone is acting," Matthew added, "I think they wish we hadn't made it at all." The soldiers escorted them to a suite of rooms that connected to a main room with a couch, water basin, and food on a table. "Now this is more like it," Matthew said eyeing the food. Once left alone, all three ate their fill, washed up, and settled down to relax.

"Your clothing is looking a little worn," Deeli said after a while. "I will see if something can be done about that." Matthew looked at himself and could see that it was true. His clothes were torn in many places, very dirty and not like anything this world had ever seen. "I am certain they have posted guards outside our door." Deeli opened the door and sure enough there were two soldiers right there. "How convenient having you two here. My young friend got his clothes all torn and dirty the other day in the clearing. You know, fighting all those Traul warriors and saving the Princess and all. Do you think there might be a way to get him something a little more appropriate to wear to the war council?"

The two guards looked at each other. Finally one said that he would see what could be done and took off down the corridor. He reappeared sometime later not only with new clothing and boots for Matthew, but for Haub and Deeli as well. "Well, well, it looks like the King is getting most generous in his old age," Deeli clucked.

"These were sent by the Princess," the guard said curtly. "Dress and I will take you to the council chamber, the war council is about to begin." With that, the guard turned and walked out the door closing it behind him. They dressed quickly, wondering where the Princess had gotten clothing big enough for Haub.

"Now you look more like you belong in our world, Matthew," Haub spoke for the first time since they had been at the castle.

"Thank you, Haub, I kind of feel like Robin Hood with a sword." Haub looked at Matthew questiongly. "Never mind," Matthew said with a smile, "just a reference to another story from my world." Matthew wanted to wear the traveling cloak he had been given, but Deeli reminded him that they were not going to be traveling anywhere yet. Deeli opened the door and they followed the two soldiers.

"Deeli, do you really think I should bring the sword to the council meeting? The fact that I'm the one who has it sure makes people mad."

"By all means," Deeli answered with a mischievous smile. "It is the best way to prove that you are the rightful heir. Besides, it's good for them."

"I hope you're right," Matthew said with growing apprehension. After a few more corridors the group came up to some high wooden doors. The soldiers opened them and ushered the three companions into a huge room with a three story high ceiling. Every eye turned on them—every conversation stopped. The room was as silent as the grave and suddenly Matthew felt very small.

"I think we have probably been the topic of conversation," Deeli whispered needlessly.

"Come in and take your seats," King Peridon ordered. In the center of the room was a huge rectangular table that had seats for at least sixty people, nearly all filled. Both the table and chairs were made of wood from the giant gold trees; light from the setting sun filtered in through the tall windows causing them to glisten. The table was hollow in the center with an opening at one end, allowing the servants' access to the guests from inside. Across from the opening was a raised area where the King of the Elves sat. Matthew, Haub, and Deeli took the only three chairs left; the seats of least honor, near the opening for the servants and farthest away from King Peridon's seat.

Matthew scanned the faces around the table. The Humans looked back at him with friendly curiosity, the Dwaries with only a little interest. The Elves would not make eye contact at all. He finally spotted King Moark, and sitting next to him was Pheltic. The two new friends made eye contact and Pheltic gave Matthew a wave and a smile. This helped considerably to put Matthew more at ease. A sharp rapping with a wooden mallet brought everyone's attention to the head of the table. Alexthna, seated next to King Peridon, was calling the war council to order.

"You all know why this council has been called. At our most sacred festival of the cycle a force of Traul and Nomie warriors attacked the clearing, slaughtering hundreds of Elves, Humans, and Dwaries. They were after the Sword of Kings, Calburnathis, to bring back to their master." Much angry murmuring arose from this statement and Alexthna had to use his mallet to regain order. "As you know they did not obtain the sword. For the first time in its sixteen century imprisonment, Calburnathis was drawn from the tree by this young half-breed." Alexthna pointed at Matthew and all eyes turned once again to him. "In the process, the Great Tree was split in half. One of our duties today will be to elect a committee to decide what should be done with what remains of the tree. The Traul and Nomie races have declared war on the Elves and all inhabitants of this valley. The question today is, who among you will stand with the Elven people in this, the final war?!"

A Human, bigger even than Haub, stood to his feet. It was Roak, head elder of Haub's village and his dead wife's brother. "I speak for the combined Human villages," Roak began. "We have always respected the Elven people and have done our best to live at peace with you. Often it seems to we Humans that you look down on us. But we know that if your peace is threatened, so is ours. I cannot speak for those Humans outside the valley; I fear they may already belong to the enemy. As for we in the valley, there are many deaths to avenge. We stand with the Elves to the end." Applause went up from the Humans gathered to show their support. Roak had also given the longest speech anyone had ever heard a Human give.

"Thank you, Counsel Roak," King Peridon stood and said. "I am pleased that the Elves and Humans will be fighting side by side again." As the Elven King sat down, King Moark of the Dwaries stood.

"I'll keep this short and simple. We Dwaries have always stood with you Elves against the evil from the north and we'll do so now." The Dwarie King sat. After more applause and voiced agreements, Alexthna stood.

"Thank you, King Moark, it seems that we are all in unity. Now comes the task of devising a plan." Alexthna sat down and suggestions began to come forth. Most of those present were not as well informed about the enemy's strength as were King Peridon and Deeli—therefore, many plans for an all-out assault on the Dark Lord came forward. For the better part of two hours plans were presented and discussed, but not one brought forward that was good enough for anyone to commit to. Finally King Peridon stood and addressed the assembly.

"We know that the enemy would like to see us annihilated and has ventured into our valley once already. From reports that I have been getting over the past few seven-days, I believe they have been gathering a sizable army for some time now. Nothing has been confirmed yet, but if they are planning to march on the valley I don't believe we have the time or resources to fight an offensive war. That is why I am proposing, as much as I hate to, a defensive plan. I put forth that we combine our efforts and sweep through the valley, finding and killing any of the enemy that might still be within our borders. Then we converge on the northern pass through the mountains and build a wall completely enclosing the opening. From atop that wall we could defend ourselves indefinitely. I believe that eventually we would be able to go on the offensive, after a prolonged siege has weakened them."

"What if he sends them over the mountains as well as through the pass?" Roak stood and asked.

"I don't think he would split his forces like that, but my plan also calls for Elven and Dwarie scouts to be patrolling the mountains on either side of the pass. From that vantage point they would be able to see every move the enemy is making. Our scouts would also have plenty of time to signal reinforcements if the enemy tried to come over the mountains. I believe we will have the advantage in numbers. It takes a lot more warriors to attack a stout wall than it does to defend one."

"Well, it seems a sound enough plan to me," Moark said slapping his palm on the table, "I think it will give us our strongest position." King Peridon nodded in acknowledgment to Moark, then turned to the Human delegates. After a little more discussion with his advisors, Roak stood and announced that the Humans were in agreement with the plan also. Then came a voice that had not been heard from yet:

"What happens if he uses magic against your wall, my reports say his power is stronger than any seen before. He also has the winged Nomies, they will be watching your every move."

"Then what do you propose, Napdeeliate?" King Peridon said in a flash of anger. "Should we just surrender to them? Does your God say that we should lay down and die, let evil take over our world?"

"Of course not, the Creator's promise will always hold true.

'As long as there are stars in the heavens, so shall my people stand.'

Your God and mine are the same, and He has not cast any of us aside. But He does want things done His way, that He might receive the glory. Our Creator has ordained that the Sword Bearer should be the one to defeat the evil that would destroy us. Your plans for the defense of the valley are good, but I propose that you allow a small group, including Matthew and myself, to make our way to the Traul stronghold. There, Matthew and Calburnathis could face the Dark One as the prophecies have foretold." The room was silent for several heartbeats, then chaos broke loose. Everyone was talking or shouting, trying to be heard. Finally Peridon grabbed the mallet from his High Counselor and began banging it on the table.

"Order! We will have order in here!" Slowly the room quieted, but before the King spoke again Alexthna stood and shouted with an angry voice.

"We do not need a half-breed to fight our battles for us!" This brought on more shouting in the room. After giving Alexthna a dark look, the King once again regained order.

"Thank you, we will have no more outbursts like that. Do I make myself clear?" No one said a word and as the King looked at Alexthna, the High Counselor slid a little lower in his seat. Then Deeli stood and the King gave him permission to speak.

"As I have told you before, Matthew is not a half-breed. He was brought here from another world for this very purpose. If he is willing to take up this quest on your behalf then your blessing and prayers should go with him." Before anyone could make a reply, a voice came from near a window behind one of the long heavy draperies.

"He is right, father, they must be allowed to go and I with them." All heads turned to see Sharineas emerging from behind the curtain. King Peridon and Gamilon stood and shouted at the same moment.

"What?!!" Gamilon said no more, but the King continued. "I may not have a choice in letting these fools throw away their lives, but you, daughter, are not going with them!"

"As Keeper of the Amulet it is my duty to go where the sword goes...I know it is the right thing to do."

"You don't even know how to use the power of the amulet yet," Peridon said as if that dismissed the whole subject.

"The boy doesn't know how to use the power of the sword yet and he is willing to risk his life for our people. Can I, their future Queen, do less?" Peridon looked at his daughter as if he did not even know her. Matthew blanched at the word *boy*. He had saved her life, yet she was not impressed with him in the least. He was also becoming a little concerned over all this talk about him throwing away his life.

"If Sharineas is going, then I am going," Gamilon said in a determined voice.

"Sharineas is not going anywhere. I am still King and my word is law! Sharineas, obey me in this or I will put you in your room under guard, the choice is yours." Sharineas gave her father a smoldering look that would have cowed any other person, but the King looked her straight in the eye and did not flinch. It was breaking Peridon's heart to treat his daughter like this, but he knew it was for her own good. The High King of all the Elves had won another battle—Sharineas turned on her heel and stalked out of the room.

King Peridon closed his eyes and let out a sigh; he did not feel as if he had won anything. After a long moment of silence the Elven King turned back to the council. "Honored delegates, I apologize for the interruption and hope you can forgive both my daughter and myself. For whatever reason, be it truly our God or some powerful magic, Napdeeliate and this Matthew control Calburnathis. Therefore, if they wish to attempt this foolhardy expedition, I give my permission. I will also give them an Elven escort to the mouth of the Great Northern Pass. What say you, King Moark?"

"The Dwaries will go along with both plans, provided we are allowed to send along one representative of our race." Peridon looked to Deeli who nodded his head in agreement.

"That will be acceptable," Peridon said to Moark. "What say the Humans?"

"We will agree on the same terms as the Dwaries," Roak stood and said.

"Good," the Elven King said. "I would also like to send along an Elf of my choosing. What say you to these terms Napdeeliate?"

"Brothers, I thank you for your support in this plan, I truly believe it is our best hope. Five is not a bad number, but I ask that no more be added. I think a small group will have a better chance of moving through the northern lands undetected than a large one. What we are about to attempt will be very dangerous, with the possibility of our not returning. So I ask you to please only send representatives that have volunteered for the mission and know the full dangers of it." When Deeli had finished, Haub stood to his feet.

"Roak, men of the combined villages, I wish to represent the Humans on this mission. I swear to uphold the honor of our race and to avenge the blood of our loved ones." Haub sat back down as Roak and the other Human council members discussed his proposal. After a few moments Roak stood and addressed Haub.

"Haub, it has been agreed upon unanimously that you would be the best to go on this mission. You will be forever sung about in the ballads of our brave. May the God you serve go with you." Deeli smiled and put his hand on Haub's shoulder. King Moark stood and addressed King Peridon.

"I will go to my most trusted warriors and have a volunteer for you by this night."

"Father, I wish to represent our people in this," Pheltic blurted out impulsively as he stood to his feet. Pheltic looked as surprised at his outburst as did his father and older brother. Telick, now battle chief of the Dwaries in his father's stead, rose to his feet.

"Father, he is too young and inexperienced and you know mother would never allow it." This last statement brought quite a bit of laughter from the assembly, which caused Pheltic's face to turn a bright red. Moark looked at both his sons, weighing his options.

"Pheltic, I wish I could grant you this, but Telick is right. An experienced warrior will be needed in this." Pheltic sat down looking as if his world had just collapsed. Matthew's sympathy for his friend overcame his good sense—he stood and cleared his throat.

"I haven't said a word during this whole discussion, even though I'm part of what you're talking about. I would like to speak now." When no one said anything, Matthew continued. "Pheltic was at the battle in the clearing and survived it. He has also proved himself to be a good friend to me, which is a lot more than I can say for the majority of the people in this room. I would trust my life in his hands and would very much like Pheltic to go with us." Pheltic gave Matthew a grateful look. Matthew did not know it, but he had just gained a friend for life.

"With a testimonial like that, maybe I should reconsider," Moark said looking at his youngest son with pride. "If the young man who drew the fabled sword from its imprisonment puts so much stock in you, how can I do less? Your mother will probably skin me alive, but I will grant your request, my son."

"Thank you, father," Pheltic replied with tears of joy beginning to well up in his eyes. Telick sat down shaking his head, but caught his brother's eye and gave him a nod of respect.

"Very well then," King Peridon stood. "I will get a volunteer from among my elite guard this night. Napdeeliate, when will you be ready to leave?"

"The sooner the better," Deeli replied. "Tomorrow morning if possible."

"I will have everything arranged by then," Peridon said. "King Moark, Roak and myself, with our counsels, will reconvene here in two hours. We will go over our strategies in further detail and choose the necessary committees then." He then nodded to Alexthna who stood and spoke.

"Is there anything that needs to be added to these proceedings at this time?" When no one said a word, Alexthna banged his mallet twice and adjourned the meeting. As the delegates were filing out of the room, King Peridon called Deeli over to him.

"I would have you know, Napdeeliate, that I do not forgive the things you have done, or your beliefs. I will, however, cooperate in this venture for the sake of my people and will provide you with everything you might need for the journey. Right now I would like you and your friends to accompany Alexthna and myself to the temple vaults. We are going to loan Matthew the scabbard and see if the armor fits him."

"The armor," Deeli said thoughtfully. "Alexthna, I think Matthew just might be able to shed some light on the mystery of the armor." Alexthna, who was not taking the outcome of the meeting very well, just gave Matthew a cold stare.

The group, with Alexthna in the lead, made their way down several long corridors. Matthew was feeling uncomfortable. No one was saying a word and all that could be heard were their footsteps echoing down the hallways. They continued on for some time, always on a decline. At one point Alexthna stopped at a set of huge wooden doors made from more of the gold wood, with symbols and markings all around the door posts. In turn, he, the King, and Deeli, all bowed from the waist and then continued down the hallway. Matthew and Haub looked at each other and shrugged their shoulders not having any idea what they were supposed to do. They caught up with the others and Matthew whispered to Deeli.

"What was that all about?"

"That was a side entrance to the outer part of the Most Holy Place in the temple."

"Oh." That did not tell Matthew much, but he did not want to ask any more questions with the King and his counselor so near. Alexthna led them down several flights of stone stairways, the air getting colder the deeper they went. Finally they were standing before a rough, wooden door—straps of iron running across it; and something that looked like a wax seal where a door knob should have been. Alexthna said some words that surprisingly Matthew did not understand. There was a tingle in the air and Matthew realized he was using magic. The seal fell away and King Peridon opened the door.

"This is the door to the temple vaults," Deeli whispered. "You two are the first non-Elven born to ever be allowed in here. The two visitors' eyes bulged as they saw all the gold, silver, gems, and holy relics that belonged to the Elven priesthood. They entered another room and there in front of Matthew was a suit of black metal armor on a stand, unlike anything he had ever seen.

"Here is the scabbard that belongs with the sword," Peridon said handing it to Matthew. It was made of leather with ancient symbols on it. There was also a leather thong at the top for tying the blade in. Matthew looked closely and saw that there was writing on the thong.

"How come the writing on this strip of leather is so different from that on the scabbard?" Matthew asked.

"That is one of the mysteries we cannot solve," Deeli answered. "The symbols on the scabbard are ancient, from the time of our first kings. The leather thong was never with the scabbard until it reappeared at the tree. But the writing on the strip of leather dates back nearly a thousand cycles before the sword was stolen."

"Can you read what the thong says?" Matthew questioned them. Deeli was quick to answer.

"It says,

'My love for you will always live, it can never die. It will be with you in-between, and at the end of time.'

We have no idea what it means or who wrote it."

"Maybe it was those two you told me about," Matthew suggested.

"It could be, I guess," Deeli said giving Matthew a "be quiet" look. "But the language used on it was not being used at the time, nor had it been for hundreds of sun-cycles. Anyway I think it is time for you to look at the armor." Deeli very much wanted the conversation to get away from any talk about Melthanis and Jaspinea.

"Napdeeliate says that he has not told you about the armor," Alexthna said stiffly, addressing Matthew. "This armor was found at the foot of the Great Tree with the amulet, sword, and scabbard. The priests of that time and all through our history have studied the armor. Still we have no clue as to what it is made of or where it comes from. Now what could you possibly tell us about it?"

"I can't tell you anything about it," Matthew answered, examining the armor. It was not like the medieval armor he had seen in the antique store. It was made from an obsidian-like black metal that bent easily in his hand. Its design was almost modern for his world, like something he would see in a futuristic comic book. What was strange about the metal was that when he bent it and then let go, the piece would return immediately to its original shape. There were small dents and scratches in places; the armor had definitely seen use. Matthew knew that dents even that small must have been caused by something pretty powerful for them not to bend back into shape.

"Our most powerful magic has almost no effect on it," Deeli added.

"I still don't know why you think I can tell you about it, I've never seen anything like it before in my life."

"When King Peridon mentioned the armor," Deeli said, "it reminded me of something that you had said when we first met. Come around to the backside and you will see what I mean." Matthew went to the back of the armor and looked to the spot where Deeli pointed. With wide eyes he read the inscription on the lower back of the breast-plate.

"Laboratories of the EPCO Corp., Gary, Indiana."

Chapter

10

Matthew lay on a mattress of down feathers, staring into the darkness. It felt as if he was lying on a cloud after so many nights without a real bed, but sleep was nowhere to be found. Every day in this world brought more questions, but he had no more answers than before. Matthew had been shocked beyond words when he read the inscription on the armor. Deeli and Alexthna began asking him questions right away, but the origins of the armor were just as much a mystery to him as they were to them.

The armor must be from my world, Matthew wrestled in his mind; *the inscription said Gary, Indiana. It would take some pretty advanced technology to produce metal that strong, yet lightweight and pliable.* Matthew had told them that he did not know of any metal like this in his world at the present time, and was certain it did not exist sixteen-hundred years ago. All the armor had accomplished so far was to make things more confused and inexplicable than before. The three of them had discussed a few theories, but with no way to prove them true or false they finally quit for the night. Deeli and Haub had helped Matthew get the armor on, and to almost everyone's surprise it was a perfect fit.

"As if it had been made for you," Deeli said thoughtfully.

"From the looks of it, I'd say this armor has been worn into battle before," Matthew added. "I must be the same size as the original owner."

"Yes, what a remarkable coincidence," Deeli said. "Or just maybe the hand of the Creator."

Now, as he lay in bed thinking everything through, Matthew realized that the mystery was only deeper. His gaze went from the ceiling to the suit of armor laying on a low couch across the room. Moonlight from an open window reflected off its black surface. As restless as he was, and with a mind so full of questions, Matthew knew sleep would continue to elude him.

He got out of bed and walked over to a window that gave him a good view of the west courtyard. The moon was still almost full and lit up the grounds well. From this vantage point Matthew could see over the wall and into the city beyond. Deeli had told him that there were two kinds of Elves in the valley. Those who lived in the city around the castle, which eventually spread out to smaller towns—and those who made their home in the forest. They were a separate community that still called Peridon king, but also had a king that they elected to rule over them locally. Their dwellings were built high up in the trees, mostly in the giant golds.

Suddenly a motion in the courtyard caught his attention. A dark figure made its way stealthily from the castle toward a low building with a large entryway. Matthew knew that whatever the person was up to—it was none of his business, but it certainly seemed suspicious that the person was trying so hard not to be seen.

Matthew shouted at the figure, which looked up at him startled. The person looked about the size of an Elf, but from that distance he could not see who it was. The dark clad figure turned and ran into the low building. He stayed at the window awhile longer, but saw no more action. Deeli and Haub were both awakened by his shout and asked him what he was doing. He told them he had seen an Elf dressed in black run across the courtyard. "Well, this is the Elven stronghold,"

Deeli reassured him. "It was probably one of Peridon's scouts either leaving or returning. I think maybe you should go to sleep now, Matthew." Matthew was beginning to feel the fatigue of the day finally catching up with him, and Deeli's explanation did sound reasonable. *I don't know what that person is up to,* Matthew thought as he crawled back in bed, *but I guess Deeli is right, it's the king's business, not ours.* He closed his eyes and slowly his thoughts changed to dreams.

The sun was just a hint of color over the mountain peaks when a servant came knocking on the trio's door. Deeli was already awake and had opened the door before Matthew could rub the sleep from his eyes.

"The King requests you to be in the main dining hall as soon as possible," the servant stated. "A Dwarie scout has come with news." Deeli thanked him and said they would be down shortly.

"Are you sure that is not what you saw last night, Matthew?" Deeli asked.

"...I'm not sure now. Until you just asked me that question I thought I had dreamt it." All three chuckled over Matthew's confusion as they cleaned up a little in a basin of water already in their rooms, and donned the new traveling clothes they had been given. Matthew wore the armor and the black traveling cloak the Princess had provided for him.

As they entered the dining hall, the smell of food brought them fully awake. Servants were running back and forth from the kitchens to the head table—carrying plates of meat, potatoes, fruit, fresh baked bread, and pastries. King Peridon and King Moark, as well as Pheltic, Alexthna, Gamilon, and an Elf they did not know, were already seated and eating.

"Good morning," Pheltic said cheerily. "I've saved a place for you over here, Matthew."

"Sit down and break your fast," King Peridon said. "We have gotten news from one of Moark's scouts." Matthew sat down next to Pheltic, popped a sausage in his mouth, and began chewing hungrily. He felt a little self-conscious when he looked over and noticed both Deeli and Haub silently praying over their food.

"My fastest runner was sent from our mountain fortress and arrived here in the middle of the night," King Moark began. "I already had my suspicions about this Enlightened One before the tragedy in the clearing.

I sent scouts north to find out what he was up to two seven-days ago. They have finally returned with news that the enemy is definitely massing its forces. The number of Traul and Nomie warriors they saw was far beyond anything we thought possible. The scouts also said that more were still arriving when they headed back."

"How long will it take them to reach the pass?" Deeli asked.

"We have no way of knowing for sure. My scouts estimate that once the entire army is together, it would take about three to four seven-days to reach the valley."

"My soldiers are gathering now, and will be ready to leave today to search our section of the valley for any more enemy spies," King Peridon spoke with a fire in his eyes. "The soldiers from each race will meet at the pass four days hence, to start building the wall. I also have laborers leaving today with building materials and tools. This is Boreshia," Peridon said, changing the subject and pointing to the Elf sitting at the table that none of them knew. "He will be going with you on the quest; along with a contingent of Elven soldiers to escort you to the pass. If you leave after our meal you should be there by late afternoon tomorrow."

"My friend," King Moark began putting his hand on Deeli's shoulder. "This will be very dangerous even with the sword, please be careful. My scouts did have encounters with some of the winged Nomies right on our own mountains. If you are even seen, the enemy will know you are coming and you will have lost the element of surprise." Deeli then proceeded to tell them all about Haub's run-in with the winged Nomies at his village and their attack on the way to the Festival.

"How long has that dog had spies in the valley?" Peridon was outraged. "He has spied on us, butchered our wives and children, and now gathers an army to destroy us. I still wish that an Elf had drawn the blade...but I am thankful that the Traul Dark Lord did not get his hands on it."

"I still say there is no hope if an Elven hand does not hold the sword," Alexthna broke in looking at Matthew.

"Alexthna, how can you continue to deny the hand of the Creator in all of this?" It was Deeli's turn to be upset. "He has used many people and things to deliver us in the past, and they were not always Elves."

"Say what you will, old fool, but the law is the law. You taught me that."

"Yes," Deeli retorted, "I taught you that. But as you just reminded all of us, I am nothing but an old fool."

"Enough bickering!" King Peridon slammed his fist on the table. "We have been forced together by God or by chance, but for the same purpose. I put more hope in our combined armies than I do an untried boy, even with the power of Calburnathis. But if there is any chance at all, Alexthna, we must let them try and give our support."

"Spoken like a true king, Peridon," Deeli said looking at the Elven King with an approving look. "I think you have it in you to become a better king than even your father was." Peridon blushed, not knowing what to say in answer to this compliment from his uncle whom he had kicked out of his own homeland.

"Let's just finish eating so we can get you five on your way and get our business started," Peridon blustered. They quickly finished their meal without much more talk and went out into the courtyard. Matthew was amazed at the way the metal in his armor bent with his body movement, but it was still going to take some time to get used to walking in it.

Servants met them outside in the courtyard with horses. They were all given packs of provisions for the journey, and bedrolls made from a soft, durable material. From atop the horse Matthew could see all the faces of those waiting to see them off. He looked, but could not see the fiery daughter of the Elven King anywhere. He did not know why he was searching for her, all he knew was that it bothered him very much when she called him a 'boy.' He saw Gamilon asking questions and looking around, presumably searching for Sharineas. *And why not?* Matthew thought. *Deeli told me they are to be married. I don't know why I even care.*

Matthew continued watching the good-byes. There was the Elf Boreshia, dressed in dark green with a dark brown traveling cloak. He was armed with a long bow and a slim sword at his side, saying good-bye to a couple of young Elf-maidens. Pheltic was hugging his father and shaking hands with a few young Dwarie males. Haub had said farewell to his brother-in-law and now sat upon his horse next to Deeli's mount. The pair sat there; no one particularly interested in saying good-bye to them either. So Matthew rode up beside their horses and the three waited alone.

Finally the farewells were over and the journey ready to begin. The five headed through the outer gate with an escort of twelve Elven soldiers. The escort was to get them as far as the Great Northern Pass and then begin preparations for building the wall. Matthew had not ridden a horse since he was a child and wished they would have given him a smaller one. They rode north through the surrounding city, Elves bustling here and there. It had been five days since the massacre in the clearing. Matthew knew it would take the people a long time to recover, but he also knew that life always continues and cannot be stopped for long because of grief. So he was not completely surprised to see the city returning to normal. *Of course I don't know what normal is here*, he thought to himself with a half-smile.

Matthew closed his eyes and allowed his horse fall in line with the others. The smell of fresh baked bread was in the air; that, along with the feeling of warm sunlight on his face and the birds chirping, gave him a sense of peace. It was hard for him to imagine that they were riding into danger. Then images of the slaughter in the clearing came flooding into his mind. He shuddered and quickly opened his eyes to the here and now, dispelling the scenes of murder.

"Are you all right Matthew?" He turned to see Pheltic riding alongside him.

"…Yeah, sure. I'm all right."

"I didn't get to thank you for standing up for me at the war council. I will never forget it. If you had not stood by me I would not have been able to go with you."

"Well, I meant what I said, Pheltic. I consider you a good friend, and I'm glad you're traveling with us. Just do me one favor, don't let anything happen to yourself. I would feel horrible if you were hurt, especially knowing that I had influenced your father's decision."

"Matthew, please don't feel responsible for me. I wanted to go more than anything. My father and older brothers are always telling stories of all the marvelous things they've seen and done. All I am able to do is sit and listen, wishing that I could go on a grand adventure of my own." Matthew just smiled at Pheltic's enthusiasm and silently prayed. *God, if You really are out there and listening, please protect my little friend here.*

Deeli had told them that the roads would be fairly well kept up all the way to the mountain pass, so there would not be any hard riding. The soldiers were keeping a sharp eye out on the surrounding forest and sky. So feeling pretty secure, Matthew and Pheltic spent much of the ride talking as if they were old friends. Matthew told his friend everything he had learned about the sword, including the fact that this was the sword Excalibur, the same sword that he had told him about in the King Arthur story.

That night they camped in a clearing along the road. Matthew was feeling very stiff as he and Pheltic laid out their bedrolls. "I think I'm going to be very sore in the morning; I haven't ridden a horse since I was a kid."

"I'm afraid I'll be joining you. I have only ridden once before in my life. We Dwaries don't have a big fondness for riding, and only do so when it's necessary."

"We'll just have to give each other pep talks along the way tomorrow," Matthew said with a laugh. "I have the feeling I might be tempted to get off my horse and walk."

They finished setting up camp, started the fires and cooked supper. Up to this point, Boreshia had mainly stayed in the company of his fellow soldiers and not said much to the four companions. Now, as they sat around their fire, he came over and joined them. The friends continued to talk, but Boreshia did not make any effort to join the conversation. He only sat and watched Deeli with an intense stare. Deeli let it go for some time, but eventually became uncomfortable enough to say something. "All right, you apparently have something on your mind, Boreshia, spit it out."

"The guys and myself have just been wondering if you are really the Napdeeliate that all the stories are about."

"...Yes. I am he," Deeli answered with a sigh.

"But my parents, our people, they were in awe of you. Our enemies feared your very name. It was said that you were the most powerful being alive and that if anyone crossed your path they had better beware. I heard my Father say that you could snuff out a life with just a glance."

"I am sorry to disappoint you, Boreshia, but most every story that you have heard about me has been exaggerated. And I have never known anyone who could take a life with but a glance. Some, however, are true. I must admit that in my younger days I was quite arrogant and had a tendency to flaunt my power." Matthew could hardly believe that the Deeli he knew was the same person they were describing. "I would ask a favor of you, Boreshia," Deeli continued. "We are going to be spending a lot of time together in the coming days. I would appreciate it if you would simply call me Deeli. The Elf Napdeeliate is dead, as is the name. *He may be humble,* Matthew thought, *but simple, never.*

"Why did you volunteer to come with us?" Matthew asked Boreshia. The young Elf hesitated, looking at Matthew as if wondering if he should even answer this half-breed. Finally he did.

"I was there when you drew Calburnathis from the tree and I knew the prophecy had been fulfilled. I don't understand why it wasn't an Elf, but I do know that this group will go down in the history of our people, and I want my name to go with it. I have always been intrigued with the stories of Napdeeliate. When I heard that he had returned, well, I could not pass up the opportunity. But if you are he," Boreshia said standing up and looking at Deeli, "I am greatly disillusioned to find that you are just a tired old Elf, nothing but a shadow of your former glory. Still, I have volunteered and will stand by you through thick and thin. I bid you all a good night's rest." With that, Boreshia turned and rejoined his comrades.

"He sure doesn't pull any punches, does he?" Matthew spoke up after the abrupt young Elf had gone.

"I don't think he'll be much fun to have along," Pheltic added.

"He is just a typical young Elven male," Deeli said. "Actually, he reminds me of how I was at that age, although I was probably more like Gamilon. You must understand, the Elven people in general can be very cold-hearted toward anyone different from themselves. They are very rigid, with little tolerance for other people. When life throws them something unexpected, they do not learn from it; just ignore it.... But enough talk for tonight—as much as I wish my people would change, I know that only the Creator can do it. I can only pray for the day to come. We had all better try to get some sleep; it will be our last night in non-hostile land for a long time."

It had only taken Matthew one night to become used to a soft bed again. He tossed and turned for quite a while listening to the cricket-song, and wondering if agreeing to this quest was going to be the smartest thing he ever did, or the dumbest. It was a long time before he fell asleep; never finding an answer to his question.

Morning finally came and Matthew did not feel as if he had slept at all. He was wet and clammy from dew, and as he got up he realized that his prediction about being sore was right. A low groan came from Pheltic who was also getting up and Matthew knew he was not alone. As they rode all morning, a little of the soreness worked itself out of their protesting bodies. Matthew and Pheltic still had to encourage each other to stay in the saddle and were looking forward to a lunch stop. But as the sun reached its zenith, the commander of the soldiers motioned Deeli forward. When Deeli dropped back in line with his companions he made an announcement: "The commander says that we are running behind schedule and the only way to make it to the pass by early evening is to ride straight through the midday meal. I am afraid that if we wish sustenance, it will have to be eaten from horseback." Audible groans escaped from Matthew and Pheltic; Deeli just smiled and said nothing.

The incline on which they had been riding began to grow steeper as the afternoon wore on. The road became a path that narrowed until the group had to ride single file. The darkening forest had closed in on either side of the path and some of the escort drew their weapons. Very suddenly it seemed, the trees fell away and Matthew was surprised to see a huge gorge ahead of them. The ground rose steadily for several hundred yards before it leveled off and became a wide pass between two mountains. The pass was easily a hundred yards wide and the walls on either side were straight up, as if they had been sheared off by a giant meat cleaver. *Perfect for marching an army through,* was Matthew's first thought. *How are they going to build a wall across that?*

The soldiers spread out along the edge of the forest to make camp and prepare their evening meals. Boreshia made his way over to the four companions so they might discuss the plan of attack. Deeli had been through the pass and into the North before so he knew what it looked like. "On the other side of the pass there is much open space before we can get to any timber. I think the best plan of action would be to wait until after dark to go through. That way there would be less chance of us being seen by any patrols on the other side."

"But how are we going to see where we're going?" Pheltic asked.

"Do not worry," Boreshia said with self-confidence while looking at Deeli. "My *young* Elven eyes will be able to guide us in the dark." Four soldiers were assigned to keep watch while the rest of the company ate and rested. As the sun set, Matthew knew the real adventure was about to begin. His anxieties were on the rise and no rest would come.

"Deeli, if it will take an entire army four weeks, I mean seven-days, to get here, we can make it there in a lot less time, right?"

"It will be close," Deeli answered. "The castle that the Trauls have used as their command center for generations is even farther north than where the scouts say the army is gathering. It is also halfway up a mountain, which will make it more difficult to enter in secret."

"Also," the almost forgotten Haub added, "as we go north the army is coming south—if we go straight through we will be killed. We are going to have to go wide around them either east or west, which will delay us even longer."

"Going around sounds a lot better than going through," quipped Pheltic. "I wanted adventure, but not that much."

"But once we're there, how do we get into the castle without any-one noticing?" Matthew asked.

"I took the liberty of studying some of my books on northern geography." Deeli answered. "I have found some things that should help us along the way. In one place there is mention of a secret entrance behind the castle. I wrote it down, now where did I put that...oh, here it is." Deeli read from a scrap of parchment:

'You can find the exit from outside. Behind the black fortress, not the front or sides. From a distance you will see, just look beneath the rainbow trees.'

"That's it?" Matthew said, with wide eyes. "That's all we have to go on? What does it mean? Is that what we're counting on to get us into the castle?"

"I know it is not much," Deeli answered apologetically, "but it is the only reference to another way into the castle that I could find. I will have to admit that I do not know what it means. I am hoping that it will make itself clear when we get there."

"Hoping!" Boreshia said stunned. "If that is our only plan then we are doomed."

"Our only other alternative is to march up to the front gate and announce ourselves," Deeli came back at him. "Is that what you would propose we do?"

"...I must prepare my things, it will be time to leave soon." Thus saying, Boreshia went over to his fellow soldiers and began rummaging through his pack. Matthew broke the silence that followed.

"I'm sorry for being so skeptical Deeli, but it doesn't seem like much to go on. What if we get all the way there and can't find a way in?"

"That is where we will have to go on faith, my young friend. Do you think the Creator would go to the trouble of bringing you here and giving you the sword, then allow you to receive the Elven King's blessing and not make a way for you to meet the enemy?"

"I guess you're right," Matthew hesitantly admitted. "I never thought of it that way. I'm sorry."

"Quite all right my boy, quite all right. It seems the young are always worried about something. If they were not, they would probably get themselves into more trouble than they already do." That brought laughter from Matthew, Haub, and especially Pheltic who always seemed to be in some kind of trouble or other.

The four began getting their gear together before it was too dark to see. Boreshia came over to them accompanied by his commander and another soldier. The group walked to the mouth of the pass in silence. Once there the commander, with a relieved voice, bid them farewell and Godspeed.

After the two soldiers walked away, Deeli asked if he could say a prayer for the journey and all agreed. Matthew was still not that comfortable with praying, and found himself looking around at the others. All four had their heads bowed, although he saw Pheltic look up twice checking out everyone. Boreshia seemed honestly respectful of Deeli's prayer, until toward the end when the name Shesea was mentioned. Boreshia gave Deeli a stony look and did not bow his head again. This was the second or third time Matthew had heard that name. He did not know who the person was or if it was the name of Deeli's God, but he made a mental note to try to find out. *Apparently Boreshia knows,*

Matthew thought. *I guess it's the same in every world, different religions fighting over who's wrong and who's right. My only complaint is that I always seem to get stuck in the middle of them.*

When Deeli was finished they began to edge their way north along the wall in single file, Boreshia in the lead. It seemed like a long walk, there in a dark and strange place. They were all a little relieved when the end of the wall came into sight and nothing had happened. Boreshia pointed out a dark mass about one-hundred and fifty yards in front of them. "That is the tree line, we must make it across this open area and regroup in the trees."

"What happens if we are seen and attacked?" Matthew asked. "We haven't even decided which way we're going to go."

"If we are seen and attacked," Pheltic answered, "we will probably be dead."

"Matthew, have your sword out and ready. That goes for the rest of you as well," Deeli took charge. "I have been through some of the land and I know to the west of here is all wasteland with absolutely no cover. I have never been to the east, but I believe we must take our chances in that direction. Once we are in the forest, travel east just inside the tree line. We will go as far as we can in the dark and then find cover for the night, leaving again at first light. Is this agreeable?" No one objected, so Boreshia gave the signal to move.

The group moved across the open area, keeping an eye on every direction. The walk seemed to last an eternity and every one of them felt as if they were being watched. Finally they reached the trees and entered into the forest a few feet, then squatted. All they could hear was their own breathing, hoping beyond hope that no one saw them cross the rocky slope.

After a few minutes with no sign of being sighted, Boreshia began to make his way northeast with the rest in tow. The group walked for a while, primarily eastward, until they came upon a little open area. Boreshia stopped at the edge, but Pheltic—with only rest on his mind—charged ahead. "Oh good, this looks like a perfect place to sit down for awhile."

"Wait!" Deeli, Haub, and Boreshia, all whispered harshly in unison. Too late; a loud screech went up and a confused yell escaped from Pheltic. Everything that followed happened quickly and was like some nightmare come true. There was a flurry of noise and thrashing leathery wings. Pheltic had stumbled across two of the mutated Nomie spies who were asleep for the night.

The creatures were as confused as Pheltic and all three were fighting to get free of each other. A claw raked across Pheltic's face, causing an explosion of white hot pain and a startled cry. By that time Matthew had leapt into the area with his sword drawn. The stone in the three pronged claw was glowing and blue lightning danced up and down the blade.

The sword lit up the small cleared area and the Nomies' eyes bulged at what they saw. Both turned to flee, but Matthew quickly lashed out and sliced a wing off one of the creatures. In retaliation the creature swung a dark claw at Matthew catching him on the side of his head. This sent him sprawling and the sword flying out of his hand. Haub, who had been right behind Matthew, put the blade of his axe through the Nomie's skull. The axe went so deep he could not get it out in time to stop the other creature who was just becoming airborne.

Suddenly there was a swishing sound in the air, then the winged Nomie shrieked and hit the ground with a thud. Boreshia's arrow had found its mark before the creature had cleared the trees. Haub went over to Pheltic and Matthew to see if he could help. Matthew was just dazed, but Pheltic looked a mess. His face was covered with blood and he was incoherent. Matthew and Haub were helping him up when they heard a gurgled scream come from where Deeli and Boreshia still were.

Two more of the winged spies had been aroused from their sleep by the noise. Boreshia's attacker had hit him from behind, wrapping its claws tightly around his neck. The second mutated Nomie hit Deeli from the side, knocking him over with the creature landing on top. Once again Deeli reacted by instinct, a short flash of light and his attacker was reduced to ashes floating away on the light breeze that filtered through the trees. Deeli sat up dazed, hating himself for what he had just done. He saw Boreshia's attacker headed for the clear area trying to get airborne, screeching for assistance.

"Stop that thing," he cried. "If it gets away we are doomed." Haub had run to Boreshia, so the creature was well past him. Pheltic still sat dazed and bleeding in the middle of the small clearing. Matthew had stayed with Pheltic when Haub ran off to assist Boreshia and was now the only one who could stop the flying Nomie.

He looked around. His eyes locked on the sword that lay a few yards away, the stone still aglow. The Nomie was already in the air when Matthew picked up the sword by its hilt. He pointed it at the black flying creature like a spear and let it fly. Excalibur streaked through the air leaving a glowing trail in its wake and sank deep into the body of the Nomie. The mutated Nomie, who had already cleared the trees, fell like a rock into the forest.

Matthew had run to throw the sword and was now on the opposite edge of the small clearing from his friends. When he saw the creature fall he sank to one knee, his adrenaline spent. No sooner had he caught his breath when a movement in the nearby trees made him turn. Out of the forest, not five feet from him, emerged a dark shape. His stomach turned to ice. No one was near, and Excalibur was somewhere in the forest stuck in the body of a Nomie. Matthew knew that he did not have enough strength left to fight and there was no chance of escape. His mission was over before it had begun.

Gamilon knocked on the door harder this time; still no answer. "Sharineas!" He yelled and let out a low growl of frustration. "Why won't you at least talk to me?" One of the Princess' serving girls started down the hall, but stopped when she heard the outburst. "You, girl," Gamilon said in a more even voice. "Will you please go in and ask the Princess to come out and speak with me?"

"Yes my lord," She replied and went into the room. A few minutes later she emerged from the room. "I am sorry Lord Gamilon, but she is not in her room this morning."

"Then where is she?" Gamilon asked with forced restraint.

"I don't know," the servant stammered. Without another word Gamilon whirled and went to look for the King. When he finally found him, the young Elf was almost out of patience even with the High King.

"King Peridon, I have been looking everywhere for your daughter this morning, have you seen her?"

"I'm afraid not Gamilon, have you tried her room?"

"Yes I have, and every other conceivable place she might be. No one, including the Queen, knows where she is.

"My daughter has not talked to me since the council," the King said sadly. "I think this is the angriest she has ever been with me."

"I am sure she will get over it, my King, you know how Sharineas is. I must get back to my father's estate and inform him of all that has transpired. If you do see her, will you please tell the Princess I wish to see her upon my return."

"Yes, of course, just be sure to be back in time to ride with me to the pass," the King added sternly.

"I will be here, you know you can count on me. If I may be dismissed?" The King nodded his dismissal. Gamilon spun on his heel to head for the stables and his horse—then home.

Chapter

11

I was afraid I'd miss you, but with all the noise you've been making the Dark One himself has probably heard you coming."

"Sharineas!" Matthew yelled. Relief flooded his body and taut muscles relaxed; a small prayer of thanks ran through his mind. Sharineas came closer and took down the hood of her traveling cloak. Matthew was so glad that his face was not being ripped apart by claws right then that he gave the Princess a big hug. Sharineas received the hug very stiffly, surprised by this outburst of emotion. If it had been daytime he would have seen her turn red, and she would have seen him do likewise. Matthew backed off, stumbling over his words.

"I'm sorry, your Highness, I was just glad you weren't a monster. I mean…you know, one of those flying things." Then Matthew realized to whom he was talking. "Hey, what are you doing *here* anyway?"

"That will have to wait," Sharineas answered sharply. "Where are the others?"

"Come on, I'll show you." Matthew led her to his companions. They found Haub piling up sticks. "What are you doing?" Matthew asked him. Haub said nothing, just pointed to the other side of the pile. There lay Boreshia's body, his throat torn out and blood all over him. Matthew's mind went numb at the sight and he noticed in a detached sort of way that the blood looked black in the darkness that surrounded them. Sharineas put her hand to her mouth and stifled a cry. Deeli and Pheltic came up behind them.

"He saved our lives. I wish we could have a proper burial for him," Deeli said. Matthew turned around and noticed Pheltic, his head half covered with bandages.

"Are you all right!?"

"Not too bad," Pheltic said a little unsteadily." Deeli put something on my face to numb the pain."

"I had no time to stitch it up," Deeli explained, "so I packed mud over healing salve and bandaged him." Then noticing Sharineas, he took a step forward. "What are you doing here!?"

"You know I belong with the sword, Uncle, do not deny it. No one will keep me from my duty," then with less confidence in her voice, "even if I don't know for sure what that duty is yet."

"But how did you get here?" Matthew asked.

"I left the night before you did and came through the pass just before dawn this morning. I have been hiding ever since."

"By yourself?" Matthew could not believe it. "It was you I saw sneaking across the courtyard the other night."

"Enough of this," Deeli interrupted. "We can talk later, right now we have to burn Boreshia's body and get out of here. I am sure the noise has aroused other patrols in the area and they are on their way here at this moment."

"The sword!" Matthew remembered with alarm. "It's still in the body of that Nomie, in the woods somewhere."

"What!" Deeli said in shock. "You left it! Go find it quickly while we take care of the body. Meet us at that edge of the clearing," Deeli said pointing. Matthew went as fast as he could in the dark to where he thought the Nomie had gone down. Tree branches were continuously slapping at his face and he took several spills, tripping over roots protruding from the ground. After several minutes of searching he saw nothing, frustration and panic began to chisel away at the edges of his mind. Suddenly, a slight tingle in his right arm made him turn—there, out of the corner of his eye, Matthew saw a glow. Matthew walked toward the glow and could soon tell it was the gem in the sword's clawed end. He saw the mutated Nomie—one hand stiffly gripping the blade of the sword—the other hand flung wide in death.

Matthew reached out and grabbed the hilt to pull the sword free. The hand of the Nomie came up and clenched his leg tightly. The creature's eyes flew open and from its mouth came a horrible screech. Matthew tried to pull away, but the monster's grip was too tight. The creature's other clawed hand now gripped his other leg and Matthew could feel himself losing balance. He fell backward, drawing the sword out of the Nomie as he went.

The Nomie, knowing it was dying, pulled itself up with every intention of killing this enemy. Matthew, in a complete panic, swung the sword at the creature. Trickles of blue lightning lit up the Nomie's face as the blade of Excalibur sliced through its neck. The creature's head rolled a few feet away, its eyes open wide. Matthew gagged and pushed the headless body off his stomach. He then got up and shakily made his way back to the others with a heart beating so hard he thought it would explode.

It was easy for Matthew to find his way back; he simply headed for the huge bonfire. As he stepped into the clearing, Deeli grabbed his arm and started pulling him behind the others eastward through the forest. "Do you have the sword? Good, we must hurry. This fire will tell anyone in the area with eyes exactly where we are."

The group traveled as fast as they could, Haub in the lead with Boreshia's bow, arrows, and sword. Sharineas was helping him with her Elven eyesight. Deeli brought up the rear with Matthew, helping Pheltic in between them. Some of the pain was returning to Pheltic's wound and he was getting more and more confused. Haub was using his axe to help clear a path which made it easier for the others to follow. Matthew had thought that now with a female along they would not be able to travel as quickly. Instead, Sharineas not only kept up, but at times would drop back to help Matthew with Pheltic.

They kept at it through the night, afraid to stop for chance of being caught. The sky began to lighten off to their right and they soon realized that they had been heading more north than east. Deeli told Haub to quickly find a place to hide for the day. Unfortunately the sun was completely up and they still had found nowhere to hide when their flight was stopped by a rapidly flowing stream. Across the stream, some thirty yards away, was a sheer wall of rock that went east and west as far as the eye could see.

This was almost too much. They were all exhausted, not having slept in twenty-four hours. Sharineas had hardly slept for two days. Haub suggested they cross the stream and look for shelter—there were boulders at the base of the cliff they could possibly hide behind. Haub crossed first, carrying the now unconscious Pheltic. Then Matthew jumped in; the freezing water made him catch his breath. He helped Deeli and Sharineas down the bank and into the water. The stream was flowing swiftly and the three had to hold onto one another to keep from being swept away. In the center of the stream the water came almost to Matthew's waist and was up over the stomach of both Deeli and Sharineas. After a short struggle in which they all became soaked—the threesome finally made it across the stream. Haub had already found a suitable place among the boulders. They squeezed in behind the big rocks that covered them from the eyesight of any passerby.

After covering any traces of the trek from the stream to their hiding place, Haub lay down in a way that he could see the area around the boulders. Sharineas fell immediately asleep, while Deeli and Matthew cared for Pheltic. Deeli unwrapped the bandages and cleaned off the mud—feeling it would be better to leave the wound exposed to the open air for as long as possible. Pheltic moaned a little during the process, but fell into a deeper sleep when Deeli was finished.

"How's he going to do?" Matthew asked.

"I believe he will live. At least the bleeding has stopped, and the Dwarie are a very sturdy race. I think he needs rest more than anything, but a little prayer on our part would do wonders." Matthew fervently agreed and they prayed together. When they had finished, Matthew was still not ready for sleep.

"Deeli, was it really necessary for us to burn Boreshia's body back there?"

"First of all, we did not want his body to be desecrated by the enemy. I was also hoping that the fire and smoke would confuse them enough to not be able to pick up our trail right away. We can only pray that they will believe it was just a strategic attack by the soldiers on the other side of the pass and not someone coming through. If they report this to their leader he will be on the lookout for us. He did challenge you to meet him, but I would rather it be on our terms."

"Boy, things sure are getting complicated," Matthew said. "Boreshia dead, Pheltic hurt, a renegade Princess, and we've only just started."

"Yes, well as far as Sharineas is concerned, I think maybe she is supposed to be with us. She does not know how to use the power of the amulet, nor has she ever been away from the valley. But I do not believe the Creator would have made the sword and amulet constant companions unless there was a good reason."

"I just hope we don't regret her being along."

"Only time will tell, my young friend, but I think there is more to my great niece than has yet surfaced. We had better get some rest now so one of us can relieve Haub on watch." They both found places to lay down using their packs as pillows. As Matthew was drifting off to sleep he heard Deeli whisper to him." Do not fear, Matthew, the Lord is with you, even if you do not recognize Him yet."

The next thing Matthew knew he was being shaken awake with a hand clamped over his mouth. His first thought was that they were under attack, but no one was moving and Deeli was whispering for him to be quiet.

"We all overslept," Deeli whispered in his ear. "Haub finally fell asleep when none of us awoke to relieve him." In the dimming light Matthew could see Sharineas and Haub sitting tensely against the cliff face, Pheltic was still asleep. He looked out between the rocks and saw eight huge Trauls at the edge of the stream. "Haub was awakened by their voices," Deeli again whispered in Matthew's ear. "My grasp of their language is a little rusty, but I think they are talking about us." Matthew strained to hear what they were saying and could just make it out despite their gruff voices.

"Hey, did any of you hear what actually happened last night?" One of the Trauls asked loudly.

"Not anymore than you," another answered. "I don't think anyone knows for sure. Only that three of the winged ones were found dead and another turned to ash, so they know magic was involved." Deeli's heart sank, both at what the enemy knew and his own inability to keep his vow to God.

"What about the body that was burning, were you around when they put out the fire?"

"Yea, there wasn't much left, but enough to tell it was an Elf. There must have been others that set the blaze. Elves are crazy, but I don't think they light themselves on fire." The other Traul warriors that were resting all laughed at this. "I just wonder," the same soldier continued, "which way the others went. They had to be pretty tough to take on four of the winged Nomies and beat them."

"I heard there are Elven soldiers gathering on the other side of the pass. It was probably some of them over here spying. They probably ran back home with their tails between their legs."

"I don't know, it didn't look like the trail led back. I wonder what those Elves are up to anyway."

"It don't matter what they do," another Traul laughed. "They have no idea what we've got in store for them, and they don't have anything that can stop us."

"Yea, well the Enlightened One doesn't have us out here patrolling for nothing. He's still jumpy about what's happening with that sword. It's still hard for me to believe that one weapon could have so much power."

"Hey!" A different Traul jumped up indignantly. "My brother was on the mission to get the sword. That half-breed with the sword slew him and about fifty others before the retreat was sounded. My brother was a decorated warrior, as were all the others. No simple boy with a plain sword could do that." The searchers quieted down after that, just resting and filling their water skins. Finally one of them suggested making camp for the night since it was so close to dark. They all agreed and began building a fire.

Matthew felt horrible inside. Up till this point he had thought of the Traul and Nomie races as evil monsters. But after hearing the one talk about his brother that Matthew had killed, he was not so sure. Every one of them had mothers and fathers, brothers and sisters just as Matthew did. Soon the smell of cooking meat was making the companions' stomachs growl. There was no chance of getting out from behind the rocks without being seen, so they resigned themselves to staying the night. Deeli was fuming under his breath about lost time when suddenly Pheltic sat up rubbing his eyes and said: "Hey what's going on?" The entire group turned and looked at him, too startled to react. Deeli recovered first, lunging over and covering Pheltic's mouth with his hand.

"Hey, what was that noise?" One of the Traul said loudly.

"I don't know," another answered, "but you better go check it out." Soon the companions heard footsteps coming toward them and saw the flickering light of a torch cast dancing shadows on the wall behind them. All sat very still—the tension in the air around the companions was almost palpable. Matthew and Haub, with hands on their weapons, awaited the moment of discovery. They listened to the lone searcher scuffling around the rocks—every muscle tensed and ready for action.

"There ain't nothin' here, it must have been some animal," the Traul yelled to his comrades as he headed back to the fire. Meanwhile, the little group behind the boulders breathed a sigh of relief. Deeli relayed the situation to Pheltic and then cleaned his wound again. After this they kept conversation to a minimum and then only whispering in each other's ears. Pheltic assured everyone that he was feeling better and would be ready to leave as soon as they were able. He told Matthew that he was not only almost as good as new, but delighted about having a scar on his face.

"In our society a scar gained in battle is a great honor," Pheltic whispered, "especially on the face." *Yeah*, Matthew thought, *it'll be a great honor if we get back alive.* The conversation ended abruptly when Pheltic suddenly fell asleep.

"I think his body needs more rest than our young Dwarie thinks," Deeli whispered. Haub took first watch; this time with orders to wake Matthew when he became tired. Matthew finally dozed off, thinking about the philosophical implications of killing a living, thinking being, also, if it made any difference that they were out to kill you.

Deeli was on watch when the sky finally started to lighten. He heard the Traul warriors begin to stir—they were groaning, grunting, and swearing about morning being here so soon. Deeli shook his fellow companions awake one at a time and once again Matthew quietly translated the Traul conversation for his friends.

"Well I don't think anything's out here," one of the Trauls grumbled loudly. "I think we'll head back to the main camp and report in."

143

"We might as well go with you," another said. "We've got some good strong chut at camp and I want to get back before it's all gone." A few of the Trauls laughed and grunted in agreement. "Okay you dirt balls, let's get a move on, we're out of here!" Noise of the Traul searchers breaking camp was like music to the five companions' ears. They were all beginning to feel a little cramped behind the giant stones. Just before the Traul warriors left, Matthew caught some more of a conversation between two that had come close to their hiding place.

"The army should be on the march by now. It'll be great to put the Elves and their friends where they belong."

"Yeah, take the valley back and rid the world of the Elven evil all in one shot." The conversation continued, but the two had moved away and could be heard no more. Haub was in position watching the Trauls leave. He crept back to the others after they had all gone.

"They have struck west, along the face of the cliffs," he reported.

"Then I guess our only choice is to go east along these cliffs and hope they do not last forever," Deeli spoke with a slight hesitation.

"You don't sound very sure of yourself," Pheltic commented. "Is something wrong?" Deeli looked at his hands, hesitating, as if not knowing what to say.

"Well…I have been praying for direction and guidance since we started this journey. For the first time in fifteen sun-cycles I hear nothing from my God, not even a feeling. I know He is still there and answering my prayers or we never would have made it this far. I was used to receiving nothing in return for my prayers before becoming a follower of the Path, but now…this silence is worse than anything I could imagine."

"I found out why you were exiled," Sharineas said in rebuke. "This is probably another punishment for your blasphemy. Your God has finally deserted you."

"Young lady, I do not know what is happening, but I know that my Lord will never forsake me. My faith will stand this test. I am only sorry to see that the Keeper of the Amulet is so blind to the truth."

"The only thing the amulet shows me," Sharineas came back testily, "is that you truly believe what you are saying, but not that it is true." Deeli sighed in exasperation.

"There is no time for these arguments and endless debates right now," Deeli said sadly. "We have already been put back an entire day, let us leave while we can." Everyone agreed, especially Matthew who did not want to hear any more arguments over religion. Haub crawled out of the hiding place first to look around and came back with a positive report. The others crept out of the boulders, gratefully stretching their legs.

The group started hiking east along the desolate looking cliff face. The stream was flowing west and was parallel with them on their right. Haub took up the lead with Matthew in back, both keeping a wary eye on their surroundings. After a while, Haub began to pick up the pace so much that Deeli finally had to say something. "Haub, please slow down. I know we have lost a lot of time, but we must remember that Pheltic is wounded, and I am getting on in cycles."

"I'm sorry," Haub apologized. "I started thinking about Marth and the children again. All I could think of was getting to this fortress and killing the one responsible for their deaths."

"I'm so sorry for what happened, Haub," Pheltic replied in a weakened voice. "I understand how you must feel, I will try to go faster."

"No, little one, I will slow the pace. As much as I hurt, I must remember to put the living before the dead."

"I think we could all use a little nourishment right now," Deeli interjected. "Why not stop and eat? Then we can clean up a little in the stream." Everyone heartily agreed with that and unloaded their packs right where they were. They ate their food cold, not wanting to start even a small fire and take a chance on attracting the enemy. Deeli once again cleaned Pheltic's wound and re-packed it with his herbs before bandaging him. "I am running low on my medicines, so no one get hurt from here on out." Deeli's attempt at humor was not that good, but it did help lighten the load a little for the others. Sharineas announced that she was going to walk a little farther upstream to wash up a bit—this of course met with immediate resistance from all the males.

"Don't worry, if I am attacked you'll hear me scream." She ignored their continued protests and walked away. They knew the only way they could stop the headstrong Princess was to physically haul her back. Since no one was quite brave enough for that, they decided to clean up themselves. While one of them waded into the stream, the others stayed on the lookout and listened for any screams from upstream. When Matthew hit the water he just about screamed.

"I don't remember the water being this cold when we crossed far-ther down."

"We were on the run and tired at the time," Haub said. "That would make your body ignore the temperature."

"Not to mention you had your clothes and armor on at the time," Deeli jibed. "Matthew may be right about one thing though, this stream probably originates in the mountains. Therefore it would be get-ting colder as we get closer to them. I hope it is flowing from the moun-tains in the far north. If so, we could follow it all the way to the Dark One's lair."

"I just hope this cliff wall ends soon," Pheltic said. "Walking so close to it is making me feel shorter than I already am." Matthew smiled at his friend as he was emerging from the stream, then a more serious thought struck him.

"What if this rock wall doesn't end? What if this stream is coming from underground and we can't follow it? We have no way to climb up a sheer wall."

"I was trying to avoid that question for the sake of morale," Deeli answered. "I guess we will just have to wait until we get there to find out." Deeli was trying to sound confident, but Matthew knew he was concerned about not having concrete directions from his God.

Deeli was the only one who had not finished and was still in the water when they heard Sharineas announcing her return. "Wait!" Deeli yelled and got out of the water as fast as he could while Pheltic and Matthew snickered behind their hands; it was the fastest they had ever seen Deeli move. Finally he was dressed and Sharineas was given the okay to come back.

"As you can see I am back in one piece," the Princess said conde-scendingly. "I am well able to take care of myself." After a slight pause she continued. "What if these cliffs don't end? How will we ever get to this fortress?"

"We have just been discussing that very thing," Deeli answered. "I have only seen the fortress from a distance. The time I did go that way, it was straight north from the pass. We are left with no choice but to continue on and leave things in the hands of the Creator. Looking back at the history of our people, I think that He prefers it that way." The group shouldered their burdens and continued east along the face of the cliffs—with no more discussion of the current dilemma.

"It seems that we have avoided the Dark One's patrols," Sharineas said to no one in particular.

"We cannot be sure about that," Deeli said. "I believe for all of his war chief's bravado, the Dark One is nervous about facing Matthew and the sword. He will have his eyes open at all times. We cannot be too careful, there could be patrols just ahead of us." That statement of reality sent a shiver through Matthew, Sharineas, and Pheltic. All three of them paid more attention to keeping their eyes peeled for the enemy. The day grew hotter with each passing hour—as did the little company of travelers. Matthew's black armor was great for blending in at night, but terrible under a hot sun.

The sun was beginning to sink in the west and the air finally starting to cool down when Deeli stopped everyone and told them to be quiet. In the distance they could hear rushing water even louder than the stream next to them. The group noticed that the farther they walked, the more choppy the stream had become. The white waters had increased so much that none of them would have tried to bathe in the stream now. None of them were sure what the noise meant, but they quickened their pace to investigate. They finally came to a place where the cliff almost reached the water. Going around the cliff's corner they saw the reason for the noise. Before them was a huge fissure in the cliff face—water rushing out and dropping about thirty feet to create the stream they had been traveling along.

Matthew, Pheltic, and Sharineas sat down in despair. The sheer rock wall continued on for as far as they could see, their hope in following the stream north, gone. Deeli, looking wary, sat down with his back to the cliff and prayed. Haub began to climb the rocks that went up into the fissure. Instead of dwelling on their predicament, Matthew observed his surroundings. They were at a place where the rock wall went in on itself, creating a kind of cove in the elbow of the stream. *A perfect hiding place*, he thought, *if that's what we were looking for*. After a short time Haub emerged from the fissure and climbed back down the rocks.

"The fissure is open all the way to the sky. It has a natural shelf protruding from the wall about as wide as my forearm and running deep into the crevice. It looks as though the shelf angles up, maybe all the way to the top. If we carry our packs in hand and are careful, I think we could walk along the shelf. That is, if it doesn't end on us."

"If it ends, then we've wasted all that time," Matthew said. "We would have to come back out and be right where we started."

"It seems that we have two choices; try the dangerous rock shelf, or continue along this cliff wall which takes us ever farther from our destination. I have been praying but…" Deeli held up his hands in frustration.

"I for one am getting sick of this wall," Sharineas said, with disgust evident in her voice. "I vote we try going through the fissure to the top of this cliff and head north." Pheltic jumped to his feet and voiced his agreement with Sharineas. Matthew felt a little shamed by their bravery and said he was willing if Deeli was. Deeli gave into the majority. Haub was glad for the decision and said so. Walking away, Haub announced that he was going to make a spear and see if there were any fish in the stream.

Deeli decided they could chance a small fire as long as no green wood was thrown on it. Camp was set up for the night in the little cove area, hiding them on three sides. It was not long before Haub came back with four cleaned fish, looking very pleased with himself. The fish were cooked over the fire and eaten along with food they had brought with them. It was a beautiful evening, with a slight warm breeze. It was the most relaxed that any of them had been since the start of this adventure. Pheltic said he was going to fill his water skin at the stream so that he would not have to in the morning. The rest of the group thought it was a good idea and followed him.

After their water skins were full, everyone sat upon rocks along the bank enjoying the sunset. A thought struck Pheltic and he let it out immediately. "What happens when we run out of the food we brought with us, Deeli?"

"I had been counting on Boreshia to bring down some game with his long bow. I guess it will be up to Haub, now that he carries the bow."

"I'm really not that good with a bow," Haub admitted, "but I will try. I'm much better at spearing fish." Suddenly a loud thrashing noise came from the forest across the stream; every head spun in that direction.

"Ha! I've finally caught you!" A voice yelled. Everyone froze. Matthew realized, belatedly, that he had left his sword back by the fire.

Chapter

12

Peridon, High King of all the Elven peoples, stood with hands on hips overlooking the construction. He was half watching the workers and half thinking about his daughter who had still not been located before his departure. Nor had Gamilon shown up, which was not like the dependable young Elf at all. *It must have something to do with his father. I'm sure he'll show up soon*, the King reasoned. Peridon had arrived late this morning; the work was already in progress. Even though Alexthna had not seemed himself since the sword had been drawn forth, the King had left him in charge of the kingdom while he was away.

It brought a certain amount of pride to see people from all the valley races working together again. Of course it was a shame that it took the Great Tree Massacre, which it was now called, to open their eyes and bring them together. Their plans were to build a wall across the entire mouth of the mountain pass. A near impossible task even with all the races banding together. Workers were already cutting and hauling massive trees for the project. Others were gathering huge stones from the hills around the area. The wall would be nearly as high as five Humans standing on each other's shoulders, and impenetrable by any means known to the allied races. *If we can get it finished in time*, the King thought.

Peridon looked to the mountains on either side of the pass. They were high, but the enemy could come over them if they were desperate enough. As unlikely as that scenario was, all three races would send well-armed parties of their best scouts into the mountains. They would keep a lookout for any advance spies and keep those at the wall informed of the enemies' movements when they drew close. There had been a few run-ins with winged Nomies reported when the troops had made their sweep through the valley. Most had been killed, but some did manage to escape. That meant the enemy knew by now that the Elves and their allies were up to something.

Roak and all of the Humans were here, but Moark had been detained. Telick had arrived this morning with the larger part of the Dwarie army and he was now in charge of constructing the wall. Both the Elves and Humans conceded that the Dwarie were much better builders than they. So they had asked King Moark if he would put his master builders to the task and the other two races would provide laborers.

Even the forest dwelling Elves were here. They generally did not have anything to do with the other races, but knew that everyone was needed to defend the valley. King Peridon had not ordered the forest Elves to help; but Hydrian, their King, had come and offered the services of his people. Peridon gratefully accepted and put the forest Elves to work. It grieved them much to be cutting down the trees, but they knew that their homes and families were in danger and this was the only means of defense.

Peridon's attention was diverted to the far end of the pass where some of the trees had already been put in place. There were people running around and yelling; an Elven worker lay on the ground with blood on his head. *Not an accident already*, the King thought as he hurried in that direction. A whooshing sound and a loud thump coming from behind him caused Peridon to stop. The King turned to see a large stone embedded in the ground right where he had been standing, he looked up and saw two of the flying Nomies circling above. There were several more over the workers and he realized the wounded Elf was no accident.

It did not take long for the valley people to recover. The Elves and Humans began to shoot arrows at the creatures with their long bows. As the Nomies that had been pierced with arrows came down, the Dwarie were on them immediately with axes and war hammers. Finally, after four of the winged Nomies had been killed, the others flew away. They headed back over the mountains to the north making their hideous screeching noises all the way.

Those stinking monsters! Now the enemy knows what we're up to, Peridon thought with rage. *They will be here every day harassing us. This wall could be harder to build than we had anticipated.* The Elven King looked to where the injured were being tended. The first Elf that had been hit and one Human now lay side by side on the ground—cloths over their faces. "More deaths on your head you evil filth!" The King was now shouting at the sky, his fist raised in the air. "You're going to pay, do you hear me? By our God and my right arm, we'll make you pay!"

Before Matthew could even rise to his feet and run for his sword, a lone figure stumbled out of the foliage on the other side of the stream. "Gamilon!" Sharineas yelled. "What are you doing here? How did you know where I was? You shouldn't have come, I…"

"Whoa, can I catch my breath first?" Gamilon said holding up his hand. "Help me get across." Gamilon was looking pretty rough, like someone who had left in a hurry without putting much thought into it. Haub waded into the swiftly rushing stream with Matthew right behind. Gamilon made his way into the water, barely able to stand in it.

Haub was in the middle of the stream and Matthew closer to the bank ready to help them both out, when Gamilon slipped on a rock. As the young Elf was being swept away, Haub dove after him and grabbed his traveling cloak. Using all of his strength, Haub pulled Gamilon to himself and anchored his feet on the rocks below. The water only came up to Haub's waist, but it was rushing so fast he could hardly make it back to the bank. Matthew had gone downstream with them along the bank, and now had gone out as far as he dared to help pull the pair out of the icy water. Twice more Haub lost his footing and was swept farther down stream with Gamilon in his powerful arms; Matthew was tagging along closer to the bank waiting for a chance to help. It was three very exhausted people who finally reached the shore. Deeli and Sharineas had run along the edge of the stream and were there ready to help them back to the fire.

The idea of leaving the fire going past dark was not an attractive one, but necessary for the soaked trio. The fire had almost gone out, so they built it up a little and gave Gamilon some food. Sharineas, Deeli, and Matthew began questioning the Elf immediately while Pheltic sat on top of one of the boulders and kept watch.

"Okay, I'll answer your questions now. Yes Sharineas, I did follow you. I searched the entire castle, but no one had seen you since the war council. I was about to start for my father's home when I went to the stables to get my mount and found one of the royal horses unaccounted for. It was then I realized where you had gone. I sent a message to my father telling him I would be delayed and not to worry. I packed what I could carry and left for the Great Northern Pass. I rode hard with little rest and reached the pass the night after you did. I let my horse head back home and made my way to the eastern side of the pass, farthest away from the camps. I had every intention of bribing the night guard to let me through, but it just so happened to be one of my good friends on duty that night. I talked him into letting me leave the valley, since his orders were only to not let anyone come through the pass from the north. He is the only one who knows I am here and will tell no one. I had no idea which way you had gone, or if Sharineas was even with you. When I got to the northern side of the pass there was a lot of commotion. Something was happening in the forest in front of me and off to the west. So I crept quietly eastward along the foot of the mountains until I felt it was safe to cross into the forest. As I traveled I kept seeing signs of patrols or search parties, so I was continually having to go farther east before striking north. I thought for sure that I was far off your course and would never find you. When I heard your voices I thought you were a band of Trauls and was about to give up and head back. You will never know how amazed I was when, just as I turned to go I recognized Sharineas' voice over the noise of the rushing water."

"We were forced to go this way as well," Deeli said. "And it is a good thing or we never would have met. The Creator must want you to be with us."

"I'm afraid you've got it wrong, Napdeeliate; I am here to take Sharineas home. I don't know how you arranged her being here, but at first light she and I are heading back. If your father had known you were going to pull this," Gamilon said turning to Sharineas, "he would have locked you in your room and never let you out. You have no idea how dangerous and suicidal this little venture is! And by the way, where's Boreshia?" Deeli very quickly and solemnly told Gamilon of Boreshia's bravery and death.

"See! You've barely begun and one of your number is already dead. Sharineas, you are going back before the same thing happens to you."

"I am not going back!" Sharineas retorted stubbornly. "I am the Keeper of the Amulet and I will not be relieved of my duty just because I'm the King's daughter." Gamilon gave Matthew a burning look, as if to say this was all his fault.

"Hey, don't look at me," Matthew defended himself. "I didn't ask her to come along. She only thinks of me as a boy anyway," he mumbled.

"Oh," Sharineas put her hand to her mouth and gave Matthew an apologetic expression. "I hadn't meant it that way, really. I guess I'm just used to being blunt. I am very grateful to you for saving me from that fall and those awful Trauls. I'm truly sorry if my hasty choice of words has hurt you."

"Uh, well...that's okay. I was glad to do it," Matthew answered, while shrugging his shoulders with embarrassment.

"I'm glad you two have cleared the air about that; it was very touching," Gamilon said sarcastically. "But it changes nothing. Sharineas, you are my betrothed and will obey me in this. You are going back!"

"I am not going back and that is final," Sharineas said, very calmly with steel in her voice. "We are not married yet, and you will order me nowhere." She then got up, went over to her pack, and started to situate her bedroll.

"I do believe, young Gamilon, that her mind is made up," Deeli broke the following silence. "You are welcome to accompany us, if you can keep your voice down. I am sure you are a better shot with a bow than Haub is." Gamilon rose to his feet and shook his head in frustration. He went over to where his bedroll was spread out on a boulder to dry. The bedding was still wet so Gamilon walked away from where Sharineas was and sat against the rock wall sulking. Deeli and Haub unrolled their bedding and lay down for the night.

Matthew told Pheltic to go to bed. The Dwarie was not looking well, and admitted that his face was still in some pain. The young Human from another world sincerely hoped his new friend was going to be all right. He picked up his sword and made his way to the bend in the stream—ready to take the first watch of the night. Fortunately the night passed without incident, for Matthew's attention was miles away. He could not stop thinking about Gamilon and Sharineas' strange relationship, and wondering why she made him feel so awkward inside.

Haub, who had last watch, sat on a rock beside the stream. The sky was just beginning to lighten in front of him. He took in a deep breath; even as dead as Haub felt inside since his family's death, this time of morning still caused a stirring in his blood. His ears pricked up at a noise; Haub kept his body perfectly still and listened intently. Again he heard the noise come from the camp and hurried back to see what it was. Sharineas was awake—her gear packed and ready to go. The others were all rubbing their eyes, wondering what was happening. Sharineas obviously wanted to make it very clear to her betrothed that she was going forward. "It's not even dawn yet," Pheltic complained, but he got up as everyone else did.

"Have you decided on your course yet, Gamilon?" Deeli asked the grumpy young Elf.

"I believe this quest to be hopeless and foolhardy, but if the Princess will not come back, then I must go with you."

"Very well then, we will be glad for your company," Deeli said. Gamilon said nothing in return. Matthew had been secretly wishing that the Elf would turn back. He did not like his attitude or the way he treated everyone. *The fact that he is engaged to Sharineas has nothing to do with it*, he answered the nagging voice in his head.

Haub led the way up the rocks. He took them past the geyser of water that was rushing out of the cliff. When the six reached the rock shelf that Haub had told them about, more than one thought of calling for another vote. There were still twenty feet of wall above the shelf and about an eight foot drop into the churning, destructive water below. The shelf did incline as far as could be seen, which meant that unless the water was coming from above and not underground, the drop would increase the farther they went. The water was rushing so fast and there were so many rocks below, that the companions could feel the spray on their faces even from that distance.

Haub led the way; jumping onto the ledge and inching his way along with his back to the rock wall. One by one the others reluctantly took their packs in hand and followed him. Deeli and a wide-eyed Pheltic were right behind Haub. Gamilon came right behind them; insisting that he carry Sharineas' pack as well as his own, and that he go directly in front of the Princess to protect her. Matthew brought up the rear, very thankful that he was not too afraid of heights. The going was slow and tedious—made more difficult by trying to watch the ledge they were on and not look at the raging water below. Each knew that if they fell in, the rocks would have them battered to pieces before dumping their bodies into the stream outside the wall. The water was coming down in a series of little waterfalls and the incline of the shelf was barely perceptible. That is why none of them realized how far they had climbed until Matthew glanced up and saw that the top of the wall was only a few feet away. He was just about to say something when Sharineas screamed in his ear.

The rock beneath one of her feet gave way and she slid down to a sitting position. Matthew dropped his pack on the ledge to his right and reached to give her a hand. Just as he did, the rest of the rock beneath Sharineas gave way and she plummeted toward the water. At that moment both of Matthew's hands shot out and grabbed her arm. The weight of her body and the force of the fall drug Matthew down hard onto his knees. Pure luck or divine intervention, he did not know, but the ledge beneath him remained solid. He held onto the Elf maiden's arm with both hands trying to pull her up, but had no leverage. It was a stalemate; Sharineas was not falling any farther, but no matter how hard he tried, Matthew could not pull her back up to the ledge.

Then Gamilon was flat on his stomach; both hands stretched out grabbing onto Sharineas' cloak. That was the extra help Matthew needed; together they managed to get the Princess to safety on the ledge next to Matthew. Shaking with exertion and fright, they held each other. When they had finally calmed down, the two rose to their feet. As they did, Sharineas whispered in Matthew's ear: "Thank you...again."

Only about two feet of ledge had given way, but Sharineas was reluctant to jump the gulf to the other side. Once Haub saw that Sharineas was safe, he had gone ahead and followed the ledge to its end. He climbed the last rocks to the top and found that they had indeed made the right choice. Haub came back along the edge of the fissure right above Matthew and Sharineas. He crouched low and stretched his arms over the edge to Sharineas. She gratefully reached up and locked arms with him. With very little difficulty, Haub pulled Sharineas safely to the top.

Matthew picked up his pack and handed it to Haub, but said he would jump across and climb the rest of the way. Deeli expressed concern over Matthew jumping and more of the rock giving way, so he allowed Haub to pull him up as well. As Matthew reached up his hands he looked over toward Gamilon. The Elf was staring at him with a look of what seemed like gratitude mixed with jealousy. Matthew had no time to say anything; Haub was already pulling him up the side. The rest of the company made their way to the top just as Haub had.

Once at the top it seemed as though they were in another world altogether. The group from the valley stood on a wide open plain, full of rocks and scraggly bushes. A few trees grew here and there with purplish needles and yellow colored pine cones. The only real vegetation they saw was along the stream they had followed up here. As Deeli hoped, the stream was running from the north. It was good they had not followed the rock wall farther, for the plain stretched in every direction except south for as far as they could see. A long way in the distance to the east were mountains, to the west and north just endless rock plain. There was not a living soul to be seen anywhere, for that blessing they were all grateful.

The small party struck north, again with the familiar stream to their right. They traveled the entire day with almost no change in the scenery. "It doesn't seem like we've gone anywhere today," Pheltic said toward evening, "nothing looks any different."

"Look behind you, little one," Haub replied. "Do you still think we've gone nowhere?" They all turned to see that the land south of them looked no different from any other direction—the edge of the cliff was nowhere in sight.

They camped that night along the stream, eating more fish provided by Haub. It was another beautiful night except for the southern wind that had been pushing at their backs all day was now sweeping in from the east and picking up speed. They set up camp west of a clump of the scraggly trees, using them as a windbreak. This wind was also much cooler—Matthew was surprised at how much colder it had gotten and asked Deeli about it.

"Even though it is springtime here," Deeli answered, "we are still in the north and it will be getting colder the entire journey. We have gone quite a way now, by the time we reach the northern mountains we will be seeing snow and ice."

"But I can just start to make out those mountain peaks from here, how can the weather change so much in such a short distance?" Matthew asked.

"I do not know what your world is like, but at the far north it is almost always cold, or so I have been told."

"You mean we're going as far north as your world goes?" Matthew asked getting more confused. "How far south of the valley does the land go?"

"The valley is the navel of the world," Gamilon said, with a fierce pride. "The land south goes about as far as the land north, east, and west."

"You mean that is the size of your entire known world?"

"Is your world bigger than ours, Matthew?" Sharineas asked; beginning to wonder if this strange Human really was from another world.

"My world is so much bigger I couldn't even begin to describe it." Matthew picked up a stick and started drawing in the dirt. He drew a big circle with a little dot on it. "If what you say is true, then this big circle would represent my world and this dot would be yours."

"That's impossible," Gamilon sneered. "Now I know you're lying." Sharineas, who was beginning to believe, found this a little hard to swallow also. Deeli was amazed at this new knowledge and asked many more questions. The only thing he and Matthew could figure was that either no one had ever fully explored this world, or it was really much smaller than Matthew's. Having no way to convince Gamilon and Sharineas, they dropped the subject and the conversation turned to other things. At one point talk had turned to names and Matthew told them that he had the same name as his father. The others thought this very interesting since that was unheard of in their cultures.

"Your names in this world are very different from those in my world," Matthew said. "I especially like the Elven names—yours is very pretty Sharineas." Matthew regretted saying that as soon as it was out of his mouth. He had meant it with innocent sincerity, but even where he came from it would have sounded like a lame come-on. Matthew winced inwardly at the look Gamilon gave him and knew he deserved it. Sharineas, a born diplomat, smoothed things over very gracefully.

"Why thank you very much Matthew, I have always been fond of my name, and a little proud of it. I was named after the very first Keeper of the Amulet of Truth. She was a great matriarch of our people and was instrumental in re-establishing the Elven kingdom after our first exile thousands of sun-cycles ago. The story of it is in the Elven Holy Words. The legend surrounding the story says that she appeared to our people with the amulet and was protected by an angel of God with a flaming sword. She was eventually martyred during a great battle and has been an irreplaceable symbol to Elven females throughout history. That's one reason I was so thrilled at being chosen as the new Keeper—the same as my namesake—almost as if I had finally met my destiny." Sharineas glowed as she talked and Matthew just sat there listening in fascination. Not only because of finding out more about this strange world, but he had never met a female with such a fiery will and strong sense of purpose.

"I am so glad you like the name I picked out for you," Deeli commented.

"You?!" Gamilon snorted incredulously.

"You, uncle?!" Sharineas said in disbelief.

"Yes, your father and I were very close at the time of your birth. If you had been a male your name would have been similar to mine. Since you were not, your father gave me the honor of picking out the name."

"No one ever told me this before," Sharineas said quietly. She was beginning to wonder about the things that had been told to her concerning great uncle Napdeeliate. The Princess was very young when he had been exiled. All she knew for sure is that no one ever talked about him in front of her father. She had heard rumors of the power he once wielded and that now he was a heretic. But now, as an adult, she had met the real Elf and found him to be wise, kind, and loving. He was also the one responsible for the name she had been given and had cherished all these cycles. Sharineas was oblivious to the rest of the conversation around the small dying fire; she had too many things to think about.

The morning came with a blustery wind out of the north and a spattering of raindrops. They ate a quick breakfast from their provisions and headed north once more. There was still no sign of any living beings for them to hide from or fight, but the constant cold wind out of the north slowed them considerably. About midday they came to a sharp bend in the stream.

"So the stream originates in the eastern mountains," Deeli said disappointedly. "We obviously cannot follow it north anymore, but I am grateful for the companionship and water it has given us so far."

They stopped there for lunch. Before leaving, everyone filled their water skins; not sure when they would have the chance again. Now the familiar stream was gone, in its place a barren plain of rock and sickly brush. Fortunately the infrequent raindrops never turned into a downpour; the clouds even began to break up in the late afternoon. The wind on the other hand seemed to only grow stronger and colder. The eastern mountain range came farther into the plain at one point. The sun peeking through the clouds lit up the lower portion of one mountain. Matthew could not make out what it was, but it looked as if the side of the mountain was on fire.

"What is that?" He asked no one in particular. "Is it a forest fire?" None of the younger people said anything—not wanting to guess and be wrong. Deeli, having been to the north before, knew what it was.

"That is a northern pine forest. And no, it is not on fire. They are called red pines and stay that color all year round. They are beautiful. This land does have some redeeming qualities." The trees were a brilliant bright red. Matthew's eyes could not make out that they were trees, but he wished there was time to go hike through the forest, or at least see it up close. "If you think it is impressive now you should see it when the ground is covered in snow. The colors look twice as bright then."

"It is so beautiful," Sharineas observed. "I wish we could go exploring. I wonder what it smells like?"

"I am afraid we cannot take time for such things now, my dear," Deeli said.

"That's right," Gamilon said. "The sooner we get this over with and back to the valley the better." Matthew noted that Sharineas had echoed his thoughts on the subject and had to fight the feeling that he would like to get to know her better. They continued on their course, but it was not much longer before Gamilon noticed that there was no more land up ahead of them.

"It looks like the world just comes to an end," Pheltic said in awe. "Come on, Matthew, let's go check it out." The little Dwarie ran ahead; his wound did not seem to be giving him much trouble anymore. Matthew smiled at his friend's enthusiasm and ran after him with the sound of Deeli telling them to be careful in his ears. Matthew yelled for Pheltic to wait up for him. He did, and they both reached the edge at the same time.

They also gasped in unison. Like the southern side of the plateau, here was a sheer rock wall straight down; but instead of forty feet or so, this one dropped for hundreds of feet into a swampy, jungle-like forest. They looked out and could see a great distance from this height. There were forests, lakes, rivers, and a lot of sandy, barren land as well. The northern mountains looked purple and much closer than before. "Is that really where we're going?" Pheltic asked looking to the north.

"I think so. They look pretty ominous don't they? Hey, what's that down there?" Matthew asked pointing in the distance to a large dark mass that covered much of the land. Pheltic squinted and strained, but could not make it out.

"We Dwarie have nearly as good night vision as the Elves from living in caves for so many generations, but in the daylight my eyes are probably worse than yours. It's likely a weird kind of forest we've never seen." Just then the rest of the company walked up behind them.

"Quite a breathtaking view from up here," Deeli said looking at the misty shrouded purple mountains, "and there is our destination."

"They are beautiful, but also scary," Sharineas commented.

"Gamilon, you Elves have better eyesight than we do," Pheltic said, still curious about the dark mass and pointing to it. "Can you tell what that is down there?" Gamilon, Deeli, and Sharineas all studied the area Pheltic was pointing toward. Recognition came to all three at almost the same time.

"By the Creator!" Gamilon whispered. "It cannot be."

"I was afraid of...something like this," Deeli stammered. "But I never thought...so many."

"What!" Matthew and Pheltic yelled together, even Haub was interested now.

"That," Deeli said with a slight shudder, "is the Dark One's army."

"But..." Matthew hesitated trying to figure this out, "if that is the Traul and Nomie army, well, it's ten times as large as yours."

"More like twenty," Haub said with a blank stare on his face.

"Even if the allied races finish the wall they won't stand a chance, they'll..." Matthew let his words fall away. They knew in their hearts that what he was about to say was truth. The Quest of the Sword, as Pheltic had been calling his grand adventure, had come north to face the evil that threatened their world. Now they were certain that if the valley had any hope of survival, it was with them. Time, was now even more crucial then they had believed. The companions stood at the edge of the cliff for several long moments. They watched in silence and dread—dark and hopeless thoughts running through each of their minds.

Chapter

13

It was Gamilon who finally broke the silence with a quiet voice: "For once in my life I hope I am wrong. Matthew, if you and the sword do not succeed, I am afraid it will mean the end of everything we hold dear."

"I cannot believe the size," Haub commented in a numb voice. "They will overcome by sheer numbers alone."

"Deeli," Matthew stammered, pointing at the dark mass, "even if we defeat the Dark Lord, how will we ever stop that?"

"I know not, my friend. I only know that the prophecy says you must meet the Emissary of the Evil One and overcome; the rest is up to the Creator. He will not forsake His people. He has used the other races to discipline the Elves throughout history, but I do not believe His intentions are to destroy us. More likely, the end of all history is upon us." That was almost too unimaginable for the others to even think about. After a slight hesitation, Deeli spoke the rest of what was on his mind. "If the time is upon us, I pray that you will all consider Shesea before it is too late." This brought an almost violent reaction from Gamilon.

"Napdeeliate, I am joining this mission and will do my best to see that you succeed. Do not! I repeat—do not—preach any of your heresies to us. Agree now or I will forcibly take Sharineas and go back."

"I will agree to say no more to you, Gamilon, but I will not be silent about what means more than life to me." Gamilon gave Deeli a frosty look, then glanced back at the dark blot of the enemy army.

"I guess that promise will have to do. We had better keep moving; that army will not wait around for us." Sharineas watched Gamilon's reaction compared to Deeli's gentle determined attitude. She, of course, agreed with her betrothed, but could not help wondering if something was missing in her life. The group traveled northeast, parallel with the cliff's edge, each wondering how they would ever reach the plains below. As they walked, well away from the edge in case of being spotted, Matthew asked Deeli to tell him who and what this Shesea was that He could provoke such hatred.

"I promise, my friend, that when we have some time alone I will tell you. I have been hoping that you would desire the knowledge enough to ask me."

"Deeli, are we going to walk all the way to the eastern mountains to get down this cliff?" Pheltic asked, eyeing the distance to the mountains.

"I hope not. There is a passage I ran across in my readings that I never understood before. Now that I am up here and have seen the situation, I believe I might know what it meant. The writings were by an old Elf who had escaped from the north long ago and made it back to the valley. It was said that his ordeal had driven him crazy and so his writings were considered worthless. I, believing that everything has a purpose, held onto them once they came into my possession. Admittedly, I did not understand much of them, but one part talked of a swamp forest he was thrown into as punishment. He said people of the north called it the Place of Fear. The old Elf talked of a dread feeling, monsters, and bogs of liquid ground. Ultimately this was how he gained his freedom. Making it through the forest alive he came upon a sheer stone wall with many stairs carved in the side. He wrote that climbing the stairs brought him to another world. When Matthew first came through the circle of light I thought of this passage, but it still made no sense. The writer was still in this world. Now though, looking at the forest below from this perspective, I can see why the top of this plateau would seem like another world. If that is the forest he spoke of down there, then maybe we can find the stairway described in his writings."

"But you said monsters are down there," Pheltic said worriedly.

"I did not say it, the crazy old Elf said it. In any event, it would take us many days out of our way to walk all the way to the eastern mountains and down. We simply cannot afford it."

"It sounds like another suicide attempt to me," Gamilon said.

"Well I'm willing," Sharineas said looking at Gamilon. "We must reach the Dark One's fortress before his army reaches the valley."

"Look on the bright side," Deeli quipped. "Maybe I am wrong about which forest it is." Matthew made a wry smile and thought to himself, *and just how often are you wrong, Deeli?*

The companions walked until the sun had almost disappeared behind the western horizon. They continued to stay well away from the edge of the cliff so that no one would spot them from below. Pheltic volunteered to go to the edge of the cliff periodically to look for signs of the stairway. It was just about too dark to see, when they decided to stop for the night with still no sign of the stone stairs. "What if we already passed it?" Matthew asked.

"And maybe this old Elf is wrong," Gamilon snapped.

"We couldn't have passed it," Pheltic said defensively, "I have been checking carefully all the way."

"I'm sorry Pheltic, I didn't mean you weren't doing a good job. I just would hate to be stuck up here and not find a way down. You haven't checked this spot yet; why don't you go look while we set up camp."

"Okay," Pheltic said, brightening immediately with the apology. He ran over to the edge of the cliff, got on his stomach, and began to scan the rock wall.

"He'll never see anything," Gamilon jeered. "It's the wrong time of day for Dwarie eyes."

"Then why don't you go help him and be of some use for a change," Matthew snapped back at him. "We don't need that kind of attitude."

"Will you two please stop it!" Sharineas broke in with a loud voice. "Gamilon, can't you please try to be a little nicer?"

"Oh, taking the side of the half-breed are you?" Sharineas glared at him in the gathering gloom.

"Hey!" A voice shouted from the edge of the cliff. "Here it is!" Pheltic was jumping up and down and waving his arms. All arguing ceased and the group ran over to the excited Dwarie. They all clamored over to the edge and began looking for the stairway.

"I don't see anything, short one, and my eyes are better than yours," Gamilon said with disgust.

"No, we're not right above it," Pheltic replied, oblivious to Gamilon's sarcasm. "Matthew was right, we had just passed it. Look back in that direction, do you see the stairs now?" All eyes turned west along the rock wall. Matthew strained, but it was getting too dark to see much. They all walked back in that direction and found the place. It did not turn out to be as much of a staircase as everyone had hoped. It was a series of protruding stones and ledges that looked as if they kept going all the way to the bottom. If stairs they were, then it was a very uneven stairway. In some places the step was only a few inches high. In others it was a couple of feet; and the drop over the edge seemed endless.

"Look Matthew," Haub said, "the gem in the hilt of your sword is glowing softly. Does that mean the steps are a danger to us?"

"The steps definitely look like a danger to us, but I don't know if that's what it means. The only time it has glowed before was during the fight with the winged Nomies. Look, the amulet is glowing too."

"Can you tell anything from the amulet, Sharineas?" Gamilon asked.

"The only thing I can tell is that there is danger or evil near. It could be the forest below, or where we just came from, I don't know." At that statement all heads snapped around looking for any signs of danger from behind them.

"It could be the forest," Deeli said at last. "Or it could be that!" Everyone's eyes followed Deeli's pointing finger. They all caught their breath at the sight of hundreds upon hundreds of campfires far out on the plain below.

"It's like looking over a small city from my world," Matthew said.

"It would be pretty if I didn't know what it was," Sharineas added.

"It looks like there is even more of them in the dark like this," Pheltic whispered. They continued to stare in silence until Deeli brought them all back to the moment at hand by reminding everyone that they had not yet set up camp. There were no trees in sight, nothing that would make a good campsite. So the group moved their things about fifty feet from the edge of the cliff and began to get themselves situated. Cold food, no shelter, and no windbreak, did not help to dispel the prevailing mood of despair. Haub started a fire using twigs from the shrubs around the area, but it was not big enough to heat any food. They had not seen a living soul or even an animal while on top of the plateau and, therefore, were not too worried about being seen.

Everyone seemed to be in a contemplative mood, just sitting quietly around the small fire. Pheltic could not stand the silence for long and began to search for something to say. "My wound is feeling much better, that is if anyone cares."

"That's great," Matthew said. "Of course we care. It's amazing how fast you're healing."

"We Dwarie are a tough race."

"I think the Creator might have something to do with it as well," Deeli ventured with a smile. Gamilon continued to frown into the fire. Sharineas thought this might be a good opportunity to find out a few things.

"Deeli?" The name sounded funny coming from her mouth instead of Napdeeliate, or a sarcastic, uncle.

"Yes, child."

"Could you tell me more about the powers of the amulet and how to use them?"

"Where to begin?" Deeli asked absently, almost to himself. "I really do not know much myself, only what Lieanea told me and what I saw her do. I know that if she concentrated when someone was talking to her she could tell if they were telling the truth or not. Also if something physical was out of place or wrong she could shine the light of the amulet on it and the truth of the matter would be revealed to anyone around.

"I still want to know how to get the amulet to respond to my commands," Sharineas said. "Did Lieanea ever use it as a weapon?"

"As far as control over the amulet," Deeli began, "I think that will come with time. I never saw the amulet used as an offensive weapon, but once I remember it being used accidentally as a defensive weapon. Lieanea was passing through the castle's courtyard when a soldier's horse became spooked. The horse broke away from its master and was headed straight for the Keeper. She fell back trying to get out of the way. The animal was almost on top of her when light from the amulet lashed out and stunned the animal in mid-stride, causing it to land right beside her. No permanent damage was done and the horse was all right once it woke up, but the amulet saved her life. Lieanea later told me that she did not consciously activate the amulet, but that it protected her on its own. If anything is going to teach you what the amulet will do, it will be a trip like this one." Sharineas just looked into the dying embers of the small fire, thinking on all her great uncle had told her. Pheltic stood up and stretched.

"Well, it's all more than I can understand, so I'm going to get some sleep." Matthew, Deeli, and Haub had to smile at their forthright little friend. Everyone decided it really was time to get some sleep and went to their bedrolls while Haub took first watch.

Sharineas awoke several hours before dawn to the sound of wind howling through the brush. Her dreams, and now thoughts, were filled with the things her uncle had said the night before. *I guess there is nothing I can do but wait and hope I can learn of the amulet's powers,* she thought to herself. The young Elven Princess got up and ushered a sleepy Pheltic to his bedroll. She decided to take her turn at watch a little early; needing the time and solitude to try to make sense out of all that had happened to her in the last two seven-days. So absorbed in these thoughts, it seemed no more than a few minutes before the sky began to color in the east and Sharineas had to begin waking the rest of the little company.

They ate some dried beef and water, trying to conserve both. All of them wished the stream was still near by so they could wash. No one except Pheltic, by his own choice, had ever gone this long without a bath. Moods were a little better after a night's sleep, but Gamilon was still very quiet. The sky was a solid gray with a light mist in the air, and the wind was blowing even harder than it had the day before. At the top of the stone stairway they paused to assess the situation. No one was very excited about trying to navigate down the stairs, especially with the wind blowing so hard. Matthew decided he wanted to go first and be ready with the sword in case anything was waiting for them at the bottom. Haub did not like the idea, but allowed him to go, saying he would go last.

Here on the open cliff face the wind was blowing even harder and the heavy mist in the air was causing the steps to be very slippery. Matthew looked down—the height was dizzying. He took one step, then another, running his hands along the face of the cliff to steady himself. *I'm cold, stiff, tired, and still hungry*, Matthew thought. *This trip is losing a lot of its appeal.* Sharineas walked up to the edge.

"I wish to go next, in case the amulet is needed." No one could argue with that and before anyone had the chance to try, the Princess began her descent. Pheltic started down next with wide-eyed exuberance.

"I can't wait to see what's down there." Gamilon, tight-lipped, pushed Pheltic aside and went down after Sharineas. "He sure is rude," the little Dwarie said, giving the Elf a dark look.

"That he is, little one," Deeli soothed. "You go next after Gamilon, I will be right behind you." Haub lay his hand on Deeli's shoulder after Pheltic had started down the steps.

"There will be trouble between the Elf and Matthew before this is over."

"I see it too, friend Haub," Deeli answered. "I only hope we can contain the explosion when it happens." Deeli turned and started making his way down the dangerous stairway.

The wind was howling so loudly that it was hard for them to hear each other talk. The going was slow and they held on for dear life to the rock at their backs. The six members of the quest, far from the safety of their valley home, felt small and vulnerable against the cliff face. Each felt as if any moment the wind was going to pick them up and carry them away. Their muscles began to ache from being constantly tensed for so long. Many times they had to stop and rest when the wind became too fierce, or the mist turned to a torrential rain and drenched them. Matthew was about halfway down the stone stairway when he heard a cry of frustration from behind him. "What's wrong?" He asked loudly over the sound of the wind.

"My hair keeps blowing in my eyes and I can't see where I'm going," Sharineas yelled back. Matthew could see that the wind was taking her long dark hair and whipping it every which way. He reached down to tear a strip of cloth from his clothes, but stopped when he remembered the armor. Matthew knew that it was too dangerous for her to continue on this way, but could not think of what to do for her. He was just about to yell for help from Gamilon when the leather thong on his scabbard came to mind. Matthew struggled with the leather strip on the scabbard behind his head, but could not loosen it.

"Sharineas!" He yelled. "Help me untie the leather thong and then use it to tie your hair back."

"I cannot use that," she protested, "it is a thing of legend, part of my people's history."

"So is the sword and the amulet, but we're using them aren't we? Besides, your getting down safely is more important than any legend." She did not argue any further, but began untying the leather strip. Sharineas felt her respect growing for this strange person. She started to tie her hair back until a gust of wind came up, almost blowing her off the step. Matthew threw his arm into her mid-section, pinning the Princess to the wall and stopping her from going over the side.

"Thank you," she said shakily.

"Are you all right?" Matthew asked.

"You knocked the wind out of me, but other than that I'm okay, just shaken." Sharineas turned to Gamilon and asked him to tie her hair. She and Pheltic held on to him with one free hand each while the Elf tied back her hair. Gamilon did not seem very pleased to be using Matthew's thong. Pheltic noticed that the backs of the Elf's ears were bright red. Whether it was from the cold wind or something else, he did not know. They continued down, the wind giving them no respite. Haub and Deeli were both praying out loud. Matthew joined them silently. *Creator of this world*, he began. *I don't understand Deeli's relationship to You, but if You hear me, please get all of us down safely. I promise to try to understand You better.*

It took almost all morning for the tired members of the little group to reach bottom. The ground was all stone slabs for about twenty feet before the forest began. Everyone collapsed on the rocks to rest. After a short time they ate an early lunch in preparation for their trek through the jungle-like forest. Pheltic talked excitedly about the climb down the cliff. The others were a little more subdued, while Gamilon was silent and fuming to himself.

After eating, they picked up their things and headed toward the forest. Looking between the trees they could see vines hanging down everywhere. Most of the ground seemed covered in moss and thick tall weeds. "It will not be easy to get through that," Sharineas stated. "May I continue to use the leather thong, Matthew, just until we get to the other side?"

"Of course," Matthew answered. "Just keep it, I don't need it back." Sharineas started to respond, but was cut short by Gamilon.

"She does not need the piece of leather! We will find her some cloth, it will be more appropriate."

"Listen Gamilon, I said she could keep the thong. It's no big deal, okay!"

"Do you have so little regard for the legends and history of our people!? You have somehow stolen the Sword of Kings, and now you spit on the sacred things of my people."

"The sword belongs to my world, too," Matthew retorted. "And I'm really getting sick of your arrogant, self-righteous cheap shots at me." Both Human and Elf were visibly angry now. The turmoil between them was coming to a head. Gamilon stepped back a pace and drew his sword.

"Please, my friends," Deeli quickly stepped in, "our mission is more important than your differences. We must continue on and work together."

"That's all right, Deeli," Matthew said unbuckling the scabbard from his back, "someone has to teach this loud mouth a lesson."

"You are not going to fight with Calburnathis are you?" Deeli asked in alarm.

"Uh, of course not," Matthew said, throwing the sheathed sword on the ground near the forest's edge.

"Here is Boreshia's sword Matthew, you may use it," Haub said with arm outstretched holding the sword.

"Haub, no!" Deeli said, aghast at his friend's encouragement. "We must put an end to this madness, not encourage it."

"Uncle Deeli is right," Sharineas said emphatically. "I'm sorry if

I've caused this, I didn't mean to. Please stop." Haub walked forward and handed Matthew the sword.

"This must be settled before we can go on." Haub then stepped back away from the two would-be combatants, Deeli looking at him as though he were crazy. Matthew had never been much of a fighter—and he certainly had not used any other sword besides Excalibur. *I've got to do something though, that Elf has got it coming.* He stepped forward to meet Gamilon, sword raised for the attack. This sword was smaller and slimmer than Excalibur, but much heavier and more awkward in his hand.

The blades met with a loud ring. Matthew's rage was growing and he went on the offensive, hammering at the Elf again and again. Gamilon pared each blow as if it were child's play. He was Elven nobility; a trained fighter and swordsman, and was enjoying every minute of this. Matthew's advances were becoming more awkward as the fight continued. Gamilon on the other hand, seemed to be just warming up—becoming more graceful and at ease with each of Matthew's increasingly clumsy attacks. Finally, Gamilon went on the offensive, and with a mocking smile drove Matthew back toward the edge of the forest. It was all Matthew could do to defend himself. At last a crashing blow sent Matthew's borrowed sword sideways, sending vibrations down his arm and knocking him off his feet.

The fall hurt him not only physically, but his pride as well. Matthew especially hated being made a fool of in front of Sharineas. Her continuous pleas for them to stop could be heard even over the clash of the fight. With renewed determination Matthew got back to his feet and went after Gamilon. He lunged, swinging the sword with all his strength, but it was not enough. Gamilon brought his sword up almost lazily and knocked Matthew's out of his hand. At the same moment the agile Elf spun around and kicked Matthew in the head almost karate style.

Matthew felt an explosion of pain in his jaw and landed on the ground—hard. One arm hit the ground near a tree and found stagnant greenish liquid. He felt foolish for being beaten so easily, his rage boiling to the top. Matthew opened his eyes to a haze of pain and frustration. He could see only one thing—Excalibur, still in its scabbard and laying where he had thrown it at the beginning of the fight. The only thing Matthew could think of was to make Gamilon pay for the humiliation he had caused him. Matthew quickly crawled the few feet and pulled the sword from its scabbard. He stood and turned to face his foe, anger written across his features. The sword in his hand giving off small flickers of blue lightning, as if trying to decide if this really was an enemy. Matthew raised the sword and started toward Gamilon with a look of hatred in his eyes.

Chapter

14

It had been several days since the bombardments began; the winged Nomies returned every morning to continue their harassment until chased off by counter attacks. After the first attack a new strategy had been developed. There was now a contingent of archers always on guard watching for the enemy, while the rest worked at the wall. They had also built small shelters that the workers could go under when the attacks became too concentrated. No one else had been killed yet. The flying attacks seemed to be designed more to keep the Elves and their allies off guard and distracted rather than to cause damage.

It was not long before Peridon, Roak, and Telick realized that the forest-dwelling Elves were the best for the job of defense. Their time living in the forest consisted of hunting for food and defending themselves from the wild animals that roamed near their homes. This had sharpened the forest Elves' agility and marksmanship far beyond that of their city-dwelling cousins. Most of the ammunition was used up, which could not be afforded with the enemy army on its way. Servants and soldiers alike were in the woods making arrows and on the field retrieving every projectile possible. The Nomie bodies that had been shot down were dragged into the pass and burned. Every day there were fewer of the creatures attacking, but progress on the wall was still being slowed. King Peridon had sent for the priests, who were originally not supposed to come until the main fighting was about to begin. He knew that without their magic to help put an end to these attacks,the wall would never be finished in time. Between those fighting and those making ammunition, the work force was greatly diminished. The King hoped fervently that the priests would be here soon. The situation was not all bad, though. King Moark had arrived the morning of the fifth day with several hundred Dwarie builders, and more Humans were showing up every day; both factors helped to bolster everyone's confidence. The evening of King Moark's arrival, the four leaders were meeting in King Peridon's tent, further discussing strategies and trying to lift each other's spirits.

"As long as we can get the wall finished in time, I believe the enemy will be not only stopped, but driven back as well," Peridon said.

"I have more warriors on the way with twenty newly designed catapults," Moark added. "We will be able to attack far into their ranks from behind the wall."

"Wonderful," Peridon said encouragingly. "I have always wanted to see one of your Dwarie war machines work."

"But how do we give chase after they have turned back?" Roak questioned. "We are not building a gate so as to give no access to the enemy, but that will also stop us from going out into the pass."

"Roak is right," Hydrian interjected. "If we can put them to flight we must be able to give chase. If we do not, they will just recover and come back again."

"Right, what we need now is a counter offensive plan," Peridon said, looking at Roak and Hydrian. "I have been thinking about it and believe we should have a way for our soldiers to easily go over the wall at the first sign of retreat."

"We could have rope ladders attached at the top of the wall that could be let down on command," Moark suggested. "Once there are enough of us on the ground we could give chase."

"It sounds like our most reasonable plan without being able to build a gate," Roak said, "provided we win the battle as easily as you believe we will."

"Don't worry about that, Roak my boy," the old Dwarie King said, slapping his hand on the table. "We have lots of surprises for them; they won't even know what hit 'em. Those black-hearted devils will probably take one look and run right back to where they came from."

"I hope you are right," Roak said, with much reservation in his voice. King Hydrian silently agreed with the Human.

"So be it, then!" Gamilon's voice was raised much above its normal level. "If you would use the power of Calburnathis against someone armed with but a normal weapon, come ahead. I will not cower." Gamilon took a stance to meet his adversary. Matthew still had only one thought in his mind, to rid himself of this arrogant, pain-in-the-butt Elf who had made him look like a fool. Matthew slowly continued his advance on Gamilon as if savoring it, the power of the sword flowing through him. Deeli, Sharineas, and even Pheltic, were pleading with Matthew to stop. Haub just watched with a hard, detached look in his eyes.

"Matthew, is this how your King Arthur would have used Excalibur," Pheltic pleaded with his friend. Suddenly the darkness that had covered Matthew's mind was pierced by a tiny sliver of light. What Pheltic had yelled about King Arthur caused Matthew to pause, and suddenly a part of the story leapt into his mind. It was when Arthur first met Lancelot and they fought in a test of manhood. Lancelot had Arthur beat fair and square, but the new King of Britain would not yield. His pride wounded, Arthur used the power of the sword to defeat the honorable knight. In the battle, Excalibur was broken in half because it had been used against a good man for the wrong reason. Arthur, realizing what he had done, was repentant and somehow the Lady of the Lake made the blade whole again.

Knowing where the weapon came from and how it got to England, Matthew now wondered how the sword had been fixed. *The same sword I'm now holding,* Matthew thought. *And I'm about to make the* same mistake with it that Arthur did. Gamilon may be an arrogant jerk, but he's not evil, or even bad. We're supposed to be on the same side. Matthew lowered his blade.

"I admit defeat, Gamilon. You are the better swordsman and fighter—the victory is yours. I'm afraid I can't turn the sword over to you, though. For some reason I was picked to carry it and I have to see this thing through to the end, although, it's obvious I'm not worthy of it." Gamilon lowered his sword also, and every member of the little party relaxed. Sharineas walked over to the two combatants.

"Now will both of you *boys* please put your weapons away and start thinking about something besides yourselves. Gamilon, our marriage was arranged when we were young, but I still have a choice in the matter. I'm not sure I will ever want to marry anyone, but hear me well. You are a bigger threat to yourself in trying to win my affection than Matthew is. We need to start working together to defeat the enemy, or no Elf will ever be getting married again." With that Sharineas picked up her pack, walked to the edge of the forest, and stood waiting for the others to follow. Matthew and Gamilon looked at each other.

"Please believe me Gamilon, I'm not trying to take Sharineas away from you. There have been so many changes in my life lately that I don't even have time to think about that kind of thing. How about a truce, at least until this mission is over." Gamilon felt foolish over the way things had gone, and about his rebuke from Sharineas. The marriage had been arranged, but his love for her was real.

"It seems I have much to learn about females," Gamilon said, looking at the ground. "I don't believe we could ever be friends, our ways are too far apart; but for the sake of the mission, and Sharineas, I will agree to a truce." Matthew stuck out his hand. Gamilon, not sure what to do, raised his. Matthew grabbed the outstretched hand and shook it, telling the Elf what it meant. Gamilon gave a nod of his head and a half smile in return to Matthew's grin. The two began to gather their things together so they could join Sharineas at the edge of the forest.

Deeli was praying silently. *My God, please forgive my trying to stop this fight. You meant it for a test and have used it to start teaching Matthew about humility. Help me Lord, not to get in the way again of Your shaping this young man.* Deeli waited for a feeling of forgiveness or word to his spirit, but nothing came. With a sigh of heartbroken disappointment he whispered, "Amen." Then he also gathered up his pack and walked toward the forest.

Haub once again said he wanted the lead position. He could not explain his intense desire to protect the others, but knew that somehow it was his duty and purpose on this quest. As Haub walked past Deeli toward the edge of the forest, he felt a hand grip his arm. "Haub my friend, your assessment of the situation was correct. I am sorry I did not understand. Thank you." Haub gave Deeli a smile and laid his huge hand over the aged Elf's small one. Haub wished he could tell his friend how much he loved him; that he considered Deeli the only family left to him. Not being good with words though, Haub just gave the small hand a squeeze and continued on toward the forest.

With the air cleared between Gamilon and Matthew, the little group started into the dank forest. As soon as they crossed over into the trees, an eerie silence fell over the group. The smell of death and decay was so pungent that everyone had to cover their noses and mouths with their sleeves. The going was very slow; Haub had to make sure he was on solid ground continuously. It did not take long to realize that the green, mossy-looking ground was just a covering for a thick, soupy liquid.

When Matthew disturbed the liquid during the fight, he thought he had smelled something bad, but did not have time to think about it then. Now, as the companions moved deeper into the swampy forest, they found that disturbing the liquid areas caused a foul odor to be released. The smell grew worse and the forest thicker the farther they went. After a time the companions' sense of smell became deadened enough that they were able to continue on without something covering their faces. Haub was not only trying to find solid ground for them, but constantly hacking vines out of the way. It seemed to him that vines hung out of every tree, and at times he would get his arms tangled in them. Haub also knew that his axe would be dull by the time they got out of this forest.

Suddenly one of the vines that he cut through sprayed a red liquid at him, and they all heard a shrill hissing sound. A long snake-like creature fell from the tree; the half with a head still attached slithered off into the swamp. A scream came from Sharineas, but not because of what happened to Haub. A long black snake had come out of the foul liquid to her right, slithered across her feet and disappeared off to her left. "This place is full of snakes!" She yelled. "I hate snakes!" Matthew looked around and saw that many of the mossy green areas were being disturbed from underneath.

"We should keep going," he said to the others. "I don't think standing around is a good idea."

"You don't have to twist my arm," Pheltic said with his war hammer in hand. "Let's get out of here." They set off again; weapons drawn and eyes searching the area. As they walked, an unnatural fear began to grip each member of the little party. No one spoke of the fear, each thinking it was just him or her and the situation; but the dread feeling grew worse. Finally Gamilon turned to check on Sharineas and saw that she was in tears, her face a mask of horror.

"Sharineas, what is it? What's wrong?" The entire group stopped now to find out what was happening.

"I'm just so scared," the Princess sobbed. "I don't know why."

"It is all right my dear," Deeli soothed." I too have been feeling a sense of dread and fear. My heart is pounding twice its normal speed, and the fear is so thick I feel as if I am about to suffocate." The others, even Haub and Gamilon, came clean and admitted the same frightened feeling. "The amulet seems to be glowing even brighter now. It may be amplifying the feeling in you."

"You said the people of this land call this the Place of Fear," Pheltic said with a quiver in his voice. "Now we know why. Even I can feel the evil here."

"I can sense magic here as well," Deeli said. "The same kind I feel around the mutated Nomies. We must continue on—it is imperative that we are out of here by dark. Everyone hold on to the person in front of you and be praying."

Pray they did. Different beliefs and levels of faith; all called out silently to be delivered from this terrible place. Matthew once again talked to a distant and nameless God. *I know the only time I come to You is when I'm in trouble, but that seems like most of the time lately. I really do want to thank You for getting us down those stairs. I would really appreciate You helping us out again and getting us through this forest alive. Uh...well, amen I guess.* Reaching out to a higher power made Matthew feel better and more secure, but when he stopped, the fear gripped him even stronger.

The deeper into the swampy forest the companions went, the larger, and more abundant, the snakes became. It was getting harder to see, and they realized that the sun must be setting. Haub did not know for sure that they were even still going in the right direction. He told them that this was not a normal forest and did not have the usual signs. The fear was almost more than anyone could bare when Deeli began to recite something from the Elven Holy Words.

"The Creator tends to me, I will lack nothing. He gives me rest in the lush meadows, I follow Him beside calm waters. He gives rest to my soul."

Haub began to recite with Deeli. Then to Matthew's surprise, even Sharineas and Gamilon joined in. The words struck Matthew as familiar, but he was not sure why.

"He shows me the proper path to use, for His glory. Even though I journey through the land of fear, the evil will not overcome me. For You are here and Your presence comforts me. You make a place of feasting for me amidst those who seek my death. You put into me the breath of life and I overflow. I know that Your love will be with me for the remainder of my days and I will abide in the dwelling place of the Creator forever."

As they were saying the words, Matthew felt a peace flow over him and the fear faded away. He thought it strange that two different religions would have the same prayer, but knew that this was not the place to bring it up. The snakes were becoming even more numerous and some were very large. Matthew and Gamilon had killed several—even Pheltic had killed one with his hammer. Haub still fought his way through the tangle of vines and snakes, his strength seemingly inexhaustible. Suddenly a huge snake came up out of the mire. It was at least three feet in diameter and the tail was nowhere in sight. The creature raised itself up, making a hissing sound like a cobra ready to strike. With fangs dripping and tongue flicking in and out, the giant reptile moved toward them.

The little group began to back away. But as they did, the giant snake came forward the same distance, watching its prey all the while. Then, without warning, the creature swiftly struck at Haub. The big Human swung his axe with all the strength he had left. He hit the snake right at the tip of its nose, just as its tongue flickered across Haub's body. Between the toughness of the hide and dullness of Haub's axe, the creature was not cut. It was, however, stunned and backed away. The unreasoning fear now had more reason—and returning to the group in full force, froze them in their tracks. Haub knew that his axe would not be sufficient against the monster.

"Matthew, if you can help with the sword make your way up to me slowly." Even before Haub said anything, Matthew had felt a surge of power go through him from the sword. It took a second or two for Matthew to fight down the icy fear in his stomach; but he finally drew the blade and made his way in front of Haub—trying not to think about what he was about to do. Excalibur crackled with blue lightning that startled the creature and seemed to hurt its eyes. Matthew made his way through the slimy liquid, closer to the giant snake. The monster did not take long to recover from being startled and with its razor sharp fangs bared, struck at Matthew.

This time the snake-like creature was not hit with a dull axe, and the results were decidedly different. Crackling with energy, the stroke that Matthew delivered knocked the monster back and took off the top part of its mouth. The creature screamed its pain and thrashed around, slinging green ichor and blood everywhere. In the dim light that was left to them, the companions could see the snake's tail. It was kicking up the slimy liquid far back in the forest. The creature came at Matthew again, tongue flicking in and out. The sword came up and the long forked tongue flew from the snake's mouth.

Matthew, trying not to let his reason get the better of him, jumped onto the creature's back. It was slippery and round, like walking on a wet log; Matthew could barely keep his balance. The monster reared up, trying to throw its assailant off and almost succeeded. Matthew fell, but managed to lock his legs around the slimy body and stay on top. *I wish I had been old enough to ride the bull back when it was popular,* Matthew thought to himself, in an attempt to curb his rising panic. *The experience would come in handy now.* As the creature reared upward to try to dislodge its prey-turned-predator, Matthew swung the sword, and with one swipe cut all the way through its neck.

The body of the monster jerked and threw Matthew into a pool of the smelly moss-covered liquid. The others, Haub in front, ran over to him but stopped short. Matthew was already dragging himself out of the pool and did not see what they did. They yelled at him to stop moving. That was when he noticed the tail of a snake hanging out of the bottom of his breast plate. He froze in fear, not knowing what to do; afraid that the snake would bite him if he moved. It seemed like an eternity, no one moving, no one talking. Suddenly Gamilon sheathed his sword. With the quickness and agility only a young male Elf could possess, he crossed the distance between himself and Matthew. Grabbing the tail of the snake with lightning speed, he yanked on it with all his strength. The snake came free, causing it, and Gamilon, to fall backward. The dark green creature, still in Gamilon's hands, thrashed about and brought a flat, diamond-shaped head around to sink needle-like fangs into its captor.

Too late. Matthew, Excalibur still in hand, brought his blade around and cut the snake in half just before its fangs could reach Gamilon. For several heartbeats everyone remained silent and still. The others all realized that they had been holding their breath. Sharineas was the first to move and came over to the two, who only hours ago had been trying to kill each other. She reached them as Matthew was helping Gamilon up out of the slime. They were both shaken, wet, and smelly; and Sharineas knew that she would always care deeply for them both. Before she could say a word, another of the snake creatures, this one bigger than the last, rose out of the slime about thirty feet back from where they had just been.

"Everyone run!" Matthew yelled as he slid his sword back into its scabbard and grabbed the two Elves near him in almost the same motion. With Matthew in the lead they quickly ran after the retreating figures of Haub, Pheltic, and Deeli. The forest was almost in complete darkness now and they could no longer see their companions up ahead. Not knowing if the monster was still in pursuit, the trio clung to each other and crashed blindly through the forest, heedless of the moss-covered liquid. They bumped into trees and ran through vines—or snakes—they knew not which. None of them even knew which direction they were going, only that they had lost the other three. Unnatural fear was compounded with the real thing and sapping them of their strength.

That same fear that worked against them also spurred the trio on; the natural instinct of survival kept them going forward. It seemed as if they ran for hours; finally, Matthew and Gamilon had to hold Sharineas up. Then without warning, the three stumbled out of the forest into a field of tall grass. They did not know what time it was, only that night had fully come long ago. All three lay down in the grass for a short time, but fear of the snake creature possibly following drove them on.

The exhausted trio walked through the tall grass until they were too tired to go on, and unanimously decided it would be safe enough to sleep there for the night. They spent the few remaining hours of the night, as well as half the morning, oblivious. Matthew awoke to the sun shining in his eyes. He rolled over to see his two Elven companions still asleep, but it was not long before they were stirring as well. The trio sat, at first saying nothing and looking at each other through bleary eyes, smelling like the swamp liquid and wondering what they should do next.

"Thanks for pulling that snake out of my armor," Matthew said looking at Gamilon.

"It would seem we are all in the business of saving each others' lives," the Elf answered with a slight grin.

"I wonder what happened to the others," Sharineas added with a worried tone.

"I don't know," Matthew said with a yawn, "but we should start looking for them. Hopefully they made it out like we did. I'll check our bearings to see which way would be the best to start looking." Matthew stood, the dewy-wet grass coming almost up to his chest. He looked in every direction and came to the conclusion that they had come out at the northwest corner of the forest. "We should probably go east from here," he told the other two. Then he noticed something in the distance coming toward them from the north. "Gamilon, come take a look at this and see if you can tell what it is." Gamilon stood and followed Matthew's gaze. The Elf immediately grabbed Matthew by the shoulders and forced him to the ground.

"That is a company of twelve Traul soldiers, you fool! And they're coming right at us."

Chapter

15

Haub had seen the huge serpent raise its head before Matthew ever yelled for them to run. He motioned for Deeli to grab Pheltic and follow him. The giant Human began furiously to make a path away from the creature. As they heard the hiss of the snake grow louder, Haub quit chopping at the vines. With a strength born of desperation, he began to plow through the heavy foliage with Deeli and Pheltic hanging onto his vest for dear life. Haub could not see where the other three were, and was indecisive as to whether he should stop to find them. Just as he was about to stop, Pheltic yelled that the snake was almost upon them. Haub knew then that wherever Matthew, Gamilon, and Sharineas were, the snake, at least, was not after them.

Haub's duty was clear to him now; he had to protect those that were here. Pheltic screamed, and Haub knew there was no other choice. He let Deeli and Pheltic pass him, then turned to face the monster. The snake stopped short at this new tactic, but did not take long to recover and strike at Haub. As with the other snake creature, Haub hit it on the snout with his dull axe. The creature was stunned and backed away. Haub yelled for the other two to run and he followed; the giant snake quickly gave chase. They kept going until the snake got too close. Then they stopped once again for Haub to fight the creature until it backed off, giving the three a chance to run some more. This cat and mouse game lasted the rest of the night; running through the dark swamp forest, not sure what direction they were even going.

After many hours the big Human knew his strength was at its end, and that he could not last through another battle with the creature. Haub told Deeli that he was going to stop, but that he and Pheltic were to keep running. He was getting up the courage to stop and face his last battle when Pheltic yelled out: "Look! The trees are thinning out, and it looks like an open field ahead."

It was true; Haub had not even noticed that the sky through the tree tops was getting lighter and they could now see what was ahead. They headed for the thinning trees, finally emerging from the forest into an open area of grass that was taller than the Dwarie. There was a loud snapping and cracking sound as the serpent broke free of the trees behind them. It was moving sluggishly, but Haub knew it could still defeat him.

"Deeli," he said in a serious tone, "take Pheltic, find Matthew and finish the quest. I will stop the monster."

"But that thing will kill you," Deeli said.

"I know. But we can't out-run it. Now go!" Haub said, pushing his old friend away and turning toward the snake. Deeli could not let his friend die for the sake of his oath. He prayed silently, *I am sorry, Lord,* and let go with a burst of magical energy. The snake recoiled, wounded and outraged, but not dead. If anything, the creature's pain gave it strength. It came at them again with more fierceness than before. Deeli raised both hands and shot forth a flash of fire that enveloped the creature's entire head. The snake screamed in pain and reared back, but was not ash as Deeli had expected.

"Someone has used powerful magic to create these monsters," Deeli said to Haub. "I do not know if I can stop it." Even though the creature was still thrashing about in pain, Haub, with his last bit of energy, ran at the giant serpent and threw himself on its back. He could see that its head was black from being burnt by Deeli's fire and hoped that the magic had weakened it. Straddling the creature's neck, Haub raised his dull axe and let fall a fierce blow. The dull weapon sank into the reptilian head, and the snake collapsed, throwing Haub off in the process. Shaking and heaving, Haub raised himself off the ground. He walked a few steps, then collapsed in the tall grass not far from the snake—and did not move again. Deeli and Pheltic tried to pull the huge Human away, but got only a few yards before they too gave into exhaustion. Knowing they could move him no further—the two lay down next to their friend and slept.

The trio started to crawl as fast and low as they could toward the east. The gruff Traul voices were coming closer now. Gamilon and Sharineas could not understand them, but Matthew could. They could get up and fight, but all three knew their strength was gone. "I would rather not fight anyway," Matthew whispered. "We don't want to draw any attention from other troops that might be nearby."

The voices were so close now that it sounded as if the Traul soldiers were right next to them, all three stopped crawling and stayed very still. From the swishing sound the soldiers made moving through the tall grass, the companions could tell that they were well east of the patrol. They lay flat on their stomachs facing west in case of discovery, but hoping the Trauls would go right by them.

"Why are we patrolling this far east?" Matthew heard one of the soldiers ask.

"Because the war chief told us to!" Another growled back. "Besides, there are others coming up behind us that are even farther east, so shut up." Matthew was intent on listening to the conversation in front of him and did not notice the Traul warrior searching even farther to the east than his companions. Suddenly he heard grass swish behind him, then felt a pain in his leg. The Traul had not seen the Human either; his foot caught Matthew's leg and he tripped. The fall was followed by a string of Traul swear words that fortunately Sharineas could not understand.

Matthew rolled over and the two looked at each other in surprise. Both started to react at the same time, but the Traul was on his knees first with his sword already in the air. Before he could use it, however, Matthew saw a silver blade grow out of the Traul's throat, and then disappear again. The soldier's eyes bulged, and a gurgle, as well as blood, came from his mouth and throat. The Traul toppled over to reveal Gamilon behind him, bloodied blade in hand.

"Well, hero from another world, I think it's time you quit laying around and got up. It looks like we have some work to do." Matthew jumped up and saw the rest of the patrol charging at them. He barely had time to raise his sword before the first warrior was upon him. Excalibur met the first broad sword attack with a crackle of the familiar blue lightning and a surge of power. A look of surprise came over the Traul's face and he backed away looking at his own sword. In his hand he held a hilt with about ten inches of blade left; Matthew's sword had cut clean through the Traul weapon. The soldier did not have long to be shocked. Without letting himself think about what he was doing— Matthew ran his blade through the Traul's heart quick and clean.

Matthew loathed what he had to do, but knew there was no other way; five more soldiers were on him immediately. *They have brothers, sisters, wives and children. I don't want to do this, but they're not giving me any choice.* Unfortunately for them, these soldiers fared no better than the first. Excalibur seemed to leap of its own accord, defending Matthew, and ending the threat. After his fight with Gamilon in which he used a normal blade, Matthew knew he was not the great swordsman that this sword made him look. When all five were down, he turned to see Gamilon fighting two Trauls at once, with another already on the ground. Matthew rushed to the Elf's aid, killing one attacker while Gamilon took care of the other. "That accounts for ten of them," Matthew said, huffing with exertion, "but where are the other two?"

"And where is Sharineas?" Gamilon added with a worried look. The two checked in every direction, but could see no sign of anyone. Then, from back in the direction of the forest, they heard a scream. They gave each other a startled look, and began to run in that direction.

Sharineas was a few yards away from her companions when the attack started. Two of the Traul soldiers separated themselves immediately and came after her. Not having any way to defend herself, the

Princess did the only thing left to her—she ran. Sharineas was running as fast as she could, but the Trauls were still gaining on her. She could see the forest looming up just ahead, but did not know where else to go. The Princess was almost to the edge of the swamp forest with nowhere else to turn, when her foot found a hole that decided for her.

She went down with a scream and rolled a few more feet, twisting her ankle in the process. Rolling over on her back, Sharineas could see that the soldiers had come to a stop and were looking at her. They were smiling and saying something in their horrible language, as if this was just sport to them. Sharineas was too frightened to do anything when they both walked forward reaching for her. Suddenly a beam of white hot light shot forth from the amulet. When she opened her eyes, the blinding light was gone; both Trauls lay on the ground stunned.

Matthew and Gamilon were both running fast, but knew that Sharineas and the two Traul soldiers were too far away for them to reach her in time. Then, just ahead of them near the forest, a white flash of light appeared for a brief second. They continued to run in that direction and found Sharineas shaking and in tears. Both noticed that the two soldiers lay a few yards away not moving, but still breathing. Gamilon held Sharineas for a minute until her shaking stopped, and then she told them what happened. When she was feeling up to it they walked her a little away from the motionless bodies.

"We can't leave them here like that," Gamilon said to Matthew. "In Napdeeliate's horse story the amulet only stunned the beast; later it was all right. If we leave them they'll come around and report this whole thing."

"I know, but what can we do?" Matthew returned.

"We have to kill them," Gamilon said without emotion. "That way even if they're found, they can't describe who we are or which way we went." Matthew knew the Elf was right, but could not bring himself to agree with him.

"I can't do it. Not in cold blood; not while they're helpless. We'll just have to tie them up with something and hope they're not found."

"Well I can do it," Gamilon said taking his knife out of its sheath. "It will be a pleasure after what they've done to my people." Without a word Matthew grabbed Sharineas' arm and started walking her away. Gamilon headed for the stunned Traul warriors. When he was through, the Elf came back to where the other two were. "We had better get going."

"Yea," Matthew answered curtly, "I heard them say that there were more patrols coming up farther east. Our only choice is to make it even farther east before they get here; hopefully we'll run into the others." Without any more talk the trio headed straight east, parallel with the marsh forest in which they had spent most of the night.

The grass was tall and hard to move through; Matthew and Gamilon had to take turns helping Sharineas walk with her hurt ankle. The going was slow and painful, but though tired and full of despair, they continued on—what choice did they have? The three lost companions had traveled for several hours when they saw a thin column of smoke rising ahead.

"Shh," Gamilon put his finger to his lips, "this might be the other Traul patrol you told us about." All three hunched down low, and then made their way slowly forward. The smell of cooking meat met their nostrils, making their mouths salivate and stomachs rumble. It reminded them in full force that they had not eaten since yesterday noon. Matthew and Gamilon were in the lead, and finally came to a place where the tall grass was flattened. They peeked through the thick grass, and there sat Deeli, Haub, and Pheltic around a small fire with pieces of meat roasting on a spit. Matthew was so relieved to see them that he jumped out of the grass and ran the few steps to his friends. Haub was up in a second, almost putting his axe through Matthew's head before realizing who he was. They were all overjoyed at the reunion, including, Matthew noted, Gamilon.

"You just about frightened us to death," Deeli said laughing.

"Sorry about that, I was just so glad to see you guys. I was afraid you didn't make it out of the forest."

"We feared the same about you," Deeli replied. "even though I know the Creator's hand is upon you."

"You should be more careful," Gamilon scolded. "If we can see that fire, then so can any patrol in the area."

"We know," Deeli answered while Haub was putting out the fire. "We hoped if you made it out of the forest that it would be near here. We took a chance on starting the fire so that you might see the smoke and investigate.

"Plus, we were hungry," Pheltic piped up smiling.

"Well, uh…yes, that too," Deeli said, pinching the Dwarie on the cheek. "I know it was a gamble, but we could have been looking for each other for days. We might have continued to miss each other, not even knowing if the other group was still alive. It has not been burning for long, that is why you surprised us so much. The food is now done, let us sit down and share while it is hot."

"There are patrols in this area," Gamilon said. "It probably isn't a good idea to stay where this smoke was. If any Trauls saw it they're on their way here now." All six gathered up their things, including the food that had been cooking, and headed farther east. After about a half-hour of walking they all came to the agreement that they were far enough away to stop and eat.

They were still in the tall grass, so everyone joined in on flattening an area. The group gratefully settled down to eat and trade stories of what had happened after their separation. Matthew, Gamilon, and Sharineas took turns relating their story first. The others were shocked by their run-in with the patrol, and it made them want to get going again as soon as possible. By the time the trio's story was concluded they were all finished eating, so they decided to head out again. The vote was to head north, but to continue veering east in hopes of avoiding any more patrols.

Along the way Deeli, Haub, and Pheltic took turns telling their tale. Pheltic, of course, remembered it as more of a glorious adventure than did Deeli or Haub. They finished the story by telling them of skinning a part of the giant serpent and cooking it over the fire. Matthew, Sharineas, and Gamilon all turned a little gray in the face, but that seemed to be the only side effect.

"I'm just glad you didn't tell us what the meat was before we ate it," was Matthew's only comment.

"I was so hungry I didn't even think to ask," Sharineas said, sticking out her tongue.

Everyone was sluggish as they walked, and with good reason. The afternoon sun was hot and beating down on them in the open field, which made the stench that clung to them even worse. Matthew noticed that Deeli was more quiet and withdrawn than usual and it bothered him. But he knew that despite all odds the little group was united again, and that would keep them going. The companions were now farther east than they had ever intended on going, but circumstances had determined that. They walked all afternoon and saw no one. Toward the end of the day they came across a beautiful small lake surrounded by trees. There were large rocks along the eastern shoreline with a sandy area nearby.

"This looks like it was made to order for us," Matthew hinted.

"I would cast my vote for spending the night here," Gamilon added.

"I think once it is dark we could even risk a small fire between these rocks," Haub said looking at Deeli. "The smoke would be less likely seen at night."

"Why are you all looking at me," Deeli said with mock seriousness. "Do you think I believe it would do any good to suggest that we continue on?" Everyone's mind seems to be made up, so we might as well set up camp." Deeli was trying to be lighthearted with his talk, but both Matthew and Haub knew something was bothering him.

"I for one need to take a bath," Sharineas announced. "I did bring along two cleaning bars, I guess I could sacrifice one of them…you boys certainly need it." Sharineas, Deeli, and Pheltic were the only ones who had not lost their packs. Matthew, Gamilon, and Haub had lost theirs somewhere in the swamp forest and had no desire to go back to look for them. After rummaging in her pack, Sharineas produced the bar of soap. Matthew gratefully grabbed it; then he and Pheltic headed for the water. Before going very far they heard Gamilon's voice protesting to Sharineas:

"You cannot go by yourself unprotected, I am going with you."

"I am only going to the far end of the lake to bathe. Besides, I have the amulet."

"And are you going to wear it while in the water?"

"Gamilon! I don't think that's any of your business. But very well, you may come and keep watch as long as you don't peek."

"Sharineas!" Gamilon protested, his face turning red. "I would never do such a thing. I am Elven nobility and would never do anything so disgraceful!"

"I know that," Sharineas answered rolling her eyes. "Do you always have to be so serious?" The Elven Princess turned and began walking to the other side of the lake. Gamilon took the good-natured rebuke with tight-lipped silence and followed her, ignoring the smiles that Deeli and Haub were unsuccessfully trying to hide. Haub went to another part of the lake to try to spear some fish, saying he would wash later, after catching dinner. Deeli joined Matthew and Pheltic already in the process of cleaning their clothes, traveling cloaks, armor, and bodies.

Matthew laid the clothing he wore under his armor out on the rocks to dry as much as possible before Sharineas came back. Deeli and Pheltic had extra clothes in their packs, but Matthew knew that he would have to put his damp ones back on. Pheltic was still splashing and having a good time in the water, so Matthew jumped back in. Deeli was a little way off being very quiet and withdrawn, so Matthew went over and asked him what was wrong.

"Matthew, my friend," the old Elf began with a sigh, "I do not know if you will understand, but I am still feeling an absence of the Creator in my soul, and in my prayers. I believe it is because of my continued use of the magic." A tear slid down his cheek, and for the first time Matthew thought Deeli looked as old as he really was. "I have failed Him too many times, and He has finally had enough. I will always continue to pray for forgiveness, but I do not know if He hears me anymore."

"I'm sorry Deeli," Matthew said. "I don't know much about your God, but I would like to learn of Him, and this Shesea person." Deeli gave his young friend a long look and finally smiled.

"Yes, I think it is time I told you all. Let us get dressed and sit upon the rocks, and I will tell you of the Path of Shesea." The two got out of the water and headed for the rocks, Pheltic tagging along behind. They had just gotten themselves situated when Sharineas and Gamilon came back.

"Gamilon," Matthew said, "I need to know about Deeli's God, something inside me needs answers. You can stay if you wish, but I'm warning you ahead of time so you won't fly off the handle again."

"I don't want to listen to this heresy, so I think it is a good time for me to go wash. Sharineas, you don't need to hear this either. Why don't you come keep watch for me?"

"I think you are old enough to take care of yourself now, Gamilon," Sharineas answered, giving her betrothed a smoldering look, then sat down on a rock to listen to her uncle. Gamilon shook his head with disgust and headed off to bathe.

"Gamilon's attitude is typical of most Elves," Deeli told Matthew. "The Elven people have always been the chosen of the Creator, and He has tried all through the ages to use my people to share His word and love with the other races. For the most part the Elves have selfishly kept it for themselves. The Elven people have always believed that God would one day send a Deliverer to His chosen, and make them the ruling race. They have been waiting for thousands of sun-cycles; for it is written that the Creator would establish His kingdom through the Elves. The Elves have always looked for this Deliverer to come in glory and splendor. They refuse to acknowledge that He already came two thousand cycles ago. Instead of coming in glory and splendor, the Creator sent His own Son in meekness and humility."

Matthew felt a tingle go up his spine, and a lightness in his head, but said nothing. "The Son of God came to this world as one of the Elven born, to teach us what our Creator wanted. He came into the world through a young maiden who had never been with a male. Not as a noble, or a king, but as a simple fieldhand's son. So now, as back then, the priesthood will not accept Shesea as the true Son of the Creator. Shesea taught us that God created and loves all of the races, and that He wished for us to think of Him as a father, so that all of the races could go to be with the Creator if they would believe on Him, the Son. Not by observing rituals, or following every letter of the Elven law, but by admitting that there is evil in us, and accepting His grace and forgiveness." Matthew's mouth was hanging open, and his brain seemed to be on fire; this was too much to be a coincidence.

"What...happened to this Shesea?" Matthew asked hesitantly. He was not sure that he wanted to face the awesomeness of this revelation, knowing what it would do to his life.

"At that time the Traul race, with their Human allies, ruled the valley and the Elven people. They gloried even then in death and destruction. The Elven priests captured Shesea. They handed Him over to the Traul government, saying that He had broken their law." Deeli became more emotional as he talked, and a tear slid down his cheek. Haub, who had silently returned from fishing and cleaning up, sniffed as well. "At that time most criminals were killed at the Great Tree from which you drew the sword."

"Yes, Haub told us all about that," Pheltic spoke up quietly.

"They nailed the Son of the Creator upon the tree with spikes, after beating and torturing him; and that is where He died. His followers buried Him in a cave somewhere in the mountains. The Elves were afraid that His followers would sneak back and steal the body, so they talked their Traul captors into guarding the cave. I know you will find this hard to believe, Matthew, but in spite of the Traul guard, three days later the cave was empty." Deeli was becoming excited now, and he began talking faster. "Shesea had arisen from the dead and began appearing to His followers. Then others began to report seeing Him in His resurrected body. Any who believe in Him, and believe that He died and was resurrected as an atonement for the evil in us, belongs to the Creator. That is what we call the Path of Shesea." Matthew had goose bumps over his entire body, and his breath was short. "I can see by your expression, Matthew, that this is too much to believe, but I tell you it is true. He has forgiven me much, and changed my life for the better. He has been directing your path all along, even if you will not acknowledge it."

"No! No, you don't understand!" Matthew was so filled by a mixture of awe and excitement that he could hardly speak. "The same thing happened in my world at the same time. At least the main religion of my world says it did…. My father swore it did," he said more softly. "In my world the Son of God was named Jesus, and He was born as one of God's chosen people. He was rejected by them and killed on a tree they called a cross. How can this be? Unless the whole thing is true! What my father believed is true," Matthew stated the fact with amazement, more to himself than anyone else.

The Spirit of the Creator of both worlds was upon Matthew now, making him feel more complete than ever before, but at the same time as insignificant as an ant beneath his feet. It seemed as though something fell from his eyes, and he could see the whole truth now. Tears of regret sprang into his eyes. All the years of searching in rebellion, and the answer had been there all of the time. The very God that he had yelled at went to all the trouble of bringing a smart mouthed, know-it-all kid to another world just to show him. "Can he forgive me, Deeli?" Matthew asked in a choked voice. "I've done an awful lot wrong."

"Yes Matthew," Deeli answered with reverence for what was going on in the young man, "He is just waiting for you to admit the evil that is inside, and accept His forgiveness."

3>

"I still don't understand why He allowed my father to be murdered. All those people in the clearing, it doesn't seem just or very loving."

"The world has much evil in it, and the Creator will let His creation run its course until time is done and the Son returns. I do not know why the slaughter in the clearing was allowed to take place, or why Haub's good family had to die. If they had not, Haub might not have come with us and saved our lives so many times. I do know that everything the Creator allows His children to go through is for their own good and His perfect will. If your father had not been murdered you might have grown up to be a very different person. You may have continued to believe in the Son, but in a complacent sort of way that would not have stood the test of time. You would not be the same man that sits before me now. More than likely you would never have been brought to this world to help us in our time of need."

"I...I never thought of it that way before," Matthew admitted.

"Many Path followers have forgotten that the Creator is sovereign, and that His will is what is important," Deeli continued. "They believe that our God should perform for them like some puppet on a string. Some even believe that whatever they speak forth will happen, whether it is the Creator's will or not. It is a sad thing to see, but these things were prophesied for the last days. Matthew, there is a true remnant that Shesea keeps for Himself. Would you like to become a part of it?"

"Yes, Deeli, more than anything. It's been so long though. What do I do?"

"Just tell the Father that you believe Shesea, I mean Jesus for you, is His true and only Son. That you need forgiveness for the evil that is inside you, and that you want to be covered with the atoning blood that His Son shed for you when He was sacrificed. Tell the Creator that you believe His Son died for you, was raised again to life, and is alive today hearing this prayer."

Matthew prayed these things out loud with Deeli, not caring who was there to hear. He knelt there, unashamed, sobbing like a child. The bitterness that he had felt since his father's murder was gone. The Spirit of God fell upon Matthew, washing his soul and lifting the burdens from his heart. This was not just a removal of guilt, as when he was younger. This was a supernatural experience; the reshaping of a life that would never be the same again. Matthew had never felt so clean and at peace before—he never wanted it to end.

"I would like to become a Path follower too," Pheltic said in a hushed voice to Deeli. "I'm not sure what everything means, just that it's the right thing."

"Pheltic," Deeli said smiling, "the Lord welcomes with open arms those willing to come with the simplicity of a child. You do not have to understand everything now, just what the Spirit is telling you." Deeli led the young Dwarie in the same prayer as he did Matthew. Pheltic was not sure of what all he just did, and knew his father would not approve, but knew that he felt an inner joy and love stronger than any he had ever known.

"Deeli, would you baptize me in the lake?" Matthew asked when he could finally speak again. "I was once before, a long time ago, but it would mean so much more now."

"You mean the burial and resurrection ritual, you have even that in your world! This is truly a mighty revelation from the Lord! That He has created both our worlds, and sacrificed His Son to redeem them both. It would be an honor to do this for you my friend and brother. What about you, young Pheltic?"

"Yes!" The Dwarie answered enthusiastically. "I would love to, if you'll tell me what it means."

"That I will, little one. And you two?" Deeli inquired of Sharineas, and Gamilon who had returned sometime during the talk. Gamilon said not a word, just turned and walked away. Sharineas was full of doubt; a lifetime of teaching that made up the very heart of her people could not easily be ignored.

"Not just yet, uncle. I don't know what has transpired here, it seems very real to you. Your words, and this strange coincidence have touched me, but you know this is no light decision for an Elf. Maybe in time…. I just don't know."

"It is all right, child," Deeli said in a soothing tone, putting his arm around Sharineas, "the Lord is patient, and never forces Himself on anyone. Will you come to the edge of the water and watch?" Sharineas nodded her agreement, and walked to the edge of the little lake with Deeli, Haub, Matthew, and Pheltic.

The four males waded out into the water. The sun was almost completely down now; orange, red, and purple colors played on the rippling surface of the lake. A warm, gentle breeze blew across the water, and the sound of birds and insects singing their praises to the Creator filled their ears. So, in a small lake, in the middle of a hostile land in another dimension, Matthew Adams, Jr. was baptized by a hundred and fifty-eight year old Elf. As Deeli brought Matthew's head up out of the water, the young man whom God had entrusted the most powerful weapon in this world to, felt truly reborn. He knew that his life now belonged to Jesus, and that he would never turn away again. Haub then baptized Pheltic. The little Dwarie was so full of the Spirit that all he could do was hug everyone and laugh.

"Now we are all truly brothers," Deeli said, knee-deep in water. "Remember you two, Haub and I will always be here for you."

They returned to where they would camp for the night a little way from shore. Gamilon already had a small fire going amidst the rocks, out of plain view. Deeli had wrapped some of the snake meat and brought it along, so they cooked it over the fire. Everyone ate some except Sharineas, who ate the little bit of food that was still in her pack. Deeli and Pheltic parceled out the last of the food they had left in their packs. They finished it all, everyone wondering where their next meal would come from.

Matthew and Pheltic kept Deeli up late that night asking questions and comparing the events of their Savior's life in the two different worlds. When Deeli was finally too tired to go on, they all turned in for the night. Matthew knew that sleep would not come easily after all that had happened to him that day, so he volunteered to take the first watch.

Sharineas might as well have taken first watch; for it took the confused Elven Princess a long time to fall asleep. She could not help wondering how the belief that the Deliverer had already come could spring up in both worlds at the same time. *Could the beliefs of my people be wrong? Am I, the Keeper of the Amulet, on my way to the underworld when I die?* When sleep did come to the young Elf maiden, it was full of troubling dreams.

Pheltic had pulled last watch; waking from a light doze, he knew that something was wrong. In the pre-dawn darkness he thought he saw movement by a boulder near the lake. He crept over to Matthew, put a small hand over his friend's mouth, and woke him. Pheltic whispered that he thought they might have company, so both quietly shook the others awake. The sky was beginning to lighten, and the companions could finally see what they were up against. They were completely surrounded on every side, outnumbered at least ten to one. As they studied the silent figures there was no doubt even for Matthew's eyes who they were. Trauls!

The band of huge Trauls was in a circle around them, keeping a distance of about twenty feet and not making a sound. "I hate to do this," Matthew said, "but we can't go down without a fight. Too much depends on what we're doing." He stood up with the sheathed sword in his hand and dramatically drew Excalibur forth. He hoped the flashing blue lightning and show of power would unnerve the Traul warriors, causing them to flee. Matthew lifted the blade high; his stomach froze. There was no lightning, no glowing gem, no surge of magical power running through his body. Excalibur was now a cold and lifeless piece of metal, just like any other sword.

Chapter

16

The wall was over halfway to completion. Progress had picked up since the winged Nomies had ceased their attacks two days before. The Elven priests had arrived, and with their aid the valley alliance was able to end the aerial harassment. Kings' Peridon, Hydrian, and Moark, along with Roak, were in their pavilion near the forest discussing the possibility of any more interference. In the last two days no more tricks of the enemy had manifested themselves and the leaders were hoping this lack of interference would help get the construction back on schedule. Suddenly an Elven scout ran into the tent, out of breath and bursting with news. "My King," the young Elf finally sputtered, putting his fist over his heart, "a large cloud of dust has been spotted in the distance to the north."

"So the enemy finally shows itself," King Moark mused. "Any estimation on the time of arrival?" The scout looked at the wrinkled face of the Dwarie King, not sure if he should answer anyone but his own liege. He looked to the Elven King, and Peridon gave him a nod of permission.

"Yes, King Moark, my captain says it will be less than a seven-day." All three leaders looked to the unfinished wall and frowned.

"All right soldier," Peridon said, "after you've rested, get back to your patrol and tell your captain that I want steady reports of the enemy's advances."

"Yes, my King." The young scout headed to the soldiers' tents weary and foot sore. Before anyone had a chance to utter a word, a servant from Peridon's household rode up outside the tent and dismounted.

"My King, a message from the Queen." King Peridon gave him the go ahead and the servant handed him a scroll with the royal seal on it. The King dismissed him and opened the scroll.

"It seems," Peridon said after reading the scroll, "that my daughter is still missing. No one has seen her since the night I rebuked her before the war council. Her mother is very worried…and I must admit that I am as well. This is not like Sharineas to pout and hide just because she did not get her own way. It is also not like Gamilon to break his word like this, to desert his people at such a crucial time. Unless…no, they would not,…could not." King Peridon called for the captain of the escort he had sent with Calburnathis. "Captain, when you escorted the Sword Bearer and his party to the pass, was the Princess or Lord Gamilon anywhere around?"

"No sire, none of us saw anyone but the five you sent out. I would have reported anything out of the ordinary."

"I know you would have captain, thank you." With a small sigh of relief Peridon turned to the other three. "This is more of a personal problem and I will settle it alone. Our duty together is to find some way to speed up construction of the wall and battlements."

"But how?" Roak asked. "We have every available person working now."

"I know of only one way at this point," King Moark said. The old Dwarie got up and left the tent with the others following behind. Once outside the tent, he made his way over to the construction area and began working along- side his subjects.

"Well it seems King Moark has set the example," Roak commented as he too, started for the wall.

"Not for the priesthood or myself," Peridon said indignantly. "If we were to work among the common people they would lose respect for the throne and their religion."

"I am just one of the common people," Roak returned as he continued on, "asked to be their voice. My duty now is to help those voices." Hydrian looked at Roak, then Peridon; without a word he turned to follow Moark and Roak. King Peridon watched as the Human and Elf walked away, then shook his head and returned to his tent. Two days later an Elven scout came to King Peridon's tent.

"My King. My captain sends word that the enemy will be at the northern end of the pass three days from now. He is not sure, but thinks that the army might be much bigger than even our latest estimates."

"Thank you, soldier. Get some rest, then get back to your outfit." The scout left and Peridon walked out of his tent to inspect the progress. The wall was coming along better now without the Nomie attacks, but did not look like it could be finished in three days. That afternoon found the High King of the Elven people, and their priests, with sleeves rolled up, hard at work on the wall. Not only did King Peridon not lose any respect that day, but his image in the eyes of the Elven people grew bigger than it already was.

Matthew was in a panic; for the first time since he had drawn it from the tree, Excalibur had failed him. Now the little group was completely surrounded by Trauls and armed with only three normal swords, an axe and a hammer. The amulet would no doubt defend Sharineas, but for how long no one knew. Matthew looked to Deeli. "What do we do now? Can you use your magic?"

"No Matthew, I am afraid not. I am through with that, come what may. Even if I did, the magic would drain me long before defeating this many."

"What about you, Gamilon or Sharineas? You're Elves, do you know any magic?" Both responded in the negative.

"Why do they not attack," Haub asked in an irritated tone. "They could have killed, or taken us prisoner before now with ease."

"That is a good point my friend," Deeli said as he stepped out of the now tightly clustered little group. His knowledge of the Traul language being very rusty, Deeli simply lifted his hand. "Greetings," he called out in Traul. A male Traul that was taller than Haub and held a staff in his hand stepped forward.

"May His peace rest upon your shoulders," the Traul said in a broken form of the valley's common language. Every jaw in the little company dropped—they could not believe what they were hearing. How could a Traul, especially this deep into the north, know their language and the traditional greeting of the Path followers? Haub recovered his senses first.

"May His peace rest upon your shoulders. Are you and your tribe followers of the Path?"

"Yes," was the reply, still in common, "we follow the Path of Shesea."

"So do most of us," Deeli spoke up pointing to Haub, Matthew, and Pheltic. Suddenly smiles broke out on all the Traul faces and the entire group began talking to one another. The sun was on the rise now and lighting up the whole area. The companions could see many females and older children in the group as well as the males they had feared.

"I can't believe it!" Gamilon said smacking his forehead. "Path-follower Trauls, how could this plague have spread so far?"

"That is a good question," Deeli said. "One I hope we can get an answer to."

"Well I for one am glad," Sharineas said, smiling with relief. "I would rather have them friendly than not." The whole tribe gathered around the little group from the valley as if they were long lost relatives, laughing and talking in a broken form of the valley language. The leader finally raised his staff in the air and a hush fell over everyone.

"There is a squad of the Enlightened One's warriors camped just to the west of here. We must return to our camp where we can talk in safety." The companions readily agreed and began following the strange band of Traul Path followers toward the rising sun.

They traveled for about two hours before coming to the low foothills of the eastern mountain range. The companions of the sword were worried about how far off course they were, but knew that once again there was no choice. The Trauls did not talk that much along the journey. As happy as they were to meet people of like beliefs, the tribe was still a little suspicious of the very mixed and out of place group. No one from the tribe asked them why they were there and what their business was. They did however exchange names and found out the leader was called Katchut. Matthew figured they were waiting to get them back to camp, and then would decide what to do with the strangers from the valley. Deeli on the other hand could not contain himself and began asking the leader questions like an excited child.

"I did not know there were any Traul converts to the Path. How did this come about?"

"Many years ago, after the Great War," Katchut began. "We and the Nomie race were a defeated people, scattered and forced back into the north to start again. Most of the leaders were dead, and the attempt to wipe out the Elves and control all of the land was crushed. I, of course, was not yet born, but my parents were left homeless and wandering the north-land trying to survive. Many Elves, Dwarie, and Humans came to our land with weapons and hate, trying to make us pay for what we had done." Matthew noticed that Deeli looked very convicted when Katchut made this last statement. "Some did not come with hate though," the Traul leader continued. "There were small scattered groups of Humans that came through to help rebuild and tell us of the grace of the Creator. Some of the Traul people believed, mainly because they saw these Humans living out what they spoke. Very few of the Nomies believed and almost none do to this day. Those who became converts began getting together and starting small communities with the help of the Humans. It was in one of those villages that I was born."

"Is that why you know our language, the Humans taught it to you?"

"Yes it is, little one," Katchut said in answer to Pheltic's question. "You must be a Dwarie, not many among my people have ever seen one of your race. Anyway, by the time I had grown to adulthood, the Traul and Nomie races started taking notice of—and hating—those who were followers of the Path. By my twentieth year, our rulers had made the Path follower religion against the law. They began to round up, kill, torture, and imprison us. Those of us still living were enslaved to work in the fields and the underground mines. Most are in the mines now, extracting metal ore for the Dark Overlord's weapons.

Those of us you see here, and our families back at camp, live in constant fear and hiding."

"And your faith has endured all this time, through all this trial and persecution?" Deeli asked in amazement.

"Our faith has grown stronger. It is the Lord who has kept us through it all. We would rather die than be without Him."

"I hope," Deeli said quietly, "that I would have the same strength under those circumstances. Once again dear Haub, it seems the Humans have turned out to be the best missionaries." Haub smiled with pride at the compliment given to his race.

Once the large group had reached the foothills they turned north and continued on until mid-afternoon. They came upon a rushing stream flowing out of the eastern mountains, and crossed over on a hand-made log bridge. On the other side of the stream was a grove of bright red pines like those they had seen from on top of the plateau. Deeli had been right; the color of the trees up close was unbelievably vivid, and the smell was sweet, almost intoxicating. They were led through the pines into a large clearing where buildings and tents had been erected. A low cliff of rock stood off a little way behind the structures and was riddled with caves. There were many more people of the tribe here at the camp; even a few Nomies walked by them and stared.

"The new ruler of our people has been too busy with his plans to conquer your home to bother with us. We have seen an increase in patrols looking for something lately, but we knew not what. Of course now we may have our answer," Katchut said eyeing the little group. "But we can talk of these things later, after the evening meal. The food is being prepared for us now."

"Thank you," Pheltic exclaimed. "We haven't had much to eat lately." The males of the tribe began to drag tables out to the central part of the compound and set them end-to-end in rows.

"We like to eat our last meal of the day together as a community. It helps us to stay close and strong in our beliefs." The companions were set down to what they considered, on this journey, to be a feast. There were several kinds of meat and fish. One of the meats was called a hopper; Matthew figured it was probably some kind of rabbit. There were vegetables, fruit, and freshly cooked bread with a red-colored honey to go on it. Matthew fell in love with this and ate so much bread that Pheltic made fun of him. They also had fresh mountain water and glasses of peach-colored juice made from fruit that grew nearby. When the meal was finished, Matthew and the south landers were as full and satisfied as they had ever been.

"I trust we have treated you with respect and honor," Katchut said to the companions. "Normally after our evening meal we have a bonfire, but because of the increase in the Enlightened One's patrols we will have to keep the fire small tonight. The whole tribe gathers around to sing songs of the faith and read from the Holy Words."

"You have a copy of the Holy Words?" Deeli asked.

"Yes, when the Humans went back to the south they left the village of my parents one copy. We now have that copy and keep it safely put away, but have made other copies in our own tongue. Would you like to join us tonight?" Gamilon remained silent, but the others eagerly accepted the invitation. Everyone at the tables helped to clear them and clean up the area. When finished, the whole tribe led the outsiders to the fire pit. This was in the center of the compound and they all gathered around it in a circle, sitting on logs. The sun was very low; crickets were playing their song in the background, and a small fire crackled cheerfully. The secure feeling of friendship mixed with the smell of smoke from the hardwood fire lent a dream-like quality to the proceedings.

"Before we start, I would ask a favor of you," Katchut said. "If we have treated you well, I beg of you to tell us who you are and why you have come here?" Matthew had been wondering when the question would be asked, but surprisingly it was put very politely and not made into a demand. As the best story teller among them, Deeli was chosen to relate their purpose to the tribe.

"You might as well start at the beginning, Napdeeliate, where Matthew supposedly fell out of the sky," Gamilon said just before Deeli started talking. At the mention of Deeli's given name the entire tribe grew very quiet and tense.

"Gamilon, I really wish you would not use my old name."

"Are you truly the terrible Napdeeliate of our legends?" Katchut asked, standing to his feet and looking like he might have to defend himself. "The one who stood beside the Elven King during the Great War, who later led the Elves in ransacking our land and killing our leaders?" Deeli hung his head in shame. Matthew could not believe it, even in the north they had heard of his friend and companion.

"Deeli," Matthew said, "does everybody know who you are?"

"I told you that I had been to the north before," Deeli answered, then turned to Katchut. "Yes, I am he. Those things happened long ago, before I became a follower of the Path. I am guilty of many wrongs in my life, many of them against your people. But I have received the grace and forgiveness of the Creator through His Son, Shesea. I only hope I can have yours." Katchut walked over and stood before Deeli, tension filling the air. No one knew what would happen next. Matthew found his hand gravitating to the hilt of Excalibur, just in case he had to do battle for his friend; though he knew the sword was now just an ordinary blade.

"The Lord has taught us to forgive as we have been forgiven," Katchut said. "We rejoice that the enemy of our people is gone, and in his place is a new being. From this moment forward let every member of this tribe strike the name of Napdeeliate from their heart and memory, and in its place will go Deeli, our friend and brother." Katchut gave Deeli a big bear hug and all of the tribe applauded and laughed. Matthew was awed at what the grace of God could accomplish. He looked toward Sharineas, who sat by a seemingly unmoved Gamilon, and saw the Princess wipe a tear from her cheek. Deeli stood before the fire and addressed everyone seated.

"Thank you for your forgiveness. I know well that I do not deserve it." After a moment of quiet, Deeli began to speak. "You must know of the attack on our valley about two seven-days ago in the clearing where our Lord was put to death. And of the great slaughter of our people, including Haub's wife and children, that took place there." Katchut looked at Haub with a sad expression, the rest of the tribe registering shock and sympathy.

"I am sorry, friend Haub. We knew of the war band that went south, but not of what transpired there. We are cut off here, for our own protection."

"Then you do not know that the sword Calburnathis has been drawn from the Great Tree!" Deeli said with shock. The entire tribe caught their breath. "During the battle young Matthew here drew the sword and ended the attack. Before leaving, the Traul war chief issued a challenge for Matthew to face the Dark One. So here we are on our way and trying to stay undetected." All eyes were now on Matthew who had drawn the sword for everyone to see. Even without the blue lightning and glowing gem it was still an impressive sight.

"I don't know how much good it will do us now," Matthew said in a dejected tone. "All the magic and power seem to have gone out of it."

"No Matthew, do you not see?" Deeli asked. "The sword knew that there was no real enemy in these Trauls. We just thought these good people were a threat, but Calburnathis knew better. There was no need for a show of power, and I am sure that the next time there is a threat the sword will respond." That had not dawned on Matthew, who had just spent the entire day worrying about it. He sat back down with a half-convinced smile.

"I hope you're right, Deeli. It wouldn't be good to walk up to this Dark Lord and find out you're wrong." Katchut was finally getting over his initial awe and was able to speak again.

"Do you mean to tell us that this is the sword of prophecy, right here in our very midst? That the time has finally come, and the sword goes to meet its destiny?" Deeli nodded his confirmation and Katchut broke into a huge grin. "Brother, you bring good news. The Lord has brought you to us and we would like to help. I know not how you got so far undetected. You must truly be what the patrols are looking for."

Deeli began his story then, by telling them that the Creator had guided their steps and kept them safe. He then proceeded to tell of their travels so far. Matthew enjoyed listening to Deeli. He was a master story teller, and it was almost as if their adventures had happened to someone else. Both he and Pheltic found themselves laughing at times, then on the edge of their seat in the next moment. The only place there was an interruption in the narrative was when Deeli mentioned the Place of Fear. The tribe began to talk among themselves, and Katchut put to voice what was on their minds.

"You have been in the Place of Fear? You have come through the forest alive? That has always been a dreaded place for our people, but even more so recently. It used to be a place where only criminals were sent, to be done away with, but that has all changed since the Enlightened One came into power. He has worked magic over that place to make it even more evil. The criminals he now uses in his experiments, making them into winged spies and an elite guard for himself. The Place of Fear is now reserved for his enemies, especially the followers of the Path."

Sharineas let out a gasp, and now it was the companions' turn to feel sorrow for their gentle new friends. "Yes, those too outspoken or too old to work as slaves are sent into the forest with only a small stone knife to protect themselves. No one comes out alive. Both of my parents were victims of the forest, as were many loved ones of those you see here." Katchut finished with a sweeping gesture of his hand. Deeli expressed his sympathy, and told about their ordeal in the forest. He went on with everything that happened after that and ended his story with the tribe finding them that morning by the lake.

The sun was even lower on the horizon now, casting long shadows of the red pine forest on the assembly. The Trauls began singing a simple praise song in their own language. Soon all the companions except Gamilon were attempting to sing along, although only Matthew and Deeli understood the meaning of the words. Gamilon, feeling uncomfortable with all the worship of Shesea, quietly got up and walked toward the forest to think. *They certainly seem happy and contented. I do wish I had more of that in my life. Sharineas seems to be fitting right in with them, but I cannot spit on my forefathers and their beliefs. These people can't be right—Shesea is only for simple fools. I know that Napdeeliate is no simpleton though, no matter how he sometimes acts—nor does this Matthew seem to be. I wish I understood all of this.* Gamilon continued struggling with his thoughts as he listened to the next song.

It was sung in the common tongue of the valley people, in courtesy for the guests. It was a beautiful worship song and before it was over, Matthew saw many hands raised in the air. Others were on their knees weeping. He was so touched by the Spirit of God that it felt as though he were floating on a cloud. Matthew looked over at the singing Elven Princess. Sharineas had no comprehension of what she was feeling, but a tear trickled down her cheek and awe filled her eyes. He knew the Spirit was at work on her and began to pray that He might have His way. Haub and Pheltic were both worshipping with the rest, but when Matthew looked to Deeli, he knew something was wrong. The Elf that had been a mentor, and almost a father to him since coming to this world, was singing the words, but with a look of sadness on his face. Matthew moved over to him. "What's wrong Deeli?"

"I know the Creator's Spirit is here," the old Elf answered with a miserable look in his eyes, "but I cannot feel Him. This absence I feel hurts unbearably."

"It's not fair," Matthew said accusingly. "Why would God desert you after all your service to Him?"

"Do not judge the Creator, Matthew. Who are we, the creation, to criticize what God does with His servants? Remember, He is sovereign over all. I know this separation is for some purpose, even if I do not see it right now. I have to trust Him to reveal that purpose in His time. Even if He chooses not to let me feel or hear Him again, I will still trust and serve until my deathday."

"I'm sorry," Matthew said admonished. "There is so much for me to learn. I am just concerned about you. I hate to see you hurting. You've been like a father to me. If it weren't for you, I never would have found the Lord and given my life back to Jesus. See, He is still using you even if you can't tell."

"The Lord is working his compassion into you my son, let it grow," Deeli said, as he gave Matthew a hug. "You are only a day old in the Lord and you are already ministering to me." As Deeli finished his sentence, a loud cry came up from one of the Trauls. Deeli and Matthew turned to see what the commotion was about. Out of the western sky flew three dark shapes.

"Mutants!" Katchut cried out. "Battle ready my people!" The females and children ran for the caves while the males went for their weapons. Matthew grabbed Excalibur. Sure enough, blue lightning flickered along the blade and the gem in the hilt glowed brightly. Three rocks came hurtling down. Two hit the ground with a thud, but one hit a Traul child running for the caves and killed him instantly. Matthew saw it happen and knew he would have no qualms about taking the lives of these monsters.

One of the winged Nomies turned northward as if to report their whereabouts. Deeli was about to yell that it needed to be stopped, but before he could open his mouth the Nomie fell to the ground with one of Gamilon's arrows protruding from its side. Haub, using Boreshia's bow and arrows, brought down another one. The creature was flopping around trying to get back up, so Matthew ran over and finished what Haub had started.

The third mutant saw what had happened to his comrades and tried to make a quick retreat. Suddenly, it screeched loudly and fell to the ground. Many Traul males quickly stopped the noises it was making. Matthew looked around to see who had brought the third creature down, and saw that it was Katchut with a sling in his hand. Deeli, Haub, Pheltic, and Matthew moved over to where Katchut was standing.

"Where is Sharineas? Has anyone seen her?" Matthew asked.

"I saw her run to where Gamilon was, over by the pines," Pheltic volunteered.

"At least those monsters cannot go report back to their master," Katchut said with steel in his voice. "All three are dead."

"Then why is Matthew's sword still acting funny?" Pheltic asked. Everyone looked at the blade that was still flickering with blue light. Before anyone could even theorize, a scream came from the direction of the red pine forest. Sharineas and Gamilon were being attacked by what looked like a twelve-foot tall Traul with leathery wings.

"By the Creator!" Katchut said. "That devil has found a way to mutate one of our kind to the point where it can fly! That thing must have flown in over the pines while we were fighting the other three." Everyone available began to run in the direction of the hideous creature, but Matthew knew that they would not reach the two Elves in time.

Gamilon had pushed Sharineas toward the pines and now stood—sword raised—between her and the monster. The mutated creature stood on two legs, towering above the Elf at least seven feet. It had nasty looking claws at the end of long muscular arms and a rough hide for skin. Gamilon was slicing at arms that were outstretched toward him, trying to buy time for reinforcements to reach them. The agile Elf danced out of the creature's reach, still slashing away with his sword. The mutated Traul, finally realizing that the Elf's weapon could not hurt him, moved in swiftly and accurately. With one massive clawed hand it hit Gamilon in the chest and sent him flying through the air. At that moment a few of the tribe reached the enraged monster. It began swatting at them like flies, but all managed to stay out of reach. The monster saw a flickering blue light coming at him and, knowing that which he sought was here, turned toward it.

Matthew was almost to the creature when it turned toward him. He was furious that this evil could attack and kill innocents like this tribe. The monster looked at him with red eyes and Matthew saw both evil and cunning there. A huge clawed hand came around out of the darkness toward Matthew's head, but he met it with the edge of Excalibur. The giant mutated Traul shrieked in pain and rage as a razor-sharp talon was disconnected from its arm. The thing backed away knowing that the sword and its bearer were too much for him alone. The creature let out a fierce snarl, and holding the bloody stump with its good hand, turned, wings flapping, trying to get away.

"Matthew," Deeli yelled. "If that creature gets away the Dark One will know where we are!" Matthew was way ahead of him though. Making a huge leap, he reached the winged Traul just as it was about to lift off from the ground. He swung Excalibur with blinding speed. Crackling with energy, the sword sliced through one of the creature's huge wings, leaving half of it on the ground. The monster fell to the ground hard, not ready for what had happened. Matthew was on the creature quickly, and with tears of frustration and anger in his eyes, he cut off the oversized head. Everyone gathered around in shock with not a word spoken until the silence was broken by a cry from Sharineas.

"Please, someone come quickly! I think Gamilon has been hurt badly." They rushed over—Katchut picked up the wounded Elf as if he were weightless, and carried him back to the fire. Gamilon's chest was torn completely open and blood was seeping onto the ground. In the flickering fire light the glistening blood looked black and alive. With a weak smile Gamilon looked up at Sharineas.

"See, I told you that you'd need me along for protection."

"Oh Gamilon," was all Sharineas could get out between her sobs. Matthew knew the Elf did not have long. Deeli's herbs and bandages could not mend this wound.

"Gamilon, before it's too late," Matthew whispered hoarsely, "accept Shesea as your Lord, please!" Gamilon did not get mad as Matthew expected, only smiled and looked up at him.

"Not you too, Matthew," The young Elf went into a coughing fit, causing the blood seeping out of his chest to bubble. "I have gained respect for you, half-breed, but I will trust in the place that the Creator has for my people. I'm sorry we can't agree on this, but I do not believe

He was God's Son." Suddenly, Gamilon's eyes opened wide in terror and his body convulsed, then went stiff. Matthew realized that the Elf had been looking at something in the next life, not this one. He reached down, and with reverence closed Gamilon's sightless eyes. Sharineas was sobbing loudly now; arms around Deeli and her head buried in his chest. Katchut's wife brought a blanket and placed it over Gamilon's body. The tribe began to recover and slowly started moving into the caves.

"We will spend the night in the caves," Katchut said quietly, "in case there are any more of these winged atrocities." As everyone was moving toward the caves, Sharineas began to get her weeping a little more under control and was finally able to speak.

"Uncle, why did Gamilon have such a look of terror in his eyes?" She asked shakily.

"I wish I was not the one to tell you this, my dear.... Those were the eyes of someone who goes to face the judgment of the Creator alone, with no one at his side."

Chapter

17

Watches were posted the rest of the night. Any sleep that did come was fitful and light. The entire camp was on edge, fearful that another monster might be roaming the skies or the forest. The day dawned with a sky full of clouds and a chill wind blowing; to everyone's relief, no more attacks had occurred during the night. The people of the little village were sad and despondent, and the weather suited them well. They took the bodies of Gamilon and the child that had been killed to a small cemetery in a clearing amidst the red pines. There they buried them side by side with a large and a small rock to mark each of their graves. Deeli knew that it would be the ultimate insult for someone like Gamilon to be buried alongside a Traul in one of their cemeteries—but knew also that there was no time to be digging a separate grave. In any case there seemed to be a certain poetic justice in it. Maybe, after all he had seen, Gamilon would not have minded so much after all.

It was a sad service for both groups. The tribe took it especially hard when one of their children died. Burying Gamilon was not an easy task for the little group from the valley either. They knew from the noble young Elf's dying statement that he had not accepted Shesea as Lord, and at least four of them believed he would spend eternity separated from God.

Sharineas was so upset and confused over Gamilon's death, that she was unable to think clearly about anything. She tried to put it out of her mind, but the look in her betrothed's eyes as he slipped into death kept coming back to haunt her. Matthew, too, was genuinely distraught; Gamilon had saved his life several times. He was actually beginning to like the brash Elf and had harbored a hope that in time they might become friends.

Deeli watched as members of the Traul tribe began to shovel dirt on Gamilon's body. *I was so much like him at that age. In time he might have come around. Why Lord? Could You not have spared him, given him a little longer as You gave me? But You understand all things better than I. Shesea, please forgive this tired old Elf his questions.* Deeli knew that if he had died at Gamilon's age there would have been no heaven waiting, no loving Savior with open arms. He had rejected Shesea at that age every bit as much as Gamilon. He too would have been facing judgment without the atoning blood and mercy of God's Son. Deeli shivered in the chill air. *I am too old for this kind of running around. I should be back home in my comfortable cottage teaching the new converts.* He walked over and put his arm around Sharineas, feeling older and more weary than at any other time in his life. "I am sorry, my dear. He was brave and self-sacrificing. Gamilon would have made a fine husband for you some day."

"...I don't know if we would ever have married," Sharineas answered without lifting her head, "but we had been friends since childhood. I can't remember a time when Gamilon wasn't a part of my life.... I shall miss him greatly." She began to weep again.

"Sharineas, why do you not stay here and recuperate? When this business is all over we will come back for you."

"No uncle, I have to stay with this until the end... something compels me."

"That something is the Creator's Spirit; He wants you for His own."

"Uncle, I have served the Creator my entire life, I do belong to Him."

"He knows that child, and it is probably why you are here. You have proven yourself trustworthy, but you still lack His Son. We all need to come to a repentance of the evil that lives in us and be cleansed by the blood of Shesea; it is the only way. I know it sounds absurd that a sweet, young, innocent Elf maiden would need to repent of evil. But no one who is born into this fallen world can stand before a Holy God on their own good works and righteousness."

"I know that my heart is not pure all of the time," Sharineas began. "I have broken some of the commandments—inside if not out. It is still hard for me to ignore all that I have been taught and believed in my whole life. Please, you must give me more time."

"I am sorry young one, I never want to force or manipulate you into this," Deeli said holding his great niece close. "A decision like this must be made from the heart and on your own, with no outside pressure, or it is not real. It is just that you mean so much to me. Ever since your birth you have been the apple of my eye, though I am sure you were never told. You were too young to remember when I was sent away. What hurt the most the day I left was knowing that I would not see you grow up, or be there for you when you needed me. Now the Lord has brought you back to me, and if anything were to happen to you without being covered with His blood...I just do not know what I would do."

"Oh uncle," Sharineas choked on her own tears. "I don't know what to think anymore, about you or your beliefs. I'm finding that all of the things I was told about you are false, and I am glad. One thing I do know is that I love you." They stood near the grave with a chilly, wet wind blowing on them. The young and old holding one another, weeping over the things in life they could not control—all the while Deeli was thanking the Lord for reuniting him with his niece.

When the service was over, what was left of the little group from the valley met in Katchut's cabin. The Traul leader, along with his wife and children, was present also. "We have been delayed far too long," Deeli announced. "The enemy could be at the pass this very moment for all we know. We must leave today and head straight northwest. Being cautious has helped, but not enough to save poor Gamilon. I believe it is time to go on the offensive."

"I have asked the tribe as you requested," Katchut spoke up, "but no one has ever heard of any rainbow trees. Nor have they heard of an unguarded entrance to the black fortress. I'm sorry my friends."

"It looks like we will have to head in that direction and see what happens."

"I believe you are right, Matthew," Deeli responded. "It seems that once again we are left with only one choice."

"You could take a seldom-used route that would keep you hidden from unwanted attention," Katchut offered, "if you will let me guide you."

"You cannot leave your wife and children," Haub said in a sudden outburst. "They will need your protection."

"It is you who are the primary target, not the village. The entire tribe is moving into the cave system where there is plenty of room; we have done this before. The tribe has already discussed this, and as leader I have the right of first choice in volunteering my services. My wife and children know and understand the danger, and they agree with me. The child that was murdered belonged to my wife's brother's widow, her only son." No one had realized how close to the home of Katchut the tragedy of the dead child was, and immediately began giving their condolences to the family.

"Katchut," Deeli began. "If you really believe this is what you must do, then I am sure that we would all be glad to have you along." Everyone agreed and welcomed the Traul as they would family, which is what the little company had become.

The Quest of the Sword ate well at the midday meal served to them by their newest member. The tribe joined together in packing them food for the rest of their journey, as well as warm clothing for the northern weather. Katchut said a touching good-bye to his family; then the companions—once again six—started on their way once more. The huge Traul, armed with a large mace and an even bigger sword, led them directly north for all of that day and most of the next. They wound their way through forests, fields, and more desolate rock-strewn areas as they came closer to the northern mountains. The air also became much colder—by the time they turned west, the party could see the evidence of their breath billowing in vaporous clouds all about them. Matthew was astonished that they could go from spring-like weather to almost winter in less than a week; he was also thankful for the extra clothing given to them by Katchut's tribe. They were all very grateful that they saw no patrols or winged spies along the way so far.

The companions walked the rest of that day and the next, straight west. Sometimes they traveled through the winding paths of the forested foothills; other times in the open country, but always on paths that had not seen use in recent history. That night was spent in a clearing amidst a cluster of pines. The moon was new and they dared not light a fire, so it was very difficult to see one another. They wrapped themselves in the furs that had been provided by Katchut's tribe and talked a little before going to sleep.

The valley dwellers got to know Katchut much better, listening to the stories of his people and how they kept their faith alive. Sharineas had been very quiet and withdrawn since Gamilon's death, but tonight she was asking many questions about Shesea and the Path follower beliefs. Matthew thought for sure tonight Sharineas would give her heart to Jesus. To his great disappointment, it did not happen.

In time, the conversations split between the younger and the older. Matthew, Pheltic, and Sharineas spent time talking among themselves as young people do, tightening the bonds of their friendship even more. Sharineas told them of a Princess' life in the Elven kingdom, as well as of Gamilon. After hearing stories about the brash Elf, Pheltic and Matthew felt as if they understood Gamilon a little more, and were sorry they would never get to know him better.

Matthew told his new friends more about his world. The other two could scarcely comprehend most of what he said, although Pheltic was intrigued by the descriptions of cities and technology. After a while the conversation of the older adults turned to gaining entrance to the dark fortress. The other three heard this and joined them. "If we storm the front gates, then all of our secrecy was in vain," Deeli said. "But if we take the time to look for the rainbow trees it may be too late for the valley. I must admit, I have no direction from the Lord on this matter. Haub, Katchut, has His still small voice said anything to you on this?"

"No, I am afraid not," Katchut answered.

"I have to be honest," Haub replied with down cast eyes. "I have been doing my best not to listen...afraid to hear that revenge will be denied me." There was a silence following—everyone knew that Haub was still going through a great deal of pain.

"A still small voice, is that how the Creator speaks?" Pheltic finally asked, breaking the awkward silence.

"He speaks in many ways, little one," Deeli answered. "But yes, that and His Holy Word is how He most often communicates with us. There are many voices though, that would clamor for your attention. That is why it is so important to study the word, so that you can discern and recognize His voice from among the others that would whisper in your ear. The Evil One will come against you all the more, now that you have given your life to Shesea. Listening to his voice will put not only your body in danger, but your soul as well." Pheltic shivered at the mention of the dread Keeper of the Underworld. The talk slowed down and everyone agreed it was time for sleep, but not before Katchut gave them something on which to think.

"We will have to decide by tomorrow which entrance we are going for. The split in the path will be reached before nightfall. It will also be getting colder, for we will be traveling farther north."

"Colder!" Matthew and Pheltic gasped in unison; leaning close to one another with mock shivers to show their distress.

"Ha," Katchut chuckled. "The young are the same no matter what race they belong to." They all had a good laugh at the two's expense and retired, once again taking turns guarding the camp throughout the night.

The group awoke the next morning shivering in the pre-dawn light; frost covered grass crunching beneath their feet. Matthew figured the temperature to be in the twenties, and was not accustomed to, nor happy about, sleeping outside in this kind of weather. After breaking their fast on cold meat and fruit, the companions traveled west and north all that day; keeping a constant eye out for the enemy. Haub walked with Katchut as he led the way. The two were becoming fast friends—realizing that even though there were many differences, they had much in common as well. Deeli and Pheltic walked at the end of the little procession. The young Dwarie spent the whole day bombarding Deeli with questions—about everything from the Great War to his new found faith. Deeli acted as though all the questioning was a nuisance, but in reality loved every minute of it.

Matthew was grateful for Pheltic's inquisitiveness. It gave him a chance to spend time with Sharineas. He was beginning to admit that his feelings for her just might be growing. The two talked all day, sharing their views on many subjects common to both of their worlds. Matthew had never known a female he could be so open with, or who was so open with him. No matter how bluntly, she always told him the truth. The small party was feeling safe. Once again they had not seen a sign of the enemy all day. The sun was on the horizon when Katchut announced that the path would split just ahead in the forest that they were about to enter.

Under the huge trees of the forest it was almost completely dark. The sun had been dipping low toward the horizon when they entered. The group had voted unanimously to look for the entrance described in Deeli's writings. Katchut said he knew of a place on that path to spend the night, so it was decided to try to make it there before night fell completely. Katchut and Haub also knew that they would be safer spending the night in the cover of the forest, rather than the open fields where they could be spotted by the Dark One's patrols. The path in the forest was extremely winding. That, together with the darkness, at times caused the companions to lose sight of each other. At one point Pheltic tripped and fell over a tree root in the path. Deeli, walking directly behind the little Dwarie, fell right on top of him. The other four were around another bend in the path and did not know the two had taken a spill. When the old Elf and young Dwarie had finally gotten themselves untangled, it was apparent that Pheltic had hurt his ankle. Deeli pulled out strips of cloth that he had gotten from Katchut's tribe and bound Pheltic's ankle for support. Finally Deeli managed to get his small friend walking again and they started out along the dark and treacherous path.

Suddenly, they heard the sound of a snapping branch come from behind them. Deeli turned his head in time to see a club strike him in the face. Everything went black. Pheltic also turned and gave a loud yell. Directly behind Deeli's falling body were two huge Trauls, a kind he had never seen before. They were even bigger than Katchut, who was the biggest Traul Pheltic had ever seen. Both had clawed hands, fangs, and moved toward him with un-Traul-like grace. Yelling loudly was all Pheltic had time to do before he too was knocked unconscious.

Pheltic's yell alerted the other four who had reached the fork in the path at just that moment.

A patrol of twelve, magically altered Trauls had spotted the companions as they entered the forest. These were a special experiment of the mysterious Enlightened One—a part of his elite guard. These Trauls were not only bigger and stronger; but had increased intelligence, speed, and were specially armed. Instead of giving immediate chase and giving themselves away, the patrol waited for the group to enter the forest, and then quietly followed. When the opportunity presented itself, they struck. The two mutants who captured Deeli and Pheltic stayed with them while the other ten ran on ahead with weapons drawn.

Katchut, Haub, Matthew, and Sharineas began running back down the path when they heard the yell. When Matthew pulled Excalibur out and saw the flicker of blue lightning and glow of the gem, he knew something was seriously wrong. The two groups met at a twist in the path with a loud clash. There was very little room for fighting, but the mutated Trauls lived for this kind of thing and knew what to do. They fanned out among the trees and came at the little cluster of heroes from three sides. They had not, however, counted on the power of the sword.

Matthew engaged the first Traul with its magically altered blade, which resulted in a shower of sparks. This blade did not break in half at Excalibur's bite as a normal sword would have. This, plus the strength and agility of the creature, caused Matthew to be less sure of this battle's outcome, although in the end, the sword of prophecy proved to be too much for them. Matthew had killed three of the mutated Trauls and was fighting a fourth when he noticed Haub and Katchut. They were having a hard time with the creatures and their magical weapons. The two were holding their own, but just barely. Two of the creatures were down and stunned by the power of the amulet. Matthew's fifth attacker backed-off after seeing the fourth one die. Matthew was thankful for the breather and turned his head to see how his friends were doing. Seemingly out of nowhere, something struck the side of his head; he had left one Traul unaccounted for. Matthew turned in that direction but—because of the darkness, and the haze before his eyes caused by the blow—he could not see a thing. In a dazed panic he lashed out with the sword creating a very impressive light show, but connecting with nothing.

The four mutated Trauls that were still standing, decided to back-off and regroup when Matthew went crazy with his sword. This was more than they had bargained for, but knew that the boy and his sword were what their master had been raving about. Haub and Katchut came up behind Matthew with Sharineas right behind them. Matthew quit swinging the sword for a moment and felt wet, sticky blood on the side of his head. He was feeling very faint now, but still managed to announce that he was going back after Pheltic and Deeli. After taking one step he fell to his knees and dropped the sword—barely conscious. Katchut tried to retrieve the blade and was amazed that he could not pick it up off the ground.

"We must get Matthew and the sword safely away from here," Katchut said. Haub was reluctant to agree, but finally did so. Deeli had been a father to him for many years, and the big Human wanted more than anything to go back for him; but he also knew what had to be done and what Deeli would want. He coaxed Matthew to put Calburnathis back in its scabbard just before the Sword Bearer slipped into unconsciousness. Then Haub, together with Katchut, carried him up the path with Sharineas in the lead. They went as fast as possible, not knowing if the remaining mutants were following. When they came to the fork in the path there was no discussion. Sharineas silently led her three companions down the path that would take them behind the dark fortress.

The same night that Deeli and Pheltic were separated from their companions, the combined Traul, Nomie, and Human army arrived at the northern pass. As soon as the first troops were spotted, a message was sent to the leaders of the valley forces. The message was brought to King Peridon first, who in turned called a meeting with King Moark, his son Telick, King Hydrian, and Roak. They groaned outwardly at the news. The wall was almost finished, but not completely. The only rea-son that it was this far along was because of the females who had vol-unteered for nursing duty during the battle. Going against orders, females from every race arrived four to six days early to help work on the wall. Knowing that the enemy was almost upon them overrode the males' pride, and the female help was gratefully accepted.

"We can work through the night," Telick was first to speak, "using torches, it's the only way to finish. But I'm afraid all of the workers are tired, especially the Elves. No offense intended King Peridon, but your people don't have the same strength and stamina as the Dwaries or Humans." Afraid he had offended the Elven King, Telick quickly continued. "Although everyone will be too tired to fight if we have to work through the night."

"Most likely they will not attack until their whole army is here," the Elven King responded, ignoring the comment about his people. "Fortunately for us they will probably stop moving them in at nightfall, which is almost upon us. Hopefully it will take them at least half a day to get the rear troops here and organized. That will give us time to rest in the morning before they attack. I suggest that we join the workers now and try to get this thing completed by then." The other four agreed and the meeting was adjourned. King Peridon's hopes were well founded and came to pass more fully than he would have liked.

The allied races worked far into the night. A few hours before dawn though, too many mistakes were made and the work was halted, the wall left unfinished. That morning, after only a few hour's sleep, the determined valley dwellers roused themselves and completed the project. It was now midday and the sounds of preparing for battle filled the air. The four leaders were expecting a message at any time, giving them estimations on the size and strength of the enemy. They spent this waiting time walking along the wall surveying the results.

The structure was a monument to Dwarie ingenuity and skill, a symbol of what the races could accomplish in unity. It was thirty feet high and covered the entire one hundred and fifty yards or so of the mountain opening. A walkway, the width of two Humans laying end to end, had been built at the top, and ran the entire length of the wall. It was sturdy enough to hold all the warriors that could fit. Huge pots of oil were being brought to a boil as part of the defenses. Piles of skull-sized rocks lined the walkway and the ground below ready to be brought up to the battlements. Many ladders and sets of stairs had been built up to the battlements. These would allow many warriors to ascend and descend at the same time. The work of making arrows continued feverishly even now, and quite a stockpile had been accumulated. The Dwarie catapults were already set up and being tested for range and accuracy. They had many rocks for the catapults as well as tar covered logs that could be set ablaze and sent over the wall. Now that the wall was completed, it seemed that everything was running smoothly.

By late afternoon, however, the troops were getting a little jumpy. There was still no sign of the enemy, or any messages from the scouts. King Peridon had been purposely keeping himself busy so as not to think about his missing daughter and future son-in-law. Now, with nothing to do but wait, he could not keep his mind from those troublesome thoughts. By sunset the only sign of an enemy army was a still-lingering cloud of dust over the northern end of the pass. The valley people were on edge and could not sleep, wondering if the black horde would attack at night. Finally, about three hours after sunset, an Elven scout arrived with news. Peridon quickly called a meeting with the other leaders to hear the scout's report. The moment the scout walked into the tent Peridon let his stress show.

"Where have you been!? You were supposed to be here as soon as the last troops arrived...well?"

"But, my King," the young Elf stammered, "I did. All day I expected to be leaving at any moment, but the army kept coming. All day, they just kept coming out of the forest, spreading out like a sea of black oil all over the ground. Finally, at dark, my captain told me to leave and report what was happening. When I left, we could see the army still coming out of the forest with torches in hand. They are even stretched out along the mountains on either side of the pass. My captain thinks they are planning to come over the mountains as well as through the pass."

"But that would be suicide," King Moark shouted. "We would have every advantage. We would cut them down as they tried to ascend the mountain."

"Yes sir," the scout countered, "but there are so many of them they can afford a frontal assault. It won't matter how many they lose, there will be more to take their place. It will be even easier for them if they force us to spread our troops too thin." To everyone's surprise, the usually quiet Hydrian let his feelings be known.

"Your scout is right in his observance of the situation. If the enemy number is really as he describes it, we have no defense."

"Sir," the Elven scout said stiffly, "I can assure you I do not lie."

"I am sorry, I did not mean to imply that you do. Can you give us any more information about what they are up to?"

"The troops that arrived first immediately began cutting down huge trees and fashioning battering rams."

"The winged Nomies have obviously reported the construction of the wall to their commanders," Telick said through clenched teeth. "Any surprise that would have been to our advantage is now completely gone."

"Sirs," the scout tested to see if he could speak further. His King gave him a nod and he continued. "One of the reasons the army has so many more warriors than we expected is because of all the Humans with them," he said looking at Roak.

"The fools!" Roak said with a grimace. "Those outside the valley would even kill their own kind for more power and possessions."

"Thank you, soldier," Peridon said. "You have done a good job, and I should not have accused you as I did. Go get some rest now. I'm sure I will need you again in the morning." The scout saluted and took his leave. The leaders planned strategies into the early hours of the morning and then caught a few hours of sleep.

An hour after sunrise found all of them on top of the walkway watching in a northerly direction down the pass. They saw the cloud of dust moving first—a dark brown stain smeared across the sky coming toward them. Soon, line after line of armor-clad warriors, stretching from one side of the pass to the other, came into sight. Out front, leading them all, was the war chief who had led the attack on the clearing; same black helmet with protruding horns, one arm raised arrogantly in the air.

The Humans, Elves, and Dwaries alike balked at what they saw. The pass was full of the enemy troops and more stretched back as far as the eye could see. Far more warriors than they could ever have imagined—the victory they had envisioned was suddenly just a fading dream. Many trembled in fear at the sight, but not one let it show outwardly. Whether religious or not, most of those behind the wall began to pray. King Peridon felt numb looking out over the ugly black mass that had come to destroy him, his family, and all those living in the valley. *It just may be,* the Elven King thought. *It just may be that judgment day is upon us after all.*

Chapter

18

Deeli opened one of his eyes a crack; wincing in pain he shut it again. He could tell that his face was swollen because his left eye would not open at all, and that same side felt as if it weighed twice what it should. The elderly Elf also knew that the sun was up and bright, but little else. Deeli continued to lie still where he was, trying to drown out the pain by concentrating on his surroundings. He was lying on some kind of crude litter, being jostled around like so much baggage. Opening his eye again, Deeli could see that the wide stretcher was being carried by four mutated Traul warriors. His hands were tied tightly together behind his back cutting off the circulation. *What could have happened? One minute I am helping Pheltic walk through a forest, and the next thing I know I am here.*

The young Dwarie was lying next to him and now began to moan. *I guess there is no sense in feigning unconsciousness any longer, Deeli* thought. "How are you feeling, Pheltic?" The Dwarie rolled over and opened his eyes, looking at Deeli uncomprehendingly. Finally his eyes focused and Pheltic realized what was happening.

"I feel like...run over by horses...or something. ...But I don't feel as bad as you look. Where are the others? What's happened to them?"

"I do not know the fate of the others. I can only pray that they have escaped capture and are all right. It would seem to me that we have been captured by the Dark One's warriors and are being escorted to him." Pheltic felt a cold fist grip his heart. *This isn't how it's supposed to happen*, he thought in terror. *We're not supposed to face the Dark Lord in chains, without Matthew and the sword!* High adventure was much less appealing than he had first imagined it to be. Thoughts of a slow ago-nizing death filled Pheltic's mind as he was bounced up and down on his way to the dark fortress.

The Trauls stopped to rest twice during the journey, giving their captives a good look at them. They were taller than Katchut and wore leather armor. In the places where there was no armor the pair could see a gray, reptilian hide. Their canines protruded out of closed mouths in a curve almost to the chin. When the mutants did look at their cap-tives it was through red eyes with shining black dots in the center. Deeli wondered how many had originally attacked them and the fate of his friends who had become more than a family to him. When he tried to question his captors, the only answer he received was a low growl and a back hand across his already bruised face.

After the final rest for the day, the prisoners were made to walk. Wrists tied tightly behind their backs and a leash on each throat; they were pushed and shoved through the barren land. The gray rock that surrounded them on every side was the same bleak color as the sky; nei-ther inspired much hope. The end of their journey found them hiking up a steep incline leading between two snow-capped mountains. The temperature grew colder as they went and even with the warm cloth-ing given to them by Katchut's tribe, they could barely keep going. Their lips and hands were turning blue, and any extra clothing had long since been lost in the forest when they were attacked. The Trauls—worried about what would happen to themselves if these par-ticular prisoners did not make it back alive—untied their hands, but kept the leashes tight around their throats.

The sun was still up, but could not be seen. The gray clouds that completely dominated the sky were now turning almost black. They were high enough in the mountains now that there were huge snow drifts on either side of the wide rocky path. It was nearly nightfall when the huge fortress came into view, towering over them even from a distance. The stone of the old castle looked blackened, almost burnt; everything around it lonely and desolate. Deeli could feel the presence of evil wash over him like a flood, and the hair on Pheltic's neck was standing on end. The two were hungry, cold, tired and sore. Feelings of hopelessness and dread had settled on both of them and increased as they drew nearer to the fortress. As they approached the gateway of the outer wall, a huge iron grid was pulled up with a loud screech by two regular Traul soldiers, allowing them entrance.

Deeli and Pheltic were shoved across a large empty courtyard, the ground frozen and hard. They stumbled up huge stone stairs and were then pushed inside the dark castle. Inside everything was in shadows with only flickering wall torches to light the way. The architecture was unlike anything either of them had ever seen, and it seemed almost as cold inside as outside. The four Traul soldiers marched them down a long hallway past wooden, iron-bound doors until they were stopped in front of one. The valley dwellers were half-shoved down a flight of stone stairs until finally ending up in a long corridor. They were forced past a few more of the iron-bound doors and then stopped. One Traul opened a door and the others shoved Deeli and Pheltic inside. The Trauls chained them to a wall with their hands shackled above their heads. Then all four shuffled out the door and slammed it behind them, leaving their prisoners in total darkness. Once the mutants were out in the hall alone, they became very talkative, laughing and grunting as they headed back upstairs.

"Did you understand any of what they were saying?" Pheltic asked.

"Not really. I heard the words *wait* and *master*, but that was all I could make out. It sounds as though we may be getting a visit from their dark-hearted leader soon."

The two could not tell how long they stood there in the dark; talking, praying and trying to encourage one another. They were doing their best to produce a confidence that neither felt. Deeli was suffering from more than just physical ailments. Even now, praying as hard as he could, the Elven follower of Shesea could neither hear nor feel anything from his God. Dark whisperings came into Deeli's mind telling him that the Creator had abandoned him. That Shesea had no more use for an old Elf who had failed him so many times. The voice said that if Shesea were real and had the power to save him, why was He not here now? Deeli struggled through, trying to pray even though it seemed a useless gesture.

Pheltic was undergoing the same kind of whisperings, but on a different level. The Dwarie's main advantage was that he was still a child at heart. He still had the innocence and complete trust of someone newly born into the Path of Shesea. Pheltic was battered by doubts, but saw them through because his Lord had put a hedge of protection around him. After what seemed an eternity they heard voices coming from the corridor. Iron scraped against stone and the door to their cell creaked open. Torch light filled the little stone room, momentarily blinding the captives' eyes. Before their eyes had time to adjust; a raspy voice pierced the silence and caused Pheltic to wish they were still alone.

"Even with your face a mess I still recognize the famous Napdeeliate. ...You look surprised that I speak your common tongue and that I know you. Well, I know every language on this planet," the voice hissed. The captives' eyes were finally adjusting to the flickering light. Before them they saw two of the Trauls that had brought them to the fortress. A third figure stood between the other two.

Deeli found himself looking into the face of his tormentor with surprise. His jailer was a mixture the Elf had never seen before, half-Human and half-Traul. He was strong, and so tall that he had to bend his neck down to look at Deeli.

"Do I know you?" Deeli asked.

"Allow me to introduce myself. I am known as the Enlightened One. And no, you do not know me, old Elf, but I know you. As a matter of fact when I had the valley finally secured I was going to come looking for you. Now you have saved me all that trouble by coming right to my door."

"Why? What interest could you have in a washed up old hermit Elf like me?"

"My, aren't we inquisitive? Luckily it amuses me to answer you. I have been brought up all my life to hate your kind and most especially you. It was you, Napdeeliate, that tracked down and killed my father after the Great War!"

"Regrettably, I tracked down and killed many after the war. Which of those was your father, I know not," Deeli said losing some of the gentleness in his voice. The master of the Traul and Nomie races lashed out with a backhand across Deeli's face. The swollen side of the Elf's face split open afresh and blood trickled down his neck.

"My father was second only to the Great One himself, Chetick. He who sired me was war chief of the greatest army ever assembled," the half-Traul, half-Human screamed with madness in his eyes. "At least it was the greatest army. My army makes that one look like a band of Dwarie females," the Dark Lord said, now laughing as if he were having a pleasant breakfast with the two. "And yes, my mother was Human; one of no consequence. Just one of the many my father owned. Normally my father would have taken no notice of a bastard child, but he saw greatness in me. I was taken away from the Human women and raised by Trauls, learning from infancy to hate Elves."

"That would make you much older than you appear to be," Deeli stated calmly.

"What is appearance?" The Dark Lord asked with a throaty chuckle. "I can change that any time I wish. I have been schooled in dark magic since childhood. I have now surpassed any that have ever lived and mastered the black power. There is only one thing I hate more than Elves…the followers of Shesea. You can imagine my delight, and the new depths of hatred I felt when I heard that you, of all Elves, had converted. My hatred for you knows no bounds, but unfortunately I need you alive for the moment. Now! Where is the sword!?"

"And what sword might that be?" Deeli asked in his most innocent voice. The Dark Lord punched Deeli in the stomach as he let out a growl. Deeli coughed up blood in great hacking shakes; nearly losing consciousness in the process.

"The sword is where you'll never get your hands on it!" The Traul master slowly looked at the mouthy little Dwarie he had forgotten until now. He smiled and began to turn away as if Pheltic was just a bug on the wall. Suddenly the evil half-breed spun back around and punched King Moark's youngest son hard in the face. The sound was a sickening crunch and Pheltic's wound, which was nearly healed, opened up once more, gushing blood.

"Get this Dwarie whelp out of my sight," the Dark Lord screamed. Then as if another personality took over again he became completely calm. "Wait, leave him here. I think I may have plans for him. Now Napdeeliate, I want two things from you. I know if you are here, the sword is also. Do those four that were with you in the forest have it?" Deeli was silent. "No matter then, I'm sure it will be here shortly. When it is in my hands I will rule all the lands with an iron fist and wipe your kind from existence!"

"What makes you think you can even lift Calburnathis, let alone use its power?" Deeli spat out.

"The one I serve has shown me a way past that little problem, but that is none of your concern. What I want most from you Napdeeliate, is to hear you deny Shesea with your own mouth. A simple thing really, do it and I will let you and the Dwarie live. I can assure you that the alternative will be unpleasant."

"I could never do that!" Deeli answered boldly. "You might as well kill me now."

"Oh I will," the evil half-breed chuckled, "but it will be very slow and painful. First I think we will have some fun with your friend here. Bring me a brazier of hot coals," he snapped at one of the mutant Trauls behind him. "Are you sure you won't change your mind, Napdeeliate?" Both Deeli and Pheltic remained silent, which seemed to please the Dark Lord as much as if they had given him what he wanted.

A many-strand whip was brought in with the coals. The two Trauls ripped off the prisoner's outer garments. Deeli watched as his enemy began slowly, one stroke at a time, to whip Pheltic. The Dark Lord smiled cruelly while the watching Traul guards laughed. Pheltic whimpered slightly with each bloody lash, but did not cry out for mercy. Deeli, meanwhile, feverishly prayed. *Dear Shesea, if you never hear me again, please answer this one prayer. Please my Lord—spare Pheltic this trial. He is so new to Your path, and Your word says that no trial or temptation would come upon us greater than we can stand. Please make a way out for him that he may not lose his salvation.* Deeli could barely see his little friend anymore through the tears. Pheltic's face was lost in blood and more blood oozed from the stripes on his chest. As Deeli finished his prayer, the whimpering sounds coming from the Dwarie stopped and he sagged in his chains. Pheltic was still breathing, but the pain had made him black out. The Dark Lord stopped his whipping and threw the torturing tool down in disgust.

"There is little pleasure in the torturing of the unconscious. I thought the Dwarie race had a much higher tolerance for pain—I will have to remember this in the future. But you," he said turning to Deeli, "you will not be so lucky. I want you kept alive and in constant pain." He then drew a double edged dagger from his belt and ran one edge across Deeli's chest, leaving two small red lines in its wake. "Now Napdeeliate, do you still call Shesea Lord?"

"Of course I do," Deeli answered through clenched teeth. That response merited him a fist across the face. Pain shot through Deeli's skull as his head slammed against the hard stone wall.

"We shall see just what you're made of, old one!" Deeli's tormentor picked up the whip and began slashing at the chained Elf mercilessly. "Where is your Shesea now?" The Dark Lord screamed, once again enraged beyond reason. "I don't see Him coming to rescue you." Deeli did not respond except for small grunts as the whip made contact. Although somewhere in the back of the Elf's mind, he was asking the same questions. The Dark Lord finally stopped, panting and sweating; spittle dripping down his chin—frustration at his captive's silence written all over his face. He picked up a hot coal with a pair of metal tongs and held it in one of Deeli's open wounds.

A scream of pain escaped the Elf's lips, but no denial of his Lord. The room was instantly filled with the putrid smell of burnt flesh that the mutated Traul guards seemed to enjoy. "I can make this pain last a very long time if you wish it," the Dark Lord gloated. "If your God really loved you, would He let you go through this? Surely He would understand your denial under these circumstances." Deeli still remained silent, so his captor ordered the Elf's bare feet held up one at a time. Laughing with delight, the Emissary of the Evil One completely burned the soles of Deeli's feet.

"Do what you will," Deeli said, with so much pain in his voice that it was almost unrecognizable. Tears streamed from his swollen eyes, mixing with the blood on his face. "I will not deny He who gave me life. My Lord is able to deliver me if it be His will. If He does not…then I am sure there is a purpose in it." The Dark Lord clenched his fists in rage.

"You will deny Him before you die, that I can promise." He spun on his heel and headed toward the door. As he reached the door post he stopped and turned back to look at Deeli with smoldering eyes. "I thought you might be interested to know the news my winged spies have brought back. My army has arrived at the mountain pass into your precious valley. It seems that your people have erected some kind of crude wall. Rest assured, it will not stand. By this time tomorrow the valley will be mine, and its inhabitants destroyed. Make sure he stays alive," the Dark Lord ordered his guards. "I'm not through with him yet." With that, he stalked out of the cell and up the stone stairway. Deeli, who had been keeping himself conscious by force of will, finally let go and sank into blackness.

Chapter

19

Haub and Katchut were dragging the almost unconscious Matthew between them. Sharineas led the way, barely able to make out the path even with her Elven sight. Night had fallen completely now and the forest was shrouded in black shadows. With the setting of the sun the air had turned much colder; and the hard, frozen ground of the path became more slick with crystalline moisture as they walked. Katchut knew that up ahead was a cave where they could stay the night and tend to Matthew, but only if they could get there before their pursuers caught up to them. They were not sure if any of the mutants were still following, but no one wanted to stop and find out.

The companions were headed north on a path that led through a ravine at the foot of a mountain. The two Trauls that had been stunned by the amulet eventually regained consciousness and went back with the prisoners and their captors. The other four had recovered from

Matthew's onslaught and were back on the trail after their quarry. They were really not eager to meet up again with the half-breed who carried the sword, but knew that this was what their master had been ranting about for the past few seven-days.

The small party from the valley finally made it to the side path that would take them to Katchut's cave. This new path was so overgrown that Sharineas missed it, but Katchut recognized the spot as he was passing by. They took the path which led them to a small hole in the side of a cliff. It was not much of a cave, barely enough room for the four of them. Katchut had found it when he was escaping the slave pits many cycles back, using it to hide from those who were chasing him.

Katchut and Sharineas pulled Matthew into the cave while Haub went back to the main trail to cover their tracks. He made it look as though the small group had continued down the main trail, then hid himself, waiting to see if it would work. Sharineas in the meantime cared for Matthew—cleaning his head wound as best she could with water from her water-skin and a dirty blouse in her pack. Sharineas then tore up the blouse and used it to bandage the wound on Matthew's head. Then she sat, leaning against the cave wall with Matthew's head in her lap, and instantly fell asleep. Katchut sat just inside the cave mouth waiting for Haub to return. Presently he saw his new friend coming down the path toward the cave. When the tall Human ducked into the hole he gave Katchut a positive look.

"It seems we were successful. There were four Trauls following us, but they continued down the main path. I pray they don't backtrack later and find us."

"We should take turns at watch," Katchut suggested. He looked toward the sleeping forms of Matthew and Sharineas. "I don't believe those two will be waking tonight. I will take first watch, at least that way we will be ready to defend ourselves. Although I do not know how much of a chance we would have without Matthew and his sword." Haub was exhausted and did not argue. He lay down, but sleep was elusive. Thoughts of what might be happening to Deeli ran through his head until an equally troubled sleep finally did take him.

Sleep was like medicine to all of them. A bright, shining sun greeted the four as they emerged from the small cave. The brilliant ball of fire in the sky was even now burning off the frozen dew; causing the forest around them to be shrouded in a thick mist. There had been no sign of the pursuing Traul mutants during the night. Matthew had a bad headache and wobbled a little as he tried to walk.

Sharineas once again was the only one in the party who had retained her pack. All four shared the last of her food, keeping a vigilant eye out for their pursuers. After eating, Matthew was feeling much better—the pain in his head reduced to a slow throb—and they were able to begin their trek northward. They traversed rugged stone mountain trails, keeping their eyes peeled for the enemy at all times. Even with the sun shining the air was crisp and cold, causing the little group to pull their traveling cloaks tighter around them. The companions walked north for half a day, always at an incline, then turned west. As evening grew closer the sky began to cloud up. They were on high ground surrounded by a forest of red pines when Katchut bade the other three to climb on top of a mound of boulders. As they climbed above the tree level, a huge blackened stone castle rose into view before them to the southwest.

"It's a lot bigger and more evil looking than I'd imagined," Sharineas said.

"It is farther away than it looks," Katchut said, pointing to the iron gate in the back. "That is the only back entrance that I know of. We have to go down this slope and half-way up that mountain to get to the entrance." Katchut made a face as if remembering something bad. "It is where they bring the slaves in and out. If we try to go in that way it will be just as noticed as storming the front gate."

The others looked closer and could see a long line of Trauls, Nomies, and even some Humans, being led up to the gate. Soldiers with whips and large sticks beat the captives as they marched, herding them like cattle. Each one was sickened by the sight and turned from it knowing there was nothing they could do about it—at least for the moment. Matthew sat shivering on the rocks, thinking back to what Deeli had said and observing the area around them. There was snow and ice everywhere at this altitude. Any of the stone around them that was not covered in snow was bleak and gray; the sky and land looking forlorn and forsaken. Even the red pines that they were near—which had been gloriously beautiful farther east—were dull and seemed lifeless here.

"Well, what did Deeli say about this back entrance; something about being below the rainbow trees?"

"The only trees even near the fortress are those two stumps over there," Katchut said pointing. They all followed the Traul's finger to see two dead trees at the top of a sharp drop-off. A little way below the trees, coming out of the cliff face, was a small stream of water. It fell over the edge in a waterfall and onto the rocks below. The water sent up a fine mist that kept a constant cover of ice on the two dead tree trunks and all the rocks in the area.

"You're right," Matthew agreed. "The only other trees are those pines at the base of the mountain. They are red, but they don't look rainbow colored to me. And the two dead tree trunks up-above certainly don't either. I guess in the morning we can investigate among those pines, but they're an awful long way from the fortress. I don't see how anyone in this world could make a tunnel that long, even with magic."

"If we do not find a way in among those trees we must take a chance and fight our way into the slave entrance," Haub said in a serious tone.

"I sure hope that's not the case," Matthew returned. "Those Trauls with the magic blades are a lot harder to fight than the others, even with Excalibur. Not to mention that all of our chances of surprising this creep will be gone. That is if he hasn't already connected Deeli and Pheltic with me and the sword," Matthew added in a hushed voice, eyes filled to the rim with tears over the peril of his two friends. He and Sharineas made eye contact for the first time that day. Both saw a reflection of their own pain and guilt at having had to leave Pheltic and Deeli behind to suffer the machinations of the evil Dark Lord.

"It's getting dark," Katchut announced. "I suggest making camp for the night, and let Shesea show us the way tomorrow." Everyone agreed with that and spent a cold, fire-less night amidst the red pines. They also had no more food with them, and saw no game this high in the mountains; there would be no supper this night. While Matthew kept watch, the rumbling of his stomach was so loud he was afraid it would wake the others.

The gray clouds that had turned almost black the evening before had moved on during the night, and a shining sun greeted them the next morning. Once again they awoke stiff and sore from sleeping on the cold ground. Somewhere on the journey north Matthew had grown out of the need to complain about his every discomfort and was learning to take the hardships in stride. Although with the fighting, a bump on the head, sleeping in the cold, and now going without any food for an entire day, he was beginning to feel very weak. Katchut found some roots that they could eat, assuring everyone that they were safe. The roots were hard, cold, and tasteless, but they all knew food was needed to keep up their strength. Katchut insisted that they bring along some more of the roots in Sharineas' pack, just in case. All three males, their minds set on the task ahead of them, headed down toward the stand of pines. Before following, Sharineas had climbed one of the rocks to see if the land below looked any more appealing in the sunlight.

"Matthew! Come here, quickly," she yelled in a loud whisper, afraid of attracting unwanted attention. They were not entirely sure if the mutated Trauls that had been following them were still in the area or not. Matthew climbed the rock with Haub and Katchut right behind him; all three a little perturbed at the holdup. "Look," Sharineas said, pointing to the two dead tree trunks they had seen the evening before. Matthew looked and his jaw dropped open in amazement. Sunlight was hitting the perpetually ice covered tree trunks, causing them to sparkle like twin prisms. Every color of the rainbow glittered right before their eyes.

"The rainbow trees," Matthew said quietly. "When Deeli's book was written those trees were probably full and covered with ice. We can only see the rainbow effect when the sun is shining through their ice covering."

"Then maybe there is an entrance below the trees," Haub said with more enthusiasm than he had shown in a long time. "Let's head down to where the water is hitting the rocks below and work our way up." Everyone agreed and they headed down the slope at a fast pace. Here was a little spark of hope they had not expected. It was a slender thread, but at least it was something to hold onto. They finally made it near to the bottom of the waterfall. As they drew close, the companions noticed a foul odor growing stronger.

"What is that terrible smell?" Sharineas asked, not really expecting an answer; but Katchut did have the information.

"This water is a stream that flows under the fortress. All of the sewage from the entire castle is thrown in here."

"Ugh, why didn't you tell us that before we came down here?" Matthew asked, wrinkling his nose.

"No one asked me," Katchut answered with a perfectly straight face. "Why, does it make a difference?" Matthew and Sharineas looked at one another with a smile and rolled their eyes.

"No, I guess not," Matthew answered." "The smell just caught us a little off guard. Actually it doesn't smell as bad as when we got out of the Place of Fear." Katchut shivered a little at the mention of that name.

"Nothing is as bad as that place," The big Traul said. They made their way to where the water was hitting the rocks, but did not see an opening anywhere.

"We must begin climbing and look for some opening along the way," Haub said determinedly. "If there is an opening, this is the only way we'll find it."

"You don't suppose it's that hole where the sewage is coming out, do you?" Matthew asked, sticking out his tongue in distaste.

"If it is," Katchut said, "we would never make it. Not only can we not climb that high, but the water is flowing too swiftly and the rocks are covered with ice. It would wash us back out and down upon these rocks."

"I will start climbing and then call to the rest of you if I find anything," Haub volunteered. Sharineas was staring at the cascading water with a frown on her face. Just as Haub began to climb she seemed to come to herself.

"Haub, wait please. It seems to me I should be doing something here, like I have a part to play; but I just don't know what it is. I've been sifting through the things that uncle Deeli told me about the amulet. Didn't he say something about the amulet being a revelator of the truth? That if you shined the light on something it would show it for what it really was?" At the moment Sharineas said that, the amulet began to glow softly.

"I do remember him saying something like that, and the amulet seems to be agreeing with you," Matthew said.

"What if the glow means danger, like it has in the past?" Haub said, drawing his axe free.

242

"It can't be, if it were, the gem on my sword would be glowing too and it's not. It must mean you're on to something Sharineas. Just try to concentrate on finding out the truth about the water, and an opening." Sharineas began to concentrate, eyes on the waterfall. The crystal brightened slightly at first, then suddenly a white beam flashed out and hit the water. Sharineas was so startled she took a step back and gasped. As she did, the beam of light died again.

"It worked for a minute," Matthew said excitedly. "Try it again." Sharineas was a little shaken with the fact that she had gotten the amulet to respond. She gave Matthew a brief smile in response to his enthusiasm and tried again. This time when the beam of light shot forth, Sharineas did not waver. They all peered at the place where the light was shining on the dark water. At first what the amulet revealed was only conformation that indeed this was the castle's sewer system. Matthew was a little disgusted with what he saw and was about to turn away when Katchut became very excited.

"Look! Behind the water, just a little way up. I can see a dark opening." The other three examined the spot and Sharineas saw it right away. It took Haub and Matthew a little longer, but finally they saw the opening as well. The light died and all four stood looking at one another. Sharineas seemed a little dazed and Matthew put his arm around her shoulder for support.

"I did it, I really did it," was all the Princess could say.

"And it's great that you did," Matthew said. "We could have looked forever and never found that."

"It will be easy to get in. We only have to walk up these few rocks and go under the waterfall," Haub stated as he began climbing up the rocks. After seeing what the amulet had revealed in the water, Matthew and Sharineas were in no hurry to get wet.

"Wait a minute," Katchut said, "how will we see once we are in the cave? Anything we bring in to use as a torch will get wet under the waterfall."

"I think I can make the amulet project a beam of light for us. I believe I am beginning to understand it better now."

"But what if you cannot?" Katchut asked sensibly.

"If Sharineas thinks she can, then we need to let her try," Matthew said. "She did find the way in for us—I for one have confidence in her."

Seeing how confident Matthew and Sharineas were about this, Katchut only shrugged his shoulders and looked to Haub; Sharineas gave Matthew a grateful look as they took a step under the rushing water. Haub had gone through just before the two young people and was already standing inside the cave mouth when they emerged from the water with Katchut right behind them. "Nobody told me when I signed on for this trip that I would have to take a shower in ice-cold sewer water," Matthew said through chattering teeth. This brought a smile from everyone, including Haub who actually let out a short chuckle.

They lingered for some time at the entrance, letting their clothes drip dry and examining their surroundings. The cave was cold and damp, but did not have an icy wind blowing as was outside. The sunlight that was coming in through the water gave a rippling effect to the walls just inside. It also gave the four enough light to see the immediate area. The ground sloped down for about thirty paces before becoming level. Where the ground leveled off again, the cave walls rose out of sight, leaving only blackness above them. There were stalagmites all around them and presumably stalactites on the ceiling. Some of those on the floor were so tall they reached into the darkness beyond even Sharineas' Elven vision. They all walked down to where the natural light faded and then the other three looked to Sharineas. Matthew gave her arm a little squeeze for support and the Elven girl closed her eyes in concentration. For a few heartbeats nothing happened. Then the amulet began to glow and suddenly sprang to life; sending out a beam of light. The beam seemed intensely bright inside the dark cavern. Everyone smiled in relief and all three males expressed their gratitude and encouragement to Sharineas. Haub insisted on taking the lead with Sharineas and Matthew right beside him. All had their weapons drawn, for the gem on Matthew's sword was now glowing steadily.

"See, I told you that I was supposed to be with the sword," Sharineas whispered to Matthew.

"You were right and I was wrong. We certainly needed you with us. I know I'm glad you're here. But please, if trouble breaks out, stay behind me," Matthew said in a protective voice.

They followed the cave deeper into the mountain for several hours, going slowly and being very careful. The ground continued at an incline most of the time. At times they would walk through giant caverns that were so wide the amulet's light could not even reach the sides. At other times the passages would narrow so that they had to walk single file. As they walked, dark voices began to whisper in their ears. The same kind of dread that fell upon them in the Place of Fear now began to grow. The voices inside talked of dark things and defeat—of fear and death. Matthew remembered what had happened to them in the swamp forest and told the others what was happening in his head. The others admitted the same attacks in their minds and all four began to pray out loud. Eventually the dark whisperings faded into almost nothing. As they entered into their fourth huge cavern, all four began to hear noises and see movement at the edge of the light. No one, not even Sharineas, could make out what it was they heard and saw.

"Matthew," Sharineas said gripping his arm tightly. "What could that be? Do you think it's dangerous?"

"I don't know. The sword's gem has been glowing the whole time we've been in the cave. It's kind of creepy knowing something else is in here with us. We've run into so many weird things and come so far, I'm always worried that our next encounter will be our last."

"Just remember what Uncle Deeli said. The Creator would not have brought you this far without letting you meet the Dark Lord."

"I know, I pray that the Lord's will be done in this. But you've brought up another thing that worries me. I was supposed to have Deeli by my side to tell me what to do. I have no idea how to go about this. I have to admit, I'm a little scared." Sharineas gave Matthew's arm a squeeze in response, but said nothing.

The Elven Princess realized that she truly did believe that Matthew was not from this world. He was so different from anyone she had ever known. In the world where she grew up a male would never admit such a weakness, especially to a female. It seemed a huge contradiction. Here he was being completely open and vulnerable before her, yet he held the sword. Matthew was possibly the most powerful person in her world, yet willing to admit his fears. Katchut's hand suddenly clasped Matthew's shoulder from behind.

"Matthew, whatever is making those sounds is now behind us as well. We are completely encircled by them."

"Do you know what they are?" Matthew asked, not sure what to do. He too could hear the scraping noises all around them.

"No, I'm afraid I do not."

"Okay," Matthew started, not used to taking charge. "Katchut, Haub, get your weapons ready. Sharineas, when I say now, quickly turn your light behind us and sweep the area. Ready...now!"

Sharineas spun around and what the light revealed was not pretty. No! Matthew thought in alarm. *Not that, anything but that.* Covering the floor of the cave was a multitude of what looked like giant cockroaches. The creatures were climbing over themselves to scurry away from the light. They were everywhere, as far as the light would shine. All Matthew could do was stare at the hideous monsters. Some were more than a foot in length. Matthew, with his complete revulsion for cockroaches, was frozen where he stood. This was his worst nightmare come true.

The light stirred up the ugly little creatures and they were now becoming braver. They began coming nearer to the four companions, and then even crawling on Matthew's feet. Katchut and Haub began to chop at them with their weapons. The creatures died easily enough, once the intruder's blades pierced the hard outer shell of their backs. At first Matthew did nothing; his mind numb with the horror of what was going on around him. *This can't be happening,* he thought over and over to himself—a silent scream reverberating in his skull. The huge cockroaches finally started crawling up his legs and that brought him around. He began kicking his legs until the creatures flew off in every direction. He brought up a hard armored boot and let it fall on one of the nightmarish creatures. Matthew heard and felt a crunching that he would never forget. He knew he could not do that again.

By this time the amulet was stunning the creatures all around Sharineas. Matthew began swinging the blue lightning-covered Excalibur. The sword whistled through the horrible monsters with ease, killing one after another. Although the creatures were not hard to kill, there were thousands of them; and they were now acting as if they had found tonight's supper. The lightning from Matthew's sword was lighting up the cavern even more. Everywhere the companions looked there were huge cockroaches coming toward them. The four knew they were in serious danger now. They would tire long before all of the creatures could be killed, and there was no place to go.

Matthew wished there was some way to kill all of them at once. As that thought raced through his head, Excalibur let out a surge of energy from the tip of its blade. The energy went out as multicolored light for about ten feet and then died away. As it subsided Matthew could see the charred remains of giant cockroaches left in the energy's wake. Matthew had felt the surge go out of his own body, as if the sword had used his energy. He separated himself from the others and tried again to will the energy forth.

Matthew pointed the sword at a mound of the crawling, filthy creatures. A blast of pure energy shot out of the sword, totally disintegrating hundreds of the giant cockroaches. The stream of energy continued to pour out with blue lightning crackling along its edges. The others began to fight through the creatures toward the nearest wall, so they could stay out of the Sword Bearer's way. Matthew directed the blast of energy all around the cavern, destroying the creatures wherever it went. Haub, Katchut, and Sharineas watched with horror and fascination at the terrible display. As Matthew let loose this power, he could feel his own energy being drained. He knew that their only hope was for him to destroy all of the creatures, so he continued releasing the energy.

The light of the sword was illuminating the entire cavern, so Katchut and Haub took advantage of this to memorize their surroundings. The cavern was shaking slightly now from the onslaught of the power beam. Many of the stalactites had fallen already, but there were still more creatures so Matthew did not stop his onslaught. Sharineas was standing between Matthew and the nearest wall, frozen in awe while watching the display of pure power. Haub, who was a few feet away from her, was checking out their best possible escape route. Out of the corner of his eye he saw movement. Haub turned his head and saw a large stalactite falling straight for Sharineas.

There was no time to do anything but run and push the Princess out of the way. Sharineas turned her head just in time to see Haub take his last leap toward her. With both of his muscular arms outstretched, Haub shoved her to the ground. Sharineas fell back, hitting the ground and getting the wind knocked out of her. All she could think of was why Haub had pushed her like he did. The Elven Princess got back up, brushed herself off, and then looked back at Haub.

The jumping light from Matthew's sword must be playing tricks with me, Sharineas thought to herself. *Please let it be.* Haub lay on the ground with a huge, broken, cone shaped rock on top of him. The energy that Matthew was still using caused the image before her eyes to continually shift in a macabre dance that made Sharineas feel sick. Then Katchut was there, desperately trying to get the rock off Haub's back and legs. Sharineas hurried over to help.

At that same moment Matthew depleted his remaining strength—the energy beam sputtered and died. The few creatures still left living, scurried into their cracks and crevices for shelter. Matthew walked toward the amulet's light on weak and unsteady legs. The sight that greeted his eyes drained the last dregs of strength from Matthew and he fell to his knees in tears. There was Katchut, with Haub's head and shoulders laying in the Traul's lap. Sharineas was wiping blood from the corners of Haub's mouth.

"What happened?" Matthew asked, totally oblivious to what had transpired behind him. Katchut, who had watched the whole thing without being able to prevent it, told Matthew the story through his tears.

"Why? Why did you do it?" Sharineas kept asking in a whisper. Haub turned his head toward Sharineas and looked at her through hazy eyes.

"My Lord said, 'greater love has no one, than to lay down his life for another.' Shesea died that I might have life. Now I have willingly done the same for you."

"Your life!" Sharineas said almost hysterically. "No! You will not die. …You're going to be okay. You have to be."

"What does your amulet tell you, Princess?" Haub asked in a weak voice. Sharineas did not answer, only broke down in sobs. Katchut and Matthew were also crying openly now. Katchut had found a soul brother in Haub and was broken- hearted at the thought of losing him so soon. "It is…all right, I can accept my fate now," Haub continued on until a coughing spell took him, causing more blood to come out of his mouth. "It looks as though I will not get my revenge now," he was finally able to say with a slight smile.

"Haub, please don't go, we need you," Sharineas said in a broken voice.

"Don't worry for me, child. My part in this is now done. I go to be with my Lord, my wife, and children. Matthew, if you see Deeli again can you tell him something for me?"

"Of course Haub, anything," Matthew choked.

"Tell Deeli that I loved him like I would my father, and that I thank him with all my heart for introducing me to the Creator and His Son." Haub paused for another coughing spell and his eyes began to look glazed-over. "Also tell him...that I have forgiven the Dark Lord for the evil he has done to me. I believe that Deeli will rest easier knowing that." Haub's voice was barely audible now and they all had to lean inward to hear his last words. The other three saw a smile cross Haub's face, and for a brief moment his eyes shone clear—but it was not this world he was seeing. "I can see Shesea, his arms are open wide," Haub said with the last of his strength, then quietly closed his eyes in eternal sleep. Sharineas lay her head on Haub's still chest and wept.

"No, this can't be. It was supposed to be me laying here." Matthew just knelt there staring. Strong, quiet, dependable Haub—who had been with him since nearly the beginning—was gone forever. It was not until this moment that Matthew realized that he had been guilty of taking Haub for granted, believing he would always be there for him to lean on in every situation. Now, both he and Deeli were gone, as well as Pheltic for whom he felt personally responsible. Matthew did not think he could keep going.

"Princess," Katchut broke the quiet of the moment. "As much as I hate to see my new friend go, I know that he was ready for death. You are not." That simple statement hit Sharineas like a physical blow. Like a hot wind from the very mouth of the Creator that made her feel as if she would melt. Here was a Traul, whom she had been brought up to believe was completely evil, telling her that she was headed for the underworld. The Elven Princess knew deep inside that what Katchut had spoken was true. The amulet at her throat burned in an instant confirmation of what she knew.

"There is such peace on his face," Sharineas stated in a whisper. "So different from Gamilon's." She looked up at Katchut, then at Matthew. "Shesea is real, isn't He? He really is the way to the Creator. I can see it all now. How can a person be so blind as to not see?" she said, putting her face in her hands.

"Yes," Matthew answered, putting a comforting hand on her shoulder, "in your world and mine. I don't know much about all of this, but

I do know that you must belong to Him to stand before the judgment of God." Sharineas nodded her head in humble acceptance.

"I do need Shesea and I want to know Him. Please show me how." Matthew thought that nobody had ever looked more beautiful than this dirty, bedraggled, Elf girl before him. Inwardly Matthew was thanking Jesus for Sharineas' seeing the light, and wishing Deeli could be there.

So in that dark, cold cave, beneath an ancient stone fortress, surrounded by dead giant cockroaches; all three bowed their heads over the body of their departed friend. A Human from another world and a Traul from the dreaded northern kingdom, led the Princess of the Elven people and Keeper of the Amulet of Truth, in a prayer accepting Shesea as Lord of her life. Haub's sacrifice had tipped the scales for Sharineas. *A fitting memorial*, Matthew thought, *for a man who lived most of his life for others. Lord Jesus, give his soul rest. He was very loved down here.*

Chapter

20

At the same moment Matthew and Sharineas were walking under the waterfall and into the cave below the black fortress, the arm of the Enlightened One's war chief came down; signaling the attack. The black hoard began to shout and stomp their feet. Five huge battering rams were brought forward and took their positions. Handles had been cut into giant tree trunks; each tree took sixteen of the mighty Traul warriors to carry it. The battering ram crews spaced themselves evenly across the entire length of the wall just out of arrow range.

From behind the line of battering rams came the sound of Nomie drums. The crudely built drums began to beat in a slow, steady cadence. At another signal from their leader, the entire army began to march in place and shout in time with the beat. The valley dwellers knew that this was all just a psychological ploy, but were unnerved by it just the same. Each time the war chief gave a signal with his left arm the beat would increase in tempo. After signaling a second time, his horse and the rest of the army began to advance in time with the beat.

"This is not what I expected," King Peridon said to the other leaders with a slight quiver in his voice. "The northern armies were never this disciplined in the past. That was always our main advantage."

"I can't believe there are so many," Telick said after a brief pause.

The pace was now quickening and the front line of enemy soldiers could be seen more clearly. Finally the war chief gave a signal with his right arm and the army began to move forward in earnest; their shouts deafening. It was a frightening sight, but every Elf, Human, and Dwarie stood their ground. Even the females that had talked the leaders into letting them be stationed on the wall did not flee, but held their positions bravely.

As soon as the battering rams were within arrow range, the Elven and Human archers let fly. For each Traul that was holding the giant tree trunk, there was another in front of him with an elongated shield. Most of the front line foot soldiers fell with arrows protruding from their bodies, but because of the shield bearers it was hard to take out the battering rams. The valley archers did, however, manage to kill a few of the warriors holding two of the tree trunks. This caused the rams to go down; but three of them continued on, picking up pace with every step. Those atop the wall braced themselves and made ready with rocks and hot oil.

Not many of the valley forces fell on the first charge, and only a few were hit with either arrow or stone. By the time the battering rams reached the wall they were covered with flaming arrows. The three remaining rams hit at almost the same time. The great wall shuddered and many of the defenders were thrown off their feet, but the structure stood firm. The Dwaries soon regained their balance and began to pour hot oil on top of the warriors below. Screams of pain could be heard all along the base of the wall and all three battering rams, as well as many of the dark warriors, were now aflame. The enemy was trying the same tactic—shooting flaming arrows at the wooden wall, but with little success. The green wood, combined with females pouring water on every arrow, made setting the wall ablaze impossible.

Long thin tree trunks were brought forward and leaned against the wall for the enemy warriors to try to gain the top. They also threw hook-ended ropes, catching them on top of the wall. Both of these attempts at scaling the wall were easily stopped by the allied valley races. The two battering rams that were not burning were picked up and brought back out of arrow range. Looking out over the black masses, the Elves and their allies could see more of the huge tree trunks being brought forward.

Their biggest hindrance was the winged Nomies back in full force. They flew above those on the wall dropping stones and shooting small arrows. This time the mutated Nomies were harder to bring down for the archers. They now wore a crude leather armor in the places their deformed bodies would allow. There were only a few of the winged Nomies, but they were able to cause much damage as well as keep the valley forces distracted from the attack below.

Peridon and Moark, looking for something positive in this, were hoping that the smaller number of flying Nomies meant the enemy was exhausting his supply of them.

The Dwaries were quick to use their invention with all the improvements they had made. They began hurtling large stones over the wall and far into the midst of the enemy forces. This thing they called a catapult was something the Dwaries had come up with since the Great War—something the enemy knew nothing about it. When the huge stones began to rain down upon them from seemingly nowhere, the Enlightened One's army began to scatter in mass confusion. They were packed so tightly in the pass that the flying stones took a tremendous toll. Almost as many warriors died in the confusion that was created as in the barrage itself.

Between an unsuccessful first attack on the wall and now the hail of stones, the enemy army had lost most of their discipline. The war chief saw this and gave the signal for retreat. The valley forces gave a loud victory shout when they saw the enemy retreating down the mountain pass. The shouting did not last long however since this was only a retreat out of arrow range where they could regroup. The outcome of this first attack did give the defenders a little more hope though, and even brought out a few nervous smiles and backslapping.

There were many dead bodies littering the ground in front of the wall. The enemy army did not bother to carry back any of their dead or wounded. Once the retreat was stopped, the enemy began their regrouping. More battering rams were brought forward and the drums began to pound once more. More troops had also been brought up; to those on top of the wall it seemed as if the enemy had not lost a single soldier. The dark army attacked once more just as it had the first time. In this second attack, four of the giant tree trunks made contact with the wall. The structure rocked violently, throwing most of those on it as if they weighed nothing. But the wall did not collapse, or even have a breach. Each warrior there was thankful the races had taken the time to build it right. The Elves and Humans who had grumbled during the building about too many Dwarie safeguards and supports, began apologizing profusely.

The outcome of this attack was also much the same as the first. Heavy casualties for the Enlightened One's army and only a few for those behind the wall—and so it continued all morning. Each time the enemy retreated they left in their wake more dead bodies on the field. Each time they returned with their original number of warriors. The valley people were beginning to think the enemy had an inexhaustible supply. The black army also left behind flaming battering rams with each retreat. These fires had to be put out by the defenders each time for fear that the wall might be set ablaze. By midday the dead bodies of the enemy were stacked high against the wall. The enemy felt no qualms about using their dead brothers as a ramp to climb up the wall. Every attempt by the enemy to do this was repelled. Each member of the defending army, whether Human, Elf, or Dwarie, male or female, fought bravely and fiercely. They knew that their lives and those of their children depended on it. Even the Elven priests were atop the wall doing what they could with their limited magic.

At just past midday, when the enemy retreated, they continued until the pass was empty. The valley forces were thankful for the respite and tried to grab something to eat. They did not have long, however. Just a short time after the last of the army had disappeared; completely fresh troops began to make their way back through the pass. As the enemy was preparing for a fresh assault, an Elven scout came riding into camp with a message for his leaders.

"My King," he said to Peridon. "Sirs," bowing slightly to the other three. "My captain wishes to report that an attack on the western mountain commenced at the same time as the attack on you. Each charge so far has been successfully repelled. But we could see from our position that even when the pass was full of soldiers and we were under attack, the enemy still had many more warriors held in reserve." This last news was bitter to the four leaders. It looked as if this was going to be a contest of endurance, and the enemy had all the numbers on their side. The report from the eastern mountain was the same—the only recourse the valley people had left to them was to try to hold their own and pray for a miracle.

The attack just after midday began as did the others. The Nomie drums began to beat, while row upon row of black clad warriors started their advance with five battering rams out front—but this time something different happened. As the warriors marched within arrow range, five black shapes began to rise from their midst. Those five black shapes turned out to be magically altered Trauls, at least twelve feet tall with fangs, claws and wings. The valley forces were stunned; they had never seen one of these monstrosities before. These five were brothers to the abomination that had killed Gamilon, and with them came more of the winged Nomies.

As the ground troops moved in, the air forces attacked those on the wall. The archers concentrated on the winged abominations this time, but to no avail. They brought down a few of the winged Nomies, but none of the giant mutated Trauls. Their tough skin resisted the allied arrows. Even when an arrow did penetrate one of their hides, it did not seem to affect them much. The flying Trauls were not content to throw stones on their enemy as the Nomies did. These creatures attacked those on the wall personally in hand-to-hand combat.

The huge monsters were vicious and seemingly unstoppable. Wherever they landed on the wall there was horrible carnage left behind. The Nomies that were flying overhead managed to take a few casualties, but were more of a distraction than anything else. This battle lasted longer than the rest, but before it was over two of the flying Trauls had been killed. The sheer number of swords and axes hacking away at them was the only thing that had accomplished this feat. The other three flew back above the wall and hovered.

Unfortunately this attack had taken attention away from what was happening on the ground. In several places the wall was on fire, and as the three remaining mutated Trauls flew clear of the battlements, all five battering rams hit the structure simultaneously. Very few atop the wall were ready and bodies flew everywhere, including off the walkway and on to the ground below. The sound of splintering wood and breaking bones could be heard distinctly over the noise of battle. This fight lasted well into the afternoon and took a heavy toll on the defenders. The outside portion of the wall was splintered in two places near the center, but still held strong. All of those on the ground ran to reinforce those parts of the wall from behind as soon as was possible.

Much of the wall was burning now. The Nomies had brought up containers of oil and thrown them at the wooden blockade. The archers behind them had sent flaming arrows into the areas, sometimes setting their comrades aflame in the process. Those still on the walkway quickly recovered and began to throw water on the flaming areas, urgently calling below for more of the liquid to be brought to them. The enemy ground troops continued their attack and many almost made it over the wall. This battle was very nearly the last, but by late afternoon the enemy knew they were gaining no more headway and the retreat was sounded.

This gave the Elves and their allies a chance to regroup and catch their breath. This backing off by the enemy seemed strange to the valley forces, but on the other hand they could afford it. The strategy seemed to be working so far; the scenes behind and on top of the wall were not pretty ones. During this break in the fighting all four leaders were walking among their people as they ate and rested, trying to keep them encouraged.

The individual who stood out most that day was a surprise to everyone. King Moark's son Telick was like a whirlwind, which was not easy for a Dwarie. He seemed to be everywhere the fighting was the heaviest. Telick had been in on both fights where the flying Trauls were killed. In many instances it was the Dwarie war chief's rallying of the troops that turned the tide of a battle being lost. Even the Elves, whose agility suited them for quickly going up and down the ladders, were impressed with how fast Telick was moving.

Another surprise was how the Humans of the valley fought. They had always been thought of as the least warlike of the three races, but as the battles grew heavier and more fierce, so did they. The other two races were a little frightened by the savagery and strength they saw in the Humans, and were grateful to be on the same side as they. Most did not realize that the Humans fought extra hard because of the guilt they felt at having others of their race fighting for the enemy.

The final attack of the day began just as the others had. The only reason the valley forces did not fall to it was due to a plan that Telick had come up with in a moment of inspiration. As before, the Nomie drums began to beat, and as before the three remaining flying Trauls emerged to wreak havoc. The mutated Trauls flew at those upon the wall with a vengeance. Their blood lust grew as they saw the puny enemy cowering in clusters before them. They did not know that this cowering in groups was for a reason. Just as the Trauls came in for the attack, the clusters broke apart. The Dwaries they had been hiding sprang up and threw their buckets of oil directly in the creatures' faces. The monsters were momentarily blinded with pain. Not being able to see, they flew up and hovered above the heads of their prey. Immediately the Elven archers let fly with flaming arrows, covering the mutated Trauls in flames. The creatures flew in every direction bellowing in pain. Two of them fell to the ground behind the wall. They were already near dead and the valley ground forces fell on them to finishing the job. The other mutated Traul flew back to his own side, so injured by flame and arrow that it was not seen again.

Meanwhile Elven archers had stopped two of the five battering rams. Better signals given to the Dwarie catapults enabled them to take out a third ram. This left two of the battering rams to crash into the wall. Fortunately neither made contact near the center where the previous damage had been done. The new damage was minimal and both of these battering rams were quickly set on fire and their bearers covered in boiling oil. The warriors below continued to stack the bodies of their dead comrades against the wall and climb up them. This practice was so repugnant to the priests and some of the more sensitive people defending the wall, that they had to turn their heads away, sickened.

With this tactic the enemy was able to gain greater heights on the wall than with poles or ladders. The pile of dead bodies was growing so high that in some places the tall Traul warriors were able to reach the top of the wall. The defenders continued to strike back with stone, sword, and axe, but it was not enough. In places where the Trauls were gaining the wall, the valley people were forced to pour oil down on them. Elven archers followed with flaming arrows setting the live warriors, as well as the dead, ablaze. This caused such a stench and such putrid smoke that many atop the wall became sick and lost what little they had in their stomachs.

The setting of the sun was a blessing to the valley races that day. Dusk came just when the defenders did not know if they could go on any longer. Finally the enemy retreat was sounded and the pass emptied of every living soul. The weary defenders went to their food and rest, leaving guards posted all along the wall. Scouts from both mountains arrived shortly thereafter with identical reports. The valley forces were still holding their positions on the mountain tops, but casualties were rising and they could not last another full day. King Peridon thanked the scouts and sent them back to their units. He did not want the mountain soldiers to know how bad things really were at the wall.

"Does anyone have any ideas for tomorrow morning's attack?" Roak asked the other leaders. "We are almost out of oil and I don't think it will last more than another day." No one spoke for several heartbeats. Finally King Moark broke the silence.

"The repairs to the wall breach are finished. Both places are almost as good as new, but any more direct hits on those spots could be disastrous." King Peridon was quieter than usual. He knew that it was his people that the enemy hated the most and wanted to destroy. He was feeling more and more responsible for the losses they had endured. The extra weight of worrying about his missing daughter and future son-in-law was not helping matters.

"Half my priests are dead," he said in a subdued tone. "I have the other half praying. I cannot believe the Creator would let it end this way. I have never been one to rely on supernatural help, but right now it seems to be our only chance. I hate to sound like I've given up hope, but they still have troops that have not even been used yet and half of ours are either dead or wounded."

"If the wall should fall, we know that the valley is lost," King Hydrian spoke. "I have drawn up a plan for a last stand in the forest. I have capable forest Elves ready to take charge of mixed groups. We would position ourselves in the trees with stones, arrows, and weapons of every kind. In that way we could take as many of the blood lusting leaches with us as possible when they enter the forest." It was a grim reminder, but everyone at the table knew they might have to face the eventuality of defeat. Each leader agreed with the plan, and they put King Hydrian in charge of organizing it.

"I cannot stand the thought of what those butchers will do to our children and females if we are defeated here," Peridon said with watery eyes. The others remained silent for some time, each contemplating similar thoughts.

Morning came without anything being tried by the enemy army during the night. All four leaders were making their way to the wall when the familiar drums began to pound. The wall looked so empty now with so many wounded and dead. Each leader wondered just how they would defend it properly. King Moark took personal charge of the Dwarie catapults. The other leaders joined Telick on the walkway to fight alongside their people. The drumming, shouting, and marching of the enemy sounded even louder today—especially in contrast to the silence of those watching the horrible spectacle once again unfold before them. The defenders watched the black hoard come at them through a sickly haze caused by the dead bodies that they had been forced to burn, and then leave smoldering all night.

This time there were no flying Trauls to worry about, but four of the five battering rams made it through the allies' barrage, and the wall was badly damaged in several places. On the ground, teams of Dwaries scrambled to repair the breaches. Fortunately there were no sections opened up enough to let any of the enemy warriors through the wall. The battle was in earnest again, catapults flinging anything they could find into the enemy ranks, but still their numbers seemed hardly diminished. The defenders on top of the wall were having a much harder time. It seemed that many rope ladders were being thrown up simultaneously, as if the enemy knew their numbers were low. The defenders did their best to cut the ropes when a hook appeared, but the enemy archers had grown smarter. Each time a rope ladder was thrown up, the Enlightened One's archers would concentrate their fire at that spot. Many of the defenders were wounded and a few killed cutting the rope ladders.

Several times during the battle enemy warriors made it up the rope ladders and over the wall. Generally only one or two would make it over before being killed and the ladder cut down. At one point however, six

Trauls managed to get over the wall and set up a defense of that ladder. Hand-to-hand combat broke out trying to stop them, but a few more managed to come over the top.

Telick saw the battle from his position on the ground and quickly climbed the nearest stairs. He threw himself into the fray with his axe swinging wildly. His rather tall—for a Dwarie—stocky frame, with its burst of frenzied energy, turned the tide of that battle. Those of the enemy that had made it over the wall were eventually beaten and the ladder cut. Sadly, one Human and two Elves were killed, along with one fatally wounded Dwarie, Telick. He had been an inspiration to warriors of all the races since the attack had begun. Now he was being carried down to his father on a stretcher.

"Father," Telick said gasping for breath. "I am sorry I won't be here...to fight with you until the end. I hope Pheltic is okay. ...Tell him and mother good-bye for me." Moark just sat there holding his son's hand and crying like a newborn baby. "I...love you...father." Telick choked out his last sentence and then was no more. Moark could not seem to move from that spot, and no one tried to make him. He felt in his heart that he could fight no more. One son dead, the other on a suicide mission to the north, and the enemy about to pour in on them.

Just then the black army sounded a retreat and backed off down the pass to re-group. It was nearing midday, but you could not tell by looking at the sky. Thick black clouds made it almost as dark as night, but it was not long before the drums began their beating again. Those behind the wall knew the time had come; as did the enemy, for their shouting and screaming was louder than ever before. They knew their prey could not last much longer. One large section of the wall was still burning. People atop and behind the wall were frantically trying to put it out, but only managed to barely get it under control. The defenders knew that this would be the last attack.

Peridon, Hydrian, and Roak were on the walkway overlooking the field of battle. An incredible number of bodies lay in the mountain pass. Neither they nor their people would have ever desecrated their dead brothers in such a way. The enemy army was now marching forward, trampling over their own dead. The leaders had called everyone who was able to the top of the wall. They knew that if even one of the battering rams hit a weakened area, it would open a way for the enemy to come through the wall. Every warrior, whether male or female, held a sword, axe, stone, sling, or bow. It did not look as if there was any less of the black hoard now than there had been in the beginning.

As the front ranks drew near enough, the valley defenders rained their projectiles down upon them. For the most part they concentrated their fire on the battering rams. Being so near defeat, the valley forces fought like cornered animals. The jubilant shouts of the attackers were mixed with the agonizing screams of the dying. Ominous low rumbling sounds began to come from the clouds above and lightning could be seen in the distance.

For all their fierceness, those on the battlements still let two of the battering rams slip through their defenses. One of them hit the wall near the center where an earlier hit had been made. A sizable hole appeared in the wall and the enemy scrambled to open it further while Dwaries ran to repair it from behind. The other ram hit the wall where it had been burning. This caused a large enough breach for the black clad warriors to start pouring through the ever widening hole. Many of those on top of the wall went below to battle at the opening. This left so few to defend the battlements, that in a very short time the enemy began coming over in great numbers.

The leaders saw that they had lost, and the pre-arranged signal for retreat was given. A loud bell was rung so that sentries halfway up the mountain could ring their alarms. It was unnecessary, however; those warriors stationed on top of the mountains were already in full retreat. The enemy had finally swarmed over the valley's dwindling numbers and they had no other option but to abandon the mountains. Those defending the wall began the retreat into the forest to make their last stand.

The breaches in the wall were growing larger now, with more of the enemy coming in every minute. Hydrian and a handful of his choice forest Elves took a stance and continued to fire arrows into the intruders to give everyone else more of a chance for retreat. Peridon, mounted atop his steed just outside the forest, could see more openings being made in the wall by battering rams. He yelled out to Hydrian and his worriers as loudly as he could. "Hydrian, come now, it is over!" As King Hydrian and his warriors broke for the forest, flames began to leap up in places all along the wall, engulfing most of it. King Peridon turned his horse into the forest to take up his position. The plan was to ambush, fight, and run; keeping this up all the way back to the Elven kingdom. *Maybe I will get a chance to say good-bye to Jasmantha before the end*, Peridon thought to himself.

Chapter

21

The trio found a slight depression in the cave floor and scraped as much dirt out with their weapons as they could. Then, with many tears and much regret, they laid Haub's body in the shallow grave and each said a prayer over him. All three then began to pile rocks and pieces of the broken stalactite on top of their departed friend.

"Let's pile them high," Matthew said. "I don't want any of those cockroach things getting at him." They had no idea what time it was, only that they were too tired to go very far. Matthew was especially drained from his battle with the creatures. "It seemed like the sword was using my energy and transforming it into the light beam," he told the other two. "I don't think I'll be able to walk far without some rest. I don't even know what direction we're supposed to be going."

"When you were fighting the cave creatures your sword was lighting up the entire cavern," Katchut said, his voice still filled with the loss of his new friend. "I was looking around during the battle and thought I saw some kind of stairway carved into the far wall of the cavern. I cannot be sure though, it could have been the moving light playing tricks with me. Sharineas, if you will shine your light that way I believe we will be able to find the place," the big Traul said, pointing into the darkness.

Sharineas did as Katchut bade her and directed the light of her amulet in that direction. Katchut took the lead with Sharineas by his side searching the area with her Elven vision. The two were not moving very fast, but it was still difficult for Matthew to keep up with them. He realized that he could only use the sword as he did against the cave creatures in extreme emergencies; it simply took too much out of him. They soon came to a wall that looked as if it could go on forever in both directions, and Katchut was not sure which way to go. He was almost certain of what he had seen, but could not get his bearings by just the single narrow beam the amulet was producing.

Sharineas was almost ready to give up in frustration; two deaths in less than a seven-day was too much for her—not to mention Pheltic and her great uncle missing, or dead themselves. The Princess made her feelings evident when she slapped her hand against the wall and touched her forehead to it; remaining that way for quite some time. Finally, at Matthew's quiet insistence, she tried once more to coax the amulet to show them the way out of the cavern. She was not certain what the amulet was trying to tell her, but believed it wanted them to go left. The trio stayed near to the wall and headed in that direction.

They would have missed the spot except that they had to stop for a pile of large stones in their path. As they were going around the stones, Katchut noticed that many of them looked as if they had been cut with a tool. He asked Sharineas to shine her light up at the wall. With the wall lit up they could see a crude stairway recessed into the stone right above their heads. The bottom portion of the stairs had broken away and were lying in a pile at their feet. Sharineas directed the beam of light up the stairs as far as it would go. The rest of the stairs looked as if they were still in good shape, and just where the light beam started to fade it looked as if they began to spiral with the wall.

"Oh no," Sharineas exclaimed, "more stone stairs."

"At least this time the wind's not blowing," Matthew volunteered. The Princess' reaction was not that positive.

"These steps look like they're hundreds, maybe thousands of cycles old; how do we know they won't collapse on us?"

"We do not," Katchut answered simply. "But we also do not seem to have a choice if we want to confront the Enlightened One."

"Well, it looks like they're heading in the direction we want to go," Matthew added, "but we're going to have to find a way up to the first stair. I hate to say it, but I don't think I can go any farther tonight—if it is night."

"I do not think it will be hard to get to the first stair, but you are right, we need to rest first," Katchut said. "Let's sleep here for awhile before we continue. I will keep first watch so that you can regain your strength, Matthew."

Both Matthew and Sharineas were reluctant to sleep anywhere near the cave creatures, but knew they had no other choices available. Both also had to admit that they were glad Katchut had insisted on bringing more of the tasteless roots along in Sharineas' pack. All three were so hungry that the root supper almost tasted good. They each took a turn at watch so all could get some rest. They did not know it truly was nighttime, and as they awoke next morning the Dark Lord's army was preparing for their second day's round of attacks on the valley.

Katchut was able to lift both Sharineas and Matthew up to the first stair with relative ease. With Matthew's help the huge Traul got a hold of the lowest step and pulled himself up. Matthew was feeling much better after a night's sleep and some more roots. He insisted on going first, and started up the steps with Excalibur drawn. Sharineas followed right behind him, shining the light of her amulet on the steps so they could see where they were going. Katchut, with his sword out as well, brought up the rear.

They climbed the stairs for hours. In some places the steps were wet with something slimy, which made them very slippery and Matthew almost fell off twice. Sharineas' light would only shine so far above them, leaving the threesome to constantly wonder how much farther they had to go. They continued to climb higher into the darkness wondering if the stairs would ever end. Matthew and Sharineas' legs were in good shape from all the walking and climbing they had done on the quest, but after a few hours they still had to stop and rest.

"I've noticed," Matthew began after they had sat in silence for awhile, "that the higher we go, the brighter the sword's gem glows. He's up there, somewhere above us. The more I think about what he's done and the deaths he's caused, the more I want to cut him in half." Matthew was sounding uncharacteristically savage and Sharineas gave him a worried look.

"Do not let hatred take you over Matthew," Katchut said. "If you do, you will be no different than the one we seek. Even righteous anger can consume you and turn to evil."

"Yeah, I guess you're right Katchut. But this is what I was brought to your world for, to kill this evil Dark Lord. I guess I'm just getting a little anxious."

"The prophecy says you must overcome him, that does not necessarily mean you are to kill him," Katchut said with a furrowed brow. Matthew did not say anything at first, but after a long pause he finally slapped both knees and stood to his feet.

"Well, I think it's time we get going or we'll never find out, will we?" Matthew began to climb the stairs into the darkness once more. Sharineas and Katchut looked at each other with worried expressions, but got up and followed their friend.

"Deeli? Deeli!" Pheltic's voice came out of the darkness.

"I am here," Deeli mumbled in return. In all of his one-hundred and fifty-eight sun-cycles, Deeli had never felt such agony. *Is this what the Lord had to go through to cleanse the world?* the old Elf thought half deliriously. *No, His suffering was greater. On top of the pain and anguish, all the evil of this world was laid upon Him. That is what truly killed Him in the end.*

"Deeli, what have they done to you? It's so dark in here I can't see you."

"I am still alive, little one—even if just barely. The Dark Lord has hurt me much, but I did not deny my Lord and for that I give thanks."

"Why didn't the Creator send down lightning from the sky or something to save you?" Pheltic asked with the innocence of a child.

"It must be His will for me to go through this, although I do not know why. You should not concern yourself with that at this stage of your faith. Just do not believe ill of the Creator or Shesea; God's ways are always right and work out for our betterment."

"Okay..." Pheltic said reluctantly. After a short pause the Dwarie did seem to have put it out of his mind. "Deeli, do you feel up to teaching me some of those praise songs you know?" Deeli began to chuckle, then to openly laugh. "What? what have I said?" Pheltic asked in a confused voice. The little Dwarie had unknowingly reminded Deeli of a story in the Path Holy Words. He told Pheltic of how two of the early fathers of the faith had been thrown in prison, and how they had spent the whole night singing praises to the Creator.

"It will be difficult for me to sing, but I think this would be a splendid time to teach you some songs," Deeli answered, feeling better already. It was thus that the Traul Dark Lord found them many hours later, singing praises to the Almighty and His Son as loudly as they could. The Enlightened One walked into the cell and punched them both in the face, ending their singing. He had one of the guards unshackle Deeli and stand him against the wall.

"Napdeeliate, I challenge you to a duel of magic for the preservation of your precious valley. If you win I will stop the attack," the Enlightened One offered in a silky voice.

"I do not use magic anymore," Deeli answered simply. Energy shot forth from the Dark Lord's hands and hit Deeli in the arm. The smell of burning flesh instantly filled the cell. Deeli gasped in pain, but did not retaliate. The evil leader was in a rage that Deeli would not be goaded.

"All right my impotent old Elf, we'll see how long you last. My army started the attack on your foolish wall this morning, by nightfall everything you hold dear will belong to me," he said with hatred in his voice. He then turned to his two guards. "I want them both whipped again, but only to the point of unconsciousness. Then gag them both, I don't want anymore concerts today." The tall half-Human, half-Traul left the room and headed up the stone stairway. His two mutated Traul guards began their grisly work with pleasure.

The two prisoners were left to hang from their shackles half dead and wishing they could finish that journey. The pair hung in the foul little cell—going in and out of consciousness from repeated beatings by the guards—throughout that whole day and night. Both Deeli and Pheltic were fully awake the next midday when the Dark Lord returned for them. He said nothing as he entered the cell, just ripped the gag out of Deeli's mouth and stared at him. Finally Deeli was the one who broke the silence. "So, do you now possess the valley?" The Dark Lord backhanded the defenseless Elf across the face.

"Not yet! It seems my war chief is still toying with your people. But the next attack will be the finale one. I have waited long enough, deny your God now or face my wrath." The end of the Dark Lord's sentence rose to a fevered pitch and energy crackled from his hands. The magic that burst forth from the maddened half-breed, caught Deeli on the side and shot past him; putting a hole in the wall. The noise made by the Traul leader's magic hitting the wall seemed extraordinarily loud, as if something had exploded near by. Everyone in the little cell also felt the stone beneath them tremble at the moment of impact. The Traul guards did not think it looked as if that much energy had been released, but knowing nothing about matters of magic, said nothing. The Dark Lord was too enraged to even notice something so trivial. He picked-up his whip once again and began slashing at the two captives.

When he finished, the Dark Lord leaned back against the cell wall and laughed; enjoying Deeli's pain. Finally his laughter subsided and in a panting voice he addressed his prisoners: "I should kill you both now, but I have a better idea. Bring the prisoners to the main hall," the Dark Lord ordered his two guards. He then spun around and headed out the door.

The two guards roughly finished unchaining their prisoners and hauled them up the stone steps. They were brought to a long hallway with many windows. Even though the sky outside was filled with slate gray clouds, the light coming through the windows still hurt Deeli and Pheltic's eyes after being in the dark for so long. They were dragged into a huge room with the highest ceiling that either had ever seen. The room itself was round; windows facing every direction ran almost the height of the walls. Each window gave a different view of the mountains below and above. Deeli and Pheltic had no way of knowing it was midday, for the gathering clouds outside were so dark and thick that it looked almost night. The lord of the castle ordered more torches and candles to be lit because the room was growing so dark.

The self-proclaimed Enlightened One sat on a throne, which in turn sat upon a raised stone dais at the far end of the room. He had three of his mutated Traul guards standing at all times on either side of the throne; many more were stationed throughout the room. Deeli and Pheltic were dumped unceremoniously on the floor to the right of the throne; near a huge mirror. Pheltic then got his first clear look at Deeli; the old Elf was truly a mess. His face was so swollen and bruised that Pheltic almost could not recognize him. Dried blood covered his face, chest, and arms; one of which had a large bloody hole in it. Deeli was naked from the waist up and Pheltic could see the burn marks made from the Dark Lord's magic. The little Dwarie did not start to cry fully though, until he saw his friend's feet. They were mutilated, scorched, and still oozing blood. Pheltic looked up at his captor with hatred in his tear-filled eyes. The Enlightened One just looked back and laughed.

"Now I want you both to look at something besides each other." The mirror, which was in a very ornately designed wooden stand, began to glow. Then suddenly a scene of battle was playing out before them. They were looking at the backs of a rushing mob of black clad warriors. The two prisoners showed surprise on their faces when a huge wall made of tree trunks came into view in front of the warriors.

"Hey! That's the wall our people built in the northern pass to the valley," Pheltic shouted. "How can we be watching that?"

"Do you not yet understand you little whelp, I have no limits!" The Dark Lord sneered back at him. "My army is now making what will surely be the last attack, your valley is lost and everyone you know will soon be dead. I have warriors that have not even been used yet, just waiting for their chance to destroy the Elves and their allies." Pheltic looked as if his life were over, Deeli's face was still a blank. "What would you say Napdeeliate, if I told you that there was still a chance that I would stop the invasion and bring my armies back here?"

"I suppose I would ask what is it you would want in return?"

"All that I want from you is to deny your God and His alleged Son. Not much to ask in return for all those lives."

"I would have to say to you that I do not believe you would stop the invasion," Deeli answered slowly. "And even if I did, I would not do as you request."

"But Deeli," Pheltic began. "Surely Shesea would understand, if you could save the entire valley. My father and mother…your relatives and friends."

"I am sorry, my friend. I know it seems harsh, but the Creator will accomplish His will no matter what I say. Under no circumstances will I deny my Lord." The Dark Lord's fists came down on the arms of his throne and he stood, glaring at the two.

"You are right Napdeeliate, I would not have called off the invasion," he screamed from atop the stone dais. "I will break you if it takes the rest of your not-so-long existence. But for now you will both sit and watch as your homeland falls to my might. Do not try to refuse, my guards have some very unpleasant ways to make you do as I wish. And as soon as the show is over we will concentrate on finding that miserable Elven sword!"

Chapter

22

It did not seem as if the stairway would ever end, and stopping for rest was becoming more and more frequent now. Every muscle in their bodies was cramping and necks were stiff with tension from always looking upward. Matthew's foot hit a loose stone, sending it skidding over the side and into the darkness below. Without any discussion all three stopped to listen out of some morbid curiosity. It was quite some time before the sound of the stone landing came echoing back to their ears. The trio looked at one another in the light of the amulet and then silently continued upward.

It was not long after this that they noticed the sound of their footsteps was changing. The echo somehow seemed shorter, and then they learned why. The little group came upon something that none of them had expected, a dead end. Matthew reached out and touched the solid stone wall hesitantly, as if hoping it was an illusion. "I can't believe it,"

Sharineas voiced all of their thoughts. "The stairs came all this way just to end in a wall."

"Matthew, look around for a lever or something," Katchut urged, "maybe it's a secret passage way." Matthew looked, felt, prodded and scraped, but to no avail—it was a solid wall. Katchut sat down dejectedly on the step below the one Sharineas was already sitting on. "It's no wonder none of my people had ever heard of this entrance, it was probably blocked off long before any of us were ever born."

"What do we do now?" Sharineas asked glumly. "Turn around and go back?"

"I don't know about the two of you, but I'm going through it," Matthew said defiantly. "Both of you go back down the stairs a little way." Sharineas and Katchut moved back down the stairs, then turned to see what their friend was going to do. When the light from Sharineas' amulet illuminated the wall in front of him, Matthew raised Excalibur. He quickly brought the Sword of Kings over his head and struck the stone in front of him; at that same instant the Dark Lord's magic hit the wall behind Deeli. The resulting explosion was deafening. With one blow Matthew sent stone and mortar flying in every direction. The stairs shook so violently that Katchut had to help Sharineas from vibrating right over the edge. When the dust settled, all three could see a gaping black hole in the wall big enough for even Katchut to squeeze through. "I don't know where it leads, but I'm game to find out," Matthew said smiling at the other two, covered in rock dust.

"I just hope no one heard that blast or we'll have a welcoming committee on the other side," Katchut said with concern.

"If the Lord really wants me to face this Hitler-reject," Matthew answered, feeling a faith in God stronger than ever before rising up inside, "then He will have taken care of the noise, and we won't lose any of the surprise."

"Well...let me shine the light through first, so we know what's there. So far no one has come out at us from the other side." They peered into the hole and saw that they were at the end of a long hallway. There were iron bound wooden doors lining the hallway on either side. Matthew was almost knocked backward when the similarity struck him. The hallway reminded him of the back rooms at the 747 club in his own world.

"This must be the fortress' lowest dungeons," Katchut whispered. *That part is the same too,* Matthew thought. *The backrooms at the club are nothing but dungeons to keep people from seeing there is another way to live their lives.*

Without saying anything about his déjà vu, Matthew crawled through the hole first, then Sharineas, and finally Katchut's massive frame made it with a little help from his friends. The trio made their way down the long line of empty cells. Everything was in total darkness except the area that the amulet illuminated. Inches of dust covered the floor, telling the companions that no one had been in this part of the castle for a long time. They slowly and quietly crept down the hallway until they came upon a set of stairs leading farther up into the castle. Matthew continued to lead the way, sword drawn and glowing, up this set of stairs. They came out in another long corridor that looked the same as the last, thick with dust, every cell empty.

"These cells are not used anymore," Katchut said with sadness. "All prisoners are now working in the mines and are held in the slave pens, or they have been mutated by the Dark One's magic." Matthew and Sharineas made no reply, but after a short, thoughtful pause, all three continued walking with a little more determination in their step. The group came to another set of stairs identical to the last. They quickly climbed them expecting more of the same, but stopped short at the top. It was another corridor just like the other two, but this one not only had torches lighting the other end, they could also hear voices coming from that same direction.

The voices and shuffling noises finally ceased and the trio quietly crept toward the lighted end of the corridor. They came to a cell door that had been left slightly ajar; Matthew warily looked into the cold, dark room. When he was certain it was empty all three entered. They found a brazier of burnt out coals and chains on the walls, with both old and fresh blood on the floor. A hole in one of the walls looked as if it had been freshly made. "Could it be?" Matthew asked aloud with a touch of hope in his voice. "Could Deeli and Pheltic have been held here?"

"Uncle Deeli might still be alive then," Sharineas said excitedly.

"To have hope is a good thing," Katchut interjected, "but this could mean a number of things." The other two looked at him as if he had just pronounced the Elf and Dwarie dead. Katchut just looked at them with his hand held to the door. "I hope you are right, but the only way to find out for certain is to continue on to our destiny." Without a word Matthew ran out the door and up the steps that were nearby; Sharineas and Katchut quickly followed. At the top of this set of stairs were hallways with windows open to the outside. The trio could see dark clouds gathering outside, and lightning crackling over the distant mountain tops. They wandered through the long halls, listening and looking for some sign of life. "It's strange that the fortress would be left so unguarded," Matthew said.

"All of the Dark One's warriors are probably either with him, or on the battlefield," Katchut surmised.

"But if he captured Deeli and Pheltic, wouldn't he suspect that the Sword Bearer is on his way, and be preparing for him?" Sharineas asked with a frown.

"Not if he thought he had nothing to fear from me," Matthew answered glumly. Then they heard muffled voices from the end of the hallway. All three quietly made their way to a giant set of intricately carved, wooden double doors. The doors were so thick that no matter how quiet they were, the little group could not make out what was being said in the room beyond. A look of frustration came over Matthew's face and he put his hand on the doors as if to open them.

"Well I guess the only way is to just go in and see what's going on."

"Wait a minute," Sharineas cut Matthew off, putting a restraining hand on his arm. She stepped back a few feet and began to concentrate. Suddenly the light from her amulet sprang forth and lit up the doors, enabling all three to see and hear what was going on in the room. No one in the huge room seemed to notice anything different, as if the companions were looking through a one-way glass.

"Look," Matthew said, taking a step toward the doors, "there's Deeli and Pheltic."

"By the Creator!" Sharineas stifled a cry. "Is that really Uncle Deeli? He's so disfigured I can hardly recognize him." It was true; their two companions were sitting on the floor, a bloody, broken mess. Matthew looked to a raised, stone dais and the figure that stood on it with smoldering anger in his eyes. The Enlightened One looked to be a mixture of Human and Traul, and was incredibly ugly. At the moment he was ranting and raving about something, spittle running down the side of his mouth. Matthew and Sharineas looked at the mirror by Deeli and Pheltic.

"Is that what I think it is?" Matthew asked Sharineas with astonishment. It was a little hard for him to see from that distance, but he finally recognized what the scene must be.

"Oh no," Sharineas said, putting her hand to her mouth. "They are attacking the wall that our people have built." The Dark Lord had now come out of his tantrum and was pointing at the mirror, saying something to his two prisoners.

"...But for now you will both sit and watch as your homeland falls to my might," the Enlightened One mocked with a sneer. "Do not try to refuse, my guards have some very unpleasant ways to make you do as I wish. And as soon as the show is over we will concentrate on finding that miserable Elven sword!"

"I think the time for secrecy is over," Matthew said, through clenched teeth. He raised Excalibur once more and struck the thick wooden doors as he had the stone wall below. Splintering wood flew everywhere and the two guards near the door were thrown momentarily unconscious to the floor. Matthew walked between what was left of the two doors that now were off their hinges and laying on the floor next to the downed mutated Traul warriors. "You want to know where the sword is?!" Matthew yelled, loudly and confidently in challenge. "It's right here in my hand, and I'm about to make you sorry you ever found it!"

Before Matthew even finished his sentence, the Dark Lord's elite guards were coming at him from every side. The gem in the sword's hilt was glowing brighter than it ever had, and blue lightning crackled with an intensity never before reached—the sword and its bearer had finally come to their destiny. Matthew was everywhere at once; fatigue melting away with a surge of adrenaline. The Traul guards had their magically enhanced swords and were putting up a tremendous fight, but Matthew met every blade with ease and grace.

Sharineas ran around to her uncle, and with Pheltic's help, pulled him farther out of harm's way. Katchut had come in after Matthew and was now fighting two of the warriors with his huge sword. When Matthew and the sword had first burst through his doors, the

275

Enlightened One's eyes bulged in fright; he had not expected this in his very throne room. But now, as the fighting was going on in front of him, he sat on his throne and watched the spectacle with an almost amused smile.

Matthew had already killed three of the elite guards and was slowly making his way closer to the stone dais and its occupant. Pheltic saw the Dark Lord make a signal to one of his guards near the throne. The mutant then began to make his way around the fighting, behind Matthew and Katchut. *He's going to attack Matthew from behind,* Pheltic thought in a panic. *I must stop him, but how?* After a brief pause the little Dwarie stopped thinking about it and ran straight between the legs of the three Traul guards that Matthew was currently engaging. He ran right past Matthew and let go with a flying tackle to the unsuspecting Traul's kneecaps. Pheltic downed him just as the guard had raised his sword to attack his enemy's blind side. The bold Dwarie ran so quickly and was so small, that the giant mutated warrior never saw him coming.

They both went over in a tumble, but the magically altered Traul was very agile. He recovered quickly and swung his sword at the little pest who was trying to scoot backward away from him. Purely by instinct, Pheltic brought a hand up to protect his face when he saw the blade coming. The Traul's sword whistled through empty air just short of Pheltic's face, but the tip caught his uplifted hand. Pheltic felt nothing at first, only saw three of his fingers go flying through the air and land on the stone floor. Blood spurted out of the gaping holes left behind in the Dwarie's hand and ran down his arm—Pheltic watched; face white with shock. Just as the mutant Traul was about to finish his helpless victim, a blade came poking out of his chest and ended those plans. Katchut had downed his two assailants and saw Pheltic's situation just in time. The Path-following Traul tore a strip of his own clothing off and tightly bandaged Pheltic's hand. He then picked up his little friend and carried the wounded Dwarie over to Deeli and Sharineas. In a flurry of lightning and sparks, Matthew was just ending the fight with the last of his attackers. He looked straight at the now standing figure on the dais before him. The Enlightened One was incredibly tall and made the impression even stronger by being elevated above everyone else in the room. There were still six of the magically altered Trauls standing guard around the throne; presumably his best. Each one stood silent and unmoving, waiting for orders from their master. The Dark Lord did and said nothing, just looked at Matthew as if he were a bug. Matthew decided he would wipe that look from his face. Raising Excalibur he pointed the sword at his enemy, intending to use it the same way he had against the cave creatures. He felt energy draining from him as power leapt out of the sword. The blast of crackling energy completely surrounded the Dark Lord, causing everyone in the room to look away from the near blinding light. He did not let up—until finally, when he could feel himself losing strength, Matthew stopped the energy flow. He could not believe what he saw.

The throne that had been sitting on top of the dais was completely destroyed, as well as the two guards that had been nearest their master. But the Dark Lord himself stood upon the dais with his arms folded and a smile on his face, untouched and unharmed. "My power is greater than that of the sword," the figure said coolly. "Now my young fool, it is my turn!" He stretched forth his arms and a stream of magical energy left his finger tips. Matthew lifted Excalibur and caught most of the deadly blast on the blade of his sword, but the force of the blast knocked the weapon from his hands. The sword went skidding across the floor and stopped near where Sharineas and the others were watching in breathless anticipation. Matthew had been knocked back and was a little disoriented, but still managed to stay on his feet. Before he could run or even think, a second bolt hit him squarely in the chest. He was thrown across the room as if he were a rag doll and landed unmoving in a heap on the floor. "There, your hero is dead," the evil half-breed laughed harshly. "Now I will claim my prize." But before the murderer could make a move for his winnings, the sound of metal scraping on stone came from across the room.

At first Matthew had thought he was dead, but when he opened his eyes the room before him was the same. His chest hurt tremendously and there was an indentation in his breastplate with a split in the metal. The armor covering his left arm was also mangled and half gone. Matthew slowly picked himself up, and despite the pain, started toward the stone dais once again.

"How can this be!" The Dark Lord stormed. "Is this your doing Napdeeliate? There is no armor made that can withstand the magic I just sent at your little puppet." Deeli gave only a slight smile in return, revealing several missing teeth in the process. He was recalling how for hundreds of sun-cycles that very armor had defied and resisted Elven magic. *We still do not know where the armor came from, but this was all in the Creator's plan. Even long ago He was preparing for this very moment,* Deeli thought, with delight at the irony. The deranged megalomaniac did not wait for any other reply from the Elf, but released yet another bolt of magic at Matthew.

This time the magic hit the armored young man from another world with a clap of thunder. Like a giant hand it picked Matthew up and threw him against the stone wall that was directly behind him. Matthew lay there in a still, crumpled pile, while his adversary laughed cruelly at his own handiwork. The leader of all the northern races was visibly drained now from using so much of his magic against Matthew, but still found the strength to gloat over his victory. Just as the evil half-breed began to rub Deeli's face in his victory, Matthew once again staggered to his feet. The armor was damaged beyond repair now and would no longer protect him, but it had successfully kept its contents alive so far.

"No! I will not be trifled with!" The Dark Lord ordered his four remaining guards to kill the weaponless boy. Katchut ran to pick up the sword of prophecy and bring it to Matthew without thinking. He met only more laughter from the Enlightened One as he tried, but failed, to pick up the sword. The remnant of mutated Trauls moved at a wary pace to obey their master. True, the boy no longer held the sword, but they wondered what other tricks he might have hidden and ready to use. The four slowly began to circle their prey with ever widening smiles as Matthew seemed to have no more defenses. This boy had caused their master much trouble and they had no intention of showing him any mercy.

Matthew, though on his feet, was stunned and confused. His body was racked with pain and it was taking everything he had just to stand. As the huge Trauls began to circle him with their weapons drawn, Matthew finally became aware of what was going on and the extreme danger he was in. Surrounded as he was, Matthew knew there was no way he could regain Excalibur. He feverishly prayed and prepared himself for the blades that were sure to come.

Up to this point Sharineas had been frozen in fear, tightly clutching her great uncle. Now though, she felt a pulsating warmth just below her neck. The amulet was glowing on and off like an urgent beacon. Looking at Calburnathis only a few feet away she saw that the gem in its hilt was pulsating simultaneously with the crystal around her throat. She sprang up, went to the sword and reached down for it. She expected the same resistance that everyone beside Matthew had experienced; but to her and everyone else's surprise, she picked up the weapon as if it weighed nothing. Suddenly she knew the main purpose of why the Keeper of the Amulet had to be with the sword. She was the only other person who could lift it; something she had never even thought to try. Sharineas looked and saw that Matthew and his attackers were oblivious to what she had just done. Quickly, before the Dark Lord could stop her, she yelled Matthew's name and threw the sword across the room. The Sword of Kings seemed to fly over the guards' heads and into Matthew's open hand as if it was guided there. And if anyone had asked Deeli's opinion, he would have said that it had been.

Now the tables had turned. Matthew, even being in so much pain, felt a renewed hope. In a flurry of moves directed more by the sword than himself, Matthew kept his four attackers at bay. Katchut saw that even with the powerful talisman back in his possession, Matthew was weak and having a hard time. The huge Traul once again picked up his own sword and joined in the fray, fighting one assailant as Matthew fought the other three. The fighting was fierce, for these were the Enlightened One's finest. As the fighting was going on, the others watched while their enemy seemed to regain his strength right before their eyes. Sharineas and Pheltic ground their teeth in frustration at being helpless to do anything. Finally the battle taking place in the center of the room ceased. Katchut killed his adversary as Matthew was finishing his third. They both stood for a moment looking at their enemy and breathing hard. He, on the other hand, was not looking at, nor even seemed interested in, them. His gaze was directed at the large mirror.

"You have beat my champions, but it will do you no good. Look, It is too late!" Everyone looked at the mirror in horror, the scene that played before them was one of death and destruction. The wall in the mountain pass now looked almost abandoned. Two holes had been made in it with battering rams, and Traul and Nomie warriors were making their way through them. Warriors were also making their way over the wall, which was on fire in many places. "Your precious valley is mine!" The Dark Lord sneered at them. "Give me the sword, boy!" When Matthew did not make a move, energy began to crackle around the Dark Lord's hands. "Give it to me now, you've lost. Do you believe your ragged suit of armor can save you yet again!" With that, another blast of energy shot forth toward Matthew.

This time Matthew tightened his grip on Excalibur and intercepted the magic with the sword. The blade caught the energy and angled it off in another direction, causing a large hole to be made in one of the stone walls. The Dark Lord though, was undaunted. He held out his hand and repeated the words more forcefully. "Give me the sword!" Slowly a chorus of hissing, maniacal voices took up residence in Matthew's head, urging him to give up the sword. Matthew clamped his teeth together and began walking toward the dais.

The evil voices in his head began to increase with each step. By the time he was halfway across the room, sweat was pouring off his face from the strain of fighting them.

Suddenly he screamed at the top of his lungs. "No! Too many voices!" As Matthew screamed he began to falter—and finally fell to his knees. The confused and battered young man knelt there, wondering where he would get the strength to continue. Then a small, quiet voice filtered through the rest. *"Matthew, I love you. Go to him."* Matthew felt peace wash over him as well as new strength. He rose to his feet with renewed vigor and started for the Dark Lord once again.

I can take him, Matthew thought to himself. *God is with me and that ugly half-breed is weak from using his magic. Even if I lose, I must try. Haub was willing to give his life. How can I do any less?* Once again the sweet voice spoke in his head.

"Matthew my servant, give him the sword."

Is this some kind of trick? Matthew thought back at the voice in his head. *The Holy Spirit would not tell me to give the sword to my enemy and God's.* Then he stopped where he was, too confused to continue. He remembered what Deeli had taught Pheltic and himself about testing the spirits. *Do you believe that Jesus came in the flesh? That He is the Son of God, and that He died for mankind's sins and rose again?*

"Yes, Jesus is the true Son of God. *Now give him the sword!*" The voice was more insistent now.

"No!" Matthew yelled aloud. "This must be some trick of Satan's. Even if it means my life I will overcome you!" No one in the room knew at whom Matthew was yelling for sure, but he once again walked forward, all hesitation gone. The sword in his hand began to crackle with lightning even more fiercely and Matthew's friends knew the showdown had finally come. Matthew stood before the Dark Lord with his sword blazing, one swift stroke and it would be all over. If the Dark Lord by some magic did not die and in turn killed Matthew, at least he would die sacrificing his life for others.

"Give me the sword, boy," the evil Traul leader said in an even tone, hand still extended forward. Matthew looked at him with a glint in his eye and a sneer on his face. He was about to answer his enemy with the edge of Excalibur's blade when the small quiet voice spoke again. It echoed words that he had heard his father use many times as he was growing up.

"Matthew, obedience is better than sacrifice. Give him the sword!" Matthew's will broke then, and finally he knew what he was supposed to do. To everyone in the room's amazement—including for a brief second the Enlightened One's—Matthew turned Excalibur around and handed it to the Dark Lord; hilt first.

Chapter

23

Deep inside, Matthew had secretly thought that the Dark Lord would not be able to lift Excalibur, but he had done so with ease. The evil being had a look of sheer ecstasy and triumph on his face as he raised the sword and took a step back. Matthew—with visions of the thing before him cutting his head off—began backing away from the raised dais.

"Now I rule unchallenged!" The Enlightened One yelled at the top of his lungs. "My control of magic combined with this sword makes me the most powerful being ever to have walked this planet!" The half-Traul, half-Human was completely over the edge now. His eyes bulged and spittle sprayed out of his mouth as he screamed. "I am now a god!"

With this last proclamation of his divinity, the sword he held began to crackle with energy. Blue lightning ran along the edge of the blade and Matthew felt the strongest surge of magical energy that he had yet experienced. *Why did I give him the sword?* Matthew thought in terror. *Now he's going to kill us all, and it will be my fault.* By now Matthew was with his friends over by the giant mirror—Sharineas came over to him and put her arm around his waist.

"It doesn't matter what happens now," she said, "we'll all see it through together."

"But it's my fault! I really believed God wanted me to give him the sword, I must have been out of my mind."

"What more can the Creator ask of his servants than wholehearted obedience," Deeli forced out through his pain. "Remember, God is glorified the most when we are at our weakest."

"I would say that was right about now," Pheltic said, with a trembling half smile on a face white with pain. He got up from his knees and stumbled over to Matthew and Sharineas. Matthew put his arm around the little Dwarie's shoulders. Sharineas was right; at least they would face the end together. Suddenly the evil laughter of the Dark Lord ceased and the expression of ecstasy on his face turned to one of pain. He looked at the five who watched in fear and screamed out in agony.

"What kind of trickery is this!?" The sword was now blazing with power, but it was not being released anywhere. The evil half-breed was desperately trying to throw his *prize* away, but to no avail—the energy of the sword seemed to be consuming him. Then a rumbling sound came from above and the very stone beneath them began to shake. The air was full of static. The black clouds that could be seen through the windows were rolling furiously—streaks of angry lightning striking all around the castle; the sound of thunder booming in their ears. Before any of the frightened onlookers could make a move, a column of fire crashed through the ceiling; totally engulfing the Dark Lord. For many heartbeats a tortured scream of pain filled the room.

Then, as quickly as it had come, the stream of fire receded into the heavens, leaving the dais completely empty. All five companions had been thrown off their feet from the blast of God's wrath upon the Dark Lord, but none of them was any worse for it. In bewilderment they began to pick themselves up off the floor. The black clouds outside were even now beginning to recede, and the sound of thunder seemed a long way in the distance. Then from the direction of the stone dais came a sweet soothing voice.

"Well done, good and faithful servants of the Most High and His Son." All heads swung around to what was a second ago an empty dais. Their mouths gaped in wonder, for sitting on the edge of the raised stone dais was a fair-haired young male dressed in white. The first thing the companions noticed was that none of them could quite tell to what race he belonged.

As the valley defenders retreated into the forest, their only thoughts were of defeat and their inevitable deaths. King Peridon had just turned his horse and started into the forest when he heard the rumble begin. The ground beneath him shook and his steed whinnied in fear. He turned the animal back toward the wall wondering what new dark magic the enemy was using now. The other leaders, as well as many warriors, stopped their retreat and looked back.

A great number of the enemy were already on the south side of the wall. Most were enjoying tearing down and burning the valley's defense while waiting for their comrades—there would be plenty of time to take the valley when they were finished. On either side of the wall, hundreds of black clad warriors could be seen running down the mountains. When the ground started shaking, the evil hoard stopped what they were doing and began to mill around in confusion. The sky had grown so dark and full of black rolling clouds, that they could barely see one another.

Then, as the valley forces that had turned back looked on, balls of fire began to rain down upon the Dark Lord's army from the sky above. The evil warriors began to panic and run over each other trying to get away. Lightning began to crackle and thunder boomed out an ominous warning. Then great blasts of fire roared down from the heavens, consuming warriors at the wall and on the mountains. The rumbling from below increased and suddenly the mountains split open as did giant fissures in the pass. The dark warriors who were not burning were being swallowed up by the ground. Those of the Dark Lord's army that were still on the north side of the pass began to flee to the safety of their homeland. Every warrior who did not make it to the safety of the northern forest, died that day under an angry sky. The valley people looked on in amazed horror at the holocaust that somehow seemed confined only to their enemies.

The thunder and rumblings finally died away and the rain of fire stopped; in their place was a profound and absolute silence. The wall had been totally consumed—not a trace was left to prove that it had ever existed. All the valley dwellers that had turned back were now on their knees; including Peridon and the other leaders. They had seen the hand of the Creator at work, and would never forget it. Then suddenly a shaft of light broke through the black clouds. It lit up a small area where the wall had been, and in the light a figure was imperceptible. Then a voice carried to them on the wind. It was very clear, calm, and gentle; but at the same time full of all the power of the ages.

"In your weakness, there I am made strong. For I Am the way, the truth, and the life. No one comes unto the Creator except through Me." King Peridon was trembling with his hands covering his face. *Those were the words spoken by Shesea. Dear God, forgive me!* Peridon, like all those gathered there, knew he would never be the same again.

Chapter

24

The person sitting on the stone dais glowed faintly as he held out Excalibur in his hands. "Matthew, you have done well and learned much in a short time. I believe this belongs to you." Matthew walked over on unsteady legs and took the sword from the young man. *This must be an angel,* Matthew thought to himself as he *looked into the perfect face. Is this really happening?* "You have all done well and have averted the end of both your worlds."

"Both our worlds?" Matthew echoed in surprise. By then the others, including Deeli leaning on Katchut, had come up beside Matthew. Deeli and Sharineas were looking into the face of an angelic Elf, while Katchut saw a strong young Traul. Pheltic was amazed at the most perfect looking Dwarie he had ever seen.

"Yes, both worlds," the angel continued. "I have been sent by the Creator to give you comfort and understanding. Matthew, you have put off for a little while the final judgment by your obedience and humility in submitting to God. This was Satan's attempt in both worlds to bring about his absolute rule. In your world the U.N. forces, combined with European and Arab armies, came against Israel. If all nations had been a part of this attack then the end would surely have come. But there were two countries that—although they did not help God's chosen— were not part of the assault, just as those who live south of the valley did not join the attack on the Elves here. At the same moment He destroyed the Enlightened One and his army in this world, the Lord God did the same to Carmine Ishmali and all those gathered against Israel in your world."

"So there won't be any judgment of our worlds now?" Matthew asked timidly. "At least not for awhile?"

"A very short time I am afraid. Even now the final Antichrist is rising to power both here and in your world. You are now in the beginning of the final tribulation that has been prophesied in the Holy Words. This miracle that God has performed will spark a revival of the Jewish people in your world, Matthew, and of the Elven people in this world. He has revealed His Son without a doubt to his chosen in both worlds; they have no more excuses."

"So Jesus and Shesea are really the same?" Sharineas asked with awe in her voice.

"Yes, oh handmaiden of the Lord," the angel answered. "Jesus, Yeshua, Shesea—no matter the language; they all mean the living Word of God—the Son. It was through only Him that the Creator redeemed His fallen creation. You have done well in giving your life to the Son, and the Creator delights in you. You have obeyed Him and fulfilled your part in this admirably. But know this, Princess; your service to Him has only just begun." The angel paused and gave Sharineas such a strange look that she feared to ask any more questions. Finally the heavenly being looked back to the rest of them. "Now, as in the days of old, the Father is going to communicate more clearly with His children. The end is so near, and times will be so hard for those walking by faith, that His compassion has been stirred as at no time in history."

"What about Deeli?" Pheltic asked, looking like he might fall over any minute. "He was beaten and tortured, why didn't Shesea help him?" The angel looked on the little Dwarie with compassion. Pheltic stared back with tears in his eyes over his friend's plight. The bandage Katchut had put on his hand was now completely soaked in blood. The red, life-giving liquid dripped from the cloth and was now forming a small pool on the floor.

"Pheltic, the Lord is well pleased with you. Even now when you can barely stand, your only thoughts are for others. You will make a fitting assistant for him whom the Lord is calling to lead His remnant in these perilous times." The angel reached out and held Pheltic's wounded hand; then reaching up with his other hand touched the Dwarie's face. The split-open wound on the Dwarie's face healed over and life seemed to come back into his body. He tore the bandage off his hand and saw that the bleeding had stopped. The places where his fingers had been were beginning to scab over.

"Thank you," Pheltic said; wonder and awe apparent on his face. Then the questioning look came back into his eyes. "But what of Deeli? Would you at least fix him up too...please?"

"Is...is my Lord angry with me?" Deeli's ragged voice came from where he leaned against Katchut, seemingly more dead than alive. The angel smiled at the old Elf and Deeli felt healing power flow into his body.

"Hear the word of the Lord," The angel began. "My most trusted servant, Deeli. I am not angered at you, for I love you from the depths of My heart. Those I love though, must be disciplined; and those who would reign with Me must suffer with Me. Magic was meant as a test in this world, to see what My creation would do with it—just as science and technology are a test in Matthew's world. Your oath never to use the magic again was made in foolishness and vanity. I never wanted you to give up your magic, but to use the gift I had given you for My glory. Every time you did use it you brought condemnation upon yourself because of the oath you had made."

"Is that why my Lord has not talked to me for so long?" Deeli asked looking at the floor in shame.

"No, Deeli. The Lord had to test you. To see that even in the darkest times, the driest deserts, and the loneliest places, you would still continue to be faithful and follow Him. You have passed that test, and now Shesea has a special task for you. The Creator wishes to use you,

Deeli, as His main instrument in the last great revival of the Elven people. He would say unto you: take My Holy Words once again to your people, and this time you will reap a great harvest in My name. Many souls will be saved if you yield yourself to My will." Deeli fell to his knees; not out of weakness this time, but in worship of his God.

"Thank you Shesea, praise be to You my Creator, my God!"

"Each of you has a part to play at this most crucial point in history, including you, Katchut. The Traul followers of Shesea will need a strong leader as never before. That, is something you will find out more about when the time is right. I must leave you now."

"Wait!" Matthew yelled in alarm, but then remembered to whom he was speaking. "...I mean," he stammered. "...I still have lots of questions. The least of which is how do I get back home?"

"Your questions will be answered by the same voice that led you to give the sword over to your enemy," the angel said as he started to fade. "As for going home; look to the sword." Suddenly, the dais was empty and the room bathed in a sublime peace and silence. Bright sunlight was streaming in through the windows—no one spoke a word for a very long while.

Chapter

25

Katchut led the small party to where the slaves were kept. They found giant holding cells near the back gate where Traul Path followers were penned together like sheep or cattle; having been treated no better than animals. Most of the Dark Lord's servants who had been guarding his slaves were already gone, frightened off when the fire bolt from heaven had come through the roof of their master's throne room. The few that were left fled outside and into the mountains when they saw the companions coming to release their prisoners. Katchut stood before the people and addressed them in a loud voice.

"My people, today the Lord Shesea has answered our prayers. The power of the Dark One has been broken and you are free!" With this announcement a great clamor arose; shouts of joy and praise to the Creator. After the crowd of former prisoners had settled down, Katchut continued. "I will lead you to others of our kind who have established secret communities in the wilderness. You will be welcomed in the name of the Lord, and will be free to live like Trauls once again. These good people before you were the Lord's instruments in bringing these things about. They too are followers of the Path of Shesea, and have extended their hand of friendship to us. We will not have to face the future alone. We will now be able to stand and face it in one accord with our brothers and sisters in the valley!" More shouts of joy followed Katchut's speech, and the released prisoners swarmed over their saviors with gladness and warmth.

The freed Trauls swept through the fortress looking for food and anything else they could bring with them. The companions found water and cleaned up as best they could. They also ate well from the food that some of the Trauls brought to them. They then packed themselves provisions for the journey back to the valley, and prepared to depart as quickly as they could. "Matthew, Deeli, thank you all for allowing me to come with you," Katchut said as he hugged each one of his new friends in turn.

"The Creator meant for you to be with us, my friend," Deeli said.

"Yea, Katchut, we never could have made it without you," Matthew added. "I know that Sharineas and I wouldn't have made it out of the caves without you." They had already told Deeli and Pheltic about what happened to Haub. Deeli had wept bitterly for some time, but seemed to be doing better now.

"I will miss you all," Katchut returned. "Especially Haub, for I know I will not see him again until the last day…which I guess will not be too much longer," he said, suddenly brightening.

"Well, you will be seeing us," Deeli said. "I will be expecting you in the valley as soon as you are able to get your people settled."

"I will be there…" Katchut looked at these people he had grown to love for a quiet moment, knowing it was time he went back to his own people. "I guess there is not much left to say but good-bye. The people we have freed are anxious to leave this place."

"I can certainly understand that," Matthew said looking around at their cold, stone surroundings. "I think I'm ready to get out of here myself." The companions from the valley finished their good-byes to Katchut with many tears—and not a few more hugs. After all they had been through together it was like losing a family member—if only for a little while. Upon Katchut's departure, Matthew and Sharineas went out to explore the stables. They found only two horses remaining and brought them to the front gate where Deeli and Pheltic were waiting. Matthew and Sharineas mounted one horse while Deeli shared the other with Pheltic. They trotted out the front gate, determined to head straight for the valley. All four were quiet for quite some time, pondering all they had been through, and the Creator's judgment they had witnessed. The image in the big mirror had faded soon after the Dark Lord had been destroyed, but not before it had shown the companions what was happening to the enemy army at the wall.

When conversations finally began, stories were told of what had happened after they had been separated in the woods. Sharineas was nearly in tears when she heard what her uncle had gone through and understood why he had looked so terrible before the angel's visit. Pheltic jumped in to tell them about Deeli's torture in the dungeon, and this time did not make it sound as if it had been a glorious adventure. "I think it's time for me to grow up and become more serious about life," Pheltic announced, when Deeli asked him why he had not exaggerated. The others burst out laughing; when Pheltic realized what he had said, he smiled along with them. Matthew told Deeli and Pheltic what had happened to them, and the details of Haub's death.

"Oh, I almost forgot," Matthew said, after he was finished with the story. "Haub asked me to give you a message. He wanted me to tell you that he had forgiven the Dark Lord the evil he had done to him and his family."

"Praise the Creator," Deeli said quietly; tears welling up once more. "He is far better off than we are."

The small group did meet scattered troops of the retreating northern army along the way. Most of them simply went around the strangers, wanting nothing but to get home. Some of the larger bands, however, stopped them and demanded their horses and food. Matthew simply withdrew Excalibur from the scabbard that was attached to his saddle. When the would-be assailants saw the sword and the blue lightning that accompanied it, they ran for their lives. They had seen enough supernatural fireworks to last the rest of their days. Matthew was glad for the effect because he had no desire to kill anyone ever again.

They traveled straight south as quickly as they could, for all of them were eager to see the valley again; including Matthew. The horses they had were the sturdy northern breed and could travel much faster and longer than the Elven steeds. So after two seven-days and one, what was left of the Quest of the Sword came to the Great Northern Pass that would lead them home. They were sure it was the same pass, but could not tell by looking at it. Both mountains to either side were flattened to only about half of their original height; giant fissures running up and down them. What used to be called the Great Northern Pass, was now only a very wide trail that narrowed the farther they went into it.

Huge boulders lay everywhere, causing the path to wind and curve around them. Dark red stains were on every stone and wall. Pools of stagnant blood that had been so big they were just now drying up, greeted their eyes and noses in many places. The horrid smell of death was prevalent throughout the pass, and pressed in on them to the point of near suffocation. But the most noticeable and grisly reminder of what had happened here were the gleaming white bones. Even though the ground had swallowed most of the enemy, there were still many bones left for the scavengers. The bones that lay everywhere had been picked clean and already bleached by the sun.

They were not very far into the pass when their horses reacted so violently to the stench of decay that the companions let them go. The animals immediately headed back north where they belonged. The four friends continued their journey through the horrible place on foot; holding pieces of cloth over their noses and mouths. Deeli, still not fully recovered from his ordeal, was having a hard time walking; so Matthew and Sharineas took turns helping to steady him. They were a dirty looking group that looked more like beggars than heroes. That is why as they approached the forest on the other side of the pass, the group of soldiers stationed there did not recognize them.

"Halt! Who are you? Where are you from, and where do you think you're going?" One of the Elven soldiers burst out loudly. Matthew was not sure what to do—he just kept looking at the arrows pointed at them and wearily wondering if he would need to pull his sword out once more. Sharineas boldly took a step forward and coolly eyed the hostile looking soldiers.

"I am the Princess Sharineas, Keeper of the Amulet of Truth, and I am going home." The soldiers' eyes then bulged in recognition, and every one of them went down to their knees.

"Please forgive us your Highness, we did not recognize you," the soldier who had asked the questions said. "We were sent here to guard the pass and were only doing our job. The whole kingdom believes you dead, no one knew where you were. Your mother and father will be overjoyed at this turn of events—they mourn you even now." Sharineas was heartbroken over the thought of what she had put her parents through. It had been necessary to sneak away in secret, but now she wanted only to let them know she was still alive.

"It is all right captain, but we will need horses to ride back to the kingdom," Sharineas answered in a much kinder voice. The Elven soldiers could not get horses ready fast enough. They scrambled for the honor of giving up their steeds to the Princess and her party. Four of the soldiers escorted them back, although the companions smiled at each other and tried to decline. *Imagine,* Matthew thought, *after all we've been through, and now they want to give us a guard.*

Two days later as they entered the streets of the Elven city, everything was quiet. No one seemed to recognize them and they were all grateful. But two of their escort began telling people on the streets, and before long people were pointing and shouting. It seemed that the news traveled up the streets faster than they did. Soon horns were blowing and people were surrounding them making it nearly impossible to get to the castle. When they finally did make it, King Peridon and Queen Jasmantha were already in the courtyard waiting for them. They rushed to their daughter, tears flowing freely, and embraced her before she had dismounted. The soldier had been right; they were indeed overjoyed at her return from the dead. All four were ushered into the castle with much fanfare, and a messenger was dispatched immediately to tell King Moark the news about his son.

"It will do your father good to see you, Pheltic," Peridon said putting a hand on the small Dwarie's shoulder. "He has not been the same since the last day of fighting. I'm sorry to have to tell you this…but your brother died in battle while defending the wall." Pheltic was shaken considerably, but did not give into the tears that tried to come. Deeli, Matthew, and Sharineas all gathered around to give him their support. When Pheltic recovered from the initial shock of the news they continued to the main dining chambers. As they walked Deeli told how Boreshia had died, and then Sharineas gave account to her father of what had happened with Gamilon. King Peridon was grieved over both deaths, especially Gamilon—who was to be his son-in-law and future King. "I am eager to hear the rest of your story, and I'm sure it will be one for the history scrolls," King Peridon stated quietly. "But I do not wish to put you through that before you have cleaned up and rested. While you are doing so I will order the kitchen servants to begin preparing a feast." He then ordered servants to take the motley little group to the bathing chambers and get new clothes for them all.

"Even for me, nephew?" Deeli asked, wide-eyed.

"Yes, even for you, uncle," the King answered with a smile. The two locked eyes in silence for only a moment, but volumes were spoken between them. The four companions were ushered away and did not return for several hours. When they did, it was to a huge room filled with people, music, and food. The hall was filled with survivors of the Battle of the Great Northern Pass, waiting to hear and tell tales of valor. Elven, Human, and Dwarie alike, were not disappointed.

The feasting went on for many hours, the four taking turns retelling their entire adventure. They told of the sacrifices made by Boreshia, Gamilon, and Haub. The Humans were very grieved over the death of one of their leaders, and a song had already been written commemorating him. The entire room listened as the Human who wrote the song sang it. King Peridon told of the battle at the wall with a little help now and then from those in the room that had been there. When the feasting and the tales were finally winding down, Alexthna rose to his feet and addressed the King. "My king, I know we are grateful for the services that Napdeeliate and Matthew have done for our people, myself not excluded." He paused for a brief second while all attention in the room focused on him. "But we do still have laws. I should think that after a good night's rest, Napdeeliate would be able to resume his exile."

"As you wish Alexthna," Deeli answered for the King, "I would force myself on no one." Sharineas stood quickly and opened her mouth to protest, but her father interjected before she had the chance.

"I do not think that will be necessary, Alexthna. The Creator has shown great mercy to His people at this time—and also that His hand is upon this small group of people that have risked everything on this quest to save our land. Without His intervention and mercy we would all be dead right now. I believe it is time that we start showing that same kind of mercy. Deeli," Peridon spoke to his uncle using his Path follower name. "Your exile is now at an end, as is the ban on all Path followers. Everyone living in the valley is welcome in the Elven kingdom from this day forward."

"But…" Alexthna sputtered. "You cannot!"

"Thank you father…" Sharineas said, looking at Peridon. "…Now I will not have to leave."

"You…" the King said with widening eyes, "have converted?" Sharineas nodded her head in affirmation.

"I told you," Alexthna burst out and pointed at Deeli. "I told you that his words would twist her mind!"

"It was many things that brought me to believe on the Lord Shesea!" Sharineas retorted. "But for my great uncle's part, it was his love, compassion, and kindness that made me see more than his words." Alexthna fumed in silence for a few seconds, then angrily stormed out of the room. The High King looked at his daughter wonderingly, then stood and addressed the whole assembly.

"My people and my friends, do not worry over Alexthna's attitude, I will deal with him later. I must confess I have never looked into the details of what the Path followers believe, but now my own daughter tells me she is one. That would seem to me a good time to learn more about this religion. But regardless of what conclusion I come to, I believe the Creator has shown us there is enough room in the valley for us all!" Most of those present cheered the King's decision. A few sat quietly with frowns on their faces; a couple of Elves even got up and left as Alexthna had, but the King did his best to ignore the fact. Being that it was already past the midnight hour, the feast finally broke up and everyone left was provided with a place to sleep.

In the next few days the four companions of the quest spent time in the quiet of the royal gardens recuperating. Deeli spent a lot of time talking with his nephew about the faith, and showing him in the Holy Words how Shesea had fulfilled so many of their prophecies. King

Moark, his wife, and a whole entourage of Dwarie warriors arrived and Pheltic was declared a hero of the highest order. The little Dwarie spent much of his time recounting his adventures to his fellow warriors. Matthew and Sharineas spent much of their time alone and sharing their growing feelings for one another. It seemed to both of them that the Lord had meant for them to be together. Those were beautiful, warm, summer days, and they all enjoyed their time of rest. Matthew though, was feeling a tug on his heart to go back to his own world—at least for a while.

"I believe I can use the sword to get back home," he said to Sharineas. "Please come with me."

"Oh Matthew, I would love to, but I just cannot leave right now. Uncle Deeli needs my help in getting his evangelism started among our people. I think my father is just about on the verge of converting, and I know my mother is. Alexthna is giving my father a very hard time, and seems as if he is about to start a revolt. Why can't you just stay with us?"

"I would much rather live in your world than mine, believe me. But now that I know what I do, I must go back and try to convince my family and friends of the truth. I promise that I will be back if it is at all possible."

"Well don't come back unless you plan on marrying me," Sharineas said, with a teasing smile and a pinch on his arm—flippant actions to cover her disappointment. Matthew turned red and smiled back foolishly.

"I thought you'd never ask," he finally said. Sharineas put her hands on her hips in mock scorn that he would say such a thing. Suddenly, as if with one mind, they both turned serious and just held each other until the shadows grew long and it was time to go inside. They spent the rest of that evening talking and planning a future that they knew was unsure and all too short. The next morning Matthew went out to the gardens to make his attempt at going home. His friends were there to send him off. He gave Pheltic a big hug; the little Dwarie was so grieved over his friend's leaving that he could barely speak. "Matthew, you are my best friend. My life will no longer be the same without you."

"Don't worry, I'll be back. And I'm going to need you to stand up for me at my wedding." Pheltic brightened at this.

"I will be looking forward to it. As a matter of fact I will begin making you a present right away!"

"That sounds interesting," Matthew laughed. "Just be sure to do a good job assisting Deeli, he's getting on in cycles you know." Matthew said this with a wink in the aged Elf's direction. He was seeing a youthful glow in Deeli that had not been there since he first met the Elf seemingly a lifetime ago.

"I will be there for him, don't you worry," Pheltic replied. "May Shesea be with you, Matthew." He had already said his good-byes to Sharineas and her family, which left only Deeli.

"I don't know what to say, Deeli." Both old and young looked at each other with tears brimming in their eyes. "It's been like having a father again, and I hate to leave that feeling. You have been responsible for changing my life around."

"No, my son, it was the Spirit of the Creator that did that, I only helped."

"But you were the one who told me of Him and didn't push. You stayed with me and helped me through 'till the end."

"Not all the way to the end, I am afraid. You had to face that alone, and you did very well, I might add. I am as proud of you as if you were my own son." There was a slight pause where neither said a thing; then Matthew broke the seriousness of the moment.

"When I come back I don't want you to be so busy getting everyone saved that you won't have enough time to be my best man," he said with a smile.

"May the Lord strike me dead if I were to miss it," Deeli replied with mock severity. They had a short laugh and gave each other one last hug. Matthew walked over to Sharineas who was standing about fifteen paces away, acting as if none of this mattered. He gave her a long hug in which she buried her head in his chest for one last cry.

"I will be back," he whispered.

"I know." Sharineas gently pushed Matthew away and walked to her great uncle's side and under his waiting arm. Matthew drew the sword and plunged it point down into the ground. *What now,* he thought to himself. *I hope this works or I'm going to look like a fool.* He touched the hilt of the sword and began to concentrate on going home. He crouched down in front of the sword for a long time; thinking about going home so hard that his forehead began to sweat.

…Nothing happened.

I wish that all I had to do was click the heels of my ruby slippers together. It would have to be easier than this. He shook his head and looked to Deeli.

"Are you thinking about a specific place?" Deeli asked and suggested at the same time. Matthew touched the hilt once more and concentrated on his own back yard. A long moment went by when again nothing happened. He was just about to give up when he felt a tug inside himself, and the gem began to glow. Suddenly, a tremendous amount of energy went out of him and he felt himself getting weaker. "Look!" Deeli said excitedly. "The passage is opening, and it is not a circle this time. The gateway is in the shape of the sword stuck point first in the ground!" Matthew looked up and was overwhelmed at this one last sign given to him by Jesus.

"That's not all it is," he said in a husky voice. "That is the sign of the Path followers in my world. It is the shape of the tree they killed our Lord on." Before him stood a tall, wide, cross of dancing, swirling colors. Those looking on were almost as amazed as he was at this revelation. Matthew hoped it was the right thing to do, taking the sword back to his world. But he knew there was no way he could ever return without it. It also felt as if Excalibur was a part of him now. Matthew could feel his strength fading fast, so he picked up the sword and moved to the light. He put a tentative foot through and got that same warm feeling he had the first time; could it have only been two months ago? He looked back at his friends who were bidding him farewell, and gave one last wave of his hand. Then those who had come to love him as their own family, watched as Matthew turned and disappeared into the dancing lights; the glowing cross slowly faded away.

Order Form

Postal orders:
John E. Webb Jr.
3014 E. 11th Road
Utica, IL 61373

Telephone orders:
815-667-9858

Please send *Lord in Two Worlds* **to:**

Name: _____

Address: _____

City: _____ State: _____

Zip: _____

Telephone: (_____) _____

Book Price: $12.99

Shipping: $3.00 for the first book and $1.00 for each additional book to cover shipping and handling within US, Canada, and Mexico. International orders add $6.00 for the first book and $2.00 for each additional book

Or contact your local bookstore